# PRAISE FOR MAG

### The Past and Ot

'Joel is particularly good at depicting the ....
family members can inflict on one another.' *Sydney Morning Heraιa*

### The Second-Last Woman in England

'The mesmerising story crackles with atmosphere and delivers some great twists.' *Australian Women's Weekly*

### Half the World in Winter

'Maggie Joel explores the way human fates as well as fictional plots can turn dramatically on a small and fleeting thing . . . a page-turner full of detail and colour.' *Sydney Morning Herald*

'If you like a robust period drama, with the occasional dash of dark humour, then you will love this.' *Daily Telegraph*

### The Safest Place in London

'Maggie Joel's *The Safest Place in London* is a beautifully written exploration of desperation and hope in a time of war. The novel captures the essence of the era with subtlety and style, while the shifting new world pushes characters to extreme lengths. A remarkable story of family, survival and how one decision can change lives for better or worse.' Jane Harper, bestselling author of *The Dry*

### The Unforgiving City

'Maggie Joel plunges the reader into the brutal heart of Federation, taking us beyond the silk curtains of lawmaking. She holds us in the harsh Sydney streets as characters—and indeed an entire country— scramble for a sure footing. Secrets and deception whisper from every page of *The Unforgiving City* and force us all to question what it means to be a united country, but also . . . how far are you prepared to stretch your heart to forgive someone?' Kirsty Manning, bestselling author of *The Jade Lily*

Maggie Joel has had four novels published. The first, *The Past and Other Lies*, was published to critical acclaim in Australia in 2009 and in the United States in 2013. Her second novel, *The Second-Last Woman in England*, was published in Australia in 2010, in the United States in 2011 and in the United Kingdom in 2013. This book was awarded the 2011 Fellowship of Australian Writers' Christina Stead Award for Fiction. Maggie's third novel, *Half the World in Winter*, was published in 2014 and in the United Kingdom in 2015. Her fourth novel, *The Safest Place in London*, was published in 2016.

# MAGGIE JOEL

## *The* Unforgiving City

**ALLEN&UNWIN**
SYDNEY • MELBOURNE • AUCKLAND • LONDON

First published in 2019

Copyright © Maggie Joel 2019

Allen & Unwin
83 Alexander Street
Crows Nest NSW 2065
Australia
Phone: (61 2) 8425 0100
Email:  info@allenandunwin.com
Web:    www.allenandunwin.com

A catalogue record for this book is available from the National Library of Australia

ISBN 978 1 76087 525 1

Set in 12/16.3pt Minion Pro by Bookhouse, Sydney
Printed and bound in Australia by Griffin Press, part of Ovato

10 9 8 7 6 5 4 3 2 1

*The author acknowledges Aboriginal and Torres Strait Islander peoples as the traditional custodians of our land—Australia— and acknowledges the Gadigal people of the Eora Nation as the traditional custodians of this place we now call Sydney.*

CHAPTER ONE

# THE NOBLE LEGACY

Evening had come already, a June evening in the final winter of the century and the rain had not let up for a week. In Macquarie Street and College Street and Phillip Street the leaves lay in great damp, decaying piles, which was odd, the trees native to the colony being chiefly evergreens, but the settlers had brought their trees with them (or how would they know it was autumn, if the leaves did not turn brown and fall from the trees?). In nearby Hyde Park (for the settlers had brought their parks with them too) the wide avenue, along which in more clement weather elegant couples strolled, ran with torrents of rainwater and soon became impassable.

At a municipal hall a mile or two to the west of the city a meeting was in progress. At the doorway of the hall young women in neat white blouses and wide-brimmed straw hats quite unsuited to the weather handed out ribbons emblazoned in large bold letters with the words FEDERATION YES! Because it was wet, and because every man to whom they handed a ribbon was wet too, the ink on the ribbons ran and everyone's hands turned black, but still

1

the men took the ribbons, because the women were young and ardent and the men wished to be obliging. Already a quantity of the ribbons had found their way onto the floor of the hall and had turned to a sodden mass beneath the men's boots and the legs of the chairs.

The hall was a functional one, distempered rather than panelled, a place of betterment and learning and, until the Methodist Hall was completed, of theological dissent too, where chairs and tables could be stacked and folded away to make room for dancing and music. This evening the chairs were in rows and the piano, a Charles Stieff upright that had not been tuned since the Queen's Jubilee, had been pushed into a corner beneath a dust cloth. At one end of the hall was a raised dais, above which a banner proclaimed in the same large bold letters as the ribbons—only this time a foot high—ONE PEOPLE, ONE DESTINY, ONE FLAG. And here *was* the flag—snowy white with a pretty blue cross on it and the Union Jack stuck up high in the top left-hand corner—a thing hastily fashioned and poorly manufactured in the manner of a flag not yet officially adopted and likely to be changed at a moment's notice once votes were cast and counted.

For a great bill had been proposed, and in twenty days the colony would vote and this time it would vote *Yes*. Nothing barring a catastrophe could stop it now. True, the very same thing had been declared the year before and the people of New South Wales had decided Federation was not for them. But a year later, with a newer bill—a better bill!—the fears that had sunk the vote a year earlier were appeased. Nothing barring a catastrophe, they said.

And so the hall was full, or if not quite full then certainly half full. Upwards of fifty or sixty men, and some women too, had made the journey on such a dreadful night to hear what the gentlemen from parliament and their own local aldermen had to say. They already knew how they would vote, but it was a thing, was it not, the men from the parliament coming out to your suburb, to your local hall? And on a night like this.

On the dais a row of uncomfortable folding wooden chairs held the by-no-means-slight figures of the mayor, various councillors and aldermen, one or two of the more important local business-men and the Hon. Alasdair Dunlevy MLA, the only member of the Legislative Assembly to have braved the downpour and made it to the meeting. But one member was better than none, and Mr Dunlevy cut an impressive figure in a black tailcoat and pinstriped trousers, a tall man in a tall black silk hat, powerfully built; a man barely contained by a tightly buttoned silver-and-black-striped waistcoat and a pale grey Ascot tie at his neck. Above the tie was a smooth, clean-shaven face that spurned the whiskers doggedly retained by the more senior members of the Assembly, a face that said it had nothing to hide, that said here is the future and it has no beard!

Alasdair Dunlevy stood at the lectern and surveyed the crowded hall. He knew these men, knew what was in their heads, knew—more importantly—what was in their hearts, understood their fears, their hopes, their prejudices, and this understanding calmed him, it filled him up, it made him powerful. His fingers gripped the lectern's smooth wooden edges, not to steady himself, but as a man does who sees an opportunity and who seizes it with both hands. The mayor, a man whose name Dunlevy had already forgotten, had spoken—trite platitudes and dry clichés for the most part—as had a councillor and one or two of the notable local businessmen, but it was not until Alasdair began his speech that the men sat forward and nodded their heads and shouted their approval, for he had shown them a vision of what their nation might be:

'You have heard my reasons, gentlemen, and I will summarise them for you. Federation will remove these absurd custom barriers between the colonies. It will mean a uniform railway gauge and new railways traversing our continent; it will finally open up the interior for settlement. Settlement for *Australians*—for Federation is the only possible way of preserving Australia for the white races. It will engender confidence in British investors. It will mean improved defences. For make no mistake, gentlemen—' and here Alasdair paused just long enough to allow each man in the room to lean an inch closer '—should there be a European war, disunion would mean disaster for Australia.'

And they all, to a man, liked what they heard.

Well, perhaps not to a man. Alasdair spotted the fellow a moment before he spoke:

'*We cannot trust 'em! We all know we cannot trust the Victorians.*'

The speaker, a storekeeper or an artisan in shabby Sunday best, jumped to his feet and a chorus of voices followed him, agreeing or not, and some of the other men now also got excitedly to their feet and their wives pulled them down again to their seats.

Mr Dunlevy held up his hand, but before he could reply the heckler, red-faced and sweating despite the cool night, spoke again:

'*If you believe the Victorians will* willingly *give up a federal parliament—not once they have got their hands on it—and let us build a brand-new capital someplace else,* you are a fool!'

'*They want Ballarat for the capital—the Premier hisself admitted it!*' called out a man in a bowler hat standing towards the back of the room. A further chorus of calls followed and some applause, a fair amount of derision too, but the tenor of the meeting had changed.

For the man had a point—*could* the Victorians be trusted? And, yes, the Premier had indeed said that about Ballarat, for all that it had been an unwise and unpropitious thing for him to concede.

A ripple swept through the hall, and the mood that a moment earlier had been one of high-minded camaraderie infused with a heady dose of patriotism now became something else entirely.

'*He's right—how can we trust 'em?*'

'*S'not just parliament—they want to take our money and put it in their own coffers and leave nothing for us!*'

'*What's the good of a Federation anyway? We managed for a hundred and ten years without one, why d'we need one now?*'

And, yes, the arithmetic was wrong (for it was actually a hundred and eleven years), but the point was made and it was greedily swallowed up, for ill forebodings are more easily gorged on than fair ones. On the dais the mayor and his councillors shifted in their chairs. Their frustration at the ill-informed truculence of their fellow citizens—whose opinions seemed to them belligerently dogged and also, somehow, fleetingly changeable—was clear.

Or it was clear to Alasdair, and the smile he allowed himself was wry, for if they anticipated this crowd—indeed, any crowd—to be rational and consistent, then they had fundamentally misunderstood their fellow men.

And so he stood, unruffled, at the lectern. He smiled. He waited. He had brought no notes with him to the meeting. His tailcoat and waistcoat had been designed in Italy. This silk top hat cost more than the collected wardrobes of every man present. This was not his first such meeting nor indeed his tenth. He had lost count of the number of Federation meetings he had attended and, the human mind being what it is, and men being essentially the same whether they be at Bondi Beach or Emu Plains or any point between, the same questions came up. Oh, patriotism and slogans and flags were all very well, but what it all boiled down to was that men feared change.

And so he smiled, he waited for a pause, and when it came he seized it:

'Gentlemen . . .' (And, yes, there were women in the audience, but none of them had questioned the Federation, had they? None of them had questioned his sound reasoning. Besides, none of them had the vote.) 'I understand your concerns. Indeed, I have shared them. New South Wales has *always* been a *champion of free trade*, and you want assurances it will remain so, that our Federation tariff policy will *not be based on protectionism*. Gentlemen, *I can make that assurance.* There is nothing in this draft constitution to suggest it. You are concerned about losing out—you worry that customs collected from *your pockets* will go into a central government coffer. Worse, that we in New South Wales will find ourselves subsidising our poorer cousins in the other smaller, struggling economies—'

'*Too right! Those South Australians, Tasmanians and Western Australians want to bleed us dry!*'

'—and that is why Mr Braddon inserted his clause into our bill which provides an assurance to *us* that customs revenue will be returned to each state *for the first ten years.* And that is why Mr Braddon assures us that *there will be a new federal capital*—a brand-new city!—and it is to be built *not* in Victoria, *not* in Tasmania, *not* in South Australia, but *here in our own New South Wales!*'

'*But a hundred miles away!*'

'Yes, a hundred miles away!' (Alasdair pounded the lectern.) 'And what is that in our country which is *two thousand miles across*? Our city, which has grown to half a million souls in less than a hundred years, will stretch out to the north and to the south and to the west to cover that hundred miles *in less than a century!*'

A cheer followed this prediction, as it generally did.

'Before it is completed, this new federal capital *will be part of our western suburbs!*'

This brought another cheer and some laughter.

'Gentlemen, look to the other brave new nations of the world that have embraced federalism: Argentina, Canada, Switzerland, the United States—'

*'And look what happened there—they all but wiped 'emselves out in a bloody great civil war!'*

Alasdair smiled and released both hands from their grip on the lectern, holding them before him, palms upwards. Someone always mentioned the American war.

'Our nation will be created out of *peace* not out of war. This, gentlemen, will be our legacy. And is it not a *sweet and noble* legacy to leave our children and our children's children? Does it not *stir the blood* to know that we here today, and at the polling booth on the twentieth of June, *will make history?*'

The red-faced man made some reply to this, but as the hall had erupted into applause and loud cheers his reply was lost.

The speeches were over. A show of hands was called: those for Federation and those against, the result being not quite unanimous but surely a clear majority in favour. The mayor beamed and his councillors congratulated each other with vigorous handshakes and jocular slaps on the back.

Alasdair Dunlevy shook every hand that was offered to him, making a point of greeting each member of the council and all the aldermen and the irritating little shopkeeper who had spoken out against him, and keeping one eye on the door and his fob watch and on his secretary, who lingered near the stage with their coats and umbrellas making hurry-up gestures, and on the photographer from the local paper who, surely, was going to ask for a picture?—yes, here was the fellow now—and striking just the right pose as the flash went off. Time for another? Yes, certainly—this time with the minister in the centre. And if the glow of victory had begun already to dissipate, it was only because Alasdair had been here at this very same hall with these very same men a year ago, almost to the day, and the mood that evening had been buoyant, celebratory, just as it was tonight, and a few days later they had lost the referendum.

∞

Outside the rain continued to fall. Evening had become night.

A short carriage ride east of the city lay the inlet of Elizabeth Bay. Here the straight lines to which men aspired and which they had largely achieved in other parts of the city were abandoned. One road led directly down to the water, it was true, but the rest followed their own path, twisting and snaking and turning back on themselves seemingly on a whim. To live in Elizabeth Bay was to be forever climbing and descending, so the horses that pulled the carriages, the tradesmen's drays and the hansom cabs that stepped lightly elsewhere, here laboured and strained and lost their footing. This was a shoreline still in the process of being tamed, where retaining walls and waterside parks and mooring for pleasure craft vied with sheer cliffs and rocky escarpments and scrub, where the newly built villas overlooking the bay perched tentatively, not quite yet master of the landscape.

On one of the newly paved streets was a row of villas made of honey-coloured sandstone, built in the Italianate style—with slate roofs and bay windows and cast-iron balustrading—by a team of Italian stonemasons brought to the colony at some expense. The new villas all had names, but they were not the Berwicks or Amblesides or Windermeres of a hundred other merchants' houses that imagined a homesickness for a mother country most had never visited; these houses were named for the men who had built them, for the men who had bought the land and subdivided it, and for the politicians who had smoothed the passage of development. (One or two even echoed the ancient names the people of the Eora nation had once used, names cut down and made palatable to the European tongue, but these were very much the minority.) The new villas had bathrooms, they had running water and the new electric lighting. One or two subscribed to the telephone service. They were houses for the new century, built in the dying months of the old one.

Inside one of these houses a maid moved from room to room lighting fires, drawing curtains, trimming wicks—for the house still retained a handful of kerosene lamps and the maid avoided, where she could, the new electric lights. This house was named Yarran, a Jewish-sounding name, perhaps, though more likely a corruption of Yarrandabby, the old Gadigal name for the headland, though it had been many years since an elder had stood on this headland and uttered its name.

Her tasks completed, the maid—whose name was Alice Nimrod—went silently upstairs to the room of her mistress.

She was a slight figure, insubstantial—not in height, for she was as tall as anyone in the house, taller than some, but in presence. She had worked five years in the large, newly built house, though she was not yet twenty, and she moved warily in the manner of one who dwells in another person's house.

Tonight her head was very full. She had got through the work of the day in fits and starts, hurrying over some tasks, lingering over others, her fingers moving restlessly, as restlessly as the thoughts in her head, and sometimes spoiling her work so that she must start afresh. Her throat was full too, she found now, full of strange words that she dared not utter and had not thought ever to utter in her life before. Yet the words fought to come out.

How full her head was!

At the top of the stairs Alice Nimrod stopped and turned about. She had no business to be here, and a maid in a place she had no business to be was in a precarious position. She walked the short distance along the landing and paused at her mistress's bedroom door, her hand raised to knock.

But she did not knock. Her hand fell to her side. She closed her eyes.

∞

Inside the room rain lashed the window.

Eleanor Dunlevy looked up from her journal. It was already quite dark outside. The curtains had not yet been drawn, and in the window she saw only the darkness of the night and her own face made indistinct by the rivers of water on the pane. The face was very white in the strange light, and featureless, the eyes blank, obscured by the little round-framed spectacles that she had recently been obliged to adopt. Her husband, a man with his nose always in a newspaper or an official document of some description and who was five years her senior, did not require such aids to his vision. She pulled the spectacles off. They were attached to a little chain about her neck and she let them fall to her chest. She had not yet told her husband she wore them, spent her evenings staring unseeing at the blurred pages of her novel until he retired to bed.

Outside leaves swirled and stuck to the pane, held fast by the force of the wind before being swept away into oblivion, and now Eleanor could make out two bright points of light in the darkness, which she thought must be the distant pilot lights of some vessel negotiating the safety of the harbour, but they turned out to be the unblinking yellow eyes of a possum wrapped around a branch of the Moreton Bay fig outside her window.

She took up her spectacles and reviewed what she had written in her journal:

*Blanche wore a feathered piece on her head, ostrich, one presumes—*

Her eyes moved down the page.

*. . . the turbot was a rather odd colour though no one remarked on it . . . R. made some fatuous observation about the Prem. that amused everyone—not A., of course, who cannot afford to mock the P.!*

What was R's fatuous remark? She could not for the moment recall. She and Alasdair had gone to a dinner at the Pykes' and some of the gentlemen had come directly from a meeting at a town hall where someone had made a great speech and someone else had proposed something and three cheers had been offered and the future of the nation was, apparently, assured. Over the fish there had been a great deal of discussion about tariffs and free trade and the new federal capital. Someone had said, *It boils down to just one thing: can we trust the other colonies?*

Could they? Eleanor did not know. She had put none of this in her journal. She had noted the ostrich feather and the colour of the soup.

*A. observed how the Prem's speech had been particularly well received and that the bill was all but assured this time.*

*Had* Alasdair said that? It was the kind of thing her husband might have said, the kind of thing he would like to have said. She had written it in her journal and so it became true. She wondered if she wrote the journal for herself or if it were not for some faceless scholar years hence, sequestered in a dusty university library researching a dull biography. Alasdair's biography.

11

On their way to the dinner at the Pykes' they had seen two constables pull a body from the bay, the sodden, clothed body of a female. It was not a common spot for suicides but any place, presumably, would do if one were determined. Sometimes they jumped from the quay and a day later were washed up in the bay by the current. Sometimes they jumped from the steamers. (Imagine sailing all this way across so many oceans simply to jump overboard with your destination in sight!) Occasionally the *Herald* reported the suicide, supplying a name and how many children were left behind; often there was no name, just a body fished from the harbour. When she and Alasdair had returned home, passing the same spot, the constables were gone. Eleanor had put none of this in her journal.

*How proud I was then of my husband, the statesman, who has stood at the Premier's side this whole time and whose tireless campaigning must surely rival that of Mr Reid himself,* she wrote and then she stopped writing and placed her pen on the blotter. Her hands were quite pale in the lamplight; a flattering light, but still the lines were visible. One could disguise the cruel march of time on one's face, one's body, but on the hands there was no hiding it. Gloves, yes, while in company, but alone there was no denying it. A flicker of panic stirred within her, consuming all momentarily, then as quickly dissipating.

She snapped the journal shut and pushed it away from her, and at the same moment a knock came at the door.

The room had become dark, but the hallway outside was brightly lit so that the opening door cast light into her room and, for a startling moment, the slight figure of the maid, Alice, appeared immense and monstrous.

No servant was ever quite invisible. Alice, who had the features of utter banality and unremarkability true to her class but a face which ought to have been free of expression and somehow never was, had never achieved invisibility. She stood now quite motionless in the doorway, not speaking, her face and hands an extension of the plain black dress and starched white apron, collar and cuffs she wore so that it was not at once clear where the uniform ended and the girl began. Her shoulders were a little stooped, a strand of hair had worked its way loose from her cap, her hands hung at her sides as though lost without something to carry.

'The curtains, madam,' she said at last.

If the kitchen had caught on fire, or a ship wrecked in the bay, one imagined she would announce it in just the same tone.

But this evening two bright red spots showed clearly, one on each side of her face.

The girl plunged into the room. She made for the window, drawing the curtains then pausing to caress the thick crimson velvet, smoothing it out so the folds fell just so. She stood back as though to admire them, though she must have drawn them and opened them every day of her life for the last five years, and nothing about the way they fell this evening was different to how they had fallen any other day of those five years.

'Thank you, Alice.'

But Alice did not leave. Alice remained where she was, taking up so little space yet taking up all the space in the room.

'Was there something else?'

Those livid spots on either side of her face.

The girl must be unwell or she wanted an afternoon off or she had broken some piece of china. Was she giving her notice? But, no, apparently it was none of these things, as Alice bobbed a brief curtsy in the vague direction of the window and said, 'No, madam.'

The door clicked shut behind her. Eleanor let out her breath. A slight weight of oppression slid away. She stared at the window.

Though it was obscured now by the thick crimson curtains, she could still hear the rain lashing the pane.

A hatbox lay opened on the bed, a number of pairs of gloves laid out beside it.

It was monstrous that one should have to go out in this weather.

She was dressed already in white brocaded satin, the bodice embroidered with gold, and her diamonds. It was the dress she had worn to the Governor-General's ball in April for the opening of the special session of parliament. *Mrs Dunlevy wore white*, the *Herald* had reported the following morning, though it had listed almost every other lady's dress in detail—Lady Darley's silver appliqué and shaded heliotrope chiffon, Mrs Barton's pale pink silk and deep flounces of lace, Mrs Dickens' embroidered netting and black trimming. But Mrs Dunlevy wore white.

The morning edition of the newspaper lay on her writing desk, where she had placed it after lunch so that she might read it alone in her room. A steamer, the *Albatross*, had gone down in the Cook Strait with the loss of all hands. It had been missing since Tuesday and now the captain of another ship had reported seeing pieces of decking and masting floating in the water. It was a wholly inauspicious name, wasn't it, the *Albatross*? Surely one was anticipating catastrophe by naming a ship thus. Eleanor saw, for a moment, the pieces of decking, the masting floating in the water. The newspaper listed the names of the perished officers and crew, recording their rank and whether or not they were married. Most were.

She picked up her pen and became aware that Alice was standing just outside the door. She held her pen above the page, and did not move. The page narrowed into a tiny white dot before her eyes. What did the girl want? Why did she stand there? She would get up and fling open the door and demand of the girl what she meant by it.

But Eleanor did not get up, she did not fling open the door, and after a time she heard the floorboards creak and Alice went away.

She had been holding her breath and she let it out now in a rush. She picked up the newspaper and read again the list of passengers. She had scanned the list already, but what if she had missed the name of someone with whom she was acquainted? For here was a Mrs Pavey travelling with her daughter—there had been a Miss Pavey, had there not, many years ago, the sister of a friend of someone? But if Miss Pavey had married, her name would no longer be Pavey; she would have some other name. There was no one, then, on the list whom she knew. She ought to be relieved.

Beneath the story of the lost steamer the paper reported an outbreak of plague at Alexandria. The rain beat at the window and she thought of infested rats in some far-off land and primitive people crowded together in makeshift dwellings. It was not Egypt, of course, to which the news item referred; it was a suburb of the same name here in this very city, a place perhaps two or three miles to the south-west. A poor place. A part of the city she had never visited.

She put the newspaper to one side and picked up her pen once more.

*How proud I was then of my husband, the statesman—*

Eleanor raised her pen to strike out the words but then could not do so. To strike out something one had written in one's journal, was that not censorship of the most insidious sort, censorship of one's own thoughts? But they were not her own thoughts. Whose thoughts were they? *How proud I was—* She hated those words! They contaminated her journal. But she could not strike them out. She closed the book and placed it in her desk drawer and turned the key in the lock.

Did Alasdair have a duplicate key? she wondered. She unlocked the drawer. Beneath the journal was a note, a single page—two or three lines, no more—on unheaded notepaper folded inside a plain cream-coloured envelope. The note had arrived with the first post a few days earlier. It was a note she was reasonably certain had not been intended for her eyes but that had, somehow, found its way to her. She had read the note just the once and put it away. She had told no one about it.

She slowly turned towards her dressing table, a fussily ornate mid-century piece of polished walnut topped by a large bevelled mirror, and regarded herself. She had dressed, had skilfully arranged her own hair, without studying herself at all, but now she made herself look. Her eyes filled her face. It was an illusion, but she could not shake it off. The pleasing regularity of her features, a strong nose and chin, a prominent brow, a clear complexion, all these things eluded her gaze. She turned to see her profile but could not quite catch herself. Were her features *too* regular? Did one tire of them over time? Did they hint at a conventionality, an absence of some kind? She had fought long and hard to hide the most secret parts of herself, but was it possible she had succeeded too well? She had turned men's heads once and sometimes did so now, though she had accepted the first proposal she had received and had not regretted it. But did one tire, eventually, of pleasing regularity?

She locked the desk drawer a second time and stood up.

An urgent tap at the window stopped her heart and she put a hand to her chest. She went to the window and threw back the heavy crimson curtain, at first seeing nothing, but a second tap proved to be the overgrown Moreton Bay fig reaching out in the darkness and in the wind and in the rain with its outermost branch towards the house, towards her. And the giant possum, a male, unmoving as the rain splashed onto its sodden brown pelt, its yellow eyes unblinking and unsurprised. They—the possum and the monstrous ancient tree—had something timeless about them, as though they had both been here a great many years, before this house and this suburb, before even the city itself. There was a recrimination in the *tap-tap-tap*, in the unblinking yellow eyes.

Eleanor let fall the curtain and turned away. She was going out. She must get ready.

The rain continued to fall. The night lengthened and the city, a place of sparkling water and dazzling light in the daytime, became a place of shivering misery from which men scurried.

Eleanor sat in a hansom cab as it splashed through the deserted streets. She had sent Alice out into the night to find the cab and the girl had taken an umbrella and gone all the way up to MacLeay Street before she had found one.

It was a filthy night, and Eleanor wondered about Alasdair's meeting and who might see fit to attend it on such a night. But they were all well attended, he said, and the newspapers said it too. Two hundred people had come, they reported, or two hundred and fifty, to hear the Premier speak, more to hear Mr Barton. Yet Eleanor was yet to attend a single one of Alasdair's meetings this time around, when she had attended a dozen or more the last time, a year ago. She had intended to go with him this evening, but in the end she had not. The rain; it was the rain that had stopped her. But there were still three weeks to go. Twenty days. She leaned back in the cab as a weariness overcame her.

They had left William Street and turned north into College Street. A void on her left, utterly black and impenetrable, was Hyde Park. Soon they would be at Macquarie Street and the moment of arriving would be upon her. She awaited with a growing dread the slowing of the cab, the opening of the carriage door, the dash through the puddles and the cold gripping the back of her neck, but it could not be put off. One could hardly tell the cabbie to turn about and take her home again. She pulled her fur closer about her.

*Mrs Dunlevy wore white.*

'We're here, lady,' called the cabbie above the pounding of the rain.

Eleanor gazed at the rain as it beat against the carriage window, drumming an insistent and incessant rhythm. It had been there for days—not the rain, though that had been present for days too, but the insistent and incessant drumming. She could pinpoint its beginning precisely to the moment she had received the note that was folded now inside an envelope in her writing desk drawer, a note that began *My dearest* and went on to confirm a meeting of which she had no knowledge; a note that was unsigned, though she recognised the florid and careless hand of her husband.

She understood her husband was having an affair.

CHAPTER TWO

# FROG HOLLOW

The distance from Elizabeth Bay to Surry Hills was about two miles, mostly by way of Darlinghurst Road and Crown Street. The maid, Alice Nimrod, made this journey in the rain not long after Mrs Dunlevy had departed in the hansom cab. It was not a journey she wished to make, but she was soaked through already from the dash all the way to MacLeay Street to find her mistress a cab so more rain hardly mattered.

The maid hastened through the dark and deserted streets, and the rain beat down on her hat and coursed down her neck and splashed up over her boots. Her coat was wet through, and her skirt clung to her legs so that her cold flesh shrunk from it. She pulled her collar tighter about her and half closed her eyes against it, but nothing could stop it, the relentless rain. On and on she went, Alice Nimrod, and it was fear that drove her on.

It was not the kind of fear one feels at a sudden loud sound in the night and that stops the heart and freezes the senses. No, this was a fear that resided daily in her breast, that beat a dull rhythm in her head and in her ears from morning to night, and was the fear of the servant who has been plucked from the pit of poverty and hopelessness and, having once been saved, whose every waking hour was shaped and determined by the threat of sinking back into it. With her mistress gone, Alice had cast off the spotless white apron and cap and snatched up her coat, but beneath her coat she still wore the ugly black dress with its stiff white collars and cuffs that marked her as a servant. She had left the house of her employer without permission, and if her mistress found her gone she faced dismissal.

She faced disaster.

For a moment she faltered, raised her eyes to the darkened sky and considered turning back.

But there was more to Alice Nimrod than her fear and her five years of service. She was not yet twenty and sometimes she stood at the shore and watched pods of dolphins playing in the bay, she observed the great ships that had crossed oceans to slip inside the heads and dock in her city, she gazed at the flocks of yellow-crested cockatoos that filled the sky at dusk.

Tonight Alice Nimrod put her head down and ran through the rain.

The road had begun to flood. A growing torrent surged along both gutters, carrying with it a detritus of mud and refuse, running off into the mean dwellings on either side of the street, dwellings that became meaner the further she travelled from Darlinghurst Road and the closer she came to Surry Hills. Something in the darkness fetched up against her foot and lodged there. She saw it was a dead rat and kicked it away; it swirled for a moment, caught in a whirlpool, and was gone. But she was on Riley Street now, and despite the rain her steps slowed.

The road had been constructed on a high piece of ground but here, at the corner of Riley and Albion streets, the earth plunged in a sheer cliff face to a crater some thirty feet below as though it had been dynamited, or perhaps dug out of the rocks with their bare hands by men in chains as, not so many decades before, so much of the city had been dug. A creek that had once crossed Riley Street to feed this pool of swampy ground and the frogs that once dwelled here and had given the Hollow its name were long gone. Instead, mean tenements, loosely constructed of rotting timber and broken bricks, of rusted sheets of tin and sometimes just mud, sprouted from the stinking mire at the bottom of the Hollow, growing one on top of the other in a chaotic and confused fashion. Frog Hollow existed on the fringe of the city, a part of it but violently separated from it, the home of the poorest and the most desperate, a place of opium and blindness-inducing homemade grog, of brutality and disease, of unwashed barefoot urchins, of rabid dogs and rats and fleas and every sort of vermin, of narrow unlit passages a foot deep in mud upon whose environs the sun never shined.

This was the place to which Alice Nimrod hastened.

Three flights of stone steps, steep and crudely carved, provided the only access down—though why someone had thought to dig out such steps and what kind of person might use them to enter such a place, who knew? Certainly the constables of Surry Hills police station did not, and nor did the various members of the clergy from the many churches in the parish.

But Alice Nimrod did. Though it was true she paused a moment to lift her skirts and perhaps, too, to steel herself. But only for a moment. She stepped down, picking her path carefully for the way was treacherous at the best of times and on this night it was a fast track to the city mortuary and a pauper's grave. If you were lucky. If you were unlucky, your body was spirited away by the people lurking below—for who knew what nefarious purpose—and you were never heard of again.

Alice made slow progress down the flights of steps until something blocked her path just a step or two from the bottom. What seemed to be a decaying pile of clothes or waste slowly took on a human form with two staring eyes. A woman, unmoving, and whether soaked by the rain or by the grog Alice felt no compunction to find out. When the figure did not stir and the staring eyes did not blink she understood that the woman had departed this earth, and her suffering, whatever form it may have taken, was ended.

Alice stepped over her and thought no more of her. There was compassion in Alice but, like everything else in life, her compassion was not limitless, it must be parcelled up. It must be rationed.

She reached the bottom of the Hollow and her boots sank in sludge and, at the same moment, a figure reared out of the darkness and lurched at her with a drunken roar. Alice let out a cry but she struck out because she was not helpless, far from it, and her own upbringing, though better than this by far, had still been filled with hardship. Her strike hit home, meeting something solid and rebounding off it so that she almost lost her footing. Her assailant staggered, reeling towards her, whether off balance or with actual intent it was impossible to tell, but Alice shoved him hard so that he fell and, before he could right himself, she fled.

Her heart beat a little faster. This was not her first visit to Frog Hollow after dark and, though she was clearly no policeman or priest or bailiff nor any of the natural enemies of the Hollow, she well understood the horrors that might befall a woman in this place. She turned this way and that, negotiating the labyrinth of narrow byways, her flight more panicked than before, but no one save herself need know it. She pulled up only when she reached the low, uneven opening at the entrance of a timbered shack.

It was a doorway, though if this was to imply that something as conventional as a door stood in this doorway that would be wrong, for all that stood there was a roughly hewn plank of rotting wood laid across the space and providing little by way of barrier or weatherproofing or privacy. It did at least keep out the stray dogs, but that was all that could be said for it.

Alice pushed the piece of wood to one side and slipped inside. The shack within consisted of a single windowless room with a dirt floor that some previous occupant had covered with layers of newspapers and straw and remnants of old matting. The only furniture was a table fashioned from four kerosene drums with a square of flattened tin on top and two wooden chairs, mismatching, and looking as though they had washed up as flotsam from the harbour. A wooden pallet on the floor against one wall on which soiled bedding was piled and a bucket in the furthest corner covered by a cloth from which a foul smell exuded made up the rest. Above, the ceiling bulged and creaked ominously and strange noises could be heard—another shack, with another family, had been built directly atop this one. How long the two dwellings would remain separate was a cause for speculation—one great downpour (a bit like this one, in fact), one violent gale or flash flood, and the shack above, along with the family and all their belongings, such as they might be, would come crashing down into the shack below.

There was no light inside other than the thin shaft that now crept in through the doorway and Alice reached out, feeling with her hands until her eyes adjusted—

A hand shot out and grabbed her by the hair and the blade of a knife flashed at her throat and Alice cried out, 'It is *me*, Milli! It is Alice!'

There was a sharp intake of breath. The knife clattered to the floor.

'As well that it is you, for I was ready to *cut your throat*! Hurry! Show me what you have brought me.'

The shadowy, shapeless figure that spoke these words rustled as though it wore a great many clothes and moved sluggishly as though hampered by some great burden. The hands snatched and twitched and could not settle. The faint glow from the doorway now afforded a glimpse of a great mass of matted hair framing a skull on which the skin was stretched taut and where the ghost of a face Alice had once known better than her own appeared fleetingly. She saw eyes that could not rest any more than the hands could rest. Whether or not this longed-for figure, her sister, would have cut her throat Alice did not know; whether Milli being nine months heavy with a child was a condition which made murder more likely or less likely she could not say. A longing had filled her head all that day and all the previous day and the day before that. It was a longing that had been dulled for the five years of Milli's absence, but now that Milli was returned it struck her mute. It had sent her, a dozen times that day, to the door of her mistress's room with a plea to be released early from her duties, with a plea—though she hardly dared formulate the words in her head—for help in whatever form it might be in her mistress's power to give. But each time she had failed, had left without knocking.

Yet here she was, and she had got away, if only for an hour or two.

'Here, Milli, see what I have got!' And with a flourish, Alice pulled from her coat pocket a linen cloth from which spilled a half-loaf of bread, two cooked potatoes and a lump of cheese. Her face burned hotly and she sat down, a little breathless. If she could not release the words of longing that filled her heart, if she could not hear those longed-for same words on her sister's lips, she could at least bring her this feast.

Two hands snatched up the food and crammed it into the almost-toothless mouth and Alice stole a glance at the sister returned to her after five years, at those restless and dimmed eyes that seemed to deny all that had once been their life together and at the same time demanded all that her younger sister could give. If there had been self-pity in those eyes at one time, or loathing, it was long gone. All that remained of Milli was those hands snatching at the scraps of leftover food.

How had she sunk so low?

Five years earlier Milli had leaned out of the window of the train at Sydney Terminal Station in their mother's old coat, clutching a carpet bag and sporting a gay red hat with a feather in the crown, about to depart on the overnight to Melbourne. Milli leaving, this time for good, to join Seamus. She had been so happy, or so it had seemed to the fourteen-year-old Alice, standing on the platform, the smoke and steam swirling about her. Alice, sad already, and desperate to be leaving too, only dimly aware of the loneliness that was to come, waving goodbye to the only family she had left in the world. Wishing she had a white handkerchief to wave, watching until the train was out of sight.

'Take me with you.' The words she had not spoken.

And now five years had passed and Milli was back. Two babies had come and been lost, both before their first birthdays, and Seamus had gone too, to Adelaide, for it turned out he had a wife already. So here was Milli, nine months heavy with a third child and so large her confinement could not be more than a few days away. The old coat that had once belonged to their mother was gone, so too the little red hat with the feather in the crown. And the bag of belongings—where was that? The happiness, the hope of a future, all of it gone. And what had returned from Melbourne was this shadowy collection of rags who dwelled in a cave and snatched at

25

the scraps on the table and pressed a knife to your throat when you came through her door.

Handsome Seamus with his Irish eyes and his Irish laughter and his solid and muscular wharfie arms and that flash of something that was thrilling and frightening all at once. Milli had said, *There's some Abo in him, Alice, somewhere back.* Alice had been a little in love with Seamus herself.

'Take me with you.'

But Milli had not thought to take Alice with her—what would she want with a girl of fourteen in tow? She had left her behind, though their mother's grave was still fresh in Devonshire Street Cemetery.

The potato had slowed Milli down; it required some tearing, some chewing. You needed a few teeth and Milli, by the look of it, had none.

Alice did not speak, though words crammed her mouth. Five years, such a very long time and such very different lives they had lived in that time, so that Alice found herself all at once filled to bursting with stories about the life she now led, the place she now lived, of the Dunlevys for whom she worked. But she said nothing. And it was because of her good fortune. Because God had seen fit to pluck Alice Nimrod from the life she had been born to and drop her into a better place, and He had not done the same for Milli.

It hung between them, Alice's good fortune.

'You took this, dint you, from the people you work for?' said Milli, indicating the scraps of leftover food. She spoke as someone afraid to be overheard. Or someone who did not wish to know the answers to her questions.

Alice nodded. Yes, she had taken it. And why should she be ashamed? The food was there to be stolen and no one would notice if it was gone or not. (Perhaps Mrs Flynn did notice; certainly she gave Alice a shrewd look every now and then. But that was all she did, for what servant wanted to know another's private business? In any case, Mrs Flynn took leftovers home to her own family.) But Alice had lately discovered that it was hard to help someone who had less than yourself, though you might think it would be an easy thing to do, and she did not understand why this was so.

'I have some money too,' she said now, and she scrabbled in her other pocket and laid a meagre pile of coins on the table.

The shame of the little pile was great and Alice sat in misery.

But Milli paused with the potato long enough to flick her fingers through the pile, to make a speedy reckoning, then sweep the lot off the table and into her pocket. Gone.

'You always did have sharp fingers,' said Milli, her voice softening and a memory flashing across her face. 'Remember the baker's on Crown Street? All them buns you nicked and that old baker never the wiser. You was like lightning.'

'Mum used to say, "Never ask where a thing comes from for it is sure to disappear if you do"!' said Alice, the brief light of remembrance shining in her own face, and for a moment they were sisters once more.

But Milli heaved herself to her feet, shifting her bulk with a groan, repositioning herself on the rickety little chair into a more comfortable position, and the shadows rose up and consumed them. The baby would come any day and what then? Alice felt the hopelessness swell and surge about them. Perhaps the baby would die.

She wondered again if she might ask Mrs Dunlevy for help—sometimes it seemed within her power to do so. At other times the utter impossibility of it struck her dumb.

A great thud from above caused them both to look sharply upwards and a shower of dust and earth came tumbling down so that Alice wondered if the ceiling might choose this very moment to finally descend on them, or if God Himself might decide to bring the roof down, for He seemed set fair on this path of cruelty where Milli was concerned.

But the ceiling did not come down. Not yet.

How many of them lived up there? Alice wondered. The woman, whose name was Mrs Renfrew and who had four or five barefoot, clamouring offspring crowded about her legs and a newborn in her arms, had spoken a civil word to her once when no one else had.

And all the time the hopelessness swelled and surged about them, but whereas Alice struggled to keep her head above the rising tide, Milli submitted to its inevitability, or this was how it seemed to Alice. She watched as her sister pushed at the matted clumps of hair that obscured her face. This was the same Milli who had once sat on a bed with a mirror in one hand and a hairbrush in the other, brushing and brushing her beautiful, soft and shining chestnut hair and arranging it and rearranging it, getting up and flouncing about the room because some lad had called out to her in the street and another had whistled at her from a tram. Milli, turning this way and that, trying to see herself full length in a mirror that showed you only your face and Alice watching her, perched on the bed and clapping her hands and laughing, and their mother seated in her chair with her withered and broken body, her eyes sunken and dulled, shaking her head and muttering dire warnings. For Mrs Nimrod had lived a life already and she had seen what happened to a girl's dreams and hopes once some man came along, and when your own life had been spoiled you did not have it left inside you to let your own child have her life. Alice had not seen it at the time—a delighted observer of her sister's exploits, a dreamer of her own future exploits—but she saw it now.

She looked away.

'What is to be done?' she said at length. And then, remembering: 'Milli, the place at Pitt Street, the Benevolent Asylum, you must go there.'

It was where the women went for their lying-in, or it had been when Alice had grown up in streets not so far away, where the sorts of women who needed such places sometimes lived.

But Milli's face was set hard. 'I went there first day I got here,' she said. 'It was full.'

'Full? But surely—'

'I went before a board, they said show us proof you are married, show us proof your husband abandoned you, or you are at the back of the queue. There was a dozen other women trying to get in. Two dozen. It was no good, so I came here.'

Alice was silenced. The asylum was the last place of sanctuary. It had not occurred to her a woman might be refused entry. If not the asylum, then what? Scraps of leftover food and a handful of coins, this was all the assistance she could render. She thought again of Mrs Dunlevy, who sat on committees and attended charitable lunches and raised funds for deserving causes. One of her committees, surely, was the Benevolent Asylum? It was what had made her think of it.

She would ask Mrs Dunlevy for help, she would!

But she said nothing to Milli, because each occasion that she had stood before Mrs Dunlevy's door unable to knock filled her with shame. Instead, she said, 'Milli, if ever there was something I might do to help, I would do it, oh, I would! And with a glad heart!'

At this Milli's arm shot out and grasped Alice's wrist in a sudden and tight grip. Her eyes fixed on her sister in a way they had not done since she had arrived, as though Milli had just awoken and had been awaiting this moment.

'You *can* help me, Alice,' she said, and perhaps she saw more than Alice meant her to, for her next words seemed to reach inside Alice's head and pluck the thoughts straight out of her. 'You must take me back with you to that grand house where you work. I can shelter there. It would be a few days or a week at most.'

Alice felt the utter horror of such a request. It struck the words from her mouth. For this was the one thing she could not do. Milli knew nothing of her life if she thought this was even a possibility.

'Or do you not wish to help me? Your only sister?'

Still Alice could not speak. The grip on her wrist tightened. Her arm was pulled sharply across the makeshift little table and would not be released.

'Alice, you must help me! I cannot stay here and not just because of this.' Milli stabbed a vicious finger at her swollen belly. 'There are people after me, people who would kill me.'

What she meant by this, and if it were even true, Alice did not know.

'But how can I take you there?' she cried. 'You do not understand, Milli. You think because it is a big house you can go there and no one will notice you, but it ain't so! There is no place where the mistress does not go, no cupboard or drawer she does not open. I cannot hide a mouse without she would find it. And then I would lose my position.'

'And end up like me!' said Milli.

And for a time the bitterness of one and the dismay of the other rose and swirled about them and neither could speak.

'I had the last baby in gaol,' Milli announced, throwing back her head—in a challenge, it seemed. As though she had been holding back this piece of information and was casting it now into the space between them to see how it might fall.

'Gaol?' whispered Alice.

Milli sneered. 'What of it? I was drunk. A misdemeanour. Twenty-one days they give me. Just enough time to get the baby out. What? You think it is any worse than *this*?' And when Alice made no reply, 'Because it is not. Not really. You get medicine in gaol and a place to sleep, and tea and bread three times a day. They let me keep the baby with me. Until it died.'

Milli turned to gaze through the doorway at the rain pouring steadily. She wore an old woollen shawl, which she pulled closer about her thin shoulders.

'You think it wicked, don't you?' she said, thrusting her face close to her sister's though Alice had said nothing. 'That is what you think, ain't it, Alice? That it is wicked? That *I* am wicked?'

Wicked? Alice was baffled by the word. She had not heard it used since Father McCreadie had rescued her from this life and put her in another. It was a word, an idea, for priests. For rich people.

Alice stared at her sister. Her lips moved but no words came. For a time neither spoke, then, 'I have borrowed money, Alice,' said Milli at last. 'And I cannot repay it. If I stay here a day longer, they shall slit my throat.' She stood up and at once sat down again. 'Where am I safe if you will not help me? Tell me.'

Alice could not speak. She remembered standing on the railway platform five years ago, waving goodbye. I just wanted you to take me with you, she thought. But Milli had left her behind. And now, for the first time, she realised just how lucky she had been.

# CHAPTER THREE

# THE RUM HOSPITAL

A line of carriages was drawn up in front of the colonnaded two-storey building on Macquarie Street that had once been the Chief Surgeon's quarters of the Sydney Hospital next door, and was now Parliament House.

Ninety years earlier the governor for whom the street was named had ordered Sydney's first hospital built, had provided the convict labour to build it, and had pulled off a clever trick with rum duties to pay for it. The resulting building was so shoddily constructed it had been declared unfit for purpose before it was even completed. When the gentlemen of the Legislative Assembly had finally moved in, the chamber's acoustics were so poor parliamentary sessions were routinely interrupted whenever troops from the nearby barracks used the Domain as a firing range. A competition to design a magnificent new Parliament House was held and a foundation stone for the new building laid amid great pomp and festivity, but afterwards, when someone actually sat down and calculated the cost of it all, the entire endeavour was quietly shelved, and a year or two later the foundation stone discreetly dug up and removed.

Such an inauspicious start to its sovereignty might have hampered other dominions, but the colony of New South Wales wore its unorthodox beginnings as a badge of honour. And as the men who had filled its legislative chambers ever since had brokered cabinet posts as favours, and made fortunes rerouting railway lines across their own land and passing legislation that lined their own pockets, all in the name of the public good, perhaps it was fitting that the parliament start its life this way.

On this particular evening Parliament House was brilliantly lit and the line of carriages, one of which contained Eleanor Dunlevy, led all the way back to Hyde Park. As each carriage drew up in the driving rain it sent water cascading in great arcs and created great puddles through which the footmen dashed. Gentlemen in top hats and ladies in elegant gowns and extravagant headwear climbed hurriedly down, shielded beneath vast umbrellas, and chose, according to their affiliation, to enter the house via one flight of stairs or via a second, the one leading to the Legislative Assembly foyer, the other to the Legislative Council foyer. It did not seem to matter that beyond both foyers the rather modest building converged into a single lobby area, this demarcation must be, and was, observed by one and all. The clerks of the house understood it, so did the grooms and the footmen, and so did the wives who accompanied the gentlemen. And lest one should be in any doubt, the Council foyer was red (plush red carpet, red wallpaper, red upholstery) and the Assembly foyer was green (green-patterned carpet, green wallpaper, green upholstery). Where these two areas converged the carpet was red, the upholstery green, the columns papered half in red, half in green.

It was enough to bring on a bilious attack, so it was as well that the hospital was right next door.

This evening the Premier was hosting a reception. Mr George Reid, recently and triumphantly returned from a series of successful pro-Federation meetings at Maitland and Tamworth in the north, was in high spirits and the mood was celebratory. The divisions that usually separated men—this party or that, Council or Assembly, those born in the mother country and those born in the colony—counted for little tonight. It was all Federation and there was no talk of defeat.

Eleanor Dunlevy entered the house via the Assembly stairs. Removing her coat and handing it to a footman, she joined a line of other rain-affected late arrivals and was swept, immediately, into the throng of ministers.

A throng of ministers. Yes, she would put that in her journal.

But the throng of ministers, though it might look droll on the page, was not so amusing in reality, and Eleanor, who had always arrived at such events on the arm of her husband, was jostled, her progress was impeded. One gentleman brushed up against her and a young lady stepped on her toe. Had it been possible, she might have turned about at this point and departed. It was not possible. She was swept into the throng.

She found herself in one of the formal chambers, high-ceilinged and richly decorated in white and gold and peppered liberally with ferns and white marble busts (of which a surprising number appeared to be Mr William Wentworth). Smartly liveried footmen in white gloves darted about balancing silver trays. The Premier was here she saw, his prominent and portly figure hard to miss, and so, too, many of the members of the Legislative Assembly and a number of the Legislative Council, some accompanied by their wives. Those who supported Federation—and there were many who did not—and who had attended meetings that evening in the more easily accessible suburbs had got here early, despite the rain. Those travelling in from the more outlying suburbs or who had been the most hampered by the weather were only now arriving and, it appeared—for she overheard someone say it—had missed the Premier's brief words of welcome and the Speaker's toast to the Federation and the little flurry of excitement as a reporter from the *Mail* was identified and ejected from the chamber.

She looked about her and saw, as well as the Premier, Mr Barton of the Opposition and his wife. She saw the Speaker, the Clerk, the Attorney-General (though she rather thought she had read that the Attorney-General had resigned, but perhaps she had got that wrong?). She saw that the gentlemen swirled about the Premier, whose voice boomed and whose laughter was audible from one side of the chamber to the other, and their wives swirled about Mr Barton, whose voice did not carry above the little crowd that gathered about him but it did not need to. He was that sort of man. The Premier was another sort.

The swell of members and members' wives closed about her and their talk buzzed and eddied about her head:

'We had upwards of two hundred at the meeting at Marrickville.'

'The rain has been so bad in the west there is a real concern it will prevent those in remote locations getting to the polling stations.'

'The *Evening News* covered my speech at the town hall two nights ago, but what they said about it in the *Herald* this morning was nothing short of scandalous.'

'I understand Reid got a fifteen-minute ovation and a bunch of roses from the Young Women's Institute.'

'I heard he was assailed by a delegation of the Women's Suffrage League and was fortunate to escape with his life.'

*Federation. Federation. Federation.*

For the colony was new. It was sparsely populated, it clung to the fringes of a great empire, eternally gazing beyond its own shores, taken up with momentous events happening elsewhere, its nose pressed forever against the windowpane of Global Affairs. But tonight these gentlemen—her husband and these others—had their own momentous event right here in this very city, in this very room. No wonder they were excited. No wonder they talked of nothing else.

*Federation. Federation. Federation.*

Relentless as a bee beating itself against a closed window, a branch tapping the bedroom window all night long. As relentless as a wife awaiting her husband's return for the length of a long, cold June night. For she blamed the Federation. It had caused this situation with her husband. Or if not caused it, had allowed it. She saw that. She saw also that a referendum was merely an event and nationhood was an idea and neither could, in themselves, come between a husband and wife. Only a husband and wife could do that.

It was possible to hold two mutually incompatible ideas in one's head simultaneously. It was what made one Human.

As she thought this, a gentleman behind her said loudly, 'I just saw Jellicoe. No, he certainly was not coming in. Looked like he was emptying his office and preparing to depart.'

Eleanor turned but could not make out who spoke nor to whom—so many bearded gentlemen all talking at once. She looked past them to the doorway of the chamber and beyond to the foyer where it seemed she must see Jellicoe in his flight. But she saw only the tall hats of a dozen jostling members and the fluffy haze of ostrich feathers from the hats of a dozen overdressed wives.

She did not wish to see Leon Jellicoe. She did not wish to see him fleeing.

It had not always been so. He had been a frequent visitor to their house once, the Solicitor-General. *Former* Solicitor-General now. His wife, Adaline, a close acquaintance with whom Eleanor had sat on a number of committees, was soon to be his former wife. Their case had been reported in the most graphic detail in that morning's Divorce Court column. Eleanor had read it in her room after Alasdair had gone out: *Jellicoe v. Jellicoe. Mr Tancredi appeared for the petitioner, Adaline Florence Jellicoe, who applied for a divorce from her husband, Leon Peter Jellicoe, on the grounds of his adultery with one Dora Hyatt.* It had turned her a little cold and she had thrust the paper aside. Leon Jellicoe's adultery laid bare to the world, his political career over—he had been spoken of as a future premier—and his wife's very public humiliation complete. Now their beautiful Potts Point home was on the market and Adaline Jellicoe was to sail for England. Or so Eleanor had heard, for she had not called on her former friend for many weeks. Probably no one had. Dora Hyatt, one understood, had been the housekeeper.

But it was no business of hers.

Eleanor looked about her for a friendly face. A footman slid past proffering jellied quinces and quails and plover eggs which the members plucked from his tray and popped into their mouths, one after another after another so that whole flocks of quails disappeared and whole generations of plovers were decimated, or so it seemed to Eleanor.

She could not see Alasdair. He was, of course, but one black-coated gentleman in a room full of black-coated gentlemen and so difficult to spot. Indeed, aside from the few ladies dressed, like herself, in white and dove grey and pearl and ivory, the only relief from the unrelenting black were the liveried footmen who darted about like exotic reef fish in a pond full of ageing somnambulant trouts. But still she could not see him.

She did see a great number of gentlemen of her acquaintance: Fraser Pyke, the tall lay preacher from Penrith whose wife was perpetually in confinement and whose family, consequently, practically outnumbered his constituents, and Charles Booker-Reid, a man of enormous girth and very little hair whose electorate was so far west of the Blue Mountains it was rumoured he had never actually been there. Behind him was Ned Dempsey, an incongruous anti-billite in a roomful of pro-billers and until quite recently Secretary for Lands (or possibly Minister for Industry; it was hard, sometimes, to remember), and his sister, Miss Marian Dempsey, he a fussy little man and she the unmarried sister who kept house for him and who probably would have made the better minister. With them was the banker Henry Rothe, who owned properties across the city and for whom politics was no more than an amusing sideline, and George Drummond-Smith, who had switched parties a number of times over the years and who puffed away complacently on a huge cigar, surveying the roomful of members with a sardonic eye.

She had known these gentlemen so many years and yet she knew them not at all. Mrs Pyke, who was a little way off in white brocaded satin and diamonds, gave her a cheery wave. Eleanor knew Cecily Pyke at least. They were friends—but *were* they? Could one be friends with a woman who had so many daughters when one had no daughters at all, and no sons either? Eleanor lifted her hand to return the wave but her hand dropped to her side. And now they were all watching her, Pyke, Drummond-Smith, Dempsey and Miss Dempsey, Rothe and Charles Booker-Reid through the smoke of his foul cigar.

Where was Alasdair? It occurred to her he was not going to come to the reception at all, that he had an appointment elsewhere.

She smiled, as it was her habit to stare dismay in the face, but there was no one to whom she might offer the smile, and as smiles went it was a pretty dismal affair. Her face was as stiff and tight as sunburned skin. The smile froze on her face. It knew it had no right to be there.

From across the chamber Cecily Pyke attempted a second wave. But perhaps it was not a wave, perhaps she was pointing, and now the ladies who stood with Mrs Pyke turned and looked her way. The gentlemen who buzzed about the Premier glanced over their shoulders at her; even the footmen with their trays of glasses stopped and stared.

Did they all know, then?

They could see her, of course, standing here in the room without her husband. A space had appeared all around her as it might for a pariah. A leper. She imagined herself to be Adaline Jellicoe, who must stand like this now, the outcast, wherever she went. But she was not Adaline Jellicoe and it was not her life laid bare in the morning newspaper.

Still she could not shake the thought: which of them—out of compassion or out of spite—had sent her the note intended for her husband's mistress?

She saw Everett Judd, the octogenarian, one of the few remaining original members of the '56 Assembly and wearing, it appeared, the same suit he had worn to that first Assembly almost half a century earlier. Judd's electorate, a large one on the shores of Botany Bay, bordered on its western edges Alasdair's own electorate and they were close, he and Alasdair, or as close as any two members of an Assembly could be.

Everett saw her and fought his way over. He placed a hand on her arm. 'My dear Mrs Dunlevy,' he said, as though he knew she was to be pitied.

And she was glad to have someone upon whom she might rest her gaze, even if it was such an ancient and tired face—but distinguished still, if a little dried up and greyish and all but obscured by his long white whiskers, and she smiled, though her instinct was to pull away. Judd's wife, a kind, quiet woman who had stood at her husband's side for forty years, had died quite suddenly only a month or so ago of a fever or a seizure, and now Everett was like a man out of step with time, constantly looking about him for the thing he had lost.

'Dear Everett,' she said, peering into his ravaged face. It was he who should be pitied, yet the tears that now pricked Eleanor's eyes were for herself and not for him. She placed her hand over his where it lay on her arm, and for a moment they were quite alone in the crowded chamber.

This illusion was abruptly shattered by George Drummond-Smith, who hailed them, pushing his way through the crowd and clasping Eleanor's hand.

'Dear Mrs Dunlevy. How delightful. But I do not see your husband. Is he not joining us?'

Drummond-Smith ignored Judd and retained hold of Eleanor's hand for longer than was necessary. He was not a tall man but tightly packed with a massive skull and forehead and eyes that fixed you and, like his hands, did not let go. There was a Mrs Drummond-Smith, a slight woman whose people had land in South Australia, but she was rarely seen and never accompanied her husband to official engagements, an arrangement that seemed to suit Drummond-Smith very well.

'Alasdair is not yet returned from his meeting,' Eleanor replied, extricating her hand and taking a small step back. Her voice was quite normal, she observed. Was it not her habit to stare dismay in the face?

'Of course. He was at Newtown, was he not? And were you at the meeting at Newtown with your husband?' Drummond-Smith might have relinquished her hand but he still stood closer than politeness seemed to warrant. 'Odd, but I could not make you out . . .'

'Says the fellow who spent the entire day at the races and never set foot in Newtown—and quite likely could not locate it on a map if called upon to do so,' observed Fraser Pyke, who apparently had overhead this exchange and now came over, leaning his lanky figure against a handily placed bust of John Blaxland and attempting to light a cigar.

Drummond-Smith ignored this and awaited Eleanor's reply with a steady gaze. He had cornered her once in the ladies' lounge, raised her hand to his lips and made a proposal as improper as it was unwelcome and took umbrage when she had cast him off.

'Naturally I would have liked to attend,' Eleanor replied, returning his gaze steadily, though he frightened her a little. 'Unfortunately there was no room in the cab, and in this dreadful rain we failed utterly to secure a second cab. I am afraid, faced with such impediments to my journey, I reluctantly took the decision to remain at home.'

'Very wise,' said Pyke.

'A most noble sacrifice,' said Everett Judd, bowing to her gallantly.

'And your husband does not join us this evening after his triumph?' Drummond-Smith went on, relentless, his unblinking grey eyes seeing everything and making certain one knew it.

'Do we know for a fact it *was* a triumph?' said Mr Pyke, puffing away vigorously at his cigar.

'What else could it be?' said Everett Judd.

'No doubt it was a triumph and no doubt Alasdair will be here,' said Eleanor, speaking as a wife does speak of her husband, with utter belief and conviction.

∞

Alasdair Dunlevy had not forgotten about the Premier's reception but he was among the last to arrive. He had only to travel from Newtown, but his secretary had failed to secure a parliamentary carriage and had been forced to find a hansom cab, a task that, in this relentless rain, had proved a challenge.

It was an inauspicious end to what had otherwise been a successful night. The meeting had gone well, the turn-out, despite the inclement weather, had been good, the mood positive, triumphant even. Yes, the mood had swung momentarily in the other direction, but it had been easily recovered. The secretary, James Greensmith, had eventually secured a cab and they had ridden to Macquarie Street.

But Alasdair had sat in the cab, Greensmith seated beside him brushing droplets of water from his coat, and felt the mood of the meeting slip away. Could they do it a second time? he wondered. A year ago victory had been assured, and the great and noble work of fashioning the new Federation, the first session of the new federal parliament in Melbourne and himself taking his place in that new parliament, had been so clear, so vivid. It had carried him day after day, week after week, from council chamber to town hall across the colony.

And then they had failed. The expected majority had not materialised. The men of the colony had proved intransigent, intractable, narrow of mind and lacking in imagination. They had proved themselves incapable of grasping a reasoned argument and too easily swayed by base fears that had no foundation in logic. They had shown themselves to be stupid.

So here they were a year later doing it all again, but somehow the glory of it was gone. Did he no longer believe in it? he wondered. Was it possible he had allowed himself to become distracted?

And he thought: I appear outwardly to be the same man I was a year ago, but I am not the same man. Not the same man at all. And the thought filled him with wonder.

And now he was arriving late for the Premier's reception. Yet he stood in the doorway and did not enter. A footman hurried past carrying a tray of wineglasses, another passed going the other way, and in the centre of the room the Secretary for Mines and Agriculture was laughing. They were serving the rather inferior colonial wine, he saw, that came direct from this same minister's own vineyards near Mudgee and for which the minister was the sole supplier to parliament at a premium price. It was little wonder the minister was laughing.

He saw Eleanor on the far side of the room standing beneath the rather disapproving portrait of Frederick Goulburn and surrounded by a little cluster of ministers. It had not occurred to him she would be here; he had forgotten she had said she would attend. She was all in white and she wore her diamonds. They sparkled at her throat and along her arms and wrists. Her face was very pale and quite without expression, and she turned from one gentleman to the other yet appeared barely aware of any of them, indeed just as though she was not really there at all, and for a moment Alasdair could not catch his breath for his wife seemed the most beautiful, the most unobtainable thing in the room.

It had been a very long time since he had looked on her as a stranger might. And even now the illusion of her beauty, her aloofness, was fading, replaced by half a lifetime of married co-existence.

Yes, now the illusion was quite gone. He looked at her again and saw, instead, his wife. He was relieved. He was a little saddened.

He remembered to be angry with her.

'Here.' And he tore off his hat and shook the rain from his coat and thrust both at his secretary and marched into the room.

And James Greensmith, the secretary, who was soaked through, having stood on the corner of King Street for twenty minutes trying to flag down a cab but who was a determined young man with great ambition and would not be another man's secretary all his life, thrust Dunlevy's coat and hat at the nearest footman and hurried after him.

∞

The important gentlemen swirled about, they made many impromptu little speeches, they uttered phrases they trusted others would copy down and repeat and that might, perhaps, be reported verbatim in the next day's newspapers, and if they were not quite making history, if they were not actually building a nation, they were at least talking about it.

It was shame, then, that the history that was made that evening, the words that were reported verbatim in the next day's newspaper, came not from a member of the Assembly or of the Council, but from quite an unexpected quarter. It was a pity that the Premier's reception, for all its portents of triumph and celebration, was to be remembered solely for the note of terror on which it ended.

Alasdair Dunlevy was not the last to arrive.

A slight young man with pinched features and wildly blinking eyes and dressed in the livery of a Parliament House footman ran up the Assembly stairs and entered the building. His right arm was stuffed inside the tunic of his uniform and this appeared to slightly impede his movement. The young man pushed his way roughly past those standing in the doorway of the reception chamber, causing a flutter of outrage. He flung off his liveried coat. He leaped onto the dais where, earlier the Premier had stood to make his brief speech of welcome.

The man was *not* a footman, it now became apparent. He let out a furious cry. He brandished a small pistol.

'*We shall never give in! You shall not take our—*'

But whatever it was that should not be taken the assembled and stunned crowd were never to learn, for the man was abruptly and vigorously cut off as a crush of constables and uniformed military men and other anonymously dressed gentlemen whose presence, up to this moment, no one had noticed and who might have been in the employ of the government or might just happened to have been passing, surged at the man and he disappeared beneath a flurry of hats and coats and arms and legs and boots. A number of the wives screamed, many of the members of the Legislative Assembly exclaimed in horror and dismay, and more than one cried, '*Save the Premier, secure Mr Reid*,' and one or two, less partisan, enquired of the Leader of the Opposition, '*Where is Mr Barton? Is he safe?*' and for a time chaos appeared to win the day.

But the man had been wrestled to the ground and was now being carried, kicking and cursing violently, towards the door. The crowd swelled, making a path which closed in again once the man and his captors were gone. A shocked silence followed— but only for a moment. The gentlemen, finding that they had not, in fact, been frightened, now quickly found their voices, and the wives recovered themselves too, all but one, an elderly lady from the country, whom it was found had fainted and to whom a great many of the gentlemen now attended. Everyone began to talk very loudly, for fear made people talk, or it did once the danger was past, and the ladies fanned themselves and held their hands to their chests and exclaimed, and the gentlemen offered solicitous and consoling arms, and huffed and puffed and became very red in the face, and several of the younger gentleman, those who had never been in the military and had never faced an enemy in battle and who had been the most frightened, laughed and slapped each other on the back and talked the most loudly.

Like all moments of danger and excitement, everything happened very fast, and afterwards people found themselves in quite other parts of the chamber from where they had thought themselves, talking to someone quite different from whom they had been talking to a moment or two earlier. Alasdair found himself on the far side of the chamber, close to the dais where the man had jumped and where the discarded livery uniform lay, a button ripped off and rolled a short distance away. He did not recall how he had got there nor how he had reacted to the man's presence. He had a sense he had moved with the crowd, had shouted and exclaimed, as they had. His heart was beating extremely fast. With whom had he been standing? What had he said? He had been badly frightened—of course, they all had—but the moment was past. The uniform lay on the floor, a button torn off, and he could not take his eyes from it and nor could he pick it up.

The lady who had fainted was being assisted to a chaise longue. A doctor had been called. And now a number of people were talking at him, among them the banker, Henry Rothe, who had helped various of the ladies and was now temporarily unemployed, and another was Charles Booker-Reid, who said, 'Anarchists!' and whose eyes bulged in his head as though he had been shot.

But where was Eleanor?

The image that presented itself to him was one he'd had over and over again in the early years of his marriage: his wife thrown from a carriage, still and pale and dead, or trampled beneath hooves, or bloodied and drained of life in their marriage bed, a nurse in the next room cradling a newborn in her sorrowful arms. None of these imagined events had ever happened, though he had feared them, almost daily, for a time. There had been no overturned carriage, no startled horse. There had been no newborn. His panic, the panic of a man consumed by love, had gradually been tempered.

The horror he felt at this moment, though it was dissipating now, was the horror of sudden death itself and not the horror of her death, his wife's.

For, really, her death would simplify things.

The sense of wonder he had felt earlier returned to him. But it was a terrible wonder, no longer filled with joy.

He saw Eleanor on the far side of the chamber. She stood near the doorway and his secretary, Greensmith, was at her side. That annoyed him. Why, he wondered, had Greensmith gone to the wife and not to the minister—his employer—whose life, surely, it was his first priority to preserve?

But something momentous and not a little frightening had just happened and the politicians in the chamber now reacted in the only way they knew how—they all began talking a great deal and making speeches to one another. Charles Booker-Reid was making one now:

'Good God, I am deadly serious, Rothe. If you indulged in a spot of newspaper reading you might be too. Complacency is rarely a sound policy.'

'Certainly there is ill feeling and ignorance in some quarters, Booker-Reid, but *anarchists*?' said Rothe, placing a foot on the fender and leaning back to survey him in a show of nonchalance that belied the shocking incident of a moment ago. 'Too much newspaper reading clearly creates a tendency to jump at one's own shadow.'

'Were the Melbourne constabulary jumping at their own shadows when anarchists blew the front of a house off in Fitzroy last year?' Charles Booker-Reid demanded.

'Youths playing with detonators does not herald an anarchist uprising. Besides, that was Melbourne.' Rothe produced a cigar and made some little performance of lighting it. His wealth was such that it surrounded and protected him so that a madman brandishing a pistol did not touch him.

'And because it is Melbourne it might as well be on the moon? I am not simply talking about the anti-billites, Rothe; I am talking about the sort of militant, anti-establishment, anti-government types who throw bombs at the Czar and attempt to wreck trains for the sake of seeing the carnage it will bring.'

And Charles Booker-Reid, who could look on with wry indifference as his unlosable seat was lost to the Opposition, was, Alasdair saw, quite purple in the face.

Henry Rothe laughed. 'My dear chap, we are not in Imperial Russia, we are in New South Wales, and so far as I am aware no trains have been wrecked and no bombs have been thrown. What do you say, Dunlevy?'

Alasdair remembered he'd been at a meeting earlier that evening, a triumphant meeting where men had slapped him on the back and shaken his hand, but he could no longer recall how that triumph had felt. 'I would say a man has just invaded the innermost sanctum of Parliament House and brandished a pistol at a room full of ministers and the Premier himself.'

'My point exactly!' said Booker-Reid.

Henry Rothe laughed at them. 'And no doubt tomorrow's papers will describe the fellow as a deranged loner acting on his own, a madman with some petty grievance and a history of instability. It is hardly a revolution.'

Alasdair had nothing to say to this and he left them. Booker-Reid's scaremongering was disturbingly compelling and he would have liked to laugh it off, as Rothe had, but he felt disinclined to laugh at anything.

The man had had a gun.

He pushed his way through the throng until he reached his wife, who had left the chamber and was now in the foyer beyond.

He found he did not know how to address her.

'Eleanor. My dear. You are unharmed? I am afraid I could not locate you in all this mayhem. Were you alarmed?'

'Alasdair. I believe I was very much alarmed. I looked for you inside.'

Eleanor did not look alarmed. Her expression was difficult to read; some immense emotion swirled just below the surface, he fancied, though he could not label it fear and had no other name for it. She watched him as though from a very great distance.

'Are you alright, sir?' said Greensmith, hovering a little in the manner of a subordinate who, in the face of danger, had found himself absent from his master's side and was now anxious to make amends. Not that anxious, perhaps, for Greensmith, a young man of pleasing if somewhat bland features, of average stature and clothed conservatively in the best coat and hat that a man on a secretary's salary might afford, remained steadfastly at Mrs Dunlevy's side as though he had been posted there.

'Quite alright, Greensmith, as you see. Come, Eleanor, let us go. There is nothing to be gained by remaining here. A lot of silly talk, in fact, that I think it might be best to avoid.'

Eleanor did not enquire what the silly talk was of and he was thankful, for he did not wish to tell her. She had her coat on already and a fur pulled closely about her neck against the chill night air outside. She had been leaving then—without him? Or had she stood here to await him? He did not know.

'It will be a devil of a job finding a cab,' he said instead, finding safety in platitudes, and he left her and went down the front steps just as if he intended to stand in the wind and the rain hailing a cab himself. Greensmith had an umbrella ready in his hands but, instead of following, his secretary opened the umbrella over his wife's head, though she was quite sheltered from the weather on the covered verandah. Irritated, Alasdair summoned a footman and ordered him to find a cab. He rejoined his wife and secretary, and they stood silently staring ahead of them, the rain beating on the roof above.

Word of the incident had spread and people—newspapermen and policemen and others who had just appeared—were arriving outside Parliament House, and at the same moment the guests were departing so that the small party outside quickly became a crowd and it was some little time before a cab was found. When one was at last secured it was the footman who held an umbrella over Alasdair's head as they splashed through the puddles to board it and his secretary who followed behind shielding his wife, who held out his hand to assist her to step up into the cab, who closed the door on them and who stood and watched as the cab pulled away.

The driver laid a rug over their knees and Alasdair leaned back against the seat and closed his eyes. His heart had not stopped its overly rapid beating. He was more frightened now, he found, than when the thing had happened, was shaking it seemed, and that was humiliating. He held his hands very tightly together and did not speak. He thought instead about the vote in three weeks' time.

He thought about the national government that would be formed in a year, or perhaps two years, and how he might be a minister in that government. Australia's first national government. That would be a thing, that would be a moment for the history books. And the parliament would be in Melbourne. He opened his eyes and pondered this, the length of time that parliament might be in session and that one would be required to be in Melbourne. Away from home.

'Alasdair, it was horrid,' said Eleanor in a low voice. 'That man—'

Alasdair started. A part of him had forgotten his wife was seated beside him in the carriage.

'Charles Booker-Reid blames anarchists,' he said, and he laughed to show her he was not at all afraid.

But Eleanor did not laugh. 'Do you believe that to be so?' Her voice was almost lost in the patter of rain on the cab's roof.

They did not face each other; the hansom cab did not allow for it. One must sit side by side facing the rear of the horse, seeing it shake its head and snort, hearing its harnesses rattle, seeing the flick of the driver's whip from above and smelling the foul coils of smoke from the man's pipe, and in this darkness, on this night, one stared ahead at nothing.

'The man was an Aboriginal, I am certain of that,' said Eleanor when he did not reply.

Was he? Alasdair tried to recall. It had all been so quick, all he could remember of the man was the uniform and the pistol. *Had* he been an Aboriginal? Perhaps. Dark-skinned, at any rate. A disquieting sense of a threat, unknown and unknowable, stole over him. A settler, downtrodden and destitute, made desperate by drink and debt and idleness—this was a type he understood, saw every day and could dismiss. But the blacks . . . One could see such a fellow every day for a year, for ten years, look into the fellow's eyes and have not the slightest idea of his thoughts, of the feelings that stirred his soul.

He stared at the water cascading all about them and turned his mind elsewhere. He could take the lease on a small furnished house in one of the better parts of Melbourne, overlooking the river, for he had visited the southern city and he had been much taken with the river and the elegant bridges that traversed it. Like a European city, everyone said, though he had not been to a European city and neither had most of the people who said it.

The rain thundered on the roof of the cab with the sound of a cavalry charge and mud splashed up from the horse's hooves and coated the windows and Alasdair pictured the small furnished house.

They said no more to each other, though there was much, surely, to be said, and after an interminable time the cab turned sharply, went downhill and turned again, and slowed to a juddering halt. Alasdair paid the driver and dismissed him and followed at a dash the umbrella that Alice, the maid, held over his wife's head.

# CHAPTER FOUR

# A HIGH IN THE BIGHT

Many miles to the west a winter mist hung low over the blue gums on the banks of the Nepean River and at the railway stations higher up the line a frost prickled the ground, but here, where the harbour met the ocean, Friday morning dawned an unwavering and brilliant blue. The sun dried out the puddles and sparkled on the water and on the windows of the new villas in Elizabeth Bay in a way that was at once delightful and blinding. The ground was still damp underfoot and in places the gutters still overflowed, but otherwise it was as though the week of rain had never happened, that one had imagined the whole thing. Such was the weather in Sydney.

In the ancient Moreton Bay fig the large possum moved up to a higher branch to catch the first trickle of winter warmth from the sun and one or two bedraggled ibis stalked the ground around the tree's great roots and poked their long bills into the gutters to see what they could find there. The milk cart had already clanked and rumbled its way down the hill to the bay and back up again, and small buttoned-up boys on bicycles had delivered newspapers and goods from the butcher and the grocer. Inside the new villas, servants had already swept the ash from the grates from the night before and lit fires in the bedrooms and breakfast rooms ready for the day ahead.

Eleanor Dunlevy was dressed in a morning gown of oyster grey silk with a woollen shawl wrapped about her shoulders, for the freshly lit fire had not yet lifted the chill from the room. She sat at her writing desk, a pen in her hand and her journal open before her. The curtains were parted just enough to allow a chink of sunlight to fall across the desk in a pleasing way. She considered what she would write. A great many images from the previous evening, snatches of words and thoughts and impressions, swirled inside her head. She tried to catch one or two, but they were as fleeting as dreams and she could not quite grasp at them.

It seemed utterly fantastic that a man had appeared and bran-dished a gun. What had he hoped to achieve? If it had been simply to frighten them all, then she supposed he had achieved his aim, for undoubtedly everyone had been frightened, though none had admitted it afterwards. She wondered if Alasdair had been afraid. It had all happened so quickly one could hardly say what one had done or thought or what others had done.

She heard a footstep outside her door and Alice came in with a brisk, 'Good morning, madam,' and crossed the room to draw back the curtains.

Eleanor paused, her pen in her hand, the page opened before her. The swirl of images, thoughts and impressions burst and vanished like bubbles. It was no good; she could not write while Alice was in the room. Indeed, she could not think. She waited, her pen poised above the page. She did not look up; she did not watch as Alice moved about the room, tying back the curtains, retrieving one or two items of clothing or footwear from one place and moving them to another place, opening and closing first one drawer and now a second drawer.

'Thank you, Alice,' she said, and finally Alice left with a curtsy and a brief, 'Yes, madam.'

The door closed. Eleanor listened to the sound of her own breathing. She lifted her head and looked out of the window and felt a moment of relief, of satisfaction, at the blue sky and the dazzling brightness of the morning, at the world returned to its natural state. Nothing bad could happen on such a day, and the horror of the man with the gun slid a little into the background, became fixed in her thoughts with the darkness and the incessant rain of yesterday. She took off her spectacles and peered at the fig tree outside. There was no sign of the possum. Instead, there was a large white cockatoo, indeed several cockatoos, released from the tyranny of the rain, wheeling and dipping and shrieking to one another high above the old tree.

But she had been writing in her journal. She looked down and the page was blank. She stared at the blank page and imagined words on it. She remembered the *throng of ministers*, how clever it was, that phrase, how pithy. That was what she had been going to write. But it no longer seemed clever. It no longer seemed pithy. It seemed dead. She could not write it. And that was Alasdair's world, not hers.

Instead she wrote: *I believe that today is the day.*

Downstairs Alasdair was already at his breakfast, seated at the far end of the table, one leg crossed over the other, the newspaper open on the table before him, a half-drunk cup of coffee at his elbow. He wore a morning suit, light grey and pinstriped, and a matching waistcoat. His choice of suit was entirely dictated by the time of day and not by the climate, he wore the same suits all the year round, no matter the season. Man had reached a point in his evolution where he controlled the elements, they did not control him—it was not something Alasdair had actually said but it was what he believed. It was something all men believed, despite the daily evidence to the contrary. For all summer long, violent cyclones buffeted the tropical northern coast and occasionally they destroyed whole settlements in a single day, and every week ships floundered in great storms and were dashed to pieces against the rocks. It was right there in his newspaper. But every day Alasdair put on a light grey pinstriped morning suit, every day he read his paper.

Eleanor sat down and poured herself a coffee. 'Good morning, Alasdair.'

'Good morning.'

He raised his head, acknowledging her presence but without, it seemed, quite seeing her. At his throat he wore a soft black satin necktie with a pearl tiepin. She had given him a gold tiepin engraved with his initials to mark the occasion of their twentieth wedding anniversary, but today he wore a pearl tiepin and she could not recall the last time he had worn the gold one. Did husbands value the things their wives gave them? She no longer knew. Children, an heir—yes, presumably husbands valued these things; but a gold tiepin—paid for with his own money—apparently not.

She observed him then looked away, and though her eyes were no longer on him she continued to see him, for she had spent almost every day of the past twenty-three years with him and there was not a phrase he could utter, a movement he could make, a thought he might express that she could not guess at and predict.

She had been seventeen when they had met. A girl, really.

Seventeen. An age when it was possible to feel fully grown and knowledgeable about the world though one has seen little and experienced less. At seventeen Eleanor had barely moved beyond the walls of her father's stone cottage in Balmain; her world had been the docks, the foundries, the shipbuilders' yards that lay between Mort Bay, Ballast Point and Darling Street Wharf. But her mother, whose first husband had been a school-master, and with an eye to improving her daughter's chances, had enrolled the youthful Eleanor in dance classes, had taught her to play the piano, had taken her, on a sweltering Saturday afternoon better spent—surely—down at the water's edge, to a lecture at the town hall.

The lecture on that sweltering afternoon had been given by a celebrated professor from the University of Sydney on the Disappearance of the Great Explorer, Mr Ludwig Leichhardt. As no trace of Mr Leichhardt had been found since his party had set out from the Darling Downs in 1848, it threatened to be a short lecture.

It had not been a short lecture and Eleanor had found it necessary to sit perfectly still and not fidget and to ignore the spreading patches of dampness under her clothes as the temperature in the hall had crept ever upwards and the professor had expounded theory after theory to account for the disappearance of the Great Explorer and his entire party. Only a brief reference to the possibility of cannibalism towards the end of the lecture had roused her, briefly, from her torpor.

At the conclusion of the talk Eleanor had left her mother fanning herself by a window and gone in search of cooling lemonade and had, instead, found a young man. This man, a tall gangly youth inhabiting a body he seemed unused to and with a manner both self-assured and diffident, had sported a cream-coloured frockcoat and a white linen shirt as would one about to set forth himself to conquer mountains and cross deserts. She had noticed—how could she not?—his thick black hair and the lively grey eyes that had flittered restlessly about the room and settled, at last, on her. And having found her, the young man had expressed to her, in words at once eloquent and stilted, his admiration for both the celebrated professor and the lecture which he had found thrilling. Eleanor had agreed at once (though she had mostly found it dull) because that was what she had been taught to do. The young man had introduced himself as Alasdair Dunlevy, and when she had appeared in no great hurry to return to her mother he had taken the opportunity to express to her his hopes of being selected himself to join a surveying team journeying into the interior in the next few months, the only obstacle being the urgent need to raise the capital which his father, inexplicably, had refused to provide.

Eleanor had commiserated and they had married four months later as the summer had drawn to a close and the European trees in the city had shed their leaves, and instead of going off into the interior Alasdair Dunlevy had gone into politics. And, on the whole, having a politician for a husband was better than having an explorer who would be forever away exploring and who might simply disappear altogether and never be heard of again.

Or so Eleanor had told herself.

'Such a relief the rain has finally ceased,' she remarked, placing a napkin over her lap.

'Indeed.'

She sipped her coffee. It was bitter and she winced but she relished its bitterness. It made her feel alive. She had more to say about the weather but she reserved her comments. Her father had used to say that if you wanted to know what the weather would be like in three days' time, you should look at what the weather was like in Perth today, as it took the weather three days to traverse the continent. And when her father was proved right, which he was around half the time, he was pleased as punch, and when he was wrong, which he was the other half of the time, he never mentioned it. For sometimes the weather got as far as South Australia and changed its mind or simply gave up altogether, and other times Sydney made up its own weather. But her father had enjoyed the weather—he had been a naval captain—and he would read out snatches of it from the newspaper over breakfast. 'A high in the bight!' he would exclaim with glee, and though Eleanor had not the least idea to this day what that meant she had loved the sound of it.

She saw that Alasdair's face had darkened over the newspaper.

'Has our adventure of last night made its way into the newspaper?' she enquired.

'It has.' And he put back his head as though to distance himself from the words, and read aloud, '*Outrage at Parliament House. Man Wields Gun at Crowded Room. Arrested Man Detained by Police. Premier and Ministers Reported Safe.*'

How curious it was. Now that it had been turned into words for the newspaper, the event, so shocking at the time, meant little to her. She felt nothing, except perhaps relief that she and Alasdair were seated at the breakfast table discussing the day's news and any possibility that a catastrophe was befalling them seemed suddenly remote.

'And what of the man? Do they say who he is? What he was doing there?'

She had no interest in the man, neither his motivations nor his fate; it was the exchange between she and Alasdair that was important.

'An itinerant, out of work, of no fixed abode. A previous arrest for disturbing the peace.' Alasdair frowned and shook out the paper a little angrily. 'Not an anarchist, hardly even an anti-billite. Merely an opportunist.'

He spoke as though he were proving a point, though to whom was not clear. He folded up the newspaper and placed it on the table, the frown still present, and it seemed to Eleanor there was something else on his mind, or perhaps there was more to the story than he had told her. Now he pulled himself back from whatever place he had gone to and saw her observing him and it seemed, for a moment, he must surely confide his thoughts to her.

But no. He placed his napkin on the table, and in a moment he would get up and go upstairs, put on his coat and leave the house. The moment, if this was a moment, would pass. Eleanor felt a quickening of her breathing, a pressure in her chest. She looked down at her lap.

He was angry with her.

How had she not realised it before now? It was not a recent anger. She raised her head and looked at him. Really, it should be she who was angry at him.

She had brought the note downstairs with her. The one that someone had gone to the trouble of sending her three days earlier. Had removed it from the desk drawer, still in its cream-coloured envelope, and closed her fingers around it, had walked downstairs with it in her hand. She sat at the table now with the sharp corners of the envelope cutting into her palm.

It appeared that, occasionally, one acted without knowing exactly why. The note was courage, she saw now. A prop. A thing that was tangible when all else seemed insubstantial, inconclusive.

But what she said was: 'What appointments do you have this morning, Alasdair? Is it the referendum?'

She saw him pause. The frown returned then was gone. His face was blank, expressionless.

'Naturally. A party meeting, a bill to redraft, a report to write and another to comment on. A meeting with a delegation of councillors from Tamworth, or Singleton—I cannot recall which. Luncheon with a man from the *Advocate* and one from the *Sunday Times*. Correspondence to deal with, preparations for this evening's meeting, a speech to write.'

On and on it went. As he spoke Alasdair looked at the news-paper before him on the table, at his coffee cup, at the door as though expecting it to open. He did not look at her.

'Alasdair, the man last night—were you frightened?' she asked him. She had meant to ask him something else entirely, about his day or last night's meeting at Newtown, but instead she asked him this.

He waited before answering. Thoughts passed across his brow; what husband desires to be asked such a question by his wife? Finally he said, 'Yes, I believe I was,' and at last his body settled into a posture of relief, for it is a great strain to be forever wary and untruthful. She saw it in his face, heard it in his voice, his relief.

Eleanor leaned a little forward in her chair, her eyes alive. 'Alasdair, do you remember when you ran your first campaign and how we travelled together from place to place? All those church halls and literary institutes and council chambers, and how we met so many people—some of them quite dreadful!—and how we stayed at all those horrid little hotels that had sawdust on the floor and how you said it would all be worth it in the end. Do you remember? And it was, was it not? Worth it?'

She paused, a little breathless. She did not know why she had said all that, where it had come from. They had not talked of such things for years. She wondered if the man with the gun last night had caused her to say it, but knew at once that it was nothing to do with the man with the gun.

Opposite her Alasdair sat unmoving, his face as empty and without meaning as the sky now that the clouds had gone.

'Certainly it was worth it,' he replied. 'I won the election.'

But, no, that was not what she had meant. That was not it at all.

Alasdair did not wait to hear what she meant. He pushed back his chair and stood up. 'I must go,' he said, and before she could think of a reply he left.

For a time Eleanor did not move. The note crumpled in her hand.

She had thought she knew every part of him, inside and out.

She got up and walked around to the other end of the table. She sat down at his seat, put on her spectacles, picked up the newspaper and studied it as he had. OUTRAGE AT PARLIAMENT HOUSE. The man's name was Peter O'Leary. It was a nothing sort of name, the kind of name one would hear and at once forget. He was a carpenter, though he was not currently in employment, thought to be twenty-nine or thirty years of age—records were unclear. The man had spent time at the Callan Park asylum. He was yet to be questioned by police concerning his motives. There was nothing to say if the man was an Aboriginal or not. The gun, the newspaper noted, had not been loaded. And so they had not, in fact, been in any danger after all. The panic that had swept the chamber now seemed misplaced, absurd.

Beneath this was a report on a signal box at Granville that had been broken into during the night. Tools and equipment had been removed, the place set on fire. Constables had discovered poles carefully laid across the railway tracks. They had been removed before the first train of the morning came through or it would certainly have been wrecked. Youths were blamed, though no one had been apprehended or charged. There had been other, similar incidents in recent weeks—whether copycat, the same perpetrators or quite unconnected, the newspaper did not speculate—but it clearly implied the Federation referendum was the catalyst. It was only a matter of time, it warned, until catastrophe.

Eleanor put the newspaper down. Who would do such a thing? There seemed nothing to be gained by it except destruction and, perhaps, death. Did men care so much about the referendum? No doubt, if you had a hand in your nation's affairs, you did care. As a woman Eleanor had no hand in it. She did see that it had cast a wedge between them, she and Alasdair. For him the referendum, this idea of Federation, was everything. For her it was . . . a wedge.

But that was to pretend it was Federation that had caused this situation between them.

She took off her spectacles and sat for a time looking about the room. She had never sat at this end of the table before, had never seen the room from this angle. Everything was slightly different. It would be warmer at this end of the table, for the fireplace was at one's back. One could no longer see the ormolu clock on the mantel or the candlesticks on either side of the clock or, above the fire-place, the William Strutt painting of terrified men and animals fleeing a bushfire. Instead, one faced the mahogany sideboard and the giant fern in its brass pot behind the doorway and the Charles Conder landscape of bathers enjoying Mentone Beach. The view from the window, too, was quite different. One could no longer see the road winding its way uphill or the frangipani tree outside the neighbouring house, but one could view the bay, distantly, and the sunlight twinkling on the water. It was quite different. And she preferred the Conder, she decided. Why should one always be staring at terrified men and animals and not at elegant ladies with parasols at a beach?

The note still held tightly in her hand.

Today then.

The door opened and Alice, as though astonished at the sight of her mistress seated at the master's end of the table, stood in the doorway, quite motionless.

A hansom cab called at the house a short time later and from her window upstairs Eleanor stood and watched as Alasdair emerged from the house in top hat and morning coat with a fat leather portfolio. He carried a rolled umbrella. The sky showed no hint of cloud but the memory of the last five days of rain was still fresh. The lawn was quite waterlogged and he stuck closely to the path. A sandstone wall surrounded the house, and guarding its solid double gates were two winged lions, cast in stone mid-roar and about to pounce. But they never did roar, they never had pounced.

They did not roar or pounce now as Alasdair passed between them, covering the short distance to the cab with that purposeful stride of his. It was a stride that had carried him all the way to the chamber of the Legislative Assembly and now looked set to carry him into a new nation and a new national parliament. It was a stride that brooked no possibility of failure, that allowed no place for hesitancy or doubt. She had admired that stride for it had carried her too, for a time.

To be so sure and certain. What did that feel like?

She watched him climb into the cab. The driver, a youngish man in a green bowler, startled the ageing grey horse with a flick of his whip and the cab set forward with a jerk.

A very short time later Eleanor, too, left the house. She had donned a long cream and ivory winter coat, sheepskin-lined boots and a hat—not the ostrich feathers of the previous night but something wide-brimmed and bland, something functional—and she had her gloves and parasol in her hand. At the front door she paused and called, 'I am going out, Alice,' and gave no more explanation than that, though as Alice did not reply and was likely in another part of the house it was possible the girl did not hear.

Eleanor had departed the house so soon after her husband that his cab was still visible as it climbed back up the hill to the main road, the bowler-hatted cab driver and his ancient horse making heavy weather of the incline. By the time it crested the hill Eleanor, moving swiftly on foot, had almost caught up to it. But now that they were on the level she could not hope to keep pace. She looked about her and, spying another cab stationary on the roadside ahead disgorging two elderly ladies, she signalled the driver and climbed nimbly inside. She held on tightly as they jerked forward, and only then did she pull up the little hatch in the roof and instruct the cabbie.

'Driver, do you see that cab before us? I should like you to follow the same route.'

And if the man thought this an odd request by a lady in a long cream and ivory winter coat and a bland and functional—though clearly expensive—hat, he gave no sign of it but sucked silently on his pipe and urged his own nag onwards, for the cab in front had suddenly picked up speed.

CHAPTER FIVE

# ALWAYS DIFFERENT, ALWAYS THE SAME

Alice Nimrod watched as first Mr Dunlevy then Mrs Dunlevy left the house. Mrs Dunlevy was on foot and this was unusual enough to be remarked upon, had there been someone to whom Alice might make such a remark. Not only did Mrs Dunlevy depart on foot, but she went bowling along the road at what might be described as a less than sedate pace. It might almost be described as a tearing hurry.

What the reason for this might be Alice could hardly imagine and did not care to try. The ways of her employers often made her wonder. If she did attempt to reason why something was one way or another, why they did this or did that, her reasoning faltered and she found herself all at odds with the world for a time, and sometimes at odds with God, too, so now she no longer tried to make sense of it.

She was satisfied simply in the knowledge that it was Friday. Of this, happily, there could be little dispute. The coalman had made his weekly delivery in the chill of a pre-dawn hour, stomping down the passage, the great sack on his shoulder, puffing and grunting and sweating. He was not quite human with his massive bulk, his coal-blackened face, his white staring eyes, more a thing arisen from the depths, and the black void of the coal hole led straight to Hell.

This was foolish but there it was. Alice could not shake the feeling. She always waited in the kitchen while the man came, deposited his devil's load and departed. After he and his horse and cart had gone a coating of coal dust lay over everything. She tasted it at the back of her throat.

And so Alice cleaned the gas stove and set the water boiling before Mrs Flynn arrived to start breakfast. She left the kitchen then for it was Mrs Flynn's domain. She beat the rugs. There was a carpet sweeper with a long handle and a roller that flew over the carpet and left a smart straight line in its wake, but really all it did was pick up threads and fluff and crumbs. All the real dust and dirt was still there and stayed there unless you did what people had always done and picked up the rug and went at it with a carpet beater. And so Alice beat the carpets. The grocer's boy came on his overloaded bicycle, and the baker's boy, and finally the butcher's lad, and she met each one at the kitchen door and made a show of checking the order was right and the butcher's lad ogled her and made a grab for her breast though he was barely thirteen, but he was already as tall as her and he leered when she took a swipe at him and left with a backward glance that said, *In a year I shall be stronger than you.*

Alice cleaned all the shoes which, after the days of rain, were thick with mud and almost spoiled. Not spoiled in a Surry Hills way (for in Crown Street these shoes would fetch a pretty penny and go through half a dozen new owners, some of whom would die with them on their feet before they finally disintegrated) but spoiled in an Elizabeth Bay way, which meant they might be worn a handful of times then discarded. And that was something Alice had learned: that things—clothes, objects, people—had different lives in one place compared to another.

She observed that Mr Dunlevy's newest pair of shoes—soft brown Italian leather—looked as though he had waded through a muddy river in them, though she considered it unlikely he had done so. She put them to one side. The laundry items got parcelled up each week and taken away by a Chinaman and done someplace else. They had been returned the previous day and had not yet been unpacked, aired or folded away, though no one had so far commented on it. And now it was Friday: the windows needed to be cleaned, the silver polished. Alice had begun the dusting, had made some real progress, but had stopped to observe first Mr Dunlevy then Mrs Dunlevy leave the house.

She sat down at Mrs Dunlevy's writing desk. It was not something she usually did, but Mrs Dunlevy hurrying out like that had unsettled her. It had set her thinking. And so she sat.

The desk was cleared but for a single ivory-handled paper knife. All else was put away into a locked drawer. Mrs Dunlevy kept a notebook in the drawer in which she wrote most nights and some mornings. It was a mystery to Alice what she wrote in the note-book but it must be important or why would it be kept locked up like that?

'They are not like us,' Maeve Gorman had warned her five years ago, taking the fourteen-year-old Alice in hand during her first topsy-turvy weeks in the house. 'Do not even try to understand their ways of being.'

These were wise words and Maeve, who had been in the Dunlevys' house for three years as maid-of-all-work and then lady's maid, had been full of wise words, or so they had seemed to Alice, who had been plucked from the world she knew and dropped into a foreign place where all was new and different and incomprehensible. And when Alice had wept for her home and her mother and her sister, Maeve had said, 'This is your salvation, Alice Nimrod,' sounding like Father McCreadie. Alice had thought she meant Jesus and the Holy Spirit and the Trinity and the Virgin Mother, but what Maeve had meant was you, Alice Nimrod, have been dragged out of the slum and shown another view of the world, you have been given a chance to have a better life. And when Maeve had given her notice and left to marry a man who sold gentlemen's suits at Mark Foys department store and who wore nice clothes and had a bit of money, Alice understood. For Maeve had come from the same place she had, once. They had even lived in the same streets, though not at the same time.

'My mum made hats,' Alice had said, when she had found out. It was the first thing she had ever said about her mum, about her old life. And Maeve had nodded. Maeve had understood, though she had offered nothing in return.

Mrs Nimrod had made hats. There was no factory so she had done piecework at home, and once Alice was old enough to wield a pin without taking her own eye out, she had made hats too, day after day, dawn until dark, until midnight sometimes, affixing ribbons and decoration to straw hats and felt hats and cloth hats and silk hats, every kind of hat delivered in huge boxes at the start of each week by a boy and taken away at the end of the week by a man who studied each item and handed over a pile of coins and took some back for each defective or spoiled item. The room in which they lived, in which Alice grew up, was strewn with straw and bits of silk and hatpins and ribbons and feathers and lace and tiny little fruit and flowers made from hand-painted plaster, and clouds of tissue paper and boxes and boxes and boxes.

They had lived in a room, she and Mum and Milli. Not the same room, far from it. They had moved often and at short notice, though it might as well have been the same room for they all had the same sour smell, the same bugs in the beds and in the nooks and crannies, the walls were always damp, the roof always leaked and the window—if there was a window—never shut properly or was sealed shut and could not be opened even in the swelter of summer. The room was always in a house that was dilapidated and ramshackle, two storeys, three storeys, sometimes four storeys high, where four or six or eight families lived, with one stand-pipe in the street outside that sometimes produced water and that sometimes the council closed off because the water was bad and might kill you, and outside was a huge iron tub and a ringer where you did your laundry, and in the corner a dunny over a foul-smelling pit. The house was in Commonwealth Street and Wexford Street and Campbell Street and Riley Street and then back to Commonwealth Street. Always different, always the same.

Mrs Nimrod's husband, Bert Nimrod, was a cooper who made barrels for the brewery, which was skilled work, and folk would always need barrels, wouldn't they, Mrs Nimrod had said, but when Alice was four there had been an accident and Bert Nimrod had been crushed to death by his own barrels. That was the time from which the moving from room to room and house to house and street to street had begun. Or so Milli had told her, for her sister was five years older and could remember their dad. Or said she could.

Mr Purley had arrived when Alice was eight. He appeared one Sunday afternoon, a large man in big boots and an oily cap with thinning hair and a strange smell. Mr Purley slept in the bed with the widowed Mrs Nimrod and in the daytime he sat in the public bar of the Brickfields Hotel. Often when he returned late from the Brickfields Hotel he shouted at everyone for no very good reason and occasionally he took a swing at Mrs Nimrod and once he knocked her down the stairs and they all thought she was dead.

It was soon after this that Milli had left.

Milli was fourteen. The night she left she had woken the sleeping Alice and explained her plan—which was no plan at all really—just to leave at once and go someplace else. When he notices you, Milli had warned, meaning Mr Purley, you must leave too, Alice. And Alice, who had been nine at the time, had not understood.

After Milli had gone things got much worse. The only times Mr Purley had not been angry was when he was asleep, and Mrs Nimrod had bruises and cuts that never quite disappeared.

Sometimes Alice hid under the stairs. 'I will not let him hurt you, Alice, I will not!' Milli had used to say when she found Alice there. But Milli had gone and now when Alice hid under the stairs no one came to find her.

One night when Mr Purley returned from the pub her mother had picked up the iron and swung at him with it. The iron had got him squarely on the forehead and they had both watched as Mr Purley reeled away then stumbled off down the stairs. The next morning they found him, stone dead, in the hallway, in a little pool of dried blood and a cut on his head. The constables had come and taken him away, and that was the last they saw or heard of Mr Purley. They had gone back up to their room and her mother had closed the door behind her and dusted off her hands just as though she had disposed of a particularly large cockroach.

After that Milli had come back. She had been away two years, she never said where. Father McCreadie had shaken his head over her, for she had not been to mass in all that time, but he had helped her to get a job at the dairy, and for the next three years they had moved only once. Then Milli met Seamus, and when Seamus said he was returning to Melbourne, Milli had announced she was going too, to be his wife. She had been happy that day, making her announcement. It was a day or so before Mrs Nimrod had come down with the summer fever, and within three days their mother was dead. But Milli had gone anyway, to be Seamus's wife, and Alice had stood on the platform at Sydney Terminal and waved her sister goodbye.

It was Father McCreadie who had come to the rescue once more. 'I have found you a position, Alice Nimrod,' he had said. 'You will go to be a maid in a big house.'

Alice ran her hand along the soft leather that covered Mrs Dunlevy's writing desk. It was a smooth dark grey speckled with lighter flecks. Like marble, she thought. She liked the feel of nice things—soft bedding and plush curtains, rich carpets and smooth silk dresses, gloves made from fine kid leather. She had been starved of nice things for her first fourteen years and now she was surrounded by them, though they belonged to someone else. Still her fingers were drawn to them, her fingers craved their feel. It reminded her of her salvation.

But today it reminded her that Milli had had no salvation.

She withdrew her hands. There was, inside her, a dull ball of knotted and confused feelings that all the dusting and shoe cleaning and rug beating masked for a time but did not quell. The fact of Milli was at the heart of this ball. Alice's own place in Milli's misery was unclear to her: if she had indeed played a part in it and was in some way to blame, or if she could be her sister's salvation, she did not know. *Could* Milli come here? But she doubted she could hide a cat in her room without it being discovered, and as for a position, it was unthinkable: the Dunlevys would never employ an untrained maid of Milli's age, let alone one who was an unwed mother with a newborn.

Could it be, then, that there was a point beyond which salvation was no longer a possibility, that a person could not be saved—or not saved in this world, at least? Alice could not believe such a thing, for it suggested an inevitability that seemed to deny God, and yet it seemed to her that Milli was at this point. Perhaps a man, some man with a position and a bit of money put by, would want to marry Milli and take on another man's child . . .

But Alice had lived in too many damp, bug-infested rooms to believe in this fantasy. She had seen too many Mr Purleys. And the time when some man—any man—might want to marry Milli was gone.

Alice sat at Mrs Dunlevy's desk. For a time she did not stir.

She thought what a fine thing it was to sit at a fine desk. She thought: Mrs Dunlevy goes to committees and sits on boards (though what a committee was and what it meant to sit on a board Alice had only the vaguest notion). She knew that one of those committees was the asylum at Pitt Street where the unmarried mothers went. Why then, she thought, should Mrs Dunlevy not wish to help an unmarried mother here, in her own home?

Alice knew she would not. She thought of Mrs Dunlevy, whose bathwater she drew, whose dirty linen she gathered up and disposed of, whose near-naked form she had helped to dress, whose frustrations and passions she occasionally witnessed, in the same way she might view a priest or the Governor-General's wife, which was to say as someone who was not quite like other mortals, whose commands you followed unquestioningly and whose infallibility was absolute.

She stood up, dusting each place her fingers had touched, and returned to the window. Mrs Dunlevy had long disappeared from sight. Mrs Dunlevy went to committee meetings and she paid visits to other ladies and she went to her dressmaker. That was what she did. But that was not what she was doing this morning, Alice was certain, though she was not sure how she knew it.

She pulled off her cap and her apron and went down to the kitchen to Mrs Flynn. She prepared to tell a lie. 'Mrs Flynn, the baker has left off half our order,' Alice announced on entering the kitchen. 'We are short two loaves. I cannot think how it happened but I shall go out now and fetch them myself.' And she reached for her coat, pulling it on.

Mrs Flynn, whose domain the kitchen was, stopped dead in the act of rolling out her pastry and stared in astonishment at her. 'They have never done such a thing before,' she declared.

It was true, the baker had not done such a thing before, but today, if anyone cared to look in the pantry, they would see that two loaves were missing. A more thorough search of the house would find the missing two loaves carefully stowed away beneath Alice's bed, but Alice was reasonably certain Mrs Flynn would not undertake such a search. Would not do anything, in fact, that was of the slightest deviation from her regular routine. Mrs Flynn was a thin, sharp-edged woman of late middle years and very rigid rules who went about her work with a furious look in her eye as though someone had once done her an injustice and she was not about to forget it. But she was not an unkind woman, and she was fair.

'I am only here,' she had announced darkly a week after Alice's arrival in the house, 'on account of my grandmother, a Scot, a wee lass from the Highlands, who poisoned her husband on their wedding night.'

Mrs Flynn had said this as she prepared a fowl for a luncheon and Alice, fourteen years old and still finding her way, had silently scraped mud off the potatoes.

'They did not hang her, on account of they needed women in the new colony. So they put her on a convict ship, and on that there convict ship she was ravished by a dirty marine whose throat she cut and whose blood-soaked corpse she tipped over the side of the ship.'

It was a grim tale, but Alice had been unmoved. Anyone could say their grandmother poisoned her husband, couldn't they? Anyone could say their grandmother cut a man's throat and tossed him overboard. Though why you would make it up, she could not say. Alice had got on with scraping the potatoes. There had been no ending to the story, and whether Mrs Flynn's grandmother had flourished or perished was unknown, though her family lived on—for here was Mrs Flynn, her granddaughter—and that was something, Alice supposed.

Mrs Flynn put down her rolling pin and shook her head.

'That daft lad is not likely to realise his mistake and return with them missing loaves.'

No, he was not likely to do that.

'There is nothing for it but you will have to go out and fetch them missing loaves yourself,' she announced as though the idea were hers.

'I shall leave at once,' said Alice. 'And I shall be as quick as ever I can.'

CHAPTER SIX

# A DEAD CLERK

Alasdair Dunlevy's mother had been a Sussman, a fact that had caused him some disquiet in the early years of his political life, though the notoriety that accompanied this name had diminished as the century drew to its close. And in a penal colony notoriety was rarely a bad thing. Indeed, it was rarely a thing at all.

His grandfather, Reuben Sussman—an Englishman whose obscure Jewish origins lived on only in his name—was a financier and small-time speculator at a time when the century was new and the markets unregulated who had found himself, while still a relatively young man, in a position of some trust at a modest but long-established and highly respectable provincial bank in the north of England. Through a series of recklessly ill-advised dealings and increasingly misguided decisions the bank, under Reuben's management, lost so much money the shareholders baulked and took fright, triggering a run that eventually caused the bank to fail. Amid the immediate sensation of the calamity a great many businesses went bankrupt, a great many ruined men took their lives and a great many widows and fatherless children were left destitute. At his trial, it was never firmly established whether Reuben intended to defraud the bank to his own betterment or whether it was simply mismanagement on a spectacular scale but, finding himself the architect of so much misery, it could hardly have come as a surprise when a sentence of transportation and penal servitude for ten years was declared.

Off Reuben went, leaving behind a young wife and three daughters, the youngest just a year old, to the fledgling colony. He served out his term quietly enough—for he was not a violent man nor an indolent one—and eventually earned his freedom. Perhaps at this point the penitent and middle-aged Reuben might have returned home to England (though it is doubtful what sort of a reception he might have got), but fate stepped in. The colony, finding itself deficient in free men with any sort of financial background, offered Mr Sussman a position in the newly created colonial treasury, an irony that went unremarked in a city where half the public buildings had been designed by a convicted forger. His wife having died during his years of incarceration, Reuben sent for his three daughters, the eldest two of whom were now approaching their majority and the youngest but eleven. His three daughters duly arrived and he installed them in a pleasant little sandstone cottage overlooking Dawes Point. Here he lived out his days, and following his death his daughters lived on. The eldest two, Athena and Delphine, never married; perhaps their father's disgrace, coming when it did in their young lives, had scuppered their chances, though they appeared to bear no grudge. Alasdair remembered his two maiden aunts fondly, seated fanning themselves by the window in their little cottage, sporting the lace caps of some previous century and starting each fresh reminisce with the words, *Do you remember how dear Papa used to . . .* And of course the youngest daughter, Lily, did marry, for she was Alasdair's mother, though the circumstances of her meeting with and betrothal to Fergus Dunlevy were unknown to him.

Alasdair's cab had traversed Potts Point and was now making its way north towards the dockyards at Woolloomooloo. The morning, which had begun spectacularly with the sort of unending blue sky that brought the whole notion of winter into question, had continued on in similar vein and now the light was so bright it creased the eyes. It was almost certainly responsible for the accident on Victoria Street that resulted in two overturned drays and a large quantity of spilled beer and a queue of vehicles all the way back to Darlinghurst Road.

Alasdair heard the shriek of metal and the shattering thud as the two carts collided and he glanced out of the window in time to see first one and then the other split and fracture and topple over, but his own cab was ahead of the smash so he turned away, dismissing it.

The harbour was ahead of him now and the masts and funnels of the Newcastle colliers and the ocean-going steam packets came into view. The air was filled with smoke and steam and gulls circling, with the shouts of the men working on the wharves, and Alasdair thought of the Dunlevys.

Compared to the colourful, roguish Sussmans, the Dunlevys were insubstantial, ethereal, crude. There was a Conall Dunlevy from County Mayo who crossed the Irish Sea sometime around the beginning of the century to work as a navvy on the canals and later on the first railway lines. This Conall had a number of children, the eldest of whom, Fergus, showed enough early promise, despite his modest beginnings, to earn himself a scholarship to a small local grammar school—at which point, Conall and the rest of the Dunlevy family fade into background and no more is heard of them. The young Fergus acquitted himself decently but found that, on completing his schooling, his expectations had been raised but his prospects remained distressingly limited. Frustrated by this lack of opportunity, and seeing little prospect of change, he came out to the colony as a free settler and went to work in a clerk's office for a legal firm where he remained and worked hard, eventually gaining a law degree. As the century reached its midway point he met and married Lily Sussman and had a son, Alasdair.

Both his grandfathers were many years dead but Alasdair's sense of Reuben and Conall burned brightly in him and had fashioned him in a way his own father had not. Of his two grandmothers, he knew almost nothing. That Conall Dunlevy had stayed in Liverpool long enough to marry a local girl, name and origins unknown, and to sire a quantity of offspring was the sum of his knowledge. As for his Sussman grandmother, she had shrunk into the mists of time, a ghostlike figure dying unnamed and forgotten in England as her disgraced husband served out his sentence on the other side of the world. His mother, Lily, seemed barely to remember her, and Lily's two maiden sisters seemed never to refer to her, or if they had he could not, now, remember it.

They were a strange pairing, his parents, Lily Sussman and Fergus Dunlevy. Lily had had a quiet presence that somehow made her the centrepiece of every room. His father, at over six foot, a large figure by any measure, and with a brooding manner that often overtook him and kept him away from the house and in his office for days on end, filled a room yet was rarely its centre. Where Lily had an almost intrinsic sense of good taste, his father strived for it and despised it in equal measure. They had moved to a large house at Ashfield as the family's wealth had grown, additional servants were employed, a carriage was kept, but where

Lily managed the new servants without appearing to do so, Fergus avoided them and preferred to dress himself. He had rarely spoken of his upbringing, never made reference to the family he had left behind or to the Irish navvy father who had not wanted his son to take a scholarship and who had refused to speak to him once he had.

The family's wealth had grown.

How oddly benign it sounded, put that way. As though wealth simply happened to one. The truth was more complicated. More subjective. His father, Fergus Dunlevy, for many years the unremarkable and unexceptional solicitor in a modest Kent Street practice, had bought at a knockdown price the estate of a bankrupt client, a great slab of empty bushland at Redmyre with barely a road connecting it to the city some seven miles to the east. It was an act of speculative brilliance, for a year or two later the railway had come, cutting straight through this land, and having successfully petitioned the government for a station to be built there, Fergus had subdivided and made a fortune. Strathfield it was called now. But that was merely the start. After this spectacular success, and with the seventies boom in full swing, his father had purchased other tracts of land, ever further from the city, and each time he had subdivided and sold for vast sums, always with the promise of new railway lines, new stations. And sometimes the promised railway, the all-important station, had eventuated. More often it had not and the speculators and builders who had purchased his land had been left with worthless plots, far from the city and quite inaccessible. The boom was long over now, the scramble to build new railways had slowed almost to a trickle, but great fortunes had been made by a great many men (and also by a great many politicians, particularly those concerned with railways and public works), Fergus Dunlevy included, though as many men, or more, had lost their fortunes. Had been made bankrupt. Such was the way of the world. Fergus had purchased the mansion at Ashfield and filled it with a legion of domestics and a stable full of thoroughbreds. Alasdair looked out of the cab's window and thought of his father, whom he had once asked to fund him on an expedition into the interior on which he had, as a young man of twenty-two, been offered a place. He was to be an explorer, that was his dearest wish.

He had only asked his father on that one occasion. The subject had never come up again.

They had left the dockside now. Grand houses had been built here only half a century earlier, their lawns rolling down to the water's edge, but now the dockyards had swallowed up all the available land and the grand houses had been subdivided, had faded, had fallen into disrepair. The grand people had moved out to Elizabeth Bay, Double Bay, Point Piper.

Alasdair had brought with him a leather portfolio which he had placed on his lap, and an umbrella which lay on the floor at his feet. He stared at these articles and could not quite make sense of them. He did not need either but habit, or subterfuge, had made him reach for both.

He thought about the man who the night before had burst into Parliament House brandishing his gun—his unloaded gun, it transpired. Did that make them all faintly ridiculous, scattering in all directions like chickens when a fox has got into the coop? Are we the men, then, to lead this nation, he wondered, that a madman with an unloaded weapon can so easily throw us into panic and disarray? He was glad that the only person to have witnessed his own panic and disarray was Charles Booker-Reid and possibly not even him. He thought, too, about the incident at Granville overnight. A signal box destroyed. A train that might have been wrecked but was not. Youths were blamed. Perhaps by the time the later editions came out someone would have been charged. Well, he was not responsible for the railways; he certainly was not responsible for the disaffected and disenfranchised few who chose to advertise their cause with threats of violence and acts of destruction. He was one man in public office and he represented the law-abiding majority. The country he was helping to create was built on solid ideals, on Christian values. Destruction for the sake of it had no place and was without meaning. Without end.

Anarchy, Charles Booker-Reid had said.

But the train had not been wrecked and Granville was a long way from the city.

*Do you remember when you ran your first campaign ... and how you said it would all be worth it in the end?*

What on earth had prompted Eleanor to say that about his first campaign, about the halls and the people, about it being worthwhile? Alasdair shifted uneasily in his seat. He had no wish to be reminded of a time that was long past when his thoughts were set clearly on what was to come. For his greatest moments were ahead, he felt it: the new nation, the new century, just a few short months away. Close enough to touch.

It had begun already, the future, *his* future.

It had begun the moment he had met Miss Verity Trent outside the offices of the shipping company four months ago. Life, of course, was filled with curious twists of fate, some minor, other portentous. If, for instance, his cab had turned into Victoria Street a minute or two later than it had, they would be stuck in that queue of vehicles right now and not sailing through Woolloomooloo. If he had decided to remain in his office that Friday afternoon in

February to finish some item of work, or if he taken some other cab via some other route that day . . .

But he had not remained at work. He had taken that cab, he taken that route and there was fate, awaiting him beneath the spreading branches of a giant golden wattle at Circular Quay.

He raised his face to the sky and let the sun penetrate his skin. How was it possible for a man to not even realise he is lost until he is face to face with his salvation? He stared at the stream of cabs going in the opposite direction, the line of horses tossing their heads in the sunlight, the drivers with their coats folded beside them and their hats pushed back, and he remembered that day.

An afternoon in early February, a Friday, the midpoint in a summer like any other yet like no other summer before it, when the sun dazzled the eyes, it pricked the skin, it turned the grass in Hyde Park a burnished yellow. It brought tiny basking lizards out onto the pavements of Hunter Street and College Street.

Parliament was closed and all the premiers were in Melbourne for the extraordinary meeting of the constitutional convention in a last-ditch attempt to break the Federation deadlock. The meeting had concluded the evening before and Alasdair had travelled by cab at dawn to Sydney Terminal to meet the Premier off the overnight express. On the platform, Mr Reid, who was not a man to disappoint a crowd, announced to the waiting newspapermen that Mr Braddon's amendments had been accepted, that the new constitution might, now, be agreeable to the people of New South Wales. The clamour of supporters and well-wishers at the station was so great it had been all Alasdair could do to shake the Premier's hand and climb with him into a waiting carriage.

And thus was the unbreakable stalemate broken, the possibility of a second referendum made real. It was a great day.

It was about to get even greater.

Alasdair accompanied the Premier to Macquarie Street then made at once for his office at Richmond Terrace where he saw, with his own eyes, the torpor that had descended over parliament since the referendum defeat seven months earlier lifted, saw men hurry from building to building and from chamber to chamber attending briefings and calling meetings and drafting documents and his own sense of purpose, a purpose that had gradually leaked out of him as the dream of Federation had faded, was renewed. All morning he attended briefings, he called meetings, he drafted documents. In the afternoon he took a cab from Macquarie Street to Circular Quay.

And there he met Verity Trent.

Of course, he had not known she was Verity Trent then. She had been merely a young woman standing outside Customs House amid the wool warehouses and the bonded stores and the government paper store that crowded along the quay, a woman standing perfectly still and alone in the afternoon heat. A barque had come in from Wellington on the dawn tide, another from Hobart. A steam packet, the *Damascus*, was preparing to set sail for Cape Town and London. Merchants and seamen and dockworkers and custom officials and shipping company clerks had swarmed, hurrying from place to place, but not she. She looked as if she was waiting. She looked as if the thing she waited for meant more to her than the brilliant summer sky or the dazzling light on the water or the day itself.

As he drew level with her in his cab she turned towards him. But, no, not towards him, towards an official—suited, hatted, overdressed in the heat—who emerged from a building shaking his head, one hand held out in apology, and handed her a document, speaking to her for a moment—no more—and departing again. And she started to follow then she stopped and gave up and her look of defeat, of utter helplessness, made him bang on the roof of the cab and call out to the driver, made him quit the cab and almost forget to pay the man. It made him go at once to her aid.

He had had in his care papers from the Premiers' Conference, though four months later he could not now recall what the papers contained nor where he had been taking them. He remembered that she wore a skirt in some pale green shade and a short, tightly fitted jacket of the same pale green, and beneath this a white blouse heavy with lace at neck and cuff, and little black boots that seemed hopelessly wrong for the climate, a hat that clung to the back of her head but offered no protection from the sun, that she carried an umbrella which she used as a parasol. He remembered that what he had taken for utter helplessness was not that at all—it was merely what he had wanted to see so that he might rescue her, when of course, really, it was she who had rescued him.

He had banged on the roof of the cab to make it stop, jumped down and pushed his way through the crowds to reach her, and her face was pale though the heat was crushing.

He touched his hat and presented himself to her:

'Madam, my name is Dunlevy. Forgive my intrusion, and my impertinence, but it seems clear to me that you are in some little distress and confusion. Please, allow me to offer whatever assistance it might be in my power to give.' He gave a little bow and immediately felt absurd.

She listened with her grave, pale face and—he saw now that he was standing before her—steady grey eyes and an unwavering gaze, a small and neatly shaped nose, a high forehead, a slightly jutting chin and a stillness. Yes, that was it: a stillness of expression and of body that told him nothing. And now he began to wonder if he had not been mistaken, for her very stillness, her calmness, her unwavering gaze, unnerved him. He fell silent, unable to gauge her response to his sudden presence. He was aware of the unceasing flow of men hurrying past and around them, oblivious, and it seemed extraordinary to him that they should fail to notice her. He wished very much to say something vital and heroic, for it seemed to him the moment demanded it, that he had it in him to deliver such an utterance.

He said, 'Let me take you for a cup of tea.'

And she accepted, but in a way that made him feel, somehow, that she was gracing him by her acceptance.

They found a teashop one street back from the quayside and ordered tea.

'My name is Miss Trent,' she said finally, as they awaited the tea. She looked down at her gloved hands. Poorly made gloves, cheap, not the gloves of a lady, but not a servant either.

He waited. She had a story to tell and so he waited as a boy might wait for a bird to hop down from a branch to peck seeds from his hand.

'I am stranded,' she said—admitted—and it seemed that this might be all she would admit. But after a pause she went on: 'I came here to New South Wales to join my fiancé, Mr John Brewster of London, who was offered a government post and who sailed out here three months ago and began his new post and then sent for me, but he caught a fever not long after, and before I even reached Cape Town I received word my fiancé was dead.'

She paused again. Not, he felt, because her tale was tragic—though it undoubtedly was—and she sought his sympathy, but simply because the waitress placed the tea before them. When the girl was gone, she resumed her story:

'I arrived in Sydney a few days ago, alone and friendless and with no means of support and no means of securing a passage home. My fiancé's family are shopkeepers from a small town, you understand?'

He did understand. The grieving parents had many sons and more daughters. They had packed their youngest son off to the New World with best wishes and, to be sure, they mourned his loss, but towards his fiancée (to whom their son was not, when all was said and done, actually wed) they felt no obligation.

'After an initial telegram,' she went on, 'I have heard no more from them. I approached the government department where John was, briefly, employed and they were most sympathetic to my loss and solicitous, even, of my welfare. Indeed, I found they had paid for John's funeral, though they were under no obligation to do so, and now I am arrived, John's fiancée, and they have placed me temporarily in a small boarding house and consider their duties fulfilled. They cannot, it seems, provide me with the funds for a passage home.'

Alasdair, who had listened in silence, now said, 'And may one enquire, do you intend to remain here? Will you try to make your way or will you return home?'

His question was simple enough, yet as he awaited her answer the sounds within the little teashop and the quay beyond faded and he heard only his own heart beating.

'I can do neither,' she replied, 'for I have no money to pay for a passage and none with which to pay my board. I have no family to return to—my father died in the weeks leading up to my departure, his illness being the reason I did not journey here with my fiancé as had been my original intention—and I know no one in New South Wales. My situation is,' she observed, 'dire.' And she might have been discussing the pot of tea—for it was a poor brew indeed—and not her own perilous circumstance.

She sat very upright in her chair, her hands folded neatly before her on her lap, and her grey eyes gazing about her at everything that must be familiar to her—the tea in the teapot, the cups and saucers, the portrait of the Queen above the counter, the kind gentleman seated opposite her in his grey suit and waistcoat, in his patterned silk necktie with the tiny gold tiepin, the waitress in her black uniform and white cap weaving between the tables—but perceiving also how everything was utterly, utterly different: the heat rolling off the paving stones outside, the cries of the curra-wongs and the butcherbirds in the plane trees, the dishevelled ibis that had just wandered into the teashop, the tiny brown-and-black skink that skittered across the floor as they talked and was now motionless halfway up the wall. A frown furrowed her brow and, though she sat with lizard-like stillness, there was a despair about her, a sort of dismayed disbelief at this cruel trick God or fate had played on her.

Or that was how Alasdair had seen it. And he had wanted to throw himself at her feet to beg her to allow him to help her.

He had paid for the tea and escorted her to her tram stop. He had offered to make some enquiries on her behalf and they had arranged a meeting for the following day. He had bowed to her again and gone about his business.

But his world had been turned on its head.

He had made some enquiries. The fiancé, Mr John Brewster of London, had arrived on the *Thermopylae* on 1 November. He had spent two nights at a hotel on MacLeay Street then taken a room in a boarding house a few streets to the south in Kings Cross. He had taken up the position of clerk at the government department's offices, but less than a fortnight into his new position had succumbed to a fever. Within a few days, his condition deteriorating rapidly and his landlady alarmed, he had been moved to St Vincent's Hospital where he had died the following day, alone and unmourned and under the care of the Sisters of Charity. He had been buried three days later at the nearby Sacred Heart Catholic Church, though there was nothing to suggest Brewster was, or had ever been, a Catholic. Clearly expediency had prevailed: there had been no one to speak on Mr Brewster's behalf, his family being in England and his fiancée being by this time halfway to Cape Town, so the Catholics had won the day—or they had opened their arms to a lost soul far from home, depending on how one viewed it.

It struck Alasdair as more than a little feeble to journey halfway across the world only to succumb to a fever three weeks after arriving. Why, he had lived in Sydney his whole life—some forty-five years—and he had never succumbed to a fever once, fatal or otherwise. That this man had done so smacked of weakness, frailty, ineffectualness. It made one wonder what exactly Miss Trent had seen in the fellow. Surely she deserved better.

A clerk! Worse—a dead clerk!

However, he had done as he had promised and made enquiries. The superintendent of the government department within whose division Brewster had, albeit briefly, been employed granted Alasdair an interview and expressed surprise at the way Miss Trent—of whose existence he had not been made aware until this moment—had been treated. He left the room, spoke to one or two people, sent and received a telegram, and announced, with some satisfaction, that the Royal Mail steamer the *Oriental* was due to sail for London in seven days' time and, if Miss Trent so desired it, passage could be reserved for her on it.

Alasdair left the offices of the government department and walked the short distance to the quayside where he stood for a time watching the ships dock and listening to the cicadas. He had secured her passage home—indeed, it had proved a surprisingly simple matter to arrange—and his heart surged as he imagined her gratitude when he calmly announced the miracle he had thus performed.

And yet when he met her at the same teashop that afternoon and reported his progress, he failed utterly to mention the department's generous offer. And when the *Oriental* sailed for London seven days later Miss Trent was not on board. Instead, Miss Trent was moved from the seamy Surry Hills boarding house in which she had found herself to a more suitable premises at Woolloomooloo, and if she had been encouraged to believe—initially, at least— that the government department of her late fiancé had somewhat tardily decided to offer recompense and were paying her board, four months later she was no longer labouring under any such misapprehensions.

The cab creaked to a stop on the corner of a tree-lined avenue of once-grand three- and four-storey residences. Most were past their prime and slipping on their poorly laid foundations, peeling and splintered, and unrepaired but still with a genteel air of faded glory. The people who lived here had known better times, too, a generation or more ago, and had watched their fortunes decline as their street had declined. But they had clung on, subdividing and subdividing again, selling small parcels of themselves until what remained was two small rooms in the top storey of a house in which the roof leaked and one girl did the work that once a team of domestics would have done. But still that genteel air, still the tradesman sent to the back door and spoken to peremptorily.

Alasdair paid the driver and stood on the pavement until the cab had turned the corner. The leather portfolio was under his arm and it felt a little ridiculous here in this street; he might be a bailiff or an inspector of some kind. He wished he had not brought it. He realised he had left his umbrella in the cab and started forward, but the cab was gone and he was not about to run after it. He did not need an umbrella; the sky was a clear, brilliant, dazzling blue. To have an umbrella was to make oneself more ridiculous.

He turned into the avenue and walked nearly its entire length and the houses that he passed had names—Tintern, Derwent, Braemar—that irked him, for they spoke of a homesickness for places long ago left behind but somehow still yearned for when the new century was only months away. It seemed to him that a man's thoughts should be of the new nation, of a future freed from the mother country. But his thoughts were not of the future. His thoughts were on the house almost at the end of the street, an imposing three-storey villa with many shuttered windows and the final vestiges of pale pink paint on its rendered walls. Outside sprouted a huge banksia dotted with spiky yellow blooms that defied the season and attracted the winter lorikeets that nestled in its foliage in a noisy blaze of blue, green and orange. Against this riot of colour the house behind appeared dull, worn. Yet here was a finely carved set of steps leading up to the entrance and wrought-iron railings, the paint gently flaking off; here was a front door with leadlight in its window and above it a delicately ornate lantern hanging in a gabled porch so that an air of quiet elegance was, somehow, maintained.

The butler who might have opened this door fifty years ago was long gone, the overworked maid with a soiled uniform and unkempt hair who may have answered the door with bad grace five or ten or fifteen years ago was similarly departed. Now the names of the residents were listed on a little wooden board nailed to the porch and the residents opened their own front doors.

Alasdair went up to the house. He observed for a moment his right hand where it rested on the flaking paint of the railing. The usual thrust of his chin, the squareness of his shoulders was gone. But every man has his secrets; it was part of what made him a man.

Or so Alasdair told himself. He pushed open the door and let himself in.

Here was a quiet that offered respite from the noisy bustle of the wharves and the glare of the brilliant sky. A coolness, too, for the sun never ventured into the dimly lit hallway. It was a grand space, or had been. One or two anonymously closed doors suggested formal drawing rooms and reception rooms now partitioned into private apartments. A magnificent staircase fashioned from Australian cedar swept upwards to a half-landing then swung back on itself to arrive at the first floor. And beside the staircase, a triumph of wrought iron and hydraulics, was an elevator cage and shaft, recently installed.

There was no one about. There was, aside from the inevitable groans and creaks of the old house, silence.

Alasdair took the stairs, his footsteps deadened by the gradually unravelling crimson Turkish carpet that must have looked impressive in an English drawing room in 1880 but here was merely oppressive. He had used the elevator just the once and its clanking and rattling had made such a terrific noise he had expected every moment that doors would fly open and every pair of eyes would gaze upon him, though none had. Since then he had used the stairs. And he rarely saw anyone. The residents—widows existing on small annuities, retired military men who had never married, men of business whose investments had not performed quite as well as hoped—had few callers. When he had happened to meet someone—an elderly lady in pince-nez; a young woman in a great hurry—they had been as speechless as he. He had tipped his hat and continued on his way. If asked he would say he was Miss Trent's brother, her business adviser, her lawyer. Not her uncle, not that. But no one had ever asked.

On the first floor a large fern in a cracked terracotta pot and one or two badly executed watercolours on the walls provided the only relief from an otherwise empty corridor and more anonymous doors. Alasdair walked the length of the corridor and paused outside the last door at the rear of the house.

He had chosen this apartment. He paid the rent on it. But he paused. After a moment he tapped on the door.

∞

The road ahead was blocked. A line of drays, carts and carriages queued the length of Victoria Road all the way back to the junction with Darlinghurst Road.

What had caused the blockage was not immediately apparent, but as Eleanor leaned out of the window of her cab she saw a dray on its side minus a wheel and a terrified plunging mare that several excited young men were now attempting to calm and others to cut free from its harness. She looked down. The road was slick with a sticky brown liquid that flowed steadily down the centre of the road and into the gutters. By its odour it had clearly come straight from the brewery via the pile of spilled and split barrels that now lay scattered across the street. Already small boys and one or two of the more disreputable local inhabitants had run

93

onto the street with caps and cups and their bare hands and were scooping up the amber liquid and pouring it down their throats. A great many men were shouting and gesticulating and a great many more were standing around, pushing their caps to the back of their heads and thoroughly enjoying the spectacle.

'Driver! Get us out of this!' Eleanor called up.

'Ain't goan nowhere,' replied the man, not even bothering to look down at her. He spat a mouthful of tobacco from the side of his mouth into the quagmire of ale below.

Eleanor leaned back in her seat. She closed her eyes. She had readied herself for action. Had steeled herself. Now this. The delay was intolerable to her. The cab they followed, the cab that contained her husband, was gone.

The shouts of the men and the frightened snorting of the horse had become distant but they came back now, louder, and she opened her eyes. They were on Victoria Street, which was a longish street stretching from Darlinghurst all the way down to Potts Point. She saw they had stopped directly outside the Jellicoes' house.

The irony of it made her smile. Made her despair.

The house, a cream-coloured two-storey villa in the Greek Revivalist style popular half a century earlier was fronted by an expanse of lawn, a gravelled drive and tall gates. It was one of a number of such dwellings in this area and Eleanor had swept through the gates on many occasions. She had handed her hat and gloves to the Jellicoes' curtsying maid. She had stood in the marble-tiled hallway with Alasdair at her side. She had allowed Adaline Jellicoe to come to her across that tiled hallway with a smile and outstretched hands.

The house was shut up and silent now. The gates closed. Though it was entirely possible Adaline or Leon—not both, surely?—were still inside. Overseeing arrangements, writing instructions. Hiding.

Yes, thought Eleanor, I would hide. I would shut up the house. I would send the servants away.

Dora Hyatt—the housekeeper! She tried to picture the woman but could conjure up merely a silent presence, plain-featured and ordinary. She shuddered. This betrayal by the servant struck her as worse than that of the husband.

But, no, the house was not entirely shut up, she saw. A figure was visible at an upstairs window and Eleanor pressed herself back in her seat, though it was absurd to imagine anyone could see her, down here in the cab. Or perhaps she was mistaken about the figure in the window, for there was no further movement and it seemed likely now it was only a shadow, a trick of the light. One's imagination run wild.

Adaline had sat with her a year ago. Eleanor remembered how the curtains in her bedroom had been half closed against the daylight and the room had smelled, oddly, of lavender, a smell she abhorred, but someone had brought something—a handkerchief or a potpourri—and placed it in her room. The doctor had come and gone again. She had lain in a fug of morphia and Adaline Jellicoe had come and had sat for a time at her bedside. Adaline had not talked but she had reached out and taken Eleanor's hand. That had struck Eleanor at the time, Adaline taking her hand. It was not something she would normally do, one felt. But Eleanor had a great wound newly stitched across her abdomen and somewhere a baby—the doctor had not said boy or girl—lay blue and lifeless and bloodied and wrapped in a cloth. She had not seen it and they had not offered it to her. It had nestled, this dead thing, in her womb for some days before they had cut it out of her. The horror of it—a dead thing inside her—had eclipsed, at the time, her horror of her first, her only, child's death.

She had barely had time to get used to the idea of her confinement, of motherhood, and it was over.

Cecily Pyke had visited her, too, and one or two others—Cecily's presence unsettling, her smugness at her own effortlessly expanding clutch of children. Though perhaps the smugness was only imagined.

She had been in a fug of morphia for many days.

Alasdair had returned home on one of those evenings to say the vote was lost. The Federation had failed. She had felt she must be to blame. The Federation lying dead inside her.

Alasdair had moved into the second bedroom at around this time. It was unsafe to risk another pregnancy, the doctor had suggested. A hushed, one-sided conversation with more left unsaid than said, and Eleanor could not remember now if the doctor had spoken these words to her or to her husband. Alasdair had remained there in that second bedroom and something else had died—though, like the baby lying lifeless in her belly, she had not realised it at the time.

The frightened horse had been freed from its harness and was being calmed by its owner and a group of men had organised themselves into a gang to raise the upended dray. They were in their element now, these men. Shouting orders at one another, putting things to rights, their faces red, their shirts damp with sweat.

She flung open the door of the cab and jumped down, tossing a coin at the driver and stepping gingerly, skirts held off the ground. She set off on foot, avoiding the chaos of horse and men and wagons, heading north in the direction Alasdair's cab had taken, though it was long gone by now.

She kept on, but after a time her footsteps slowed. She looked about her. The villas here were a little less grand as she neared the docks; the space between each one had shrunk. She would have liked to sit down but there was nowhere. She had a sudden fear someone of her acquaintance would see her from a passing carriage or an upstairs window.

A cab was now coming towards her pulled by an ageing grey, the driver a youngish man in a green bowler hat, and she saw it was the very cab Alasdair had caught, though empty now of its fare.

She stepped out and flagged down the man. 'The fare you just dropped off,' she called up to him, 'a gentleman in a top hat whom you picked up in Elizabeth Bay—I wish you to take me to the same address.'

The driver nodded resignedly and barely waited for her to climb in before awkwardly turning the cab around and starting back the way he had come.

For a some minutes this extraordinary stroke of luck took up all Eleanor's concentration and she stared out of the window without seeing the rows of houses that flashed past, the docks that now came into view. Someone had left an umbrella in the bottom of the cab. It rolled against her foot. She pushed it away with her toe.

But already the cab was slowing.

'Wait!' cried Eleanor. 'Just wait.'

# CHAPTER SEVEN

# THE CLEVER LIE

The world was a different place this morning and Alice Nimrod stopped at the top of Elizabeth Bay Road to raise her face to the day and feel the sunlight enter her skin and flood her body. A hatred of rain, of cold, ran deeply in her. She felt her body close in on itself during the three months of winter and open up again as the first hint of spring filled her air. The sun had brightened and warmed this day in a way that made Alice believe the words of priests, made her believe that the light that streamed through the stained-glass windows of the cathedral was a glimpse of Heaven. But to know that it was the second day of June, to know that winter had barely begun, was a weight that hung heavily, and she could no more ignore it than Man could ignore his own mortality, and so she was a little saddened.

She set off again, walking briskly; the jubilation at her clever deception of Mrs Flynn was fading a little. Her plan was to find her sister. The sense of urgency that she felt could not easily be put into words but it caused her heart to beat too fast and her breath to come in short gasps as she hurried along Darlinghurst Road. And now the first doubts crept in: what if Mrs Dunlevy returned home and found her not there?

What if she lost her position?

Alice faltered. She wavered. The shadow of the black and bottomless pit out of which she had dragged herself was at her shoulder, but if she walked briskly she might outrun it. She was collecting the two missing loaves, was she not? There was no reason her clever lie should be discovered.

Alice pressed on, comforted and enveloped in her lie, though each step was charged with dread.

As she made her way southwards the stream of elegant carriages and sleek horses became draymen's carts and coalmen's carts, and men with nothing better to do than lounge on the meanest of street corners and outside gin houses stared at her and called out. One stepped into her path and would have waylaid her but she shoved him roughly aside. She approached the Hollow cautiously, as she had the night before, and in the sickly yellow semi-daylight of a smoke-filled Surry Hills morning all the nameless and unseen terrors of the place seemed no less terrible. Indeed, they were worse, for now a person could see them more clearly: the angry-hungry eyes of men who watched her, keeping one hand inside their coats on the blade of a razor; the vacant faces of women selling themselves for a shot of gin. A young mother too weak to stand, huddled in a doorway with her children clustered about her and with barely the strength to hold out a hand to beg for help.

Alice hurried past. She had escaped this and they had never, she and Mum and Milli, not ever sunk as low as this. Alice had her dignity, though it would have surprised her to realise it.

She slowed her pace to descend the stone steps as she had done the night before and the woman who had lain dead on the lower steps was gone and Alice was glad. She stepped carefully because the mud, which elsewhere had dried out, was ankle deep here, and she lifted her skirt rather than soil her clothes.

'Milli?'

She had found her way back to the shack and someone had pulled the plank away from the entrance, perhaps to let the sunlight in, though little enough light of any sort penetrated this dismal place even on the longest day of the year. But someone had removed the plank. A flicker of fear flared inside Alice's head and ran the length of her spine. She stepped inside and the place was deserted. There was not a stick of furniture: not the makeshift table nor the rescued chairs nor the wooden pallet bed; all of it was gone. And no sign of Milli. For a moment Alice stood peering into the gloomy interior, disbelieving. Then she ran outside and called out, 'Milli! *Milli!*'

A head appeared above her in the doorway of the shack that was balanced, precariously, on top of this one.

'Yer too late,' said this neighbour, Mrs Renfrew, dully, as though such calamities—if such this should prove to be—were to be expected. Her head shrunk back inside.

'Too late?' Alice felt her heart fluttering. 'Please, where is Milli?'

The head reappeared, a weary face, a face so ground down it did not seem capable of words.

'You're her sister,' said Mrs Renfrew at last, as though the thought cost her a great deal. One of the rescued chairs from Milli's shack was balanced perilously on the ledge on which Mrs Renfrew stood. The makeshift table was wedged in beside it.

Mrs Renfrew frowned as a second thought now occurred to her. 'She ain't long gone. Perhaps you will catch her?'

'I seen her, missus,' said a child, one of the Renfrew brood, its small head appearing suddenly beside its mother. The child held in his hand a small, hard potato at which he had been gnawing. 'I seen her,' the child said, 'goan up Crown Street.'

Crown Street is just the other side of Riley Street, a busy thorough-fare connecting Cleveland Street to the south and Oxford Street in the north, gateway to prosperity or poverty, depending on which direction the traveller chooses to go. On that June morning Alice Nimrod turned south towards Cleveland Street and Redfern and the crumbling tenements and warehouses and railway works that lay beyond.

She hurried, as much as any servant might hurry in a uniform that reached to her ankles and was made of some unyielding mater-ial that resisted movement, and in a pair of lace-up boots that had uneven heels and thin soles. But the notion that this was the moment when she might save her sister drove her on, it filled her heart with both fear and courage so that she could not catch whatever breath the obstinate and constricting uniform might allow her to take. And so Alice ran, this way and that, the length of Crown Street all the way to the junction with Cleveland Street and back up the other side, passing the pub and the brewery stables and weaving between the drays and carts that crowded the street.

When it seemed to Alice that she was too late, and the hope that had sprung up inside her and allowed her to imagine a future where she, alone, might be her sister's salvation had begun to fade, she saw her.

Milli stood on the corner huddled in her woollen shawl and clutching a single bag of belongings in one hand. She stood quite still, heavy with the child she carried, and the busy and diverse populace of Crown Street surged and swarmed about her.

That she was leaving was as clear as the child she carried in her swollen belly, and for a moment the utter dismay of her sister's betrayal took the breath from Alice's lungs and she could not find her voice.

'Milli?'

'Go *away*, Alice!' shouted Milli, seeing her sister, and she turned and began to hasten away.

But Milli was large with her child so Alice, despite her clothing, soon caught her up.

'What are you *doing*? Are you leaving again? Is that it? You would *leave* me—'

'Do not try to stop me, Alice, for I have made up my mind.'

Alice tried to think. She did not know how to stop her sister leaving her again.

'But you have no plan. You have no place to go, you said so—'

'And perhaps I have made a plan, Alice. Perhaps I have found a place.'

Alice was confounded by these words. There was no comfort in them. She saw, finally, that in Milli's other hand she held a brick. An old broken brick probably manufactured at the brickworks right here and fallen from some wretched hovel in this very suburb. But why would you carry a brick?

'What if Father McCreadie saw you now?' said Alice, though she hardly knew what she meant by this.

And Milli laughed, an ugly laugh, a laugh that was entirely at home in Crown Street and among the people who inhabited it. 'What do I care if Father McCreadie sees me? I *want* him to see! Priests and nuns—what do they know? They do not live in our world, yet they tell us how to live our lives!'

Alice had no reply, for what reply was there in the face of such an undeniable truth?

'What if Mum saw you?' she said finally.

'Mum is dead these five years,' said Milli, strangely flat and listless now, as though this fact no longer conveyed much to her, and the fire that had flared briefly in her seemed extinguished. She did not look at her sister or at the street on which they stood; her gaze was turned towards the smoking rooftops and beyond, to the spires of the distant university. If she would only look at Alice now, if she would only meet her sister's gaze and reveal her soul, she might be saved. But Milli did not look. She did not reveal her soul. Instead, she started forward, sudden purpose in her step. A police constable was approaching on the other side of the street.

Alice watched with a helplessness and an inevitability that the poverty of her youth had instilled in her as Milli dived across the street, all but falling beneath the hooves of a startled ironmonger's horse, and hurled her brick at the plate-glass window of an unfortunate butcher.

The astonished constable did not react at once, seeming unprepared for a hugely pregnant female to arrive at his feet and hurl a brick through a shop window. But he recovered himself and seized her. And Milli did not attempt to flee nor to resist arrest but submitted quietly enough to the cell that awaited her.

Instead it was her sister, Alice, who cried and wrung her hands.

# CHAPTER EIGHT

# A PLACE I CAN NEITHER SPELL NOR PRONOUNCE

Alasdair rapped on the door of Miss Trent's apartment and waited. He was aware of the silently closed doors of the other four apartments on this floor, aware of the potential for any one of those doors to open and an enquiring face to appear and questions to follow. But the doors remained silently closed. The questions he feared were not asked.

Yet some person was abroad for, as he stood there waiting, the newly installed lift jerked into life and rattled wheezily upwards, passing him and going on to the top floor. Its doors clanged open then shut again, and the lift wheezed and rattled its laborious way down once more. The lift clattered to a halt on the ground floor and at the same moment the door before which he stood opened.

Verity was not expecting him.

This was clear to him the moment she opened the door and stood in the doorway in her pastel green skirt and her little matching jacket, her hat already pinned into place on her head, her hair neatly arranged. Behind her on the console table lay her gloves and her reticule. And even if her apparel had not told him this, her face did. A look part confusion, part consternation crossed her face, her lips parted then at once closed again. The confusion, the consternation was quickly gone. She met his eyes and then she looked away. She was quite pale.

Despite this, his senses intensified at sight of her, his being soared, and the fear that lived permanently in his soul that other men would see in her what he saw flared agonisingly. He had a curious feeling that many lives had been lived by him and by her until their fates had, finally, in this life, collided. It was curious because he did not, in any way, believe in such things, yet still he felt it.

'You were expecting me? You received my note?'

She shook her head. 'I received no note. If you recall,' she went on, 'I told you I have an appointment this morning.'

Indeed, she had told him this and he had quite forgotten, or had chosen to forget. But he had sent her a note three days ago. It unsettled him that she had not received it. That his plans had been spoiled.

He nodded and said, 'Yes, of course,' because no man wishes to look foolish.

She had given him no explanation of the appointment and seemed disinclined to provide one now, and Alasdair would not demand one of her, though he rather thought he deserved one, that it was his due.

He was a gentleman, even if she was not, quite, a lady.

She had told him her father had been a watchmaker with a shop in Tunbridge Wells—though he could just as well have been a publican or a tailor or a cobbler. The family had lived above the shop and done quite nicely; there had been a servant who did the manual work. But the family's fortunes had declined as the father had aged and was finally forced to give up the business, so that they had found themselves in lodgings in a not so pleasant part of town. The servant had been let go. They had sunk and then they had sunk lower. Alasdair had seen all this in the moments after he had first gone to her assistance and he had been relieved (he did not wish her to be a lady, for this would make their arrangement impossible), but the specifics—the father who was a watchmaker, the servant who did all the work—these things he had learned later and they made very little difference.

She was not a lady, yet there was something about her that lifted her above the common class. For Miss Trent had that rare ability to adapt. Was this it, then, the thing that had attracted him? She could look about her at the ladies strolling with their parasols in the botanic gardens, seated with their straight backs and shoulders high, and she did the same. She listened to their phrases, she heard the words they used, and she used them too. It was a skill that was beguiling, for he could not decide if it were deliberate or instinctive, if it were a mask or a parody.

'I had thought to see you before your appointment,' he said.

Miss Trent, standing in the doorway and dressed for an imminent departure, hesitated and her lips moved silently then became still and she looked at him then looked away. She had pale grey eyes that occasionally offered him glimpses of who she was but for the most part remained obscure and closed from him. It left him often floundering in her presence. He raised his chin, consolidating his position in her doorway.

'Come in, of course,' she said, as she must, and she stood aside to let him enter.

He glanced at her gloves on the console table, at the satin and pearl reticule he had bought her a month or so ago and that she had been pleased with, or had appeared to be. She glanced at them too as she preceded him, and he stood aside and followed her into the little drawing room. The apartment—the one he had found and now paid the rent on—consisted of this little hallway and two rooms beyond: a large drawing room, high-ceilinged and looking out through wide French doors and a tiny wrought-iron balcony to an overgrown garden below; and a bedroom, smaller, and similarly overlooking the garden from a pleasant little bay window. The apartment came furnished with a collection of stuffed upright chairs, one or two writing tables and sewing tables and occasional tables, a faded chintz settee, an array of brass-potted ferns, an over-sized sideboard and an even larger dresser. This, combined with the striped crimson-and-white wallpaper and the faded Turkish carpet, all added to the sense of a place twenty years past it prime.

Alasdair seated himself on the settee. He was already dissatisfied with how the visit was going. Her welcome was less than he had hoped for, less than was his due. Really, it was hardly a welcome at all, and he felt himself harden a little against her. He wondered how he might punish her, but all the ways in which he might do so struck him as petty and ridiculous. He decided not to punish her.

Verity remained standing. She was distracted, he saw. She walked over to the French doors and looked out, and Alasdair remembered the very first time he had visited her here, a day or so after he had found the place, tucked away in Woolloomooloo, and he remembered how nervous he had been and how serene she had appeared when it ought to have been the other way about. Detached was perhaps a better word for how she had seemed that day.

'You have moved me to a place I can neither spell nor pronounce,' she had said that first day, standing at the window and gazing out at the tangle of overgrown garden below and at the funnels of the steamships docked at the nearby wharves.

'No one can spell it,' he had said with a laugh. 'And anyway, my dear Miss Trent, to whom are you intending to give your address? And come to think of it, to whom are you intending to write?'

'To no one,' she had replied. 'No one at all. It was merely an observation.'

He had still called her Miss Trent then.

'And which novels are the good citizens of Sydney purchasing?' he asked her now. For she had lately found a position three afternoons a week in a small second-hand bookshop in College Street. She had found the position herself and had told him about this change in her circumstances only once the deal was done, as it were. He had been a little surprised. He had been a little put out. Why had she done this thing behind his back? Why did she need the money when he gave her all that she might need? He had said nothing, though, lest it sound petty, belittling. But he might yet say something, he decided; the subject was not closed merely because he had let it pass initially.

She turned away from the window towards him. 'Mr Thackeray, Mr Wells, Mr Hardy, Mr Conan Doyle,' she recited as though she were often asked such a question and could answer it without thinking. 'And all the old novelists remain popular here, as they do in England: Scott and Stevenson, Mr Dickens and Mrs Gaskell. But I can find no novels written by New South Wales authors. Are there any?'

It was a simple enough question, asked with a simple honesty, but Alasdair found himself irked. For did it not imply something rather lacking in the menfolk of his own colony?

'We have our own novelists, Verity, as you will discover: Mr Rolf Boldrewood and Mr Marcus Clarke are two fine examples. And our bush poets—Mr Paterson and Mr Lawson and others—are, I am told, held in high regard. I have little time for novels myself, tending more towards the historical and philosophical. When I was a boy, my father read to me each night from the journals of Mr Watkin Tench—of whom you will have heard?'

But, no, Miss Trent had not heard of Mr Watkin Tench.

'Then I trust you shall know the pleasure of discovering his accounts of the earliest days of the colony. They certainly made a strong impression on my youthful mind. And I am named for him, too—my baptismal name is Alasdair Watkin Dunlevy.'

He bowed to her as he said this as though he were meeting the Governor-General. And it was a fine name, he had always thought so: Alasdair Watkin Dunlevy—it was, surely, the name of a future prime minister. Of a great prime minister.

Verity had left the window and now at last she sat down, though not on the settee beside him but on one of the upright chairs. Again he noted her eyes sliding away from him, the unnatural pallor of her face.

What was it she did not tell him?

Was she dividing her time between him and another gentleman? No, it could not be. He had arrived unannounced at her rooms on too many occasions and her always at home and no sign of any other gentleman for it to be even a possibility. And, besides, he would simply not believe it of her, for she was an honest woman, he felt it instinctively, for all that she was conducting this illicit affair with him. Or was that how she considered it? She was curiously difficult to read. And that, he realised, was another reason for his attraction. And his unease.

But still it was galling that she hid some part of herself, hid this appointment, from him.

'You will have read of the incident at Parliament House last evening?' he enquired, because she had as yet made no mention of it.

'I am afraid not,' she replied. 'Was there an incident?'

And now, because she had called it an incident, his own word turned back on him, it seemed ridiculous, absurd.

'A madman stormed the chamber as the Premier hosted a reception and climbed up onto the dais brandishing a pistol. He was swiftly dealt with, but it was cause for a certain amount of alarm among the more skittish of our number.' And Alasdair smiled to indicate he did not count himself among them.

'Heavens!' she replied mildly. 'Why did this man do such a thing?'

'His motive remains a mystery. I suspect we shall find out his faculties are impaired and he had no more idea of a motive than any such impaired soul does for any action they undertake.'

'Perhaps that is so,' she said thoughtfully. 'But to prepare such an action and then to undertake it suggests a certain amount of lucidity.'

A frown crossed her face as though the thought troubled her. And had he himself been in any danger? she might have asked. Had he participated in the man's capture, had he acquitted himself heroically in saving the ladies present or in throwing himself before the Premier or Mr Barton? But she did not ask these questions. Instead, it was the madman and his motivations that troubled her.

Had his wife been there? she might have asked, but she did not. To his recollection she had never once asked about Eleanor and that was entirely proper, though she must, surely, be a little curious?

'I shall be a good deal engaged with the referendum these next few weeks,' he said. 'There are more Federation meetings at which I am to speak.'

Indeed, he had spoken at such a meeting last evening, as she very well knew, though she had not enquired about it. Instead what she said was, 'They work you very hard, Alasdair. I hope it all proves to be worth it.'

It was a curiously empty phrase and his dissatisfaction grew. *You said it would all be worth it in the end. Do you remember? And it was, was it not? Worth it?* Eleanor's words over breakfast. They had unsettled him. It unsettled him now that Verity had uttered almost the same thought. Were they so much alike then, his wife and his mistress? Must he be, forever, justifying his work to them? Did they not see that the work was noble, it was honourable, that it was, in fact, an end in itself?

But what came into his head was himself returning home in a cab a year ago, the evening the Federation vote had been lost—irrevocably, it had seemed at the time—and entering Eleanor's room to inform her. She had been lying in bed, quite pale and stricken, though her face had had no expression (how could that be, he wondered?). The doctor had just left and the look she had given him as he delivered his news had told him she understood. Their child was lost before it was even born and his despair at the Federation was how he would get through it. It was how all men got through such moments. He did not know how women got through them. He suspected women, in this way, were stronger than men.

But Verity was watching him. He stared at her and for a moment had no idea who she was or why he was here. He made himself smile.

'Naturally, my work is worth it. It is the creation of a nation. You are new to our shores, Verity, you cannot be expected to fully appreciate the importance of our task.'

'Oh, but I do,' she replied. 'Men in parliament are always engaged in great and important tasks, and if this particular task may result in the creation of a new parliament, even greater and more important than the current one, then of course it must be worth all the effort you are putting into it.'

He smiled at her, for she had missed his point—entirely and charmingly. She was young—twenty-two—and he was, therefore, more than twenty years her senior, which was as it ought to be. (There was something distinctly unbalanced about a man's wife being almost the same age as himself. It was unnatural. He had not considered it so when he and Eleanor had met and were first married, but now it struck him forcibly whenever he was with her.) So he smiled at Verity and forgave her ignorance, forgave the secretive appointment.

'Come here,' he said, indicating the place beside him, and remembering his uncertainty the first time he had kissed her, the very first day he had come here to visit her—for nothing had been spoken between them and his offer of assistance, his setting her up in a place of residence and paying for the first six months' lease on the place, might have been merely the generous gifts of a gentleman moved to help a young lady in distress and with nothing expected in return. But it had not been the generous gifts of a gentleman, it had most certainly been the price to pay for something that was very much expected. And the fact that he had never done such a thing before and he was fairly certain she hadn't either only made it all the more open to speculation and misunderstanding. But he had kissed her on that first day and it had very soon become evident that the nature of their association was clear to them both and that there need be no more speculation nor misunderstanding between them.

Verity got up now from her chair and came over and sat beside him on the settee and he kissed her, which was what he had wanted to do since she had opened the door to him, since he had sat in the hansom cab, since he had sat at breakfast reading the newspaper.

He kissed her and he took her in his arms to show he forgave her the secret appointment, her less than satisfactory greeting and the job at the bookshop.

But it had never quite left him, that uncertainty he had felt the first time he kissed her.

CHAPTER NINE

# TRAVERSING THE DOMAIN

A steamer recently arrived from the Clarence River was docked at the wharf and the shouts of the men as they unloaded her carried across the air. Otherwise, the street was utterly still and silent, not a curtain stirred nor a door or window opened. It seemed to Eleanor, seated in a stationary hansom cab halfway along the street, that the great and important business of the colony was being attended to, earnestly and with enthusiasm, but it was happening elsewhere. In this street, the arrival of a tradesman with a delivery would shatter the stillness; might, indeed, cause a number of the older establishments to quake on their flimsy foundations.

She leaned forward. No tradesman arrived but a gentleman had just emerged from one of the houses.

The man stepped smartly down its front steps holding a leather portfolio tucked under his arm. He might be a man of law, a businessman, a purveyor of insurances, though his hat—a tall hat covered with good silk—suggested otherwise. He disappeared momentarily as he passed behind the monstrous banksia but now reappeared and set off the along the street in the direction of the wharves. He did not pause to look about him, yet there was something about his gait, the movement of his head, the tightly controlled way in which his arms held the leather portfolio so close to his body that suggested an awareness of the world about him and hinted that his place in it, at this moment, was not altogether legitimate.

Or so it seemed to Eleanor as she observed from the cover of her cab fifty yards up the street.

The gentleman was her husband.

He had been inside the house perhaps half an hour. It could not be much longer. Less time than she had anticipated.

She studied the house. It was large, extravagant even, but worn, faded, its best days behind it. What sort of young lady lived here? The answer, of course, was no lady at all. Some other sort of woman.

She had brought with her the note, still in its envelope, that someone—*who?*—had sent to her four days ago. She pulled the note from her reticule though she did not read it. She knew its contents. She had brought it with her as talisman or warrant or weapon, she did not know which, but to legitimise her presence at any rate.

She felt that she had been waiting six months for the note, perhaps longer. Anticipating its arrival with no idea she was doing so.

This house. The note. Her husband's rapidly diminishing figure. She had her proof. She did not know what to do with it.

What had Adaline Jellicoe done when she had uncovered her husband's betrayal? Eleanor did not know. She had not spoken to her friend about it. It was possible Adaline had known of Leon Jellicoe's affair a year ago as she had sat at Eleanor's bedside offering her silent comfort, that it was this that had driven her to Eleanor's side, had prompted her compassion.

Calamity, it seemed, struck people differently.

Eleanor sat perfectly still in the cab, one hand clenched on the faded upholstery of the seat, one on the strap that hung from the ceiling. The hat she wore had a fine gauze veil attached to it that she had pulled down on first entering the cab. She viewed the world, she viewed this street, through the delicate film of gauze and was protected by it.

'Where to, missus?' called the driver, grown impatient, his horse tossing its head and pawing at the ground. 'Where to?'

She did not answer him, instead hastened to open the door, struggling with the handle because her fingers would not do as she wished, had grown stiff and clumsy. At last she got it and the door swung open and she stepped down from the cab. With no warning, the ground surged up, it became as malleable as water. For a moment the world went black. She steadied herself against the cab, aware of the horse, its massive hindquarters, its nervous twitching head, its eyes swivelled around to view her.

'Y'right, lady?' The cab driver, peering down from his perch.

She pulled herself back. It was intolerable that he should see her tears.

She paid the man, handing him the coins and not caring if it was too much or too little, and turned away at once because his eyes on her face, even with the veil, was unbearable. He was a witness.

She did not wait for the cab to depart but set off along the street and her legs were foreign and unfamiliar to her and did not do as she wished. She stopped when she came to the old house, thrusting aside the teeming banksia with its host of noisy lorikeets, and after a moment's pause taking the steps that her husband had come down a few minutes earlier.

At the front door she paused, not quite able to catch her breath. She put a hand against the peeling paintwork of the house to steady herself. Beneath her fingers a large flake of paint came away, revealing powdery brickwork. The flake of paint drifted to the ground. She placed the toe of her boot on it and it shattered into dust at her feet.

Something made her spin around, a sound, eyes somewhere watching, but the street was deserted. The cab had gone. She turned back to the house. A wooden signboard was nailed to the wall before her on which the names of the residents were inscribed. Her eyes ran over the list of names, drawn to and repelled in turn by each one. Maj. T.H. Jenkins, Mrs T. Fowler, Mrs S. Longfellow, Mr T.E. Barnes, Capt. K. Littlejohn, Miss V. Trent, Mrs and Miss U. Tiptree. She went back to Miss V. Trent of flat 6, for she was the only Miss on the list aside from the Miss who resided with her mother, or possibly with her married sister. On the whole, Miss Trent appeared the most likely.

She gazed at the name for a time. Miss V. Trent. One could tell everything and nothing from a name on a signboard. Was the V for Violet? Veronica? Vivienne? Victoria was the most likely, the most conventional, and she pictured the patriotic parents far from home bestowing on their newborn daughter the name of their distant consort. How proud would these same parents be now if they knew how their dearest Victoria made her way in the world? It pleased her to think this, but with a bitter pleasure as one might bite into a sour apple simply to prove it was sour.

The door opened by her pushing it. Eleanor stepped inside and her heart beat a little faster. She must have a story at the ready, something she might say if she were stopped and questioned. She would say she was visiting someone.

But there was no one about and no one stopped her. And did she not have a right to be here, as every wife had?

She looked about her. The hallway was high-ceilinged and elegant but papered in a lurid crimson-striped design, the floor covered by a worn and ugly Turkish carpet. Two doors—closed—faced her and a wide, sweeping staircase led up to a first floor. There was also a lift; she could hear its uneasy clatter as it approached the ground floor.

And what if it were her, inside?

I will know her at once, thought Eleanor, and the words she might utter clogged her throat.

But the lift doors did not open and no one emerged. The lift had simply arrived, as though in anticipation of her arrival. Eleanor availed herself of the lift, stepping into its cage and dragging the double doors shut behind her so that they locked, studying the buttons, pressing 1 and lifting her face and testing the air about her as though she had arrived at a foreign land.

The lift lurched and began its slow and rattling ascent. It arrived at the first floor with a clunk and the doors released. Eleanor pulled them open and stood for a moment. A long corridor greeted her, a number of oversized ferns in brass pots and five anonymous doors painted a uniform white. At each end of the corridor was a window, the one at this end small, round and high up, facing the street, the one at the rear of the house reaching floor to ceiling and creating a square of sunlight on the carpet. She stood for a moment, listening. The shouts of the men at the wharves and the booming of the great ships and the chattering of the lorikeets were gone and there was, instead, a strange quiet to the place. She became aware of her own position as imposter, trespasser. She felt the same way entering a cathedral or any ecclesiastical structure, could not comprehend how such places made some people calm. They always induced in her the most intense anger.

She would like to be angry now.

This end of the corridor was cool and encased in winter shadow but despite this her hand was slippery with perspiration on the handle of her parasol. Her skirts were heavy around her legs. Directly opposite was the door to flat 6. She peered at the door, at the space immediately before the doorway, as though she might discern some essence of her husband, some residual part of him that remained after he had gone, just five minutes earlier. She drew in a breath, pushed back her shoulders and strode towards the door, the parasol gripped in her hand, her reticule in her other hand.

She heard a latch click somewhere behind the door and it began to open.

She darted back, retracing her steps and retreating into the safety of the lift as Miss Trent herself emerged.

Or one presumed it was Miss Trent. Eleanor peered through the grating of the lift. It was a very young woman, surely not more than twenty-one or twenty-two, slight of frame, almost too slender in a way that suggested economies being taken and the occasional straitened circumstance. She was of no more than average height, her hair a dull brown, her complexion unspoiled, to be sure, but pale in a way that made one think she was, or had been as a child, starved of sunlight; it was not the translucently pale and prized complexion that a lady of means and position might cultivate. Certainly her features were very regular, though the nose was perhaps a little too sharp, a little too narrow. A high forehead, an unremarkable chin. Her eyes were pale too, their exact shade elusive in such a fleeting moment. But her hat! It was a sorry little thing, too small, too insignificant, too many years past its prime—if, indeed, it had ever had a prime, which was doubtful. Her jacket too, which was short and narrow at waist and cuff with fussy little cap shoulders, was serviceable but of a feeble shade of green that had been popular with a certain class of female two or three seasons before; and her skirt, very high at the waist, not quite narrow enough at the ankle, was of the same green stuff. Her reticule, though, was of satin and pearl and very smart and, to Eleanor's eyes, it struck an incongruous note.

Was this her then? And was she a beauty? No, decidedly she was not, but was there something—what? Her face was, perhaps, a little unusual, her bearing not that of a lowly woman at all, for she carried herself with purpose—was it this then? Eleanor did not know. It was so fleeting, her sighting of the woman. An impression, no more.

Miss V. Trent now stooped to place her door key inside the brass pot of the largest of the oversized ferns. She straightened herself up and adjusted her gloves, took a quick, sharp breath and departed down the wide staircase.

Eleanor did not move. She did not speak. The words she had prepared and rehearsed were gone as Miss Trent was gone. She stared at her hand on the rounded ivory handle of her parasol, at the hem of her coat as it brushed the floor of the lift. She put out a hand to the side of the lift to feel its cold metallic reassurance but her fingers felt nothing. She felt her powerlessness as she had once or twice experienced grief. It washed over her, sweeping aside all else and leaving her without a breath in her body. She had thought herself stronger than this, but somehow her husband's betrayal felt like her own failure.

Downstairs the front door opened and then closed.

She wrenched shut the lift doors and stabbed her hand at the button, and the lift lurched as it began its labouring descent.

\*

Miss Trent—if indeed it was she—now proceeded on foot. She made her way in a surprisingly short time to the end of the street and turned into a busier road, heading west. She was hurrying, but where or to whom Miss Trent hurried one could only speculate, or one might if one was not entirely consumed with keeping up with her, at a discreet distance of some twenty yards or so, as Eleanor was.

Miss Trent skirted the wharves and entered the Domain where, on this sunny morning, carriages circled at a leisurely pace and young ladies strolled arm in arm and, in warmer seasons, couples picnicked. But Miss Trent did not stroll, nor did she strike a leisurely pace, and she certainly did not pause to picnic or to gaze at the young men in shirtsleeves noisily playing an unseasonal game of cricket. She traversed the Domain in a surprisingly short time and emerged at the rear of the hospital and onto Macquarie Street. She continued onwards until she reached the tram stop at Elizabeth Street. A green-and-cream-liveried tram approached and trundled to a halt and Miss Trent stepped on board.

Eleanor, some paces behind, would have lost her quarry right there had not a fraught young woman of the lower classes with a baby at her breast and two resistant little boys at her skirts spent such a time boarding that Eleanor had time to catch up and enter the tram by its rear door. Here she took a seat and, because she wore a veil and no other woman on the tram—or, indeed, on any tram—wore such a thing, every pair of eyes at once flew to her. Except those of Miss Trent. She sat a few rows in front and seemed intent only on her own thoughts. Eleanor fixed her gaze on Miss Trent's vulgar little hat and where they were bound she did not know, but she paid a fare to the conductor that he did not challenge and resigned herself to the ride.

The tram continued on its way down Elizabeth Street for a time before swinging into Oxford Street so that it seemed Miss Trent's pressing appointment must, after all, be in the pleasant and leafy eastern part of the city. But abruptly the tram turned south down Crown Street and in no time at all they were in Surry Hills, and the elegant four-storey houses and newly built offices became, instead, the mean streets and warehouses of the poorer part of the city, and suddenly Miss Trent's appointment took on a very different hue altogether.

Just before the tram reached Cleveland Street Miss Trent stood up and, as the tram slowed, stepped off. A moment later Eleanor followed.

This was a place of market stalls, of street sellers pushing their wares before them in barrows, of public houses and places purporting to sell gin and very little else. The window of a butcher's shop on the corner was broken and glass littered the pavement and was crunched beneath the feet of the passing people. Beside the butcher's was a tobacconist's and a small non-conformist church tucked in between a pawnbroker and a dusty antiquarian bookshop, and on the far side of the street an apothecary and a doctor's rooms, all of which, if not exactly prosperous, did at least suggest an air of ordinary mercantile respectability amid the poverty. The women who inhabited this part of the city wore shapeless, grime-encrusted garments and clutched parcels of shopping or small children or wares for sale, and the men wore boots that let in the daylight. They slouched against walls and on corners and regarded Eleanor in a way that made it clear she was the interloper. A smell hung over the place of three-day-old fish and discarded oyster shells, of cheap gin and cheaper tobacco, of straw and sweating horses and manure.

But all of this was of a moment's impression, for already Miss Trent had crossed Crown Street, dodging between an overloaded drayman's cart and a timber merchant's wagon and avoiding the horse droppings, looking to left and right, then going into the doctor's rooms.

This was a surprise, though no more so than if she had gone into the apothecary or the pawnbroker or, come to that, the small church. For none of these places suggested appointments to which one hurried. But it was to the doctor's rooms that Miss Trent had gone, entering down the laneway between the bookshop and the grocer's, for the doctor's rooms were, it appeared, upstairs and reached by way of the laneway and a dark flight of stairs.

Miss Trent had gone and Eleanor stood for a moment, pondering the sign: DR J.M.H. LEAVIS, MD.

What now? Already her mad dash after this woman, her journey to this part of the city, seemed absurd. The powerlessness bubbled up again and she stood in the street, lost.

A hansom cab sidled into Crown Street clearly in need of a fare and Eleanor hailed it and climbed in. She called out an address to the man and sat back, having no wish to be seen, and was relieved when the driver urged his horse on and in a short time she was leaving Crown Street and Surry Hills behind, heading north once more.

When at last she dared to turn and look out of the window, the cab was passing a young woman hurrying along the street. A domestic judging by the woman's uniform, and at large, perhaps, without her employer's knowledge. The servant looked just like Alice—but from behind they all did, and Eleanor reached up to pull down the little blind.

\*

She returned to the same Woolloomooloo street, its faded mid-century elegance no less noticeable and no less poignant in the middle of the day than it had been earlier in the morning. There seemed to be not a soul about and at the shuttered windows of the silent houses, each set in its overgrown oasis of lawn and shrubbery, no one stirred.

On this second visit Eleanor ordered the cab pull up right outside the house and this time she entered boldly through the front door, she took the wide staircase rather than the lift. She reached the first floor and she stooped beside the brass pot and her fingers found the key at once. She stood and slid the key into the lock—a cheap key, she saw, and a cheap lock, but suitable, no doubt, for someone who had little of value and little worth stealing. The door swung open and she stepped inside, pushing the door shut with a click behind her.

For a time her breath came unevenly, for there is nothing so thrilling or terrifying as standing illicitly in another's home.

She stood quite still, listening but hearing only the steady tick of a clock whose whereabouts she could not identify. And because there was this almost-silence it was the smells that she noticed: old timber and crumbling plaster and ageing rugs that had not been properly beaten in a while. It was a smell of not-quite-dry laundry and furniture polish and, faintly, of mothballs and cheap soap. Smells familiar and yet here, in this place, utterly alien. She reached out a hand. At her side was a narrow console table on which lay a worked brass tray, a repository for keys or letters, though it held nothing now, and beside it a cut-glass vase, though it too showed no evidence of having been recently used. The hallway was little more than an alcove and before her the apartment opened up into a generous room. She took in the crowd of mismatching tables and chairs, some of them quite good, others cheap and worthless, so that one got the impression an assortment of relatives, of varying means and tastes, had all died at once, leaving the apartment's occupant the contents of their homes. On the walls, perhaps in an attempt to minimise the effect of the oppressive crimson wallpaper, were a collection of reproduction Landseer horses and stags and pre-Raphaelite women in various states of religious ecstasy. But there was nothing here of a personal nature. This furniture must surely predate Miss Trent by thirty or more years.

Eleanor turned about and saw a large fireplace set in the back wall, its hearth hidden behind an ornately worked iron fireguard, beside it an ash bucket and a collection of pokers and paper spills, and on the mantel two empty brass candlesticks and the clock, a small gold carriage clock, the source of the loud ticking. She walked over to the hearth but it was swept clean or had not been used for some time. Still nothing.

Where was Miss Trent in this room? She picked up the carriage clock, which looked to be of good quality though utterly unsuited to fill the space on the mantel, which wanted a much larger timepiece than this little thing. She turned it over and saw an engraving: *To my little Verity with all my love—your dearest Papa, 1876.*

And here at last was Miss Trent. But Verity, and not Victoria at all. This required a rethink. Eleanor had pictured the parents quite distinctly but now they became vague and insubstantial. Verity. It was rather a cheap name, a music hall name. And yet this clock was charming.

She replaced it on the mantel and saw the doorway to a second room. She crossed the room and opened the door. And perhaps because this door was closed and because, therefore, one did not know what was contained within—though one might guess— she held back even as she pushed open the door and viewed the room beyond. It was a bedroom, as of course it must be, and she understood that this was the reason for her reluctance. This second room was much smaller, though a bay window with a cushioned seat built into it and overlooking the garden below gave it a charm and sense of proportion. A large fireplace opposite the window was similarly swept clean with a mantel similarly free of objects. And between was a chest of drawers and a bureau with one or two books on it, a trunk on the floor near the door, and a bed.

The bed. It was a simple enough affair, the bedstead and footer made of plain iron struts painted black and topped with brass, and a counterpane heavily embroidered. Another counterpane beneath it and the corners of a rug testified to how cold the room got in these winter months—particularly if one did not light the fire. Eleanor had not moved from the doorway. Aside from her mother's she had never set foot in another woman's bedroom— unless one considered the servants' quarters in attics, which one rarely had occasion to visit and were not the same thing at all. And so the utter strangeness of it struck her. Even the smell was different in here. It smelled more of *her* and less of the house, of other people's furnishings. But what was it? Soap again and rose water or lavender or some kind of potpourri and a smell of both washed bodies and unwashed bodies. She looked at the bed and felt faintly nauseated. Its plain iron bedstead and embroidered counterpane swam before her eyes.

In a rush she went to the bed and flung back the covers, layer after layer, until she had revealed the mattress. Stains—were they? Or just shadows, just laundry marks? She could not decide. She turned away and put her hands to her face and found her face cold and her hands cold too. She pressed her fingers into her eyes until lights danced before her. She dropped her hands to her sides. She made herself turn around and face the chaotic pile of covers, the pillows spilled onto the floor, the mattress, laid shockingly bare, exposing a part of someone's life that only a servant should ever see. And slowly, methodically she replaced the covers, she retrieved the discarded pillows, she returned the bed to its original state, and what did it matter if a stranger had viewed your most intimate secrets if you never found out about it?

*Would* one know if another pair of hands had gone through one's most intimate things, if another pair of eyes had viewed one's most private secrets? Eleanor felt soiled by it and a wish to wash her hands came over her, very intensely.

Her eyes went to the books on the bureau—a small Bible, not new but not well thumbed either, and three or four volumes of poetry and a book on modern painting by Mr Ruskin. Was this the normal sort of fare for a woman such as Miss Verity Trent? She did not know. The only thing left in the room was the trunk by the wall, a great old sea trunk complete with leather straps and some previous owner's initials stamped on it. It was unlocked and she kneeled and lifted the lid to find nothing more than empty boxes and tissue paper. But, no, for right at the bottom, and wrapped in tissue so that one had to be careful not to tear it, were two photographs in cheap frames. One was a family group—an elderly man, a tradesman heavily bewhiskered in Sunday best, and his wife, petite with her hair piled high and ill at ease in a new gown, and their daughter, sixteen or thereabouts, with a clear smiling face made stiff and formal by the arduous photographic process. The second photograph was a young couple. It was the same girl, a few years older, now with a young man, bowler-hatted and suited, a drooping moustache, a waistcoat and a stiff white collar—a bank clerk, perhaps, or a draper or a draftsman. He was proud, though, it was there in his eyes, and perhaps this was because of the fine-looking young woman on his arm. And she was fine looking, unsmiling but serene, her chin lifted high, defiant almost in her gaze at the photographer, her composure evident even as her face was locked in the agony of a long exposure, frozen in that moment for all time.

Eleanor stepped back. It was her, Miss Trent, in both photographs, but who was the bowler-hatted young man?

And for the first time she thought, Is this the wrong woman? Have I come to the wrong flat? And then she thought, But why are these things put away in the bottom of a trunk and not on display on the mantel? These people were dead, then, or they were something to be hidden away. Or perhaps both. She carefully wrapped them again and placed them at the bottom of the trunk and replaced the tissue paper and empty boxes and closed the lid. She stood up. She looked around the room. *Was* this the wrong woman? She did not know. She felt keenly the precariousness of her position.

And then she saw it. On the bureau so that she had almost missed it: a gold tiepin. She walked over to the bureau, not taking her eyes from the tiny gold object. She knew before she had picked it up and studied it that it had his initials engraved on the head. She had gone to the jeweller herself in Hunter Street to make her commission and a man, an elderly Jew with a pronounced Mittel Europe accent and a straggling greying beard, had put a glass to his eye and peered at the tiepin and nodded and said, '*Ja, ja,*' and she had returned the following day to pick it up.

And here they were, the initials: *A.D.*

CHAPTER TEN

# THIS IS NOT IMPERIAL RUSSIA

Alasdair instructed his cab to drop him in Macquarie Street. From here he walked the short distance to Richmond Terrace, an attractive avenue overlooking the Domain but whose unfortunate proximity to Parliament House meant that its row of elegant mid-century merchant's houses were gradually being bought up and converted into ministerial outposts. The offices of the Secretary for Public Monies were here, squeezed into a narrow and already rather cramped three-storey terrace. It was a temporary measure, Alasdair presumed, though whether temporary because larger and more appropriate accommodation on Macquarie Street would be forthcoming or because the ministry was itself a temporary measure and would soon cease to exist, the Secretary for Public Monies did not care to speculate.

There were only thirteen ministerial positions in the Legislative Assembly. When the new ministry had been announced the previous year, the Premier had seized for himself the offices of Colonial Treasurer and Minister for Railways. That left only eleven to be distributed between the other members of the Assembly, and when one took out all the ministries allocated to the various members who had assisted the Premier to get into office and those who had assisted him to stay in office and those who might assist him in the future, this left very few positions indeed for up-and-coming young members who burned with ambition and whose futures were ahead of them but who had very little in the way of political power to wield in the meantime. It meant Alasdair Dunlevy, long-time member for an electorate not too many miles from the city and therefore of moderate importance, had been promised Secretary for Lands and had seen it go to George Drummond-Smith, he had heard rumours he might get Public Works when it had been retained by Charles Booker-Reid, and there had been hints he was next in line for Railways when the Premier himself had grabbed that portfolio.

Eventually, and only when a member had died suddenly in office, the Premier had appointed him Secretary for Public Monies. Alasdair had been provided with a small staff and this office, the house in Richmond Terrace.

He had thought he had made good time, was disconcerted to find it was well after ten o'clock, closer to eleven, and he had missed one meeting and a delegation was seated in an adjacent room impatiently awaiting his arrival.

He thrust his hat at James Greensmith, his secretary.

'Good morning, Mr Dunlevy,' said Greensmith, jumping to his feet.

An impressive stack of papers and completed correspondence lay before him on the desk and a great deal of work appeared to have been done.

'The Premier's secretary delivered some confidential papers which I have placed on your desk, Mr Dunlevy,' Greensmith announced. 'Three telegrams came in, two of which require a reply. A number of reporters from the daily newspapers have requested comments relating to the incident last evening. I sent them packing, naturally. The delegation from Goulburn are awaiting your presence, as you see. The ones from Orange were here and waited some time but have now departed. And Mr Judd was looking for you.'

He was very well dressed, James Greensmith—perhaps a little *too* well dressed for a man who was another man's secretary. Alasdair noticed this; he had noticed it before but now it struck him anew. And Greensmith had sent the newspapermen packing, had he? That was a little high-handed of him. There was something about the fellow's eagerness, his excessively smart attire, that caused Alasdair to suspect his secretary had been making the most of his employer's absence to plan his own future, that some portion of the completed correspondence was on his own behalf to men whom he had identified could advance his own career—including, no doubt, some well-connected member of the Legislative Council whose eldest daughter Greensmith had identified as a potential future wife.

It was unpleasant to feel one was being made a fool of.

'They will have to wait,' announced Alasdair, regarding the three-man delegation from Goulburn with distaste. 'I have a meeting with the Premier this morning.'

He went into his office and closed the door, leaving Greensmith to fumble through the ministerial diary. He would find nothing. The meeting had been arranged in a hasty aside in the corridor of Parliament House two days earlier as the Premier had hurried from one place to another, its purpose off the record and undis-closed—though a place on the Premier's next tour of the north seemed, surely, the most likely reason.

There was also, of course, the small matter of the Solicitor-General's position, which was now vacant.

His meeting this morning with the Premier. It was the reason he had gone to see Verity. He had said nothing to her, naturally, but the knowledge of it had driven him to her. Curious, the impulses that drove a man. Her scent was all about him, her essence in his head. He would carry these things with him into his meeting with the Premier.

He sat at his desk and for a time did not move. The confidential papers lay on the desk before him, the three telegrams, two of which required a reply. He swung the chair—which was new and had a clever, if occasionally unnerving, swivel feature—around to face the window, and from this vantage point he observed the currawongs in the plane trees outside and the constant stream of officials and parliamentary staff at the rear of Macquarie Street who moved from one wing of Parliament House to the other, from the dining room to the stables and into the kitchens and back again. So much bustle! Such important work! And this on a day parliament was not in session.

He sat up. Where had Verity been going at such an hour, in such a hurry—and in so clandestine a way?

For it *was* clandestine.

He stood. The currawongs, sensing his presence, flew off.

What secret could she have from him?

A knock at the door and the face of his secretary interrupted these unsettling thoughts.

'Mr Judd is here, Mr Dunlevy. Shall I send him in or are you occupied just now?'

Mr Dunlevy was 'occupied' standing at the window, though his secretary's question contained no hint of irony.

'Yes, yes, by all means. Send him in,' said Alasdair, waving the secretary away and resuming his seat, which chose that moment to swivel away, leaving him stranded in undignified mid-air.

Everett Judd, whom Alasdair had last seen standing with some solemnity amid the chaos that was the immediate aftermath of the incident at last night's reception, carried his cadaverous frame into the small office with apparent difficulty and eased himself into a chair. Judd had been tall once, not so very long ago in fact, vibrant and vital, a man with energy, passion and a love of politics that had carried them all along in his wake. But the man seated before him was diminished, a widower whose wife of forty years had died, and the passion, the energy, was spent.

'You have seen the newspaper, Dunlevy?' said Judd, dispensing with any preliminaries. His voice was quite flat and devoid of emotion, as one for whom emotion, feelings, have run their course and he has no further use for them.

'The report of last night's intruder? Yes, of course.'

'That, yes, and the incident at Granville,' said Judd, shifting himself in the chair as if his bones distressed him.

'The break-in at the signal box? Yes, I saw. What of it?'

'It means some person or band of persons out there is so intent on derailing the Federation they would derail a train to do it.'

Alasdair laughed. Somehow he had not anticipated this. 'Hardly that, Judd! Another deranged and disgruntled soul who has lost his position and whose wife has left him and who seeks comfort in a bottle of gin.'

'You think so?' Judd fixed him with a sharp eye. He leaned forward. 'And could such a man destroy a signal box and ransack its contents and conspire to wreck a train?'

Alasdair leaned back warily—he would master this damned chair; it would not be master of him! 'If driven to it, no doubt. And who, precisely, do you believe they are, the fellows perpetrating these outrages?'

Judd spread both hands, palms up. 'A well-organised, funded and ruthless gang who will stop at nothing to disrupt the bill . . . Or one opium-addled malefactor with a grudge. Who can say?'

Alasdair got impatiently to his feet. 'But it is ludicrous! Does the public vote for or against Federation because a signal box is destroyed, a railway line incapacitated?'

'The act is an end in itself,' said Judd patiently. 'Destruction, fear, chaos—it is its own objective. A civilised and democratic vote on a question of nationhood is anathema to such men. The outcome of the vote is irrelevant; it is the process itself they wish to destroy.' And the very calmness of his voice as he outlined this dystopian vision was chilling. One might be discussing railway timetables.

Alasdair gazed out of the window at the kitchen orderlies and the currawongs. He snorted derisively so that Judd should be in no doubt as to his opinion. But his thoughts went to revolutionaries in Riga and Moscow who threw bombs at the Czar, who blew up railway lines, who destroyed telegraph lines—their aim was to change the regime and, presumably, once this was achieved, they wished to create a new regime in its place. Or was that not the aim? Was it simply destruction? And were these men now come to New South Wales?

He turned back to the old man. 'But this is not Russia, Judd, and Englishmen do not do such things.'

'We are not in England.'

Alasdair dismissed this. 'It amounts to the same thing.' He resumed his seat. He wished Judd gone. 'We are a nation that decides its fate in parliamentary debate, in gatherings of men in municipal halls.'

Judd shifted again, closing and opening his fist, spreading the fingers each time as though they were stiff. 'Feelings are running high, Dunlevy.'

Alasdair sat back and observed him. 'Is that what you came here to tell me, Everett?' He sighed. 'The people have accepted that the bill will be passed. Nothing can stop it. Why, they are more anxious to find out where we will choose to place our capital! Look at these . . .' And he scooped up the pile of correspondence on his desk. 'Submissions and proposals and entreaties from the council-lors, the aldermen, the mayors and the wives of the mayors of every single insignificant town and settlement in New South Wales south of Sydney staking a claim to become our federal capital. See here: Bathurst, Goulburn, Cooma, Orange, Wagga Wagga, Blayney—I do not even know where Blayney is!—but every single one claims *their* town and only their town is perfectly placed to take on the role, that no other rival has a case to make. *This* is where feelings are running high, man, and it is nothing to do with nationhood and everything to do with self-aggrandisement and self-interest.'

Judd made no reply. He eased himself to his feet. Frowned for a moment at the neat rows of parliamentary periodicals and law books that lined Alasdair's shelf. Seemed to have nothing further to say. Then: 'You mention the capital, Dunlevy. Do you recall the words spoken in parliament at that same session? That federal parliament would, in the first few years of Federation, be held in Melbourne; and if Melbourne then refused to relinquish the federal parliament, if it decided to go back on its word, what was our recourse as New South Welshmen?'

He did not need to say it. Alasdair had been there. He had heard the reply: The only solution would be war.

*

There was a definite police presence in Macquarie Street. Alasdair had failed to notice it an hour earlier but here it was, now that one's head was clearer. Not the usual fellow who tipped his hat and said a respectful, 'Good morning, sir,' as you arrived at Parliament House, but clusters of uniformed constables in twos and threes patrolling the length of the street, their countenances stern, without expression. No tipping of hats. No respectful greeting. He passed two of them now and they peered right through him and saw directly into his head so that he looked away, picked up his pace a little.

Was this, then, a sign of how it would be? Judd's words come to pass so quickly. A new world, certainly, but not necessarily a better world? No, one could not believe such a proposition. It rendered all of Man's endeavours worthless at best, devoid of meaning. Judd was lonely, his recent widowhood hanging heavily. Why, the man had been clasping Eleanor's arm last night as though she were his wife. They had all witnessed it. It had seemed endearing then. Now it seemed a little—sad to admit—pathetic. And, yes, perhaps a little . . . indecent.

Alasdair slowed as a black cab rattled passed him, turning his face away so that its occupant would not see him.

Judd had arrived, unannounced, at his office not to voice his concerns about the referendum and the recent spate of protest. He had come to discuss Eleanor.

Alasdair stopped in the street. True, nothing whatsoever had been said by Judd during their curious meeting to suggest this, and yet the idea, once formed, would not be dislodged.

He set off again, quickened his pace. He thought about his meeting with the Premier. Made a brisk review of the year thus far in his ministry, the triumphs, the—

No, one did not think in terms of defeats. The challenges, then. The opportunities. There were many. For it was a curious office, the Secretary for Public Monies, falling as it did, uneasily, between Colonial Treasurer and Secretary for Public Works and covering much of the same ground as those two portfolios while having none of their power. And as practically everything that happened in the colony had something to do with public money, Alasdair had found himself on every committee, responding to questions, making speeches and drafting reports on every subject from infectious diseases to drought relief, from snagging in the Darling River to the registration of goat ownership. In the last session of parliament alone he had been appointed to a sessional committee dealing with foreign seamen and he had reported back from another sessional committee on the phylloxera vine pest that destroyed the European wine industry and now threatened the colony. He had fielded questions concerning next year's Paris Exhibition—would the colony be represented? (Apparently not, for no one admitted to having organised anything, certainly Alasdair's department had not, after which the usual concerns had been voiced lest it was found that Victoria had stolen a march on its neighbours and were themselves to be represented at the forthcoming exhibition.) The question of the City Railway (or lack thereof) had come up, as it always did, and there was the usual and very vocal consensus that the railway was both imperative and necessary—to which Alasdair had added his own voice—but that, due to various reasons which were equally vital and compelling, it could not happen yet. Or any time in the next ten years. Perhaps twenty years. He had made a speech in response to the long-awaited report of the Board of Health on the provision of infectious diseases, a report that had stalled for some years as it attempted to identify which diseases should be considered infectious within the meaning of the Act and which should not. And he had responded to an ardent speech made by a fellow member concerning the carriage of fruit on trains—a practice that flagrantly contravened Sunday trading laws.

This subject of the carriage of fruit on trains was a vexing one that came up with surprising regularity (or perhaps it was not surprising when one considered that the members of the Assembly who raised the issue invariably turned out to hold a substantial financial stake in the particular railway concerned or in the fruit industry or both). That such shameless partisanship and self-interest should rule parliament no longer struck Alasdair as odd. He had become inured. He had come to suspect that the Board of Health's report on infectious diseases (which recommended the creation of a weekly updated map identifying street by street and house by house the sites of such infections) was simply a method by which the members and their wives might know which places in the city to avoid on the weekends as they made their way to the theatres and recital halls.

Such was the business of the Office of Public Monies. And yet it was vital, if not the work itself, then the ownership of the office, for if one aspired to be elected to the new federal parliament, one needed to be a minister in the Legislative Assembly. And so Alasdair made speeches in the chamber, he drew up reports, he attended committees.

And today he met with the Premier.

A knot of determined pressmen greeted Alasdair at the steps of Parliament House and he ran through in his head one or two pithy statements he had prepared on the short walk over.

'What does the Premier have to say on the outrage last night?' one man demanded, pushing to the front of the little crowd.

'Is Mr Reid alarmed by the rise in violent protests?' cried another, and it became clear it was the Premier and Mr Barton that interested them. A minor minister—and they did not get more minor than the Secretary for Public Monies—did not.

But the Premier was not here, was he? And the minister was. Alasdair held up his hand for quiet:

'Gentlemen.'

He held them then, just for a moment. Just long enough to allow a silence to fall, the jostling to cease. Respect to be established. He lifted his head so that the men at the rear might catch his words.

'I am about to meet with the Premier and I can assure you neither he, nor indeed any member of his ministry, will be cowed by these childish and uncoordinated acts of disorder and lawlessness. The vital work of the Federation—'

'But surely last night's attack *was* coordinated.'

'Bloke went to the trouble of disguising himself as a waiter.'

The days when a gentleman, when a minister of the Crown, might speak uninterrupted and unimpeded were, apparently, gone. Alasdair held up his hand once more. He raised his voice:

'Gentlemen, if you care to recall the Premier's own words at Tamworth on Wednesday, as reported in your own newspapers—'

But no one cared to recall the Premier's words, at Tamworth or anywhere else.

They had just spotted Leon Jellicoe.

The former—now disgraced—Solicitor-General had just stepped down from a cab and was making his way, head down and at a quickened pace, towards the other doorway. The little knot of pressmen spied him at once, deserting the minor minister and descending on him.

Alasdair looked on. It was unfortunate timing, but parliamentary careers rose and fell on timing, good timing or poor, fortuitous or regrettable. Jellicoe's, undoubtedly, was regrettable. And Jellicoe, at whose Potts Point house Alasdair had frequently dined and whose cellar he had enjoyed, saw Alasdair in the moment before he was besieged by the excitable men of the press, and gave him a confused look, as though not quite able to place him. He was a muscular figure, clean-shaven with a steady gaze. The sort of fellow who looked well on a horse, his strength and vigour being of the most basic masculine kind but also of the intellectual kind, of the kind that can, in time, make its possessor a leader of men. But this Jellicoe, surrounded now by a multitude of clamouring pressmen, was a shadowy and hollowed-out facsimile of that other man. The strength, the vigour faded. A poor copy of the man who had once been talked of as a future premier.

It was unsettling. One had no wish to witness another fellow's downfall—this ghastly affair, this very public divorce—though undoubtedly Jellicoe had brought his present calamity down upon his own head. Still, it was unsettling. One was aware of living in a glass house, metaphorically speaking.

Alasdair looked away. He frowned. His conscience did not often prick him. He thought of his umbrella, left behind in the hansom cab. To lose an item in his possession under such circumstances became, somehow, at this moment, significant, crucial, when surely it was the most trivial thing in the world. But still he thought of the lost umbrella.

He took the steps up to the entrance of Parliament House two at a time. He was vigorous. He was strong! He thought about the Solicitor-General's position which was now vacant. It was a prominent position—more prominent, certainly, than Secretary for Public Monies.

The thought pleased him and made him, at the same time, a little uneasy.

*

The parliamentary reception desk was unmanned. A handful of faceless clerks and functionaries could be seen moving along distant corridors and in the outbuildings that bordered the Domain, but of the other members of the Assembly there was not a sign.

Except for one.

'Dunlevy. Not expecting to run into the Prem, are you?'

George Drummond-Smith emerged from one of the chambers. The fellow fairly burst from the room, as was his wont, a bulldog of a man, barrel-chested, with a vast plain of a forehead and a skull that was all bone and no flesh at all. He sported an immense walrus moustache on a scale to rival that of the Premier's own and had such bulging, staring eyes one's natural inclination was to step back as though one had stumbled across some brutish hound, chained and slavering, at the gate of a house one had intended to visit. And once Drummond-Smith had got your scent in his nose he did not let go.

He had got Alasdair's scent.

'Because Reid departed by train at dawn. Selling Federation to the northern townships—Murwillumbah, Lismore, Byron, Grafton, those sorts of places—and he took Rothe with him. You didn't know?' And with an amused smile Drummond-Smith leaned against a conveniently placed bust of William Wentworth. 'Had you arranged a meeting with him? Ah, I see. You imagined the Premier would take *you* with him on his Tour of the Regions? How priceless.'

Alasdair had stood perfectly still as Drummond-Smith spoke these words. Now he advanced on the man. He had not realised how tightly wound he was. Felt his fingers clench into a fist, the air around them both growing hot then cold.

'Careful, Drummond-Smith. You sail too close to the wind.'

141

Drummond-Smith lifted his chin a little, fixing him with an appraising eye. 'Indeed? How so?'

'Do not come the fool. You have played with fire. Do so again, you will get burned.'

Drummond-Smith let out a shout of laughter. 'Two clichés and a threat! Priceless. And you, Dunlevy, are the fire? How absurd you sound.'

No doubt he was absurd but, oddly, it seemed not to matter. Alasdair's thoughts, at this moment, seemed extraordinarily clear. I am ready for what he says next, thought Alasdair.

Though, of course, he was not.

'Your dear wife,' said Drummond-Smith, stroking his monstrous moustache, 'how is she? I thought she was looking a little unwell last night, even before that preposterous incident with that chap and his toy gun.'

For a moment their eyes locked. Alasdair saw the little vignette at the Premier's reception last night. He saw Eleanor standing with Judd and Pyke and this man, Drummond-Smith, at her elbow, at her ear—saying what?

It was Drummond-Smith whose gaze dropped first. But only so he might turn his gaze on another.

'Well, now, here's a sorry tale,' he murmured just loud enough for his words to reach the ears of Leon Jellicoe, who had escaped the throng of pressmen and was now crossing the lobby.

Jellicoe evidently heard, for he paused and turned. He returned their gaze coolly. For a long moment it seemed he would not speak, then: 'What is it you want, Drummond-Smith?' he demanded, a flash of the old Jellicoe present, or something akin to it.

'Business proposition,' Drummond-Smith replied loudly with barely a pause. 'I hear your place at Potts Point will soon be on the market. I might make you an offer. Cannot promise you market value, naturally, but I expect you would be glad of what you can get in the current climate. Am I right?' And when Jellicoe's eyes narrowed and he took a step towards them, 'Oh, no need to make up your mind now, old man. Think on it.' And he pulled a match from his breast pocket and proceeded to light a cigar.

Jellicoe did not hesitate but came up to Drummond-Smith and thrust his face at the other man, and even at this late stage of his demise he still retained that steady gaze, that formidable jawline, that extraordinary Iron Duke nose.

'Your behaviour does not become you, sir, as either a gentleman or a member of this house.'

Jellicoe turned, not awaiting a reply, and left them, and Drummond-Smith, having succeeded in lighting his cigar, choked, though whether from the acrid trail of smoke or the words Jellicoe had spoken to him was unclear.

'Really! A lecture on manners by a fellow fallen so low? Now that I call rich,' he declared at Jellicoe's retreating figure.

But Alasdair had eaten at Jellicoe's table. Had consumed the fellow's finest wine. And he had heard the man speak a dozen times in the chamber.

'You make enemies too readily, Drummond-Smith. A man who wielded that much power in the state is not a man whom you should make an adversary.'

Drummond-Smith afforded him a sideways glance. His eyebrow crawled its way up his massive forehead. 'You envisage a phoenix-like rising from the ashes by our fallen minister at some distant point in the future, do you? My dear Dunlevy, there are some pales beyond which no man may return.' He puffed once, twice. Knocked ash onto the carpet. 'A reputation is a fragile thing. The most fragile thing a gentleman possesses. More fragile than the love of a woman.' His eyes narrowed speculatively.

Alasdair looked away, his face burning. A functionary hovered with a dustpan and brush. The little pile of grey ash lay on the carpet at their feet. Alasdair glared at the man, who slunk away.

'You have a reputation to lose too, Drummond-Smith.'

'I think we both know you have more to lose than I, old man.'

CHAPTER ELEVEN

# ANGEL OF MERCY

The little gold carriage clock chimed the hour and Eleanor raised her head to listen. She had sat on the settee in Miss Trent's drawing room for a long time. She was not certain how long. She held the gold tiepin in her gloved left hand. Her fingers closed over it then released it. She wished to hold it tightly and at the same time to take it to the window and hurl it far from her into the tangled garden below. She did neither. The chimes ceased. She sat.

She thought of the clock on the mantel—a present from a loving father, and the old sea chest in the bedroom.

Miss Trent's people were dead. She was alone here, perhaps had journeyed across oceans by herself. It struck Eleanor that they were alike in this way, she and Miss Trent, for her own parents were many years dead. She still thought from time to time of her mother, the schoolmaster's widow. Almost never of her father, because the loss was so much greater. But he came to her now, William Tremaine, his callused hands, his sea-salty smell, an impossibly tall man, or so he had seemed to her as a child of three, four, five years old, with steel-grey hair, a sun-coarsened face and eyes permanently squinting after a lifetime at sea scanning distant horizons. A man who had lived his life and settled down to old age before his first and only child had come along, travelling to New South Wales to take up a land grant in the inner harbour suburb of Balmain. He had built himself a two-storey sandstone cottage with a crow's nest in the roof from which lofty vantage point he could sip his rum of an evening and train his spyglass on the many and varied vessels on his doorstep. He had also taken a wife, his neighbour, Mrs Eliza Bass, widow of a schoolmaster whose husband and three children had perished in a single year from typhoid. The widowed Mrs Bass, who was well into her middle years and must have considered herself past the age of marriage and motherhood, at the age of forty-eight had found herself married once more and mother to a thriving baby girl.

There had been no further children. Eleanor had grown up the child of two ageing parents who had both experienced the best and the worst of life and were content to count their blessings and enjoy their quiet good fortune.

*Were* they alike then, she and Miss Trent? Were their origins, were the paths they had followed, so different? Eleanor had loved her father with an intensity that occasionally made her stop and gasp at his loss even now. But it was her mother who had made the decision, that hot December afternoon twenty-three years ago, that they attend the lecture at the town hall. And now Eleanor was the wife of the minister.

And Miss Trent—what was she?

The clock chimed again, the quarter-hour this time.

Eleanor stood up. Miss Trent had not returned. And now Eleanor did not wish her to return, did not wish Miss Trent to come through her door and find a stranger seated there. But

146

not, perhaps, a stranger—for Miss Trent must, surely, be aware of Eleanor's existence. It was vulgar, suddenly, the idea of their meeting, and Eleanor crossed the room and flung open the door and returned the cheap little key to its hiding place and she left. Her haste turned to humiliation and her humiliation grew as she fled down the wide staircase and through the front door and down the steps. To be found out now, to be seen fleeing, was hateful to her. She reached the street without meeting anyone and set off in a direction, any direction.

And there, not twenty yards ahead of her, was Miss Trent.

But not the same Miss Trent whom Eleanor had observed setting out from her house that morning. There was none of the urgency that had swept Miss Trent along the street and across the Domain and onto a tram a few hours earlier. Now she walked with a flagging step that spoke of exhaustion or illness or some great disturbance of the mind. Her face was a curious pale grey and her gaze was gripped by the ground before her as though she didn't trust it not to crack apart or trust her feet to carry her safely. Something made Miss Trent look up with an instinctive sense that she was being watched. Or perhaps Eleanor had made some sudden movement, made some involuntary sound. Whatever it was, Miss Trent raised her head, raised terrible eyes to the face that observed her.

And she stumbled. Her legs gave way beneath her and her body crumpled and she lurched forward. She threw out both hands and let out a cry as she fell.

Eleanor watched as though from a great distance, at first frozen in horror at the sight of the one person she least wished to see coming at her and then by the extraordinary sight of Miss Trent falling.

She ran forward, was at Miss Trent's side in an instant, though she was aware of no conscious decision to help, simply found herself running to the young woman's aid. Eleanor kneeled down and took her elbow, got the stricken woman to her feet, retrieved her reticule from the gutter, and ascertained with anxious questions if she could stand? (She could, yes, but unsteadily.) And did she require assistance to get home? (She did, most certainly.) And so assistance was rendered and they made their way at a cautious pace towards the very house that Eleanor had a moment earlier fled.

'Here? This is your home?' she asked, and Miss Trent nodded, her eyes closed, leaning on the angel of mercy who had appeared from nowhere. They negotiated the steps and the front door, they chose the lift over the stairs and stood in silent and grim communion as the hydraulic lift rattled and wheezed its way up to the first floor.

But she has recognised me! thought Eleanor with a horror that turned her flesh clammy. She knows who I am and that is the cause of her collapse! And now they were trapped together, she and Miss Trent, in this cage.

But it could not be, she reasoned. The girl was unwell before they had met, the girl's collapse had come when her eyes were fixed solely on the ground at her feet. There was no danger, then— though what she had thought that danger might be, Eleanor could no longer think. Exposure, perhaps. Her unveiling.

'This one—this is my door,' Miss Trent gasped. 'The key—it is in the pot.'

And her angel of mercy scrabbled around in the pot of the giant fern and soon located the key, and she opened the door and helped the young lady inside. She took her to the little chintz settee and lowered her gently down.

And now what?

Eleanor did not move. She felt the absurdity of her situation. She observed in a bewildering rush the host of mismatching tables and chairs, the crimson wallpaper, the Landseers and the pre-Raphaelite women on the walls, the French doors and the little balcony beyond, the mantel and the clock and the door to the bedroom. She had left the bedroom door slightly ajar, she saw now. And the clock, was it exactly in the centre of the mantel or had she replaced it a little too far to the left?

'Thank you. I am a little better now, I believe,' said Miss Trent in a low voice, not lifting her gaze from her hands in her lap.

She did not look a little better. Her face was a ghastly grey and her hands showed a tremor. Perspiration stood out on her face as though a fever had overcome her. And there were spots of blood on the fingers of her gloves. And on the hem of her skirt. More than spots, a fresh splash of blood, though its origin was unclear.

'Is there someone I might fetch for you?' Eleanor suggested. 'A neighbour, or a friend? Your . . . husband, perhaps?'

'No. No one, thank you.'

'Then may I get you something? A glass of water? Or brandy, perhaps, if you have such a thing?'

'Perhaps a glass of water . . .'

She sat rigidly upright, her hands one on either side of her, pressing down on the upholstery. Her eyes were closed.

'Of course,' murmured Eleanor.

There was no kitchen, only a gas stove, a tiny sink, a wall cupboard in a corner. Eleanor ventured over. She did not wish to touch anything. She wanted to handle each and every thing. She opened the cupboard, surveyed a small array of crockery and some glassware. Someone else's crockery, someone else's glassware—there was nothing of Miss Trent here. She selected a glass, filled it with water and returned to her patient. She held it out to her, watching closely as Miss Trent opened her eyes, raised her face in a tight little smile, took the glass.

Eleanor sat, unbidden, on the edge of the settee. She watched as Miss Trent took a sip. Miss Trent's hand shook. She closed a second hand over the glass, steadying herself. She did not look up again, seeming discomforted by the silent gaze of her visitor.

Her lashes were wet with tears.

'What is your name, my dear?'

After all, one wished to be absolutely certain.

'Miss Trent.'

Eleanor nodded. She did not offer her own name, or any other name, in return, and if Miss Trent thought this odd she did not say so. How could she?

'You are from England, I think,' said Eleanor. She did not explain how she knew this. Let Miss Trent wonder.

'I—yes, I am.'

'And how long have you been in New South Wales?'

'I arrived in February.'

Four months.

'And have you no family at all here?'

Miss Trent shook her head. She did not speak.

'You are alone then.' Eleanor paused, let the words sink in. 'But why stay, if you have no one? Have you not considered returning?'

'I have no one there either.'

'Then you are truly quite alone.'

The colour, such as it had been, was quite gone from Miss Trent's face. Her very essence drained away, so that one could not judge what this woman might be like ordinarily. And Eleanor did wish to know, she wished it very much.

Eleanor stood up. She went to the French doors, where it was safe. She stood looking out at the tangle of garden below.

'How old are you, Miss Trent?'

There was a faint pause. 'I am twenty-two.'

'I am forty.' Eleanor addressed the French door, the tangled garden. 'I have recently begun to wear spectacles for reading, though I have kept this fact from my husband. Curious the secrets between a husband and a wife.'

Miss Trent made no reply.

Eleanor turned and faced the room. She stood behind the little settee, behind Miss Trent. This upright posture of Miss Trent's was not quite natural, she observed, even if one accepted the girl was unwell. It was not the bearing of a gentlewoman brought up for drawing rooms and a good marriage. It was the posture of a girl expected to work, who had worked, in some capacity or other, for much of her twenty-two years. Her answers, too, were the unconsciously diffident responses of someone more accustomed to serving than being served. But not quite a servant, no. An artisan's daughter, perhaps, or a clerk's.

But fallen.

Eleanor paid no heed to the lashes wet with tears, the hand that shook. Here was a woman who had compromised herself—and for what? So that she might have another woman's husband? Or because circumstances demanded it? Eleanor had sat on the board of the Benevolent Asylum, she was not without knowledge of the sort of woman who found herself in such a precarious position, but that was not Miss Trent—there was no child, so far as one could ascertain, no deserting or drunken or violent husband. She was not in poverty. Why, then, had she thrown her morals aside? Spoiled her chances, such as they may be, of a normal life?

Unless she had no morals to lose in the first place.

She thought of the Jellicoes' housekeeper, the faceless, the omnipotent Dora Hyatt. A destroyer of marriages, reputations, lives, and all for her own nefarious, sordid ends.

Or so one presumed.

Miss Trent turned her head, but short of twisting herself right around she could not meet the gaze of the stranger standing behind her. It was awkward; her discomfort was evident. How much more powerful I am than you, thought Eleanor, and she felt her power—she did!—as it surged through her, and in the same moment found she had no power at all. For what could she do? What was there to do?

'Oh, see what I have found on your carpet!' Eleanor exclaimed. She came around and resumed her place on the edge of the settee, holding out before her, so that Miss Trent might see it, the gold tiepin with the engraved initials: *A.D.* 'It is a gentleman's gold tiepin,' she added, so that there be no mistaking it.

Miss Trent peered at the pin. It was not quite dismay on her face but something close to it. She looked away. She said nothing. What could she say? A gentlemen's gold tiepin in her apartment.

She did, then, have some modicum of respectability, some modesty.

'It looks to be quite valuable,' said Eleanor. 'Perhaps it was left by the previous occupants.'

She was not sure why she had presented the girl with this way out.

Miss Trent nodded weakly. 'Yes, perhaps.'

'I shall hand it in at a police station,' said Eleanor. 'No doubt the gentleman who lost it will be glad of its return.'

And Miss Trent said nothing, but her eyes followed the tiepin as it disappeared inside Eleanor's reticule and was gone.

Having rallied for a moment, Miss Trent now seemed a little worse. She closed her eyes once more and leaned back, resting her head, where before she had not allowed herself to do so.

'May I get you a cushion?' offered Eleanor at once. There were none on the settee. It would mean going again into the bedroom. Would Miss Trent allow such a thing? What might her visitor find there? More tiepins?

'No, I shall be quite alright. Thank you. You have been most kind.'
Miss Trent clearly wished her angel of mercy to be gone.

Eleanor stood up. She brushed a speck of dust from her skirt.
'You are certain there is no one I might ask to sit with you?'

'No, thank you. No one.'

Miss Trent answered in a low voice, her head down. There
was no one. To whom would Miss Trent go for help? Eleanor
gazed down at the crown of Miss Trent's dislodged hat, observing
the strands of dull brown hair that had come loose and partially
covered the back of her bare white neck. It was a beautiful neck,
she saw, pale and youthful and unadorned. She observed the gloved
hands clasped rigidly together in her lap, the whiteness of her lip
where she bit down on it as though to counter some awful pain.
Miss Trent was very young. She was very alone.

'Then I shall leave, if you are quite sure you will be alright?'

'I shall be. Thank you. You have been so kind.' A slight flush of
Miss Trent's cheeks showed her relief that her saviour was, at last,
departing. She had not asked her saviour's name. It was entirely
possible that, in her distress, Miss Trent had not even observed the
face of the woman who had come to her aid. She was a stranger
and would remain so.

Eleanor left, abruptly, without looking back, pulling the door
shut behind her. She had noticed the spots of blood on the carpet
at Miss Trent's feet. They had not been there when Miss Trent
had sat down.

Outside the sun had begun to lower in the western sky. Three
weeks shy of the winter solstice and the days were short but there
was, as yet, no chill in the air and the sky remained a vivid winter
blue with not a cloud in sight. A lorikeet swooped overhead in a
brilliant flash of blue and green and orange.

Eleanor walked rapidly away from the house for the third time that day, not noticing in which direction she walked. The day had not gone as she had imagined it would—though now she was uncertain what, exactly, she had imagined. Her idea of how things might go seemed, at best, misguided. That one might believe one could predict, perhaps even dictate, how something would be was absurd, deluded. One was an observer, a player in a larger game that someone else—God or fate—was controlling. Perhaps there was no game at all and life was simply a series of events, one leading on from another, utterly random, utterly unpredictable.

But she was, surely, more than simply a passive instrument of fate?

On she walked. And on.

But I feel nothing, she thought. Nothing.

What did one do now? Collapse, as Miss Trent had done? Sit down and reflect? Pull out the letter and read again those same words: *My dearest* . . . ? She had gone to Miss Trent's aid. She did not know why she had done so. Except that Miss Trent might have died. Would that have been preferable?

One could not commit murder.

Eleanor walked south and eventually she found a police station. She was not sure if she was in Woolloomooloo or Kings Cross or Potts Point, but here was a police station with a blue lamp over the doorway and a drunken man lying sentry beneath it. She sidestepped the man and walked up the steps and spoke to the constable at the desk. She was taken to a room.

Here she sat for a time on a hard wooden chair before a wooden table, another chair facing her. She waited. This was a punishment, she saw, this waiting, leaving her in this room for a longer time than she could endure. For it turned out that she did not feel nothing. It turned out that the difference between feeling nothing and feeling it all was an instant, a moment, a breath. She placed her hands on her lap and pressed down on her thighs.

She had never felt such terror.

When the policeman came in she informed the man she wished to report a crime. She wished to report an illegal abortion performed that very day by a Dr Leavis of Surry Hills on a Miss Verity Trent of Woolloomooloo.

CHAPTER TWELVE

# HARD LABOUR

On that same day, the first Friday in June, the Premier's Tour of the North arrived at Murwillumbah. On Saturday it moved on to Lismore then Byron Bay. Sunday being a day of rest, it was Monday when the party arrived at Grafton.

It was on Monday, too, that Alice Nimrod, late in the afternoon, stood gazing up the daunting edifice that was Darlinghurst Courthouse.

It was a formidable structure, this courthouse. With its Doric-columned portico, a pedimented gable entrance and those colonnaded wings, it was worthy of any great city in the empire, worthy of Ancient Greece itself. It completely dominated and obscured the colony's first purpose-built gaol, which had been erected directly behind it. In less civilised times, on a day when a public hanging was underway, the more squeamish citizens might stroll along Oxford Street and take solace in the elegant lines and smooth sandstone, in the tiled marble floors of the magnificent courthouse and so forget the horrors behind.

It was meant to be daunting, it was meant to be formidable. Alice Nimrod, late on Monday afternoon, shrinking before its magnificence, understood that. It was meant to strike fear and awe into the hearts of every wretched man and woman who was brought through its doors.

Her footsteps slowed as she approached. There seemed to be very few people about: two police constables nominally standing sentry who silently observed her approach, one or two court officials coming out of one side door, crossing the courtyard and disappearing inside another. The vast double-height front doors remained solidly closed as though to repel all intruders like the gates of some great medieval castle. Alice stopped before these doors, presuming some way inside would present itself. A sign affixed to the wall suggested that a Jury Assembly Room, Sheriff's Office and Court Keeper's Office were somewhere within but gave no clue as to how to enter nor how to reach these obscure places.

The two constables observed her. She abandoned the massive front doors and went instead to a side door. Here was a glass case just inside the doorway within which was a typed sheet headed *Court 3* and beneath this *Crown v. Nimrod*. There were other cases, too, being heard that day—nine in all, which seemed a heavy workload for any courtroom—but it was here that Alice's eyes went and stuck fast and got no further.

*Crown v. Nimrod.*

Somewhere deep inside her the fading but always present figure of her mother moaned and wept inconsolably for the shame that had befallen her eldest child.

*Crown v Nimrod.*

It was as though Milli had offended against the Queen herself and though Her Majesty, seated on a throne in a castle on the far side of the world, could know nothing of this one particular case, yet still it was a shame almost too great to endure.

Alice pulled her shawl over her head. The middle part of the day was past and the sun had dipped already towards the warehouses and church spires of the city. The rain had held off and for four days the sky had radiated a light so vivid, so blue, it hurt the eyes. But as the winter day waned the warmth drained from it with a swiftness that caught a person out. You needed a shawl and Alice drew hers closer about her shoulders.

She entered the courthouse and no one stopped her; indeed no one was abroad at all, though she could hear voices behind distant doorways. She found herself in a vestibule carpeted in crimson and gold—not the rich carpets of the Dunlevy house, but a functional and hard-wearing carpet that stamped its authority on the person who walked upon it. The walls were painted a deep forest green and a pale cream that ought to have had no place in a chamber carpeted in crimson, but here was a room that thumbed its nose at good taste. This building had a job to do and, if its walls clashed horribly with its carpets, what of it? A silent and dimly lit corridor led off to the left with, about halfway along its length, a coldly uncarpeted staircase fashioned from some ancient timber so dark and knotted it might have been salvaged from a medieval manor house. There was a smell, too, of musty disuse, which was curious for a building not much more than half a century old.

Alice took the corridor rather than the staircase, passing long, hard wooden benches on which no one sat and a series of closed doors, and the signs above the doors—COURT OFFICIALS ONLY, BARRISTERS ROBING ROOM, PUBLIC DEFENDERS—suggested worlds beyond her knowledge, and her fear grew. The corridor twisted and turned, throwing up corners at random intervals, and she found herself outside in a courtyard. The sudden sunlight made her stand and blink. It was a small, square, sandstone place walled in on all sides, and apart from yet another unwelcoming bench it seemed to be a place to pass through rather than one in which to linger.

But where was Court 3?

Alice sat down on the bench, which was half in the sun and half in shade, one part of her warm, the other part cold. She did not know if Milli had been called before a judge already, for the afternoon was fading and surely, Alice thought, she must be too late.

And so even in this she had failed her sister.

She lifted her face to the patch of purest blue above and she wished with all her heart Milli had not done this thing. She wished she might help her sister, though it seemed to her there was nothing she could do. Milli had made her own plan without Alice's assistance, without her blessing.

She does not need my help, thought Alice as she sat on the bench.

The first Alice was aware that something was happening was the muffled shout she heard from some distant part of the building. A shout, a scream, a cry—one followed the other, and whether man or woman or both was impossible to distinguish. And a disturbance—for such Alice took this to be—in a courthouse where so many wretched and desperate souls were confined must not be a rare occurrence, but Alice jumped up, she followed the sounds. Her heart beat a little faster.

She hastened from the courtyard, retracing her steps along the twisty-turny corridor. More shouts followed, urgent now rather than muffled, and Alice arrived back at the chamber she had started from and it became clear that the noises came from above, up the ancient staircase. She set off up two short flights and came almost at once to a bare and unfurnished waiting room and she understood that she had found the site of the disturbance, if not its cause.

And when it had seemed to Alice that the courthouse was utterly deserted and herself the only occupant, here now was a great and clamouring mob of persons—men and women of the common classes like herself—and all crowded in a doorway, pressing and pushing and creating the utmost commotion. The door, a solid affair with a frosted-glass panel, was wide open and beyond, though she could see only the high ceiling, was a courtroom—or what she took to be a courtroom, for she'd not had cause to view one before now. And she saw among the crowd a number of court officials and clerks pushing the people aside and cursing them and struggling to restore order, and a constable too, for she saw the top of his tall hat.

But what could be the cause of such excitement?

'Holy-Mary-Mother-of-God! It is too late!'

'Give the woman some air!'

'It is not air the lass needs!'

'Get these people away, for the love of God!'

'She will die, like as not.'

'Aye, they will both die.'

Words came tumbling one on top of another from a dozen mouths, so that Alice could perceive neither their sense nor their substance and her head buzzed with it all.

'She is dead! 'Tis certain the lass is dead!'

At this the crowd surged forward once more and someone screamed and someone else fainted and a cry went up—'Send for a priest!'—and Alice craned to see. Someone had fainted; a young man, it seemed, which was curious, for people usually spoke of young ladies fainting yet this was a man. But as the young man slithered away to the ground a gap appeared in the crowd and Alice thrust her way into it and saw the courtroom. She had a confused impression of wood panelling and cream-coloured walls, of a very high ceiling and a row of wooden benches on which, at present, no one sat. She saw that the faces of the clerks were a peculiar greyish hue and several of them were kneeling down and one or two were standing back in horror and there in the middle of them all was her sister Milli, in the final stages of childbirth.

Alice cried out and threw herself at her prostrate sister, but the court officials and the constable made a final effort to shut out the crowd and Alice was forced back and found herself on the wrong side of the door as it was slammed shut. She regained her footing and flung herself once more at the door, but with the futility of a fly at a window.

'*It is my sister!*' she cried, banging on the door. '*She is my sister! Let me see her!*'

She banged her fists again, but the door was solidly built and would not give.

The crowd, deprived of the spectacle that had kept it amused, grumbled a good bit and began to drift away, all but one woman. This was a stout elderly soul in a patched tartan shawl and features as scoured and coarsened as stone on a windswept hillside, but perhaps this woman had known motherhood or remembered the warm embrace of her own mother for she broke from the dispersing mob and came to Alice's assistance.

'Hush, lass, you shall not help your sister by banging on the door and carrying on,' she said, putting a restraining hand on Alice's arm. 'It is her time and the baby is coming, ready or not. Come now, calm yourself. Is it her first?'

And the hands she placed on Alice's arm were deformed by age and by work but no less kind for that.

Alice put out her own hands to steady herself and allowed the old woman to seat her on one of the hard wooden benches. She stared into the woman's face and shook her head numbly.

'No, it is not her first.'

'Well, then, she knows what to do, don't she? I have had six and, let me tell you, you know what to do after that many.' And the woman nodded to herself and seemed pleased, as though Milli lying on the floor of the courthouse in the final stage of her confinement was an entirely ordinary occurrence, perhaps even one to be applauded.

'They said she was dead!' said Alice, searching the woman's face. Reassurance, if it came, would come from here, she felt.

'Dead! What does a man know about it? A sight of blood and they go all to pieces.' The woman aimed a contemptuous glance at the young man who had fainted and was now being fanned by his girl and his mother. She turned back to Alice. 'Serves them right, anyhow. Look what she has done to their fine court—gone and given birth in it! Ha! That is what I say. Serves them right, God forgive me.' And when Alice stared at her, uncomprehending: 'Did you not hear, dearie? Where you not there in the court? That old devil—God forgive me—of a judge give yer sister three years' hard labour. For breaking a winda! No wonder she keeled over and went into her confinement.'

Alice heard these words from very far away, a tiny voice in a great void. The rest of her shrank and she heard nothing more.

The bench on which Alice and the elderly woman sat had been built for poor people. Every expense had been spared in its design and construction with the expectation that the persons who would avail themselves of it would be the family, dependents and associates of criminals. The lowest of the low.

The elderly woman in tartan patted Alice's hand and smiled a sad and distant smile. Alice felt as though the woman had been talking all this while—her thin lips forming words, perhaps in an effort to alleviate the very suffering and indignation they described—but Alice had heard nothing. There was a buzzing in her head.

'Poor child. You have had a shock.' And the woman nodded and patted. She had no teeth and perhaps had no need for any. She smelled of boiled cabbage and sour sweat and sawdust and a dozen other things.

'Three years' hard labour,' said Alice, from very far off.

'Yes, dear.'

They had not sat long when the door to the courtroom opened. Alice jumped up and started forward; a shudder of fear flooded her heart and caught in her throat. A woman emerged, a matron or nurse, carrying sheets, blankets, bloodied and soiled, and went down the stairs. She looked at no one: important, busy—or ashamed.

Alice ran to the doorway but pulled up sharp, for there was Milli on the floor and Milli was not dead. She lay, her body covered for modesty by a large blue cloth which, to the onlookers, appeared curiously patterned and providential (for what courtroom antici-pates its clients halting proceedings to expel a child?) and turned out to be the British flag that hung in each court, torn from its hooks and pressed into emergency service. If Milli was cognisant of the assistance rendered her by the empire, she did not show it; her eyes were closed and her breathing was laboured and uneven, her hair matted and bedraggled, her face drawn and exhausted and grey. When her eyes opened she let out a scream, shrill and piercing and dreadful, that seemed to express not gratitude for help rendered, but outrage that her child had been taken from her.

'*Milli!*'

Alice ran to her sister and fell at her side, but at once an official hauled her up and shoved her away.

'Do not approach the prisoner!'

A second man joined the first, for it took two of them to drag Alice from her sister and attempt to bundle her from the courtroom. She bit the hand of one, drawing blood and forced her way back inside, and in the general commotion that this caused Milli stopped her scream and her gaze fell, instead, on her sister's face.

'*Alice, the baby! Do not let them take it away or I shall never set eyes on it again! Alice! Do not let them—*'

But the door was closed on her and Alice, reeling, understood that the baby was born, that the baby was somewhere, might indeed be living.

She shook herself free of her captors, cursing and screaming at them so that the two guards backed away, one nursing his injured hand. They advanced but seemed undecided whether to forsake her or to arrest her, and as they delayed the woman in tartan clutched Alice's arm and led her very smartly away down the wooden staircase.

'*But Milli—the baby* . . .' cried Alice, and she would have turned and run back up but her saviour propelled her downwards. Reaching the bottom of the stairs they paused and Alice saw what it was they pursued: just ahead of them, disappearing around a corner in the corridor, was the matron who had passed by them with her bloodied consignment. This woman had made slow progress, for she moved with the waddling gait of a very fat person, wheezing as though she might expire at any moment, but—they could both see it!—was still clutching her cargo.

And they set off after her, Alice only dimly perceiving why they did so.

The matron, some yards ahead of them, had entered the small interior courtyard, sun-filled a short time earlier but now in shade. Tired by her exertions, she sank down onto the bench to fan herself, though the warmth had gone out of the day. She lay the bundle gently upon the bench beside her. She closed her eyes and leaned her head against the wall. Her excessive and fleshy body was disinclined to action.

She had laid the bundle gently and not, as one might expect a bundle of bloodied and soiled sheets to be laid, with careless disregard.

And Alice, at last, understood and stifled a cry. She did not pause. She divested herself of her guardian angel, the elderly woman in patched tartan, and striking out on her own she made her way along the silent corridor at such a smart pace that in a moment she had reached the shady little courtyard and the bench on which the fat and wheezing woman rested. In another moment Alice had ducked back inside and was gone, and the place where the bundle had lain was now bare.

A very short time later a slight young woman who had arrived at the courthouse carrying nothing now departed holding a most precious bundle, and could be seen hastening out of the side door of the great building and down the driveway and out of the gate and was soon lost among the throng of people on Oxford Street.

# CHAPTER THIRTEEN

# CORANGAMITE

After the deed was done Eleanor had gone home and awaited Alasdair's return. She had thought to greet him at the door, her excitement—yes, it was excitement, or something close to it—had thrilled through her, it had filled her up. She had stood at the door to greet him.

But in the end he had returned so late from a meeting she had given up and gone, alone, to her bed.

And so it had been on the second evening too. The third day, a Sunday, Alasdair had breakfasted without her, worked in his study all day, gone out in the evening, returning in silence. When she sat across from him at the dinner table he had been somewhere else. Her excitement, if that was what it was, had wavered. But this evening, a Monday evening, it had soared again. Three days had passed since she had done her deed and something, surely, must break.

Eleanor dressed slowly and purposefully. She chose a deep blue silk gown, the bodice sheathed in the palest tulle. She attached diamonds at ears, throat and wrist.

But every hour she feared a policeman at the door.

The terror that had overtaken her at the police station seemed to have taken root. But it could be channelled, she had discovered. Its energy could be diverted. She had reported Miss Trent's crime to the police—the deed was done and could not be undone, and the police, one presumed, were duty-bound to investigate. At the police station a man had demanded her details and she had given a false name, which a second man had carefully written down, and an address that did not exist, but the witness to the crime was of no consequence. The police would find the doctor—she had been precise about the doctor's name—and they would find Miss Trent. The evidence was there, it was undeniable. The carpet was stained red, the place smelled thickly of her blood. Miss Trent may lie but her body could not.

And if Miss Trent should tell them who the father was?

Eleanor felt certain she would not. It was not in her nature. The girl was frightened. She would be very much more frightened. She must remain silent and steadfast or incriminate herself. How odd that Eleanor knew this for certain, or felt that she did. No, she would not believe she had placed Alasdair in danger. Surely, whatever outcome now befell Miss Trent, no scandal could be ascribed to him. She was glad she had retrieved the little gold tiepin. There could be nothing that connected her husband to that woman, to that place.

As to Miss Trent's likely fate . . .

Well, it was not one's place to speculate. Miss Trent had transgressed and must pay the price that society, that the law, deemed appropriate.

And as to her husband . . . She lifted her face to the mirror and studied herself. She did not flinch. As to Alasdair, surely there could be a return now to how things were. Was it naive to think she might suggest, in a day or two, he move back into her room?

Their room.

$\infty$

Alasdair was, that moment, some miles away in the west of the city, speaking at a Federation meeting at the public bar of a hotel in Leichhardt.

A great many men attended the meeting in noisy solidarity for the bill, and in another hotel across the street a great many other men—perhaps not as many—met to denounce the bill. At the conclusion of both meetings, which either by bad luck or malicious intent had occurred simultaneously, the two groups spilled out onto Norton Street, where opinions were passionately exchanged, a punch thrown, a bottle smashed, and it was only due to the heavy presence of the local constabulary that prevented the event descending into pitched battle. Amid the chaos the secretary, James Greensmith, managed to secure a cab, and all the way back to the city he sat exclaiming in thrilled dismay at the sudden and dramatic turn that events had taken.

'Do you think, sir, it was paid agitators who kicked the thing off?' he asked, his clothing a little disarranged, for he had been briefly manhandled by the crowd.

'No, I do not,' Alasdair replied shortly, and though they were hardly into George Street he signalled for the driver to stop and he turned his secretary out into the night to make his own way home.

Alasdair sat back in his seat but he was unsettled. This was not democracy; indeed, it was not the way of Australian men to care strongly enough about their politics to fight in the street. To take against those of a different race, yes, it was part of a man's nature to do so, but Australian men were all of the same race, the same species, for the most part, if one ignored the obvious difference of Anglican and Papist, Englishman and Irish, rich and poor. He was unsettled, he was disappointed. Tonight it had been the Black Labour issue that had fuelled men's tempers. The proposed dissolving of the barriers between the six colonies would trigger a flood of black workers from the north; Chinamen and men of the other Asian countries toiling in the comfortably distant northern cane fields were just waiting for their chance to swarm south. This was the prospect the anti-billites presented. The white men in the southern colonies would be put out of work at best, overrun and diluted at worst, and it was an easy fear for the anti-billites to fan, for all white men did fear this, though the more rational ones among them saw it for what it was: a baseless fear fanned by a scared opponent.

And was it fear, above all else, that drove men? Alasdair wondered.

The moon had climbed above the rooftops and bats circled, twittering excitedly in its glow. Above him the cab driver made clicking noises with his tongue to encourage his reluctant horse, and the cab stopped and started, lurching alarmingly as it failed to negotiate a pothole in the street and Alasdair experienced each sound, each vibration magnified tenfold. It was disagreeable to be in a cab going home in the dark with a distinct chill in the air and he wished to be free of it, but instead of being cheered as the cab began its descent to the bay an oppression came over him. He called out to the driver to stop and let him out. He would walk the remainder of the way down the hill. He tossed a coin at the man and set off.

But his footsteps slowed as he approached the house.

The oppression came over him, it consumed him.

He had spent the day replying to correspondence, had spoken to a journalist from the *Herald* and another from the *Mail and Advertiser*. He had met delegations of town officials from Goulburn and Bathurst and Cooma, provincially clothed self-satisfied men, each convinced of their own importance, each convinced their town and their town alone should be made the federal capital. He had listened to their arguments, he had pointed out that the referendum had yet to happen, that there would be no federal capital at all if it did not pass.

'Gentlemen, we are building a nation!' he had said to the town officials and again to the journalist from the *Herald*, words he had spoken a hundred, two hundred times this twelve-month, but today the words had fallen from his mouth like a platitude, empty, devoid of meaning.

For Miss Trent was nowhere to be found.

He had gone to the house at Woolloomooloo on Saturday evening and had stood at her door and she had not answered. He had returned the following evening, though it was a Sunday, but the outcome had been the same. He had walked around the exterior of the house, looking up at the windows, some lighted, some in darkness, had waited for a time in the shadows, had started forward as a carriage appeared, as a figure had approached the house, as another had emerged from it. Had slunk back into the shadows at each fresh disappointment. He had left, finally, debased and shamed. And yet he would go there again this evening, though he and Eleanor were to attend a dinner first.

The dinner was at the house of Charles Booker-Reid, a man he despised, a dinner at which nothing of importance would be uttered and at which his presence would make no difference, and yet Booker-Reid wielded some influence still, had the ear of one or two prominent men. And so he would take Eleanor to dinner, though his heart strained within its cage so that he stood for a long time, unmoving, outside his house.

Eleanor opened the front door to him. He wondered if she had been watching for him. It irked him that she had done so—did they not have servants?

'My dear, you look fatigued,' she said, standing in the doorway to deliver this charge. 'How went your meeting? Come inside, the fire is lit in the drawing room. Let Alice bring you some refreshment.'

And at last she stood aside to let him enter.

His wife was dressed already in a lustrous blue silk gown, diamonds at ears, throat and wrist. Her colour was high and her eyes shone, two points of light as bright as the yellow eyes of the bats that circled above, of the old possum that lived in the fig tree outside. There was a bright, almost brittle quality about her; it had been there these last three days and Alasdair was glad, now, that he had accepted the invitation from Booker-Reid. To sit opposite his wife at their own dinner table with her profuse gushing was a prospect suddenly untenable.

The servant, for whatever reason, was not in attendance, and so he removed his own hat and coat and gloves.

'The meeting went badly and then descended into a pitched battle,' he said in answer to his wife's enquiry.

He did not, as a rule, report the outcomes of his meetings to her, for it seemed to him she rarely showed an interest, but this evening he wished to shock her from her complacency. *Was* it complacency? It seemed more like a sort of hectic agitation, the cause of which he could not guess.

'Heavens!' she exclaimed. And she searched his face as though to see whether he was in earnest or in jest. 'Was anyone hurt?'

'I certainly hope so,' he replied. 'At any rate, I hope so of the dunderheads who peddle their nonsense and whip the common masses into a frenzy of such irrational fear they can no longer tell their heads from their feet.'

'There were people who disagreed with you, then?' said Eleanor.

'It is hardly a question of agreeing or not agreeing, Eleanor. Naturally a man is free to disagree, but when his head has been filled with so much nonsense he cannot make a rational decision . . .' He gave up. She did not understand, could not be expected to.

She had gone ahead into the drawing room. The fire was lit and she stood before it, smiling. 'Come inside, Alasdair,' she said.

But he could not look at her, he could not come into the drawing room. 'I must dress for dinner,' he replied briefly. He went up to his dressing room and closed the door.

And after a time he did dress, slowly and meticulously, taking some little while to knot a new tie and at last pausing and staring at himself in the mirror. He could not find one of his tiepins, a gold one engraved with his initials. He searched, turning first one drawer inside out and then another. At last he flung open the door and called, '*Alice!*'

It occurred to him the maid had taken it. She had never taken anything before, to his knowledge, but it was simply a matter of time. They all stole eventually.

It struck him that he ought to have a valet, though he had never perceived this lack in his household before. But a gentleman ought to have a valet. This fussing about dressing oneself was petty, it was undignified. In London a gentleman of his standing, a minister of the Crown, would have a valet, unquestionably. And a butler. His parliamentary colleagues, those who had been born in England, who had been educated there, thought nothing of keeping a manservant to dress them, a butler to open their front door, a liveried footman, a carriage. But those, like himself, born in the colony scorned such ostentation, they mocked it, and perhaps this was simply to mask their discomfort. His grandfather had been a navvy, had built canals and railways with his bare hands, could not sign his own name on a document. And his father had had so many servants they had been housed in a separate wing, yet he had never learned how to deal with a single one of them until the day of his death. This incongruity between his grandfather and his father troubled Alasdair occasionally. It troubled him now. He felt that he took an uneasy middle path between them.

There was no sign of Alice.

He abandoned the search for the gold tiepin. He dug out another pin and stabbed it in his new tie. It stuck out inelegantly, in the wrong place, at the wrong angle. He sat down on a chair and stared at himself in the mirror.

Where had Verity gone?

And to whom?

∞

Charles Booker-Reid's house at Woollahra was a late Regency mansion constructed to imposing and ultimately overambitious proportions by an English merchant who had come to the colony, made his fortune then promptly lost it all building a lavish and increasingly costly house worthy of his position. With its portico and Doric colonnade it rivalled the Rothes' Hyde at Potts Point, and how Booker-Reid had ended up with it was a mystery to Eleanor, though oddly in keeping with what one did know about the man, which was, for the most part, unfavourable.

Alasdair said nothing in the cab, remained closed off from her and unfathomable, when she felt herself fizzing and bubbling and light-headed beside him, the blood pulsing through her veins and throbbing in her ears. She imagined herself making light-hearted conversation with him here in the cab, imagined herself making a clever and humorous observation—for all her troubles were over and his, though he did not yet know it, were over too—but she said nothing. No observation, clever or otherwise, presented itself to her, so she sat in silence. But inside she felt herself fizzing and bubbling.

She imagined, over and over again, the constable arriving at Miss Trent's door.

Nine places had been set around the table, which by any measure was an odd number, and only three of the dinner guests were ladies. This curious arrangement struck Eleanor, who was one of the three ladies (Cecily Pyke and Blanche Rothe were the others), and from her place seated between Fraser Pyke and Judge Thistledon she wondered why Alasdair had accepted Charles Booker-Reid's invitation. There was, surely, little political capital to be gained from a man who had lost the safest seat in New South Wales and who, on being newly elected, seemed unable to recall the exact location of his new constituency.

'Eat up, eat up,' said Booker-Reid, rubbing his hands together and presiding over the julienne soup and the medallions of foie gras, the roast loin of mutton and the lobster cutlets, the iced pudding and the out-of-season glacé strawberries with an almost pantomime glee while touching almost nothing himself. He drank a good deal though. He was a widower, his young wife perishing barely a year into the marriage of some unnamed and unknown illness.

The dead wife's father, the explorer Sir Bertram Egremont, was here, and one of the dinner guests. Clearly the old gentleman bore no ill will towards the son-in-law who had driven his only daughter to an early grave, for he was seated, quite at ease, at the foot of the table, a brandy in one hand, the other resting on the arm of his chair. The man must be in his seventies at least but he cut a fine figure, lean and leathery with a shock of snow-white hair, seated perfectly upright in a tight fitting if outdated collar and cravat and sporting a splendid set of bushy mid-century whiskers. Sir Bertram was speaking, Eleanor saw, in that way that all men of his age had: dully and at great length and with an unshakeable belief that his audience hung suspended from his every word.

'We set off from Melbourne heading west,' said the ageing explorer, 'why, it must be nearly fifty years ago, and we went on horseback where we could, and on foot when the bush became too impenetrable—which it was most of the time, dense enough to lose the man in front of you though he was but five yards ahead, and terrain rough enough you were lucky to cover ten miles in a day, half that on some days. We had mules and a few goats and a couple of blacks to guide us, though the mules died soon enough—one fell and became lame and a second was bitten by a snake—and the goats were driven off one night by some blacks, and the blacks that were to guide us left after a week or so. After many days of no fresh water we set up camp on the shores of Lake Corangamite. And a bitter day it was, let me tell you, when we ran into the cold waters of that lake to slake our thirst only to find the water was brine though we were many miles inland. And that is what it means, of course, in the local Aboriginal dialect.'

'That is what *what* means, Sir Bertram?' asked Blanche Rothe, leaning a little over the table towards him with an intentness in her face, though Eleanor had seen her eyes wander during the old explorer's words.

'Corangamite, dear lady. It means bitter. Or thereabouts. A rough translation, at any rate.'

And Mrs Rothe was gratified, or looked to be. At any rate, she smiled.

Bitter. Yes, one would be bitter journeying all that way and finding only salt water. But why go all that way—for what reason? Eleanor felt she had missed the point of the story. It seemed to her that Sir Bertram told them a story from another time, another century, when such things as explorers still existed, when there were still uncharted places left to explore. She recalled Alasdair had wanted to be an explorer, too, at one time. She looked across the table at her husband—he had been placed opposite her. He looked impatient, as though the elderly gentleman's reminiscences irritated him. She had a feeling Alasdair would not wish to be reminded of his earlier aspiration to be an explorer, though it was a noble enough calling—perhaps less so in these modern times, when such an ambition might seem faintly absurd, but twenty or thirty years ago, yes, it was noble—heroic, even. Certainly, she had thought it so at the time. She remembered the story of Mr Leichhardt embarking on his great expedition and the celebrations and speeches that had accompanied his departure, and he had gone and been lost and, finally, forgotten. But they had named a suburb after him and that was something, was it not?

Alasdair looked annoyed. Or preoccupied. She tried to catch his eye but he avoided her, frowning at his brandy glass, glowering at the coffee the maid was now pouring into his cup. He was wearing a new silk tie, grey with black stripes, and a tiepin with a small diamond at the head. It was not quite in the right place, his tiepin; it was slightly off centre.

The gold tiepin with the engraved initials that she had taken from Miss Trent's room was in her reticule. It nestled in a compartment of the little bag on her lap and, as she thought of it, it seemed to grow in size and then to diminish. She wondered why she had taken it, why she had not left it in that bedroom to be found by him the next time he was there.

But perhaps there would not be a next time?

And now here they were at dinner and the discussion around the table had moved, inexplicably, to art and literature.

'Surely it is about time', Alasdair was saying, leaning forward in his chair and unaccountably animated, 'that one of our own men produced a work of literature worthy of the great works of Mr Dickens and Mr Hardy, of Mr Trollope and Mr Thackeray?'

And Eleanor was astonished. Alasdair had never spoken of literature before. He had never expressed a preference for this author over that, had never admitted to an admiration for the literary classics, yet here he was exhorting his fellow New South Welshmen to produce a work of fiction worthy of Dickens, of Hardy.

'Oh, but Mr Dunlevy, we have the Bush Poets, do we not? Mr Lawson and Mr Paterson and others,' replied Cecily Pyke, moved to utter the first words she had spoken all evening that did not concern her daughters, of whom she had a quantity. And then, perhaps regretting her outburst, she looked to her husband for confirmation.

'Oh, certainly,' agreed Fraser Pyke, who, as well as being a member of the Assembly, was also a pastoralist and an occasional Methodist lay preacher and who surely had no more idea of who Lawson or Paterson were than he had the members of the Imperial Russian court. He looked pleasantly bewildered by this turn in the conversation. He had previously been discussing the Premier's Tour of the North which, one gathered, had been a great success and from whence Henry Rothe—in his London-made clothes and the largest mansion on the point—was that afternoon returned. Why did Alasdair not get invited on these trips with the Premier, Eleanor wondered—but only for a moment. Her husband's career was in many ways a mystery to her, and it seemed to her that one of them, or perhaps both, had deliberately cultivated it to be so.

'Speaking personally, I only have time to study law books and legal journals,' said Judge Thistledon, lifting his distinguished head and addressing them with a faint note of censure in his voice. 'Though I do not deny I read some Dickens as a younger man.'

He managed to make this sound like a vice of which he was now cured, and Eleanor gave a little laugh as if the judge had made a joke, though she knew he had not. Thistledon was a neighbour of Booker-Reid's, a bachelor forty years on the judiciary, a man who rarely smiled and looked out on the world through eyes that did not blink. A heavy brow and a neatly trimmed white beard went some way to compensating for the absence of hair on his domed and shiny head and somehow added to her impression, long held, that the judge lived outside of the normal plane of human endeavour.

'When I was a young fellow I had my Bible in my saddlebag and that was all I required,' said Sir Bertram, stretching out in his chair and unconcerned that he no longer held the attention of the room. 'It served me well enough—though I recall as a child being utterly absorbed by the journals of Mr Watkin Tench.'

'Alasdair is named for Mr Tench, Sir Bertram,' said Eleanor. 'It is one of your baptismal names, is it not, Alasdair?'

But her husband had shrunk a little since he had made his initial appeal to literary endeavour and at each response the skin had tightened on his face and the clothes stiffened on his body so that they resembled items made of wood or stone within which he was trapped, or so it seemed to his wife. He gave Sir Bertram a tight smile, though it was Eleanor who had made the observation.

'That is so, sir. A whimsy of my father's,' he said, and these words appeared to cost him a great deal.

'Which did not inspire you to take up exploring, Dunlevy?'

'No, Sir Bertram. I have always known my destiny was to serve the people of this colony as their representative.'

And Eleanor thought: he has forgotten who he once was.

She was regretting her decision to wear the blue silk gown. It was too similar to Blanche Rothe's peacock blue brocaded satin, though they were seated some distance apart and her own gown had a tulle-sheathed bodice whereas Blanche's was trimmed with silver embroidery and grey chiffon. But the shade of blue was uncanny, as though they had gone to the same dressmaker—which they had—though who was there at the table who would notice it? None of the gentleman, and Cecily Pyke had shown only a glancing interest in her appearance even before the advent of motherhood; now it was debatable whether she knew which decade she was in. And Blanche herself, a beauty at seventeen and still a beauty almost three decades later, who had been born into great wealth and married into greater wealth and found all things amusing, would not care a jot. But still Eleanor regretted her decision.

The discussion had moved on.

'If they had only built the City Loop back in the seventies when it was really needed, when all the other railways were being built, we would not now be faced with this impossible dilemma,' said Henry Rothe, who had found himself briefly Minister for Public Works a year or two back and so talked of the railways.

Opposite him Blanche Rothe, in peacock blue, took a neat little bite from a square of toast and caught Eleanor's eye as though they shared a joke.

What was the impossible dilemma? Eleanor wondered. She sat back in her chair feeling the energy of a few moments earlier drain from her. What was the joke she shared with Blanche?

'But my dear Rothe, there was no money in it,' said Booker-Reid in his bored way. 'Why build a railway underground at unimaginable expense and to the general disgruntlement of every George Street storekeeper and every city tram operator when you can make an absolute fortune building a railway—or promising to build a railway, at any rate—in an area far outside of the city in which one (or one's brother or one's wife's brother) happens to hold a vast, untapped parcel of land? It is economics of the most basic kind.'

'A somewhat cynical view of our city's public works,' observed Fraser Pyke, the idealist pastoralist.

'Cynical—yet utterly true. We lived through it, did we not, Dunlevy? Came in at the tail end, anyhow. And your father benefitted from the policy greatly, did he not?'

Alasdair started slightly as though he had not been paying attention to the discussion, and now a frown shadowed his face. 'The seventies was a boom time, Charles. Anyone who owned land did well out it.'

'Even swampy land with no drainage and no natural water some ten miles from the city, what? But no matter—so long as one could convince an enthusiastic and train-gorged public that a railway was coming, the speculators queued up to purchase it and paid whatever was asked. And if most of those proposed and promised railways failed to get built or languished for years in parliamentary debate or were thwarted by lobbyists demanding other routes and different lines, what of it, eh, Dunlevy?'

'In case you have failed to notice it, we do have a working rail network,' Alasdair replied in a tight voice, 'and a fine and extensive tram network.'

'Which we are still paying off and have been in recession because of ever since.' And Booker-Reid laughed as though this was the greatest source of amusement to him. He signalled the maid to top up the gentlemen's glasses.

Alasdair tried, and failed, to look as if he were not annoyed.

'Have we heard anything more from these so-called anarchists?' enquired Henry Rothe. 'I have been in the north with the Prem so I fear I may have missed something.' In any other man, this would have been conceit, but Henry Rothe had no need for conceit. He had a beautiful wife and a magnificent house and a satisfactory, though not particularly taxing, parliamentary career.

His wife, speaking almost at the same moment and aiming her remark at the other two ladies, said, 'I saw Adaline Jellicoe this morning. She was cancelling an order for a dress. It was rather sad, really. I cannot think why she did not send her maid to do it.'

And Blanche did look a little sad when she spoke of Adaline Jellicoe, who was divorcing her husband, and this was no affectation either. It suited her dramatic looks.

'Poor Adaline,' said Cecily Pyke desperately. 'I do wish there was something we could do for her.'

But there was nothing they could do for her.

'The Premier is to speak at Newcastle on Saturday,' said Rothe. 'I've declined that particular excursion—too much on—so I believe Drummond-Smith is to accompany him this time.'

Alasdair shot Henry Rothe a look of such tightly contained fury that Eleanor felt its ripples from her own side of the table. Did it matter to him so much that another man accompany the Premier and not himself? Apparently it did.

'Alasdair's meeting at Leichhardt descended into a riot this evening,' she announced, because it was important the room understand her own husband's contribution to the Federation, even if the Premier, evidently, did not.

'Hardly that!' Alasdair cut in, clearly irritated, though he himself had described it thus to her earlier. And as is the way at such gatherings and at such moments, the rest of the company fell silent so that his words fell with a crash they surely had not intended.

'Judge Thistledon, I heard a woman gave birth in your court,' said Fraser Pyke, stepping into the void that had followed Alasdair's outburst. 'Can it be true?'

'Indeed, it is true,' said Thistledon, refolding his napkin and placing it neatly on his plate. For a moment he held Pyke in his gaze and his eyes did not blink. 'And if one did not know better, one might actually believe the wretched women did it on purpose. She had already shown her utter contempt and misuse of the judiciary, so it is not absolutely outside the bounds of possibility that she planned the whole thing.'

'Misuse of the judiciary? However did she do that?' asked Cecily Pyke with a curious half-smile. One never knew with the judge if he was speaking in jest, though it was perhaps safest to assume he was not.

'I am afraid to say it, Mrs Pyke, but they all do it. That is, the poorer class of female who finds herself approaching her confinement having made no provision whatsoever to shelter or support herself. They commit some minor misdemeanour and get themselves incarcerated for a week or two and have their confinement in the comfort of a prison infirmary at the expense of the taxpaying citizen. Then off they go, pleased as punch. This wretch had done it twice already—although she had not come before me prior to today or she would have paused to think again. And you can be sure I did give her pause—I informed the woman in no small way I knew what her game was and that I was not going to put up with it. Gave the woman three years' hard labour.'

Mrs Pyke started. Her husband said, 'For what offence? What is it they do to get themselves arrested?'

'This particular wretch had broken a window. A butcher's shop window, I believe.'

This was met with a silence.

Mrs Pyke, in a quiet voice, said, 'Do you mean to say that when she heard her sentence it caused this woman to commence her confinement?' She looked down at her napkin and not at Thistledon. Two spots of bright colour had appeared on either side of Cecily Pyke's face.

'Who may say what caused it, for am I no physician, but that was the moment at which it happened, yes,' said the judge, and he plucked a cigar from the box before him on the table. They were American hand-rolled cigars.

'And the woman and her child,' said Fraser Pyke, shaking his head when the box of cigars was turned towards him, 'how did they both fare?'

'The woman is serving her sentence at Darlinghurst Gaol. As for the child—' Thistledon paused to strike a match '—that I cannot say. I *can* tell you my courtroom had to be cleared and was not fit for use again for the remainder of the day.'

'Scandalous,' observed Charles Booker-Reid, leaning back in his chair and regarding his dinner guests through the blue trail of smoke from his own cigar.

Mrs Pyke looked up with very bright eyes, the flush still on her face. 'I do wonder at the depths of desperation to which such a woman must have fallen to be driven to such an extreme,' she observed to no one in particular.

'No doubt the woman *was* desperate,' Eleanor countered, weary of Cecily Pyke's veiled and rather pious reproaches, weary of her quantity of daughters. 'It is hardly the act of a rational, God-fearing person who has lived a moral life.'

And at this, Mrs Pyke, who was her friend, flushed again and Eleanor turned her gaze away for she did not, altogether, believe her own words.

'And do we not feel even a moment's compassion for this woman?' said Alasdair, stirring as though he had just that moment woken from a sleep. 'Can each of us say, in all honesty, that we have never committed an act some might consider immoral?'

He made this statement to the table in general yet Eleanor felt a flush creep over her own face for the rebuke was aimed solely at herself.

CHAPTER FOURTEEN

# THRIVE

The baby did not thrive. Instead it cried piteously, expelling a sound from its lungs to echo the suffering of ages and a black muck from its bowels that was as viscous and primeval as Hell itself. And then it fell silent. It lay limp and unresponsive as though it had tasted life and had found it wanting and turned its tiny, red-creased face away from such torment.

Alice Nimrod thought it dead. She snatched it up and held it to her breast and felt, faintly, its heart still beating, the blood still moving sluggishly about its little limbs. The baby lived, though it did not thrive. It would not live much longer if she could not get it to feed.

She could not think what she would do. She had taken the baby and that was perhaps a crime, she did not know. If the baby died in her care, was that too a crime? And what if they should hear the baby cry downstairs? This was her biggest fear.

She had returned to the house with the baby under the cover of darkness and had fled up the stairs to her room at the top of the house. Here, she had swaddled the baby in a shawl and laid it in a drawer and run downstairs to be the housemaid once more.

In the kitchen Mrs Flynn had looked up and observed her with a thoughtful and disapproving silence that spoke of a hundred young maids who had engineered their own downfalls and in whose image she clearly saw Alice. Then she had packed her bag, pulled on her coat and left for the day. Mrs Dunlevy had returned from a fitting at her dressmaker and gone at once to dress for dinner. Sometime later Mr Dunlevy had returned. Alice had missed the moment of his return as, in a sudden terror of what she might find, she had run upstairs to her room, where she had scooped up the baby, motionless and silent and wrapped in the shawl, knowing it was dead but finding it lived still.

She was frightened to leave it. Had stood at the window as Mr and Mrs Dunlevy had departed in diamonds and silk, leaving her alone in the house with the baby that did not thrive.

She unbuttoned her dress and placed the baby's mouth to her breast but no milk came. So she carried up milk from the kitchen in a cup and dipped her finger into the milk and placed her finger on the baby's lips, inside its mouth, over its gums, but the tiny, squirming, wriggling thing dribbled the liquid out, it turned its head away, it wailed in fury. She tried a dab of sugar on its lips, and honey too, and finally, in desperation, a drop of gin from a bottle she found on the lowest shelf of a cupboard in the scullery. The baby would not take it; it seemed not to know how to feed, how to swallow, and Alice held it and her body became as stiff as the baby's. It shamed her to realise she did not know how to care for it. Would she know, she wondered, if she had given birth to it?

The crying became louder and fear shook her body.

She did not know what to do.

She wondered for a time about Mrs Flynn, whose domain was the kitchen and the scullery three floors below and who returned home to her own family each night, sloughing off the house in Elizabeth Bay, and returning, different and changed, at dawn to prepare the day's meals. She wondered if Mrs Flynn would keep her secret or if she would shrug her old and bony shoulders and betray her. In the pantry the meat hung, a goose or a lamb or half a pig or a side of beef, dangling lifeless from a hook waiting to be cut into pieces. Sometimes the blood dripped onto the cold hard floor and congealed there. Sometimes it stained Mrs Flynn's apron. Alice imagined that Mrs Flynn, if asked about the baby, would say: 'Drown it!' Drown the baby. As though it were a cat or a stray dog. And not because she was cruel, not because she was callous, but because she was practical.

Alice held the baby to her breast. It was her sister's baby. She felt her sister's blood pulse through the baby's tiny veins, she saw the blood purplish-blue beneath the transparent skin of its eyelids. She thought of her sister locked up this cold June night and every night for three years in a cell in Darlinghurst Gaol.

And then she closed that door and did not open it again because she could not endure it.

The clouds had rolled in from the west to obscure the moon and Alice turned away from the window and looked about at her room beneath the eaves, a sloping room cut from a space in the roof that was usually reserved for bats and birds. A narrow bed pushed close up against the sloping wall filled most of the space, crowded beside it a chest of drawers and a small, roughly hewn table on which a water jug stood. The window jutted out into the night and the doorway opened onto the little landing and the narrow staircase down which you crept at night without a candle at your peril.

Might she ask Father McCreadie for help? The old priest had come to her aid once before when she had found herself alone and unprotected, but five years had passed. She had not returned to the church, had not once attended mass. Did not know if Father McCreadie remained still at the church. Was even alive. He had been an old man then, stooped and unshaved and smelling already of the decay and the dust of the dead. *I will take the child into the orphanage, Alice. I will hand it over to the Sisters of Mercy,* he would say. *It is for the best. It is God's will.* And that would be the last she would see of it, Milli's child.

At her breast the baby shuddered and let out a wail. It began to cry. It went on crying. It did not stop. It was hungry or thirsty or dying, Alice did not know which. She patted its head, and stroked its downy cheek, she jiggled it on her knee, propping up the head, which seemed impossibly large for its body and in imminent danger of wobbling right off. She lay the baby down, she picked it up. The baby cried.

Panic-stricken, she put it down and ran from her tiny room down the narrow staircase to the floor below then downwards to the hallway and the closed doors of the dining room and the drawing room. She opened each door to reveal the empty unlit fireplaces and the polished unlaid tables and the silverware in the cabinets and the paintings on the walls and the rows of untouched books on the shelves. She threw back the curtains. There was no one here. She did not know what it was she searched for. Silence, perhaps, peace—for, distantly, she heard the crying of the baby. It did not stop. The Dunlevys would be home this hour or the next, the empty house would not remain empty for long. And then what?

She did not know what to do. Everything sped up inside her, the beat of her heart, the blood in her arteries, the breath in her throat, the thoughts in her head. She ran back up the two flights of stairs and flung back the door to her room to scoop up the crying thing—

But someone was there before her. Someone was in her room holding the baby.

'Why do you not feed it, Alice? The baby will perish if you do not tend to it.'

Mrs Flynn. Her sleeves rolled up and her coat and hat on as though she had thought to leave for the night but had changed her mind. Spots of animal blood on her arms. Her lips set firm around her toothless gums. The baby in her arms.

'I do not know how to,' said Alice, and her shoulders sagged and the breath went out of her at her own failure, at this blessed and unhoped-for relief.

'It needs mother's milk,' said the elderly and toothless cook. She did not say, *And who is the mother and why is she not here?* She had lived too long in the world to bother with such questions.

'But where?' said Alice helplessly. 'Where do I get such a thing?' Her own failure, her lack of knowledge, hung heavily about her.

'From a nursing woman,' was the simple reply.

The baby did not stop its crying but Mrs Flynn did not flinch. She held the little shrivelled thing to her shoulder and nursed it as best as a wizened and dried-up old woman could.

'You must find a nursing mother if the real mother cannot nurse it,' she said again.

Alice nodded. She knew where she must go—it was as preordained as Christ's death on the cross—and she readied herself to go out into the night. The clouds had rolled in to obscure the moon and it seemed likely the rain would come again. But not yet, and under Mrs Flynn's silent gaze she hurried down to the scullery and gathered such items as she might need and tied them in a cloth. She wrapped a shawl about her shoulders and over her head and took the baby, which Mrs Flynn held out to her, enclosing it inside the warmth of her arms, and set off.

Alice returned to Frog Hollow and to Mrs Renfrew, a woman who had four or five children already and a sixth at her breast, whose husband had lost his job because of his drinking and who would never get another and whose bitterness at his own failure was displayed daily on the swollen faces and bruised and bloodied bodies of his wife and offspring. 'This is where you come when you cannot sink lower,' Milli had said once, meaning herself, but it applied equally to the Renfrews and to all the others too, for the Hollow was large enough to swallow up countless unfortunates and many families found their way there eventually.

But at least Mrs Renfrew had her freedom, at least she was not locked in a cell at Darlinghurst Gaol. And so Alice hurried to her, through the lengthening night, carrying her valuable prize.

She negotiated the descent down the flight of stone steps and picked her way as carefully as she could. A child, ten years at most and pale as a corpse, darted past her and slipped behind a square of sackcloth pinned across the doorway of the shack that four nights ago had been Milli's. This place, the Hollow, and the souls that inhabited it, did not remain stagnant for a moment. A space had become vacant and had been filled almost before it was cold.

Someone at some point had fashioned a rudimentary ladder up to the Renfrews' shack and Alice grimly attacked this ladder, hauling herself up one-handed, clutching her precious bundle. As she neared the top she called, 'Hello? Anyone inside?'

A head appeared, dark against the dark sky.

'Who's there? What d'you want?'

190

'It is Alice Nimrod, Milli's sister. I have come to see Mrs Renfrew. It is terrible important I speak with her.' For the head, the voice, was not a woman's but a man's.

'Terrible important, is it? Then you had best come up.'

Scorn—but also an invitation.

Alice pulled herself up, stood unsteadily for a moment atop the little ladder, swayed and might have fallen had not a hand shot out and grabbed her sleeve, hauled her inside.

And Alice baulked. For here, in a space no bigger than Milli's little shack below, Mrs Renfrew and her brood lived. A quantity of this brood were here now, sprawled or huddled, every space taken, the smallest ones perched like doves in a coop on shelves that had been hammered into the timber walls and the furniture stacked one thing atop another so that you wanted to step right outside again to draw breath. The little ones watched her, rows of eyes in the gloom staring, unblinking, as though she was a ghost or a phantom. The watching eyes and the chaos and the roof-high piles of clutter on the brink of toppling was oppressive, a great weight pressing on the chest. How did they stand it? Alice wondered. The smell of too many bodies, of rotting food scraps, of night-time slops in such a confined space almost made her gag.

'It is the Nimrod girl's sister,' said the man who had pulled her up. A tallow candle burned and the light it gave out was feeble and flickered madly on the walls and danced about in the breeze, distorting all that it touched. A sea of staring faces, a mass of shifting bodies was all she could discern.

'Alice, is it?' said a woman's voice, and she recognised Mrs Renfrew emerging out of the dark, creeping, as though the roof were low or as though she expected it to fall in on her at any moment. Mrs Renfrew straightened herself up and peered closely through yellow eyes that blinked in the candlelight. Her lips were split and covered in scabs.

'You are brave, coming here,' she said in wonder, as though 'brave' was not a word she had much cause to use very often. 'Or you are foolish.' And she sighed. 'You know they are after your sister for she owes them money?'

'Quiet, woman!' said the man, Mr Renfrew, emerging out of the gloom and striking his wife a blow about the face. She tottered and almost fell over but otherwise seemed barely to notice.

'Please, I have come to ask for your help,' said Alice, and at her breast the baby stirred and let out a wail.

'Zat Milli's baby?' said the man, moving into the candlelight so that Alice saw the whites of his eyes in a blackened face, saw the sluggish shuffle of a body broken by drink and poverty but still with a strong right arm on him. He reached out with long callused fingers that twitched as though they longed to feel the newborn's flesh and Alice shuddered.

'The child is born then,' said Mrs Renfrew, as though a prophecy had come true.

'I cannot nurse it,' said Alice. 'But you can.'

She looked at the woman, at her yellow eyes, at her split and bloodied lips.

'And why would she do such a thing?' said the man, testing her, searching for the profit that might be had.

'I have food and a little money. It would only be for a few days. While I decide what must be done.'

'Is Milli not returning then?' said Mrs Renfrew simply, as though a mother disappearing after her child is born was a common enough matter—and perhaps it was, here. Perhaps it was everywhere.

'No,' said Alice.

'How much money?' said the man.

It was a simple enough transaction. Alice gave them what money she had brought with her, which was little enough but more than nothing so it was greedily accepted. And then she brought out the small bundle wrapped in a cloth and tied with a knot so that she could lay it upon a table and untie the knot and let the contents fall out and dazzle them: bread and cheese and the drumsticks from lunch and leftover game pie and a little wine in a bottle sealed with a stopper. And they fell on the food, like dogs, until the man swatted the children away and curses were thrown and a little blood spilled.

'It is just for a few days,' said Alice, holding the baby, still wrapped in its shawl.

Mrs Renfrew reached over and plucked the baby from her and put it under her left arm as her own baby was under the right. Alice would have asked, Do you have enough milk for two? Will the baby live? But she did not ask for she did not trust that the replies she got would be the truth. The man, she saw, wolfed down the food when she had brought it for the mother, but she said nothing.

'We have no room for an extra mouth beyond these three days, mind,' said Mrs Renfrew.

And what she meant was: *We cannot say what will happen to it after that time, if you do not come for it.*

The man would sell it, Alice presumed. Or worse.

'God bless you,' said Alice, reaching out to touch the woman, to touch the stunned baby, which had not uttered a cry since she had handed it over. The woman said nothing and it seemed unlikely that God did bless her, or indeed any of them, and Alice made ready to leave, taking one final look at the child.

'It is a boy,' she said, from the top of the ladder.

*

She had saved the baby, for now. And Alice almost tripped and fell in her scrambling haste to descend the ladder and at once her feet sunk into the mud at the bottom. Her dress dragged in it and her boots were sucked into the quagmire up to her ankles. All about her the tumble of shacks and huts crowded any which way and no one but herself was abroad, though every pair of eyes in every dark corner watched her.

She was leaving the child in this fearful place. But Alice Nimrod could not afford second thoughts. Second thoughts were for rich people.

A dark figure now sprang from the shadows to block her way. A second figure came at her from behind and grabbed a handful of her hair, jerking her head back.

'YOU. OWE. US.'

The light was such that Alice saw only the whites of a man's eyes and the moonlight flash dully on a rusted razor blade held an inch before her eyes. But she felt their combined bulk, holding her in a grip from which she could not even struggle; she felt hot breath on the back of her neck, the arm fast around her middle, and now the blade of the razor softly nuzzling the delicate skin on her cheek, moving down and scraping against her throat. Fingers, too, closed around her neck and Alice stood perfectly still.

'I do not owe you nothing!' she said calmly and steadily, though fear clogged her throat and her bladder had emptied, sending a trickle of warm liquid down her leg. The razor pricked at her skin. The man standing behind her let out a snarl and pulled tighter at her hair, jerking her head back further, exposing the whiteness of her throat.

'Your *sister*,' whispered the first voice, 'she borrowed money from us and now we have come to collect. If she is gone then *you shall do just as well.*'

'I have nothing. Look—' Alice held out her hands, though they shook, she lifted up her arms, showed the pockets of her coat.

'Then we shall take this as down payment.' They stripped the coat from her shoulders, laughing as she fought them, twisting this way and that to stop them from taking it, laughing when she slipped and fell.

'Next time we will not be so gentle.' And they ground her face down into the mud and left her.

# CHAPTER FIFTEEN

# THE RESPECTABLE ESTABLISHMENT

The journey from Charles Booker-Reid's house at Woollahra to Elizabeth Bay was a long one if judged not in miles travelled but in words spoken and silences accumulated. For the latter part of the journey the flickering lights of ships on the harbour were distantly visible to the north, and across the night air could be heard the tinkling of rigging on the yachts moored at Rushcutters Bay. The fine weather held. The clouds that had rolled in earlier in the evening had moved offshore and the sky above was clear, if crisp. One needed gloves, one needed a muffler. But there was no danger of a frost. There was never any danger of a frost. This was Sydney, after all.

Alasdair Dunlevy turned his face away from the lights on the harbour, he blocked his ears to the tinkling of the rigging. It was intolerable, this cab journey. Why must he be forever in one cab or another, going from one desolate place to another?

'Cecily Pyke is rather a silly woman,' observed his wife, seated beside him and evidently having given the matter some thought, for she had sat silently since they had left Booker-Reid's house.

Alasdair stirred restlessly but did not turn his head towards her. 'Because she does not tend to your point of view?'

Eleanor laughed at this, though he had not intended it as a joke. 'I merely meant she is rather naive, always jumping to the defence of the poorer classes as though she has a better understanding than others of what such lives are like.'

'Her husband is a Methodist preacher when he is not a parliamentarian and their congregation are tenant farmers and drovers and their wives. Perhaps she feels this gives her some insight.'

'No doubt she does think that, though I am equally sure it is misplaced. Can she really believe she has a superior understanding of such things than Judge Thistledon? Than men who sit in parliament?'

'I really cannot say.'

This was intended to close the conversation, but it had the opposite effect. Eleanor sat up, turned a little towards him, seemed about to confide in him, though what she might confide he could not for the life of him imagine.

'Alasdair, what did Charles Booker-Reid mean when he alluded to your father benefitting greatly, when we talked about the railways?'

'How can I possibly say what any man has on his mind? Why do you not ask him?'

'I am asking you, as my husband. He implied there was some irregularity. I merely wish to know why he would suggest such a thing—it is not unreasonable.'

'Not *unreasonable*?' And now he turned to face her. 'My father bought and sold land and became moderately wealthy, as many men did at that time—is that what you wish to know? My father came from humble origins but he made his way by sheer hard work and some good fortune. He did not spend his time sitting on a roof gazing at ships in the harbour through a telescope—'

His wife gave a tiny gasp at this allusion to her father but he went on:

'—and if you wish to cast aspersions on my dead father's name, you would do well to remember that it is his money that set me on my political career and paid for the house in which we live.'

'My dear, I merely—'

'And, furthermore, if the wife of a dear friend happens to express her sympathy for the plight of a poor unfortunate wretch who has been forsaken by society, then I, for one, do not find it naive; I find it admirable evidence of Christian charity.'

It was curious how the words now tumbled out of him. Words he had no wish to utter yet here they were.

'No doubt you already knew Drummond-Smith was to accompany Reid on the tour to Newcastle—'

'*I*? How could I possibly—'

'—and no doubt it pleased you immensely.'

'Why should you think such a thing?'

But he would not answer her question. Would not humiliate himself further.

The cab had by now reached Elizabeth Bay. Through the fronds of the palms on the esplanade the moonlight shimmered on the water.

Alasdair rapped on the roof of the cab. 'Stop here!' he called, his voice carrying across the still night air all the way to Beare Park and beyond.

Eleanor started, and when the driver jumped down and flung open the door she stood up, stumbling a little and dropping a glove.

She climbed down the step, but when the driver stood aside to let Alasdair out he dismissed the man with a hand. 'I am remaining, you will take me onwards,' he commanded, and he saw Eleanor turn back in surprise.

The cab lurched forward and Alasdair leaned back in his seat and did not observe as his wife stood in the road and watched him go.

'Where to?' asked the driver, who was no stranger to odd behaviour, not least among his fares.

And when they were gone up the hill and the still night air could no longer carry his words, Alasdair leaned out and replied, 'Woolloomooloo.'

Perhaps he had drunk a little more of Booker-Reid's brandy than he had realised. The cab lurched from pothole to pothole in the streets nearing the wharves, and Alasdair found it increasingly difficult to retain his seat.

'Here, stop here,' he called, having only a vague sense that this was the right neighbourhood but not wishing to prolong the ride in the cab. He climbed down and waited, standing in the middle of the road as the cab trundled away and was gone into the night.

He turned about him to get his bearings, picking out the bulky silhouettes of the wharves and the warehouses that lined the dockside, listening to the mournful calls of the ships entering and leaving the harbour. He set off confidently, the blood running faster in his veins. It was good to be outside finally. He sucked in the crisp, salt-rich air.

Here was the house, unmistakable, with its steep gables and many chimneys, the overgrown banksia spilling onto the pavement. A light flickered in an upstairs room. Her room? He could not be sure. Perhaps not. He went up to the front door. He had come and gone at a late hour before this and the front door had never been locked, but perhaps on this occasion it was? No: he pushed it and it swung open. He entered, taking the stairs softly in the gloom of a single gas light turned down low. Quiet reigned inside the house, as it always did, and he paused to listen. Floorboards creaked and nothing more. The house was as silent as its ancient timbers and straining roof joists ever were, and whatever the residents did within their various apartments they did so noise-lessly. He had wondered at it each time he had visited Verity, had wondered at the ferocity of his passion and love-making in such a church-like place, yet once inside the secrecy of her bedroom he always forgot such thoughts. He wanted to make love to her now, right at this moment.

The thought that this might not eventuate could not be borne.

He took the stairs two at a time, reaching the first floor and going to her door.

He kneeled and felt with his fingers in the pot of the large fern where the key habitually resided, inching around the circumference of the pot as he had done each time previously. His fingers found nothing. He got to his feet and stood close to the door, listening. Beyond was only silence. He tapped softly.

'Verity.'

He waited.

'Miss Trent.'

The silence lengthened. It swirled about him, lapping at his knees, tickling the back of his neck, prickling his scalp.

'*Verity!*'

He pounded again and again on the door, over and over.

But she did not come.

Others did come, however. Footsteps thudded and distant voices mumbled and lights flickered and somewhere a door opened and

Alasdair, his shame rising up to consume him, stumbled away down the staircase and out of the front door to stand, breathing heavily, outside.

But despite the shame, or because of it, he was not ready to admit the misery of his defeat.

He stole down the side of the house where an overgrown path led into the garden at the rear. Here he negotiated the bougain-villea and the frangipanis that grew unchecked and through whose ghostly branches he could hardly make out the house above him. Here were her rooms, or he took them to be, the bay window and little French balcony, and at neither door nor window was the curtain drawn. And no light at all from inside. She was not there, it was as clear as the moon in this cloudless night, but still he would not admit his defeat, stooping down and finding a stone and hurling it, like a love-stricken schoolboy, at her window. It bounced off the window and he waited, breathless, but no light went on, no door or window opened. The apartment remained in darkness and silence. He stooped again, but a light went on at another window, not hers, and a man appeared, some object—a firearm, perhaps—in his hand.

Alasdair fled, stumbling and righting himself and stumbling again. The house did not want to let him go, reaching out its branches and its roots and its shadows and trapping him, but finally he escaped, running out into the street and standing there, in the middle of the road, like a drunken man who has lost all that he valued.

But a cab came by at last and he flagged it down and got in.

∞

Three weeks shy of the shortest day of the year and the sun did not make an appearance the next morning until the church clocks

201

had struck seven. Those final minutes before dawn put a dew on the lawns of the houses in Elizabeth Bay. By a quarter past the sun had warmed the rocks on the little bay and most of the dew had gone. A host of seasonally confused currawongs, magpies and butcherbirds, believing spring to have come early, now set up such a racket that it was futile attempting to remain another minute in bed.

Eleanor got up. She dressed quickly, choosing a morning gown of palest yellow that seemed to complement the season's sudden rush towards spring. She would arrange a little tea party for that afternoon, she decided, and was at once taken up with the preparations for it.

But no sooner had she dressed herself than the extraordinary burst of energy dissipated. She sank down onto the chair. The gown of palest yellow now seemed ill-advised. Precipitous. It hung heavily on her frame. The tea party, foolish.

Downstairs the front door opened and closed, and she sprung up and stood at the window in time to witness Alasdair's early departure.

She thrust both fists at the windowpane and for one teetering, blinding moment found she might pound on the window, might even break the window, stand at the broken pane, perhaps bloodied, screaming loudly like a madwoman. The impulse was gone in a moment, but it left her breathless, dismayed.

Alice tapped on the door and came into the room with hot water and a hasty, curtsied, 'Morning, madam.'

Eleanor kept her face turned away. She stood very still and rigid as the maid moved about the room. She wished to tell the girl to leave at once but could not speak. Did not trust herself to sound quite normal. And so she waited.

'Will there be anything else, madam?'

'No.' She shook her head. Still did not turn.

The door closed. The room became her bedroom once more and not simply a place where servants came and went.

Eleanor sat down. Alasdair had returned very late last night. Now he was gone out again before the hall clock had chimed the half-hour. She had not suggested, last night, that he might think about moving back into their shared bedroom. The dinner at Booker-Reid's, the cab ride home, had not been favourable. And then he had ridden off into the night.

To find her, presumably.

It only now occurred to her that Alasdair might not know what had happened to the woman, Miss Trent. That he might go to her flat and find the police there. Or that the police had come and gone. The woman arrested. She realised she had shut her mind to it. To the possible implications, outcomes. Her own part was over and done. What happened now to this woman, her own husband's part in it, no longer concerned her. It happened offstage. She stood at the window. The new beginning she had anticipated, had engineered even, had not eventuated.

'Alice, I am arranging a small tea party today,' she announced to the maid as she came downstairs a short time later.

There would be a tea party. It would be a simple affair but it required arranging. She began to make those arrangements.

But her plans were put into disarray when Adaline Jellicoe called.

Her friend's presence was announced by a card on a tray handed to her in her room by Alice.

'What does this mean?' enquired Eleanor sharply of the servant.

But Alice, not comprehending the question nor, probably, the circumstances, could provide no answer.

And so, thought Eleanor, seated at her desk, all her efforts to avoid this had come to nothing. The object of her fear had come to her, was seated in her drawing room, or waited outside in a cab.

'Very well,' she said, standing up.

She went to the window and saw that Adaline Jellicoe waited outside in a hansom cab. She emerged now from the cab wearing a veil, and if she had come directly from a funeral at which she was the sole mourner she would look thus: cloaked in a solitude that kept her apart from others. She might look out at the world and the world might look in at her but there was no possibility of communion, or so thought Eleanor, who stood at her window and dreaded her friend's arrival. But it could not be put off. She left her room and went downstairs.

'Mrs Jellicoe,' she said, entering the drawing room and at once setting the boundaries for the visit. The last time they had met she had addressed her as Adaline. 'Do, please, sit down.' And Eleanor smiled, because it cost her nothing to do so. Alice hovered in the doorway awaiting instruction. 'Tea, I think,' she said, and the maid departed, leaving behind her in the room a disturbance and unease of which she was perhaps dimly aware, for it crackled in the very air.

Eleanor was silent. She waited. She would not be rushed in her own drawing room by a caller who was unexpected and hardly welcome. Her visitor wore a buttoned jacket of lavender grey, tight at the waist and arm, capped at the shoulders, over a high lace collar, a skirt of the same stuff, white gloves with tiny pearl buttons at the wrist and pearls at her throat. Her hat, very small and round and pinned to her hair, was also of silver-grey silk, and no doubt the wearer had sat before her dressing table this morning and dressed herself with the same care and attention as did any lady of their acquaintance, but here the comparison ended for Mrs Jellicoe was not the same as any lady of their acquaintance and never would be again.

Mrs Jellicoe sat. She slowly rolled back her veil, which was made of a thin gauze. Look on this face, she said, though she uttered no words.

Eleanor gazed upon the woman now uncovered, but unlike the smile it cost her something to do so. There was some trickery here, for the face she saw was the face of a friend as familiar to her as the twisting roads and pretty little bays that surrounded her own home, but the person who stared out at her from behind the grey-blue eyes was strange to her. A face, dark-browed, straight-nosed and full-lipped and surrounded by a mass of glorious chestnut hair, and striking to some men, less so to others, and with both poise and bearing intact. But it was a face, a body, from which the essence had been gouged.

'Eleanor,' said her visitor at last, her voice very low, 'I understand how disagreeable it is for you to receive me in these circumstances. Distasteful, even.'

It *was* disagreeable, it *was* distasteful, but to have it remarked on in as many words made it plain to Eleanor just how far her friend had fallen. She offered a hopeful smile while knowing the situation was without hope.

'Leon is being difficult,' said Adaline, staring down at her lap. 'About the children. About the settlement.'

The tea arrived on a tray, with lemons and sugar in a silver bowl, in the tentative hands of Alice, the maid. These things offered reassurance and normalcy and Eleanor fell upon them greedily.

'Here, Alice,' she said, indicating, 'place the tray here,' and then watching as the girl departed and the room turned cold once more.

'I wondered if perhaps Alasdair—who is his friend—might speak with Leon,' said Adaline, as though the arrival of the tea was nothing. 'I wondered if he might . . .'

But her words, her plea for help, hung in the air, unfinished. She attempted to complete it with her hand, lifting it into the air and describing an arc, but when this too failed she sat immobile on the settee. Her tea went undrunk.

Beyond the room the maid moved from place to place. In the kitchen sounds could occasionally be heard.

'You are quite well?' enquired Eleanor, as though the plea had not been made. As though this was like any other call from any other caller. She saw Adaline at her bedside a year ago, placing a hand on hers and holding it tightly. She recalled the sudden stillness of the bedroom at that moment. The calmness that had descended for a time when all about her had been, up to that moment, chaos. 'And the children? They are well?'

And when Adaline nodded once, a slight jerk of her head, and said in her strange brittle voice, 'Yes, quite well,' Eleanor felt the shame of her questions.

It struck her they were same, she and Adaline. Miss Verity Trent, and the housekeeper, Dora Hyatt. Leon and Alasdair. That this must draw them closer, this shared horror. And there was a moment, as Eleanor sat on the very edge of her settee, nursing her cup of tea, when it seemed the space between herself and Adaline could be traversed. That the relief that this would bring her would be worth the horror—

But the moment passed. She stared it down until it wilted and was gone.

'Alasdair has been so busy, of course, with his meetings,' she said. 'The Federation,' she added, lest Adaline, in her despair, had forgotten.

She saw then how unimportant it must seem to Adaline, the Federation. This colony which she was soon to leave, or so one understood, with its absurd referendums. These politicians, squabbling. But politicians squabbled in England, too, one presumed.

And it had done the trick. A wall had come up, protecting them both. Adaline's face was quite composed, her hand quite steady. The danger was passed. Soon she would get up to leave. Eleanor would not speak to Alasdair, and Alasdair would not speak to Leon Jellicoe, who had been his friend. And in all likelihood neither of them would see Adaline Jellicoe again, for she had a passage booked, they had heard, to England.

In the meantime, Mrs Jellicoe's tea was undrunk. It grew cooler and cooler as the moments passed. A moment would come, quite soon now, when she would be gone and the teacup would be removed and washed up and put away. Eleanor thought about this moment. She clung to it.

∞

The letting agent for the house at Woolloomooloo was a man named Orange whom one might imagine would sport bright red hair and fiery red whiskers or perhaps heralded from Ulster or the Low Countries, but in defiance of his name Mr Orange had an olive complexion and fine glossy black hair and dark lashes over eyes that had no more rested on the floodplains of Holland than they had the moon.

'This is a respectable establishment,' the agent said, searching among a ring of keys to select the correct one and, like the establishment which needed to proclaim its respectability, Mr Orange, who was not quite a gentleman, needed to wear an expensive suit of clothes and gloves made by an Italian tailor.

Alasdair stood behind him and stared with loathing at the little man, the letting agent, who was not little at all, who was in fact a fine specimen of manhood, but who must proclaim his position in the world through his ownership of this large ring of keys and hence anything and anyone behind the door he might open. Alasdair waited impatiently while the man found a key and fitted it into the door. It proved to be the wrong key and Alasdair turned away rather than watch the man forage again for the correct one. He ought to have taken this step days ago, he realised, struck by his own intransigence, but until last night he could not really believe in Verity's disappearance. He was not entirely sure he truly believed it even now, when they were at the stage of breaking into her rooms, when his life and hers were about to be thrown wide open for the world—for this man, at any rate—to see. They were about to see the room emptied of her things, Miss Trent gone, the walls echoing to her silence and to his folly. His loss.

It was intolerable to stand here, waiting.

The correct key was at last located and fitted smoothly into the lock and the door swung open. The man, Orange, went first into the room and Alasdair held back, delaying the moment he must enter, delaying the moment of his loss. His folly.

'Miss Trent?' the man called, but it was a courtesy, no more. Neither expected her to be here. And so it proved. The two rooms were empty of her presence.

Though her things remained.

At first Alasdair did not understand. *Were* these her things? Had he misremembered? The furnishings came with the apartment but the clock on the mantel, the coats and hats and umbrellas and gloves in the hallway, the clothes in the bedroom, the great sea trunk, the little crowd of objects by the bedside table, all were hers. The bed was made, the clothes neatly put away but all still here, nothing to even suggest a departure, planned or otherwise.

He went back into the main room.

'Well, she is not here but neither has she done a flit,' observed the man, Orange, whose eyes ran swiftly and critically over furnishings, wallpaper, doors and windows and locks as befitted an agent paid to take care of another's property. 'Ay, ay—what's this?'

He kneeled before a rusty brown stain on the carpet near the sofa. A second stain could be seen beneath the legs of the sofa when he pushed it a little to one side. The man exclaimed and stood up, pulling away the cushions on the sofa and finding further stains, larger this time, discolouring the fabric.

'What has happened here?' the agent demanded, turning to Alasdair.

Alasdair stood behind him and said nothing. He felt the disbelief, the confusion clouding his head.

But Mr Orange was insistent. 'I must ask you, sir, what has been going on in this apartment?'

Alasdair pushed the agent aside, kneeling down to see for himself. It was blood, though neither had spoken the word out loud.

'How can I say? You know as much as I.'

But the agent was outraged. 'This is a respectable establishment, sir. Whatever has occurred here, whatever has happened to this young lady, it is not allowed. I am afraid she will have to vacate at once.'

And Alasdair sprang to his feet. '*Damn* you—the young lady has *disappeared*! Do you not understand this fact?'

'That is no concern of mine,' countered the man, and he drew himself up stiffly in the face of this sudden truculence. 'I have a duty to my client. I shall be forced to terminate the lease henceforth. Please remove the lady's items immediately.'

Alasdair advanced a step towards the man.

'These rooms, sir, are paid for until the end of the year. And *I* have paid for them. If you do not wish to receive a legal writ and a visit from my lawyers, if you do not wish to see your position with your employer terminated forthwith, you will get out—'

'I shall do no such thing—'

'Go! Get out *now*!' And Alasdair grabbed the man by his collar and shoved him bodily out of the apartment and slammed the door after him.

It was blood. Her blood. He could not know it for certain, though it seemed the obvious conclusion. She had hurt herself or been hurt. But what kind of injury caused such a wound? He walked again about the room and back into the bedroom, going to each of her things—searching for what, he did not know.

But there was nothing.

He went to the chest of drawers in her bedroom where, oddly, he now recalled leaving his gold tiepin on his final visit—but it was not there. He stood staring at the spot where he had placed it, uncertain now of himself, uncertain of everything.

He tried the French doors and the windows but they were firmly locked. The front door to the apartment had been locked. It seemed to imply no one had forcibly entered her rooms, that she had, instead, simply gone out. Or let someone in.

He left the apartment, wary of the man, Orange, but he had gone, or was waiting downstairs in the street till he might reclaim his client's property. Alasdair went to the door of the apartment next door and rapped on it, throwing to the wind the caution, the subterfuge he had employed all these months.

It was opened at once by a tiny, frail old woman with milky eyes and scant hair and a pinched face that hinted at straitened circumstances. The promptness with which she answered his knock suggested she had been standing just inside the door. And perhaps she often stood there. Perhaps by standing in such a position she could hear all of what occurred on the landing outside.

'Who are you? What do you want?' she demanded in a high, querulous voice. Her milky eyes squinted and did not quite find his face.

'Do excuse this intrusion, madam. I am enquiring after the whereabouts of the young lady next door, Miss Trent.'

'I know nothing of this person and I certainly do not involve myself in other people's business,' the woman retorted, her sightless eyes scouring for him feverishly but unable to settle. 'Kindly remove yourself from my premises at once.' And the elderly lady—for she was a lady, or had been, which perhaps made her circumstances a little sadder—retreated behind her door with all the furious indignation of one habitually frightened and almost always alone.

The stupidity of the old woman—for Alasdair, in his rage, saw only stupidity where another might have seen fear and loneliness—almost caused him to pound an angry fist on the slammed door, and for a brief time this fury swelled and enveloped him. It abated as swiftly, leaving him deflated and without a plan. He turned bitterly away.

Almost at once another door opened directly across the hall, and a hand appeared and, somewhat surprisingly, signalled to him. The hand belonged to a young woman of bookish appearance, her russet hair severely restrained and a pair of rather ugly wire spectacles perched on her nose behind which two very intense eyes stared at him. She wore a faded slate-grey silk morning dress that had seen the end of too many darning needles but she seemed unconscious of the fact, or indifferent. Alasdair went to her and at her behest stepped inside her doorway. She looked to the left and right and then behind her, as though there was another in the apartment whom she did not wish to overhear her.

'I am Miss Tiptree,' she hissed, as though that explained all.

'Good day to you, madam—'

'Hush—please! Mama is asleep but she sleeps lightly. You are enquiring about Miss Trent? I thought so. You have not heard, then, what happened a few days ago?' And not awaiting his reply: 'It was on Saturday, very early in the morning, that we heard a commotion. For that is the only way I can describe it. Mama and I were not yet breakfasted when we heard the noise—or noises, really . . .'

'Please, Miss Tiptree, what happened?'

'A police constable—or, rather, *two* police constables!—came to the house, came specifically to Miss Trent's apartment. They could not get in, for she did not answer, she was already gone out, or so we believed, but we let them in—'

'Let them in? How?'

'I have a spare key. Miss Trent entrusted me with it. For emergencies. This was the emergency—though I confess when one is handed a spare key for an emergency one does not really anticipate there will be any such emergency, does one?'

'No indeed. But Miss Trent?'

'I was made to wait outside—indeed, I was urged by the constable to return to my rooms, but I confess I did not. I lingered, as who would not?'

Miss Tiptree paused here to blink rapidly a number of times.

'They closed the door, but after a short time one of the policemen emerged and departed, leaving the other inside. Alone, you understand, with Miss Trent. I nearly went to her aid but I did not like to as they had bade me gone. At any rate, the first constable returned after some little time and brought with him a nurse and a doctor, or such I took them to be, and after a short time again they *all* emerged and this time poor Miss Trent was with them and I cried out in dismay when I saw her, for she was in a dreadful way, quite unconscious and needing to be carried. What the matter was, nor how long she had been in such a way, I cannot say, nor what transpired afterwards, for they did not return and there was no one to ask. It has been quite a mystery. Though . . .'

And here she paused, wrinkling her brow and placing a finger on her bridge of her spectacles.

'There was an incident last night. A drunken man came to her door and then, I believe, later attempted to break in via the rear garden—but whether it was the same man outside as the man who came to the door, I cannot say.'

She faltered as it seemed to dawn on her that the man who had come to the door last night was quite likely the man she now faced in her doorway. She looked at him doubtfully, and withdrew a little into her hallway.

Alasdair almost advanced after her but held back. 'But where did they take her—do you know?'

'It would be the hospital, would it not? The Sydney Hospital.'

'And she was alive, you said, when they brought her out?'

'Yes, to be sure. But that was three days ago.'

213

# CHAPTER SIXTEEN

# CINNAMON BISCUITS

That afternoon three ladies called for Mrs Dunlevy: Mrs Pyke, breathless in a hat crowded with clusters of glazed fruit; Mrs Rothe, who had never been breathless in her life, magnificent in white lace and ruffles; and Miss Dempsey in a prim white blouse and skirt. Like a shop girl, thought Alice, who was doubtful about any woman who kept house for an unmarried brother rather than find a husband for herself, though she liked the brother, Mr Ned Dempsey, as he had smiled at her once and placed a coin in the palm of her hand. In the drawing room Mrs Dunlevy waited with the silver tea things and Mrs Flynn's cinnamon biscuits, freshly baked that morning.

'That Miss Dempsey do not like my cinnamon biscuits,' observed Mrs Flynn darkly when Alice had returned to the kitchen and relayed the names of the callers to her. 'She complained last time they were not moist enough for her liking and though she liked cinnamon as a rule, she did not care for it in a biscuit.'

And Mrs Flynn, who was in the midst of preparing a duck for that evening's dinner, brought her chopping knife down on the neck of the unfortunate fowl with a violent *thwack!* The feathered head with its glassy sightless eyes rolled from the table and dropped with barely a thud onto the tiled floor at their feet. She flicked the severed head aside with the toe of her boot, grabbed a handful of feathers and proceeded to tear them from the unprotesting corpse of the duck. Alice stood and watched as the pile of discarded feathers grew and the grey, mottled flesh of the bird was revealed.

Mrs Flynn had not said this morning, nor at any time since last night, 'Where is the baby gone to, Alice?' She had not made any allusion to the unusual turn that events had taken, except to say, 'You did not clean all the pots and pans nor take out the slops last night, Alice. I had to do them myself this morning and my knees are gone now because of it.'

Her knees did not look gone. She stood at the great scrubbed wooden table and tore and tore at the flesh of the duck and did not look gone at all.

Alice had not cleaned all the pots; she had not taken out the slops. She would work twice as hard today. But it was not just the kitchen. The silver tea set that Mrs Dunlevy was at this moment offering to her callers was dulled where she had failed to give it its weekly polish. The clean linen was piled in unruly heaps about the house and was not put away and the bedding was not properly aired and in some rooms the dust lay thick and undisturbed. As each task went undone Alice felt the weight of it pull at her limbs and thump in her head, and her exhaustion was such that the very skin covering her muscles ached. But it could not be helped. There was Milli. There was the baby.

There was, besides, a nick on her throat where a razor had pricked her skin and there was also this second mark, much deeper, and unseeable (unless one peered very closely and no one did peer closely for Alice was a servant) that had been made in the dark by the two men holding her life in their hands and tossing it carelessly between them as one might a trapped fly, choosing to release her simply because it was in their power to trap her again whenever they wished. In the last five years Alice Nimrod had become complacent; she had forgotten the tenuous and fleeting nature of life. To be reminded it of now had left its mark on her.

The drawing room bell rang.

'That will be her now,' said Mrs Flynn, pausing grimly in her task. 'Wanting something else instead of the biscuits. Wanting a sponge cake or a muffin, as if such things grew on trees and did not have to be measured and mixed and baked and set on a tray to cool.'

It was an inconvenience to Mrs Flynn, always having to prepare food, always having to cook. She shook her head and resumed her plucking.

In the drawing room the ladies were seated, two on the settee, one on the upright armchair and Mrs Dunlevy in the other armchair nearest to the little side table upon which the tea things were arranged.

'Her mistake was to confront her husband,' said Mrs Rothe, and, 'She was the *housekeeper*!' exclaimed Mrs Pyke.

Mrs Pyke was perched on the very edge of the settee, a teacup and saucer balanced on her lap. She fell silent as Alice entered. They all fell silent. The feeling in the room was sharp and thrilling and rather terrible, as though something had been said or done that could not be undone.

'Alice, see if Mrs Flynn has any cake or muffins,' said Mrs Dunlevy. 'Miss Dempsey does not care for cinnamon.'

'It is not the cinnamon per se,' corrected Miss Dempsey. 'It is the presence of cinnamon in a biscuit I find not to my liking.'

Miss Dempsey was a slight figure in her prim white blouse, very upright, but it was the uprightness of a thin layer of ice that would shatter if a single drop of rain fell on it. The flesh of her face was stretched tightly over muscles constantly contracting and releasing, eyes alighting and darting away and alighting afresh someplace else. Mrs Pyke had exclaimed, 'She was the *house-keeper!*' and Miss Dempsey's discomfort, her horror, was writ large. Miss Dempsey took refuge in the failing of the cinnamon biscuits.

'Told you, didn't I?' said Mrs Flynn with grim satisfaction when presented with this request. 'She can have the last of the almond cake from last week, and if it is stale and nasty I shall not be the one to blame for it.'

And she cut a slice of this almond cake, which Alice duly delivered, though to enter the room in which the four ladies sat induced in her such a reluctance she afterwards fled to the solitari-ness of the dining room. It unsettled her, this sudden reluctance, and she could not account for it. Mrs Pyke had exclaimed, *She was the* housekeeper! and Miss Dempsey had spurned the cinnamon biscuits and they sat, the four ladies, perched on the very cusp of their chairs like birds about to take flight.

In the dining room the lunch things were only partly cleared away, another task unfinished. Alice moved quickly, though her body was sluggish and unwilling. She saw Mr Dunlevy's news-paper on the table where he had left it that morning and she opened the newspaper, though this was not a part of her duties. She cast her eye over the very pages, the very words Mr Dunlevy had cast his eyes over and there was no difference between them, Mr Dunlevy the parliamentarian and Alice Nimrod the servant, for they both read the newspaper, they both saw the same things. Or so it seemed to Alice, for whom the unfinished and unattended tasks of the day nagged only vaguely in some distant room. She read advertisements for patent medicines and agricultural tools and ladies' corsets, advertisements for men seeking employment and other men seeking workers, for possessions lost and possessions found. And this was what Mr Dunlevy read! It was extraordinary to her. She saw—though she had not sought it—an advertisement that read, *Childless couple seeks baby to adopt or to care for. Good Christian home. Reply to Mrs Flowers at the address given.* She saw that there were many other similar advertisements beside this one: more couples wishing to adopt, and they were all good Christians, it seemed, and women seeking couples who wished to adopt. These women too were all good Christians. And so were their babies, though this was implied rather than stated. So many babies, so many childless couples. A veritable trade in babies was going on amid the pages of Mr Dunlevy's newspaper. But this one, this Mrs Flowers, was the only one that offered to care for and not simply adopt. At a cost.

For the first time, Alice saw this wondrous thing, her sister's baby, that only the day before she had snatched from the courthouse with no thought as to the consequences and for which she now found herself solely responsible, as the burden it surely was. And would be for the next three years.

She had failed, she realised, before she had even begun, for she could not hope to keep it. But she would not give it up! Not her sister's child, she would not! But if she could send it away to safety, to be cared for, to have a better chance than she and Milli had had, perhaps, even to be loved—

Alice tore the page from the newspaper, folded it and thrust it into the sleeve of her uniform. She straightened her cap and smoothed down her apron and emerged into the hallway to find her eyes brimming with tears and a lump in her throat because she had thought of her mother who had been dead and gone these last five years but who had come back to her all in a rush, so that the loss of her, just as though it were happening all over again, was almost too much to bear.

But no one noticed because Mrs Dunlevy's guests were departing.

Indeed, Mrs Dunlevy had about her the look of someone held together by tissue paper. But all she said was, 'Alice, please inform Mrs Flynn the almond cake was a little stale.'

'Yes, madam.' Alice stood at the front door and handed each of the ladies their coat and hat and gloves and mufflers, and Mrs Pyke smiled and said, 'Thank you, Alice,' Mrs Rothe took Mrs Dunlevy's hand and gave it a quick squeeze as though she were at the funeral of someone she did not know very well, and Miss Dempsey, whose brother had once placed a coin in Alice's palm, left first because she had just seen a cab go past and wished to be the one to secure it.

'Gone, have they?' said Mrs Flynn standing over a great steaming dish at the stove and waving the steam from her face.

'Yes, Mrs Flynn, and Mrs Dunlevy said to tell you the almond cake was very nice.'

'Nice, indeed!' said Mrs Flynn, who thrived not on compliments but on grievances. 'What is that you have, Alice?' she added as a sheet of newsprint fluttered to the floor and lay at Alice's feet.

''Tis nothing,' cried Alice, snatching at it, but Mrs Flynn, who had earlier complained that her knees were gone, had already stooped to retrieve it and was peering short-sightedly at the tiny newsprint. She turned the page over and over again, waiting for its mysteries to reveal themselves to her. After a lengthy perusal, she placed the page on the table without a word, an advertisement for a revolutionary corset design uppermost and, when she saw this, primly turning the sheet the other side up. Mrs Flynn had lived a hard life in an unforgiving city and was not easily shocked, but an advertisement for a ladies' under-garment was a step too far.

Alice said nothing. She left the kitchen. She went from room to room. She thought of the baby whose future she could not see beyond the wretchedness and squalor that was the breast of Mrs Renfrew. When she returned to the kitchen the page from the newspaper lay where Mrs Flynn had placed it, still with its revolu-tionary corsets and its Mrs Flowers. Alice wished she could be left alone to do her work in peace, but this Mrs Flowers had wormed her way into Alice's head and would not be dislodged, so when Mrs Flynn went for a moment into the scullery Alice reclaimed the page of the newspaper, folding it carefully and tucking it once more into her sleeve.

'You oughta think real careful before you do that, my girl.'

Alice spun around and met the inscrutable and unblinking eyes of the cook, who had re-emerged from the scullery with all the stealth of a housebreaker, looking very much as though she had sprung a trap and was come to claim her spoils.

'You know what a baby farm is, don't you?' Mrs Flynn said.

''Course I do! I weren't born yesterday.' It was an unfortunate thing to say given the circumstances.

'You hand that baby over, Alice my girl, along with whatever sum of money they demand of you, and you will never see its face again this side of Paradise, of that you can be sure.'

'You don't know that!' Alice spun away.

But Mrs Flynn would not be silenced. 'They will do away with it first chance they get,' she went on with a sort of grisly relish, 'and they will go on taking your money just as long as they can get away with it. And when at last you get your suspicions they will be off and nothing to show they was ever here except a tiny corpse stuffed in the drain or buried in the yard for the coppers to find a year or two later.'

'Stop it!' cried Alice, for who can bear to hear their own fears voiced—and with such grim satisfaction—by another? 'That ain't so! Not nowadays. There's laws against it.'

'*Laws?*' Mrs Flynn laughed. She laughed so hard she had to pull up a chair and heave herself into it.

And it *was* funny, hilarious even, the idea that the law existed to protect people like themselves.

Alice went back to her work. She cleaned a tea stain from the carpet so that you would not know it was there. She polished the silver. She cleaned all the shoes that she had not cleaned over the last few days.

She answered a summons from Mrs Dunlevy.

∞

Sydney Hospital was in Macquarie Street on the site of the old Rum Hospital. That notorious structure, built by convicts to house convicts, had been constructed on a grand scale but with a breathtaking disregard for workmanship. It had suffered repeated outbreaks of typhoid, and on hot summer days the smell from the drains was so foul it disrupted parliament next door. As the century drew to a close the old hospital had finally been pulled down and this new building constructed, this time of solid no-nonsense colonial sandstone with a handful of turrets, elevated colonnades and cast-iron lace balustrades thrown in to add a dash of whimsical high Victorian romanticism. The members of the two legislative chambers could breathe easily once more.

In Macquarie Street the working day was ending, the road and walkways congested with merchants and shop workers and clerks and lawyers heading to the quay and the tram stops, and it was under the cover of these crowds and the fading daylight that Alasdair Dunlevy ascended the two flights of steps and entered the hospital through its green double doors.

Here, on the other side of the doors, was a foyer beneath a distant and lofty ceiling, a floor tiled ambitiously in marble, and walls richly panelled in dark cedar. A staircase of the same timber, wide and resplendent, rose to a half-landing that was walled entirely by stained glass, before dividing in two. The effect was half English manor house, half gentlemen's club and the occasional nurses, stiffly dressed and with covered heads, who silently crossed and recrossed the space were as spectral nuns in a medieval convent, so that Alasdair stood for a moment, confused by the silence, by the calm, by the improbable scale of it all. Here to his left was a boardroom, its door ajar, showing tall, arched windows that gazed with a certain sedate benevolence at the mercantile bustle of Macquarie Street below, and nestled discreetly beside the doorway was a modest reception desk.

A clerk stood behind the little reception desk, waiting, and Alasdair, who made speeches in the Assembly chamber and routinely addressed a hundred or more men at Federation meetings, could feel the young man's gaze upon him and was disconcerted. He had hoped to find his own way—to request assistance was, at this moment, abhorrent to him—but the impossibility of this was apparent. The corridors to left and right told him nothing, they might lead anywhere.

At last the clerk could wait no longer. 'May I assist you, sir?' He sounded a little impatient. This gentleman plainly needed assistance yet refused to ask for it, and clearly this irritated the young man, who appeared to have no other function than to assist those who did not know their way.

Alasdair turned to the man—who was slight and pale and brittle in the manner of one who is the first in their family to wear a collar and not toil all day with their hands—and addressed him. 'I am enquiring after a patient,' he said. And then he raised up his heart, for it still caused him a moment of breathlessness to utter her name: 'It is a Miss Trent, whom I believe was brought here sometime early on Saturday morning.'

Offering no comment, the man consulted a large ledger opened on the desk before him, moving his finger down a list. And as this was his sole purpose, the pinnacle of his function as it were, he did so with a flourish and a solemnity that was impressive, or was intended to be. He turned a page, he moved his finger down a second column and then the finger paused. A tiny frown creased the man's features. He looked up at the gentleman making the enquiry. He looked down again and the frown deepened. A slight flush appeared on his face.

Alasdair felt a tightening in his stomach.

'Would you oblige me, sir, by waiting here one moment?' said the clerk, and without awaiting a reply he emerged from the reception desk and scuttled across the tiled foyer and up the staircase.

Alasdair now understood that Miss Trent had died. The frown on the clerk's face, the finger poised on the page, the slight flush to his face, leaving his post to seek assistance—all of it told him she was dead.

He wondered at the great wave that now rushed over him, for it swept up every part of him, leaving nothing in its wake, and yet he remained here in the marble-tiled foyer, at the reception desk. He saw the thick cream-coloured pages of the ledger, the neatly entered columns of names. He saw the clever workmanship of the desk, how the corners had been worked so that the joins were invisible. He saw the names of the hospital board and its bene-factors engraved on a great panel on the wall. He saw all these things, though his mind seemed gone.

The clerk returned accompanied by a second man, much older and more senior, in thick white whiskers, a stiff high collar and an old-fashioned frockcoat, carrying pince-nez which he placed on his nose as he approached. There was a coldness about this man, a disapproval striving to appear as blandness.

'Would you come this way?' the man said with no preamble, no introduction, as though he dealt habitually with people of no consequence. But Alasdair found himself following, for it was easier to have someone else decide what he must do, even someone like this man.

They ascended the wide and resplendent staircase to the floor above and walked in silence for a time along a featureless corridor until they came, finally, to a door. Beyond was an office, plain and thinly carpeted and airless, a place of bureaucratic func-tions and small tasks. The hospital official entered the office, sat down at a desk and leaned forward a little. He had mastered his features now. He was businesslike.

'My name is Gregson,' he announced, when Alasdair had followed him in and taken the seat opposite. 'You are enquiring about a patient, I believe. A Miss Trent?'

Alasdair was. They knew this. He inclined his head. He had not removed his hat. It was not that sort of a place, not that sort of occasion.

The official, Gregson, did not continue at once. Instead, he studied his visitor through slightly narrowed eyes, stroked his beard, ran a fingernail over his front teeth, and Alasdair despised him.

But the man was talking. What was he saying? Alasdair brushed the man's words aside. He cut him off.

'Does she live?' he demanded. 'Does Miss Trent live or not?'

Gregson sat back, affronted. 'Certainly, sir, she lives, though she remains gravely ill and her recovery is in no way assured.'

He said more but Alasdair found himself at the window, and after a moment or two found he looked out upon the courtyard at the rear of the hospital, at a circle of lawn and a fountain mounted on a sandstone plinth. He tried to make sense of the scene but could not. He turned back to the room and to its jumble of chaotic images which now sorted themselves once more into a man seated at a desk, talking.

'You are aware that Miss Trent was in police custody when she was brought here?'

But the man's words made no sense. Alasdair sat down, seizing the chair as a sinner seizes absolution. 'I think not. You have made an error, sir.'

The realisation that they were talking at cross purposes, that this man was speaking of some other woman entirely and Verity might, after all, be lying in the morgue, was an agony beyond endurance.

Gregson frowned so deeply he was required to place his fore-finger and thumb on the pince-nez so that they did not fall off. He studied again the records laid before him.

'Miss Verity Trent of Woolloomooloo. Brought in on Saturday morning last, under the charge of two constables. Suffering severe loss of blood and possible internal injury and infection.'

Alasdair shook his head. He did not speak for a time. 'I do not understand,' he said finally.

And Gregson gazed steadily at him. The man was old, so old he might have worked here when convicts walked the hallways of the original building, so old his white beard was as yellow as ancient parchment. His eyes were not unkindly, but they had looked for too many years on too much hardship and desperation to be anything other than dimmed and remote. He reached up and removed the pince-nez from his nose and slid them into a pocket, a gesture that had, perhaps, assisted him through the ages to navigate difficult interviews.

'Sir, what is your connection to this woman, if I may enquire?'

'You may not.'

Gregson gave a sad, almost imperceptible nod of his whiskered head. 'Then I am afraid I can tell you no more.' He closed the book that was open on the desk before him.

Alasdair slammed both hands down on the desk that separated them. 'You will not tell me of what it is Miss Trent is charged?'

'I will not—unless, sir, you have some connection to Miss Trent, the nature of which you are willing to divulge.'

'How dare you, sir!'

Alasdair found himself on his feet, his chair toppled backwards. It was ludicrous to take offence when what the man seated before him had hinted at was undeniably true. Yet here he was, offended, denying.

He righted his chair. He sat down. He met the man's gaze. 'Very well then. Miss Trent is a member of my constituency. That is, her fiancé was. The fellow was a recent arrival to our shores who took up a position and found a place to live within my constituency. And then promptly died. She arrived—Miss Trent—from England a few weeks later to find her fiancé deceased and herself in a very invidious, precarious even, position. She tried various places and people, or so I understand, but none would aid her. At last, and taking the advice of whom I cannot say, she presented herself at my office and my secretary took her particulars. Made cognisant of her plight, I instructed my secretary to render what small assistance we could. It was, I am ashamed to say, little more than the address of a boarding house where Miss Trent might safely reside and one or two other names of persons who may be able to assist her. She had no family, it seemed, here or in England. That was the extent of my contact with the unfortunate lady until yesterday, when we learned she was no more at the boarding house and was understood to be here at this hospital. If some awful occurrence has befallen her, then, having taken some initial interest in her case, I feel duty-bound to render my assistance.'

Alasdair raised his chin and stared the man down. There was enough truth in this drawn-out explanation to allow a glow of self-congratulation at the compassion, the benevolence of his actions. If his actions had very soon gone beyond benevolence, well, that was no one's business but his own.

The ageing Mr Gregson remained impassive, unmoved by this speech, other than to remark, 'Am I to understand you are a member of parliament, sir?'

Alasdair inclined his head.

The old fellow appeared to consider and then to make up his mind. 'Very well then. Miss Trent, I am sorry to say, appears to have found herself in a certain condition.' He looked directly at Alasdair as a man did who wished his meaning to convey more than his words could.

And they did convey meaning.

Alasdair reeled. 'She is with child?'

∞

Alice found her mistress seated at her writing desk, though there was no paper before her on the desk and no pen in her hand. Mrs Dunlevy sat very upright, looking towards the window.

A branch of the big tree outside tapped softly against the glass and for a moment they both observed it.

'Alice,' said Mrs Dunlevy, 'you went out last night and you took something with you, something from the house, and you returned very late. Can you explain what you were doing and what it was that you took?'

The branch tapped again, softly, the merest brush of leaves against glass, but insistently, as though its destiny was to overrun the house and return this place to its original state, if not today or next year, then eventually. What was stone and brick and glass compared to God's own work, compared to a tree?

Alice felt a coldness spread through her body. 'I did go out, madam, yes.'

Though how Mrs Dunlevy could know of it when Alice had gone out after her and returned to the house before her, she did not know. And even as she wondered this a curtain twitched in the upstairs window of the house opposite and the elderly lady who lived there, who never left her house, who sat hour upon empty hour at this very window, appeared briefly—triumphantly!—and was gone.

'I am very sorry I did not ask before I went, madam, but I was desperate.'

Mrs Dunlevy turned very slowly to face her, and lifted her eyebrow enquiringly. 'Desperate?'

'Yes, madam. What I mean is I had forgot some of the laundry, and so when the girl came to take it away some got left behind. I realised it and I bundled it up and I went out, late, after you and Mr Dunlevy had gone out for the evening, and I took it there myself. I know I should have told you, madam, but I had made a mistake and I did not wish it known.'

Mrs Dunlevy turned back to the window. She did so with a single smooth movement that involved head, neck, shoulders, her expression not changing, the eyebrow returned to its normal position. She does not move like we do, thought Alice, like most people; she moves like a swan. Alice had not seen a swan, but she had the sense that this was how one would move: slowly, gracefully, without the ugly, jerking, hurried movements that other people made, that she herself made, could not help making. It was the difference between them. One of the differences.

Alice's hands shook. She clenched them tightly into fists behind her back.

'This is just the latest, then, in a series of errors you have made recently, Alice,' said Mrs Dunlevy, turning once more and studying her steadily, gravely.

Alice waited. Her gaze, no match for her mistress's, sunk to the floor.

'Things have been left undone, or they have been done late—the laundry, the dusting, the beds, the silver. The list goes on. Do not think I have not observed it. Your work has become sloppy.'

It seemed extraordinary to Alice that the thing she had feared—this very meeting with her employee, these exact words spoken—had come to pass. And because she had imagined it, had feared it and now it was happening, she felt very far away, watching herself from elsewhere, another Alice Nimrod, not herself.

'It is true I did get behind, madam,' said the other Alice, 'but I have worked double hard today to catch up. And I have caught up now, madam.'

'I am glad to hear it, for I will not put up with laziness. You have a good position here and mark my words, Alice, I will not be made a fool of, do you understand?'

Mrs Dunlevy's expression did not change, nor did her gaze fix directly on Alice but at some distant place that only she could see. A cold place, it seemed to Alice.

'Yes, madam. Of course, madam.'

'Then you may go. We shall say no more about it. For now.'

Alice left, both the Alice in the room with Mrs Dunlevy and the Alice observing from a great distance and now, all in a rush, the two Alices collided once more into a single Alice who found herself filled with such a jumble of different emotions she could not think. She stumbled once as she walked across the landing.

Much later she went up to her room in the attic. She did not have a writing desk nor paper nor pen. But she did have a piece of an old laundry bill and a pencil. And she did have a little table beside her bed, and if she moved the water jug to the floor she could make a space to write. She considered for a moment and then she wrote, as she had always known she was going to from the moment she had picked up Mr Dunlevy's newspaper:

*Dear Mrs Flowers . . .*

∞

Verity was with child. It had not occurred to Alasdair. And yet why should she not be with child? *His* child.

The elderly clerk watched him, watched his face, seeing all or seeing nothing, it was impossible to tell.

'Yes, I am afraid so,' the man said, with a sigh for all of Man's failings or, more precisely, for all of Woman's failings. 'I fear you were sadly deceived by Miss Trent, sir. She was not set upon the moral path you must have presumed. Or if she was, she has strayed very far from it.'

'Indeed,' said Alasdair.

But a child! His ears rang with it. And she had told him nothing, though they had lain together so intimately, her nakedness a thing of wonder in his arms, her breath on his chest, the softness of her flesh beneath his fingers. He had done this, given her his most precious gift, and with it she had created a child. *Their* child.

He would not think of that other child, the one his wife had carried inside her for eight months and that had reversed the natural order of things by dying before it was born.

But the joy and the grief—they made him giddy!

'She has been offered spiritual support but refused it, I believe,' continued the clerk in the manner of one for whom the rejection of God's love was, clearly, incomprehensible.

'Then I shall see her myself,' Alasdair declared, rising once more and casting himself, in both their eyes, the hero.

But there was something, a cliff edge it was, that he remembered he stood at, balanced precariously. He peered over its edge and felt the dizziness of vertigo.

'She has not said who the father is, I take it?'

The elderly clerk shook his head. 'She has not. As I say, she remains in a state of unconsciousness. Though perhaps she has said something to the police? I cannot say. And perhaps the wretched woman does not, herself, know.'

'Good God,' said Alasdair, as this seemed expected.

The precipice was gone. But at once a second opened up to take its place, this one right beneath his feet and he almost could not speak.

'But, Mr Gregson, you mentioned the police. I still do not understand why the police are involved. There was an injury to Miss Trent, but—no, I am afraid I do not understand.'

Or perhaps he did. Perhaps he had known from the moment he had arrived at the hospital, for when the old man replied his words were the words he was always destined to speak, words that might have been revealed by a prophet centuries earlier in a Book of

Revelation: 'Miss Trent attended a doctor who performed a certain illegal operation on her person and now the child is no more.'

Yes, here were the words, and they were not the word of God, they were the word of Man, a man bewhiskered and benign and seated at a desk, a man who believed in compassion yet spoke with loathing.

'The operation, naturally, was done without the blessing of law or church,' Gregson went on, relentless and precise, 'and for her sin she has found herself gravely ill and in the custody of the police. It is, sad to say, not an uncommon story in our colony. If Miss Trent lives, she will go to prison. If she dies—well, one does not wish to speculate on her likely fate.'

He had finished, rather pleased with himself, as is the minister in his pulpit who contemplates the sins of his congregation and sees himself above them.

Alasdair did not move. The breath had been driven from his body and he seemed no longer to hear properly. Words came and went, some audible, most very faintly. He saw the man's lips moving and even those words he did hear ceased to have any meaning attached to them. He understood something very dreadful had happened and that it would pass, as all things did. He sat very still waiting for it to do so.

CHAPTER SEVENTEEN

# THE WIFE OF THE MINISTER

## CONSTABLES ATTEND
## UNCONSCIOUS WOMAN

### Near death of female sought by police

A woman was brought to the Sydney Hospital on Saturday last in an unconscious state and in the custody of two police constables.

The woman, whose name was not released though it is believed she heralds from the Woolloomooloo area, was said to be suffering greatly from a loss of blood and is at present described as gravely ill. A charge of using drugs or instruments to procure abortion contrary to Section 58 of the Offences against the Person Act was levelled on the young woman, who is thought to be of about 21 or 22 years of age and a recent arrival to our shores.

The police constables had gone to arrest the woman at a boarding house at the above-mentioned district when they discovered her in a state of unconsciousness having apparently lost a great deal of blood.

It is thought that, had the constables not arrived when they did and immediately rendered assistance, the woman, who was weak and close to death, would surely have perished before the day was over.

The story was hidden away on page five of the *Herald*, in among the Divorce Court listings, the reports from the quarter sessions and an advertisement for a family cough mixture, and Eleanor, seated at breakfast with a cup of coffee, almost missed it.

A heat flared up in her so fiercely her face grew hot and red. Her hands shook and in her haste to turn the page she tore the newspaper. But the story was gone now. In its place, page six was safe and calming, a refuge filled with the upcoming Federation referendum—though, even here, those insistent black headlines swam before her eyes, stripped of meaning. On her face her flesh burned. It betrayed her.

Well, and what of it? There was no one but herself to witness it. Alasdair had breakfasted early; he was now upstairs in his study preparing for the day ahead. She breakfasted alone.

She placed the newspaper on the table, she removed the reading glasses her husband did not know she wore.

The maid, Alice, burst into the room brandishing muffins fresh from the oven and butter in a little dish. (Or it seemed to Eleanor that the maid burst in and brandished. All was extreme and excessive this morning.) Alice curtsied. She placed the muffins on the table and Eleanor searched for hidden meanings in the maid's mumbled, 'Madam.' After a time Alice withdrew.

Eleanor picked up the newspaper. She turned back to page five.

It was there still. The words remained. She read them again—slower this time, for what if she had been mistaken the first time? She was not mistaken. It was Miss Trent.

Eleanor closed the newspaper and looked to the window. The frangipani was bald at this time of year, and on an upper branch a large black-and-white currawong was perched, whistling and trilling with an urgency that suggested some predator was about. It turned its head this way and that emitting an urgent warning.

It had not occurred to her that Miss Trent might die. There had been blood on the carpet, a spot or two. Perhaps more by the time she had left. If she had thought Miss Trent might die, that Miss Trent was in mortal danger, what might she have done? Eleanor did not know. Perhaps nothing, perhaps something.

She had gone to the police. They had waited overnight and then come for her and, it seemed, had saved the girl's life. If the police had not come, who would have? Perhaps no one.

So, did I condemn the girl to death or did I save her life? Eleanor wondered. She did not know. She had wished to play with fate, hadn't she? To alter destinies. Now that she had played God she felt a little sick. A little frightened.

She saw that her own part in the incident was not mentioned in the newspaper. No one knew of it except herself and the girl, Miss Trent.

The predator that had set off the currawong's urgent warning was a carriage attended by her husband's secretary, Mr James Greensmith, come to take them to the railway station. They were to attend a pro-Federation reception at Penrith as guests of the mayor and the mayoress.

'It is Mr Greensmith, madam,' said Alice, appearing in the doorway and looking startled, though he was a frequent enough visitor.

'Show him in, Alice. Mr Greensmith, please sit down. Have you breakfasted?'

Her husband's secretary, that ambitious young man, pleasant of feature with a keen eye for a fine suit of clothes and a smart gentleman's hat, blushed furiously, as he was wont to do when alone, however briefly, with his employer's wife.

He appeared now to cast about for an appropriate response. 'I have breakfasted, thank you, Mrs Dunlevy.' He stood just inside the door, so that Alice had to move around him to get out. He carried a letter for the minister that he crushed in his hand then hastily smoothed again.

'But you will join me in a cup of coffee. Or tea perhaps?'

Faced with further alarming questions, Mr Greensmith nodded. 'Coffee would be most welcome. But please, let me.' And he darted forward, perceiving coffee pot and cups on the table and availing himself of both before resuming his position by the door.

'Please do sit, I beg you, Mr Greensmith. I am not nearly ready, as you see, and shall need to abandon you for a time while I go upstairs. My husband will, I am sure, join you soon.'

She excused herself, taking up the morning newspaper, and withdrew with it clutched in her hand, and the way James Greensmith observed her one might think he had never before in his life seen his employer's wife with a newspaper.

They were to catch the eleven o'clock train, so why Mr Greensmith had arrived to convey them to the station at nine o'clock was a mystery. It meant he had a very long wait indeed while Eleanor readied herself and gave some thought to selecting the most appropriate hat. Something bright and large and grand, she decided, for they were to travel to Penrith and the elegant hats she had purchased in the city this season could hardly be appreciated by the drovers' wives whom one met in such places. As the wife of the minister, the people must be able to see her from some distance and they should feel that though she understood, was sympathetic even to their concerns, yet she was separate from them and would always remain so. The hat she selected was plum-coloured and wide of brim and sported a large ostrich feather that sprouted from the crown and trailed opulently behind her.

She had once, as a girl of perhaps fourteen or fifteen, seen the wife of the new Governor. The Governor had been in the colony just a few months and the whole district had come out to see his wife (for the last Governor's wife had been killed at Parramatta when her carriage had overturned in the driveway of old Government House—a thing of wonder still, all these years later). The wife of the new Governor had come to open a garden fete, or some such occasion, at the wharf in Balmain. Eleanor had seen her through a crowd of people, fleetingly, a figure slight and slender and elegant in a gown of purest sapphire blue beneath a white parasol that someone held above her head. She had laughed a little and inclined her head and the people had gazed upon her as they might a queen or a deity. Eleanor had gazed at her. After a short time the Governor's wife had left in a carriage and the sun, which had been unrelenting all afternoon, had dipped behind a cloud.

Eleanor placed the plum-coloured hat just so on her head. She looked at herself. She was no longer red-faced and hot. She was quite pale. She was, she realised, a little frightened.

Alice stood in the doorway. 'If you please, madam, Mr Dunlevy is enquiring if you are almost ready yet.'

Eleanor turned and regarded the maid, who had clearly been sent to hurry her along.

'You may tell Mr Dunlevy I am quite ready, thank you, Alice, and shall be down directly . . . Is there something else?' For the maid hesitated.

'Will you be out all day, madam?'

'Yes, I have already informed Mrs Flynn we shall not be back until late afternoon. It is not an excuse to slacken off, Alice.'

'No, madam,' said Alice, and she left at speed.

Eleanor stood up but she did not immediately depart. It was warm outside—she had got Alice to open her bedroom window—but Penrith was thirty miles inland and at the foot of the mountains and it was sure to be cold. She wrapped a possum fur about her shoulders and took up a muffler and left her room without a backwards glance.

Alasdair would not look at her. He stood at the front door, impatient and tapping his cane against his leg, his hat already on, gloves in his hand, and Mr Greensmith stood wretchedly at his side. The letter or telegram brought by the secretary was in Alasdair's hand and, as Eleanor now appeared, was thrust wordlessly into his pocket.

'Our train departs at ten o'clock,' Alasdair said. His lips hardly moved as he spoke and he addressed the door, his cane, the wretched Mr Greensmith.

'My dear, I believe you informed me it departs at eleven.'

'No. I certainly did no such thing.'

'Oh, but,' and she turned to Greensmith, 'I am sure I am right. Mr Greensmith, you can vouch for me—do you not recall Mr Dunlevy said eleven?'

And the secretary stared and blinked rapidly at her, appalled to find himself in a such a position.

'For God's sake, Eleanor! You are not a child. Do not expect me to treat you as one!' Alasdair placed a hand on her upper arm, his fingers closing around her so that she almost cried out, and marched her out of the house and deposited her at the steps of the carriage. He released his grip and they boarded and sat side by side, Greensmith facing them with his back to the driver. No one spoke.

On the longest platform at Sydney Terminal Station the train was ready to depart, the doors already closed, a uniformed porter stowing the final bags into the carriage, the guard with the whistle between his lips and the flag in his hand. But at the sight of Mr Greensmith running at him and waving both arms he paused. And whatever Mr Greensmith said, whoever's name he mentioned, was enough to make the guard lower his flag and fling open a door and even allow himself a little bow and a mumbled, 'Sir,' and, 'My lady,' and one or two people stuck their heads out of windows and wondered at the tall gentleman and his smart wife who had held up the train yet swept into the first-class carriage with all the dignity of the Governor himself, though the man scowled darkly and his wife stared before her as though she saw nothing and was not really there at all.

At last the whistle was blown and the flag waved and the train set off on its journey westwards to the mountains and beyond.

For a time no one spoke. They had reserved a compartment and having found it and seated themselves—Eleanor at the window, Alasdair opposite with Greensmith beside him—they sat in silence

239

as the railway yards at Redfern flew by, followed in quick succession by the suburbs of Stanmore and Petersham and Lewisham. Alasdair studied some documents then lit a cigar. At Ashfield Greensmith offered to go in search of refreshments. It was not known if refreshments were available or not but he seemed anxious to go in search of some, even if meant jumping off the train to do so.

'And, for God's sake, find me a newspaper,' Alasdair called after him. 'Dashed if I know what happened to mine.'

The door slammed shut behind him and a moment later they set off again and it was not known whether Mr Greensmith had rejoined the train via another carriage or been left behind.

A train travelling in the other direction sped past, causing the windows to rattle and the compartment to fill with noise. They passed large merchants' houses with long, shady gardens that dipped down to the railway line. In one of these gardens two little girls in white dresses and wide straw hats waved at their train. Eleanor watched the two little girls, their smiling, upturned faces, the shady strip of lawn dotted with trees on which they stood, the solid respectability of the large merchant's house behind them, and she felt that she envied them a little. In an instant the two little girls had gone and she had not returned their wave.

'How *dare* you rebuke me in front of others, Alasdair.'

She turned to face her husband as she spoke, not knowing, really, that she would speak but, now that she had, a great flood washed over her and it seemed the few words she had spoken barely touched on all she felt, all that she had endured.

Alasdair did not move and it seemed that he would make no reply. But his hands, shuffling through the pile of papers, became still. 'You are my wife. I shall rebuke you if I choose.' He did not look up.

She turned away and stared straight ahead at the window and another train rushed past with a whoosh of steam and noise, and when the train was gone the whoosh of steam and noise went on, it seemed, inside her own head.

The houses were less densely packed now, the streets wider. The train stopped at Granville and Mr Greensmith re-entered the compartment triumphantly with tea that no one drank. They went through Blacktown, Rooty Hill, St Marys and Werrington. Now the streets were unpaved, then there were no streets at all, just tracks, and the trees were all eucalypts and paperbarks, the creeks dry, the homesteads sparse.

Outside Kingswood the train screamed to a halt and the undrunk tea spilled from the cups and splashed onto Alasdair's papers and Eleanor was flung forward and only Mr Greensmith's quick thinking saved her from falling.

'Good God, what the devil do they mean by stopping so suddenly?' said Alasdair.

'I shall go and see, Mr Dunlevy,' said Greensmith, already pulling open the door.

Eleanor regained her seat. Some part of her was bruised and tender though she did not attempt to find out which part.

Through the window blue gums stretched from ridge to ridge as far as the eye could see. If Penrith lay a mile or two up the line, it was well hidden. She and Alasdair had come this way, Eleanor remembered, in the early days of their marriage, when Alasdair was campaigning for his first seat. They had stayed the night in a pub, sleeping in a wretched and rickety old bed that looked like it had come out with the First Fleet and been slept in by every convict and emancipist who had come this way since. An old Aboriginal woman who cleaned the place had said, *The Governor slept here once*, though which governor she had been unable to say. She had left them with a shrug and a candle and they had fallen, with the fury of youth, onto the bed because it was the early months of their marriage. And Eleanor remembered how the bed had shaken and the plaster had crumbled from the wall. She had been coy at first about their nights together, because it seemed this must be what her new husband wished her to be, but when she had not been coy he seemed to like it more and so she abandoned coyness and she had abandoned herself, enjoying her nakedness and relishing the moments when she shocked him. And while his thoughts had seemed often elsewhere during the daytime, and she had known they dwelled occasionally on other women, at night he had always returned to her. Now it seemed to Eleanor she could as soon reach out and touch the tip of the furthest blue gum as she could reach her husband across the small space of the train compartment.

'It is a great log!' cried Mr Greensmith, returning to the compartment and full of the news he brought. 'Laid across the tracks and put there deliberately, they are saying. A railway official has come down the line from the next station to warn us and had the driver not seen him and stopped in time we would be wrecked for certain!'

'Good heavens!' said Eleanor. 'Are we quite safe, Mr Greensmith, in your opinion?'

And: 'This is monstrous!' said Alasdair, setting aside his papers, standing up and taking the cigar from his mouth as though there were an important decision to be made and he was the one to make it. 'Is it generally known that I am on this train, Greensmith?'

'There has been no announcement, Mr Dunlevy, but it might reasonably be ascertained by anyone acquainted with your schedule. Or it might merely be coincidence.'

Greensmith looked at his employer unhappily. A sense that this might in some small but vital way be his responsibility seemed to weigh heavily on the young man's shoulders.

He turned to Eleanor. 'Yes, Mrs Dunlevy, I feel sure we are safe enough. The station is sending down a carriage to take us to Penrith. Though, as there is no very good road nearby, I fear it may take some little time to reach us.'

'Then I suggest,' said Alasdair, 'that we wait in the relative safety and anonymity of this compartment until such time as it arrives.'

'We shall be very late for the mayor's reception,' said Eleanor.

They were very late. The carriage when it came could get no nearer than a drover's track that passed close to the railway some five hundred yards up the line and so the party was required to alight from the stranded train and make its way on foot along the track to the place. Their journey along the five hundred yards of railway track in the chilly air of the lower mountains was made for the most part in silence, Eleanor—a step or two behind her husband, who had set a demanding pace—holding her skirts with as much decorum as the situation allowed for and leaning heavily on Mr Greensmith's arm. And when it generally became known that a carriage had come to take the stranded passengers on to Penrith there was a great rush of persons exiting the train and making their way along the track only for a nasty scene to follow when it became clear there was only one carriage and only four passengers could be taken. It also transpired that two officials—councillors from neighbouring districts—were aboard the train and were also making their way to the mayor's reception, which meant Mr Greensmith found himself turned out of the carriage and told to make his way as best he could by other means.

News of the incident had proceeded them.

'You poor dear things!' exclaimed the mayoress, who was a mature lady with a great many children and so understood about mishaps and unforeseen circumstances, even if they did not usually involve wrecked trains and stranded ministers. Cups of warm punch of an alarming red colour were produced and the special guests and the two councillors from neighbouring districts—who had made themselves indispensable during the bumpy thirty-minute carriage ride to Penrith pointing out various local landmarks—were made welcome.

'Well, well, no harm done,' said the mayor a number of times, clapping one or two people on the back as though it were a big sporting occasion at which a cup had been played for and lost. He was a large, bluff, red-faced sheep farmer who wore a suit that had seen many seasons and looked like it might originally have been borrowed from a passing swagman. He proudly wore a stockman's hat on his head and spoke as fondly to the three blue cattle dogs that ran at his heels as he did to his wife and many children, who ran about at his heels every bit as much as the cattle dogs did.

*Had* no harm been done? Everyone was very keen to laugh loudly and make light of it, but had they not almost died? Eleanor smiled and touched her gloved fingers to a great many people's hands and said a great many polite things to a great many people but it all seemed a little unreal. Had they almost died? She did not know. She wished someone would tell her. She could see that her shoes were ruined and this was irrefutable proof of something—but what? And she was shivering, could not stop in fact, but that was likely due to the cold.

It soon became clear that the official reception—a sit-down luncheon followed by official speeches—was to be held outside, and certainly the sky blinded with its brilliance and the sun shone and this was Sydney, after all—or close to it—and so they must sit and endure outside and never mind that it was very chilly indeed and there was clear evidence of a frost from earlier in the day.

It was not Sydney; it was thirty miles from Sydney. A flock of noisy cockatoos swooped and circled overhead, sheep wandered in and out of the reception, and in a neighbouring paddock a mob of ten or twenty kangaroos had gathered at a dam to drink. The local landowners and the drovers and the squatters and their wives and children milled about eating ice cream and drinking great quantities of lemonade and smiling at one another and tipping their hats as though they had never before ventured outside in their best clothes except to go to church. They gazed at the minister from parliament but mostly they gazed at his wife, who had about her an ethereal and otherworldly quality they could not put their fingers on much less put into words—a grace, was it? an elegance, an aloofness?—and who wore a hat the like of which they had never seen in Penrith before. But for the most part they strolled about giving scant attention to the dignitaries seated at the table, their loosely swinging limbs, their louche expressions, clearly said, Do not come here from the city and offer us the World when you will surely hand us a stone. The talk was of the price of wool and very little else, and when they did venture to talk of the upcoming Federation referendum it was in terms of how it might affect the price of wool and some of the men thought it might affect it and some thought it might not and some thought this a good thing and others a bad. And when Mr Greensmith finally joined them, out of breath, red-faced and missing the handkerchief that had started the day in his top pocket, he did so just in time to be handed a small bunch of wilting grevilleas presented to Eleanor by a small, shy child in a grass-smeared white smock.

The lunch, great slabs of steaming grey meat cut from the carcasses of several sheep that had been roasting on spits all day, was served to the official guests seated at a row of cloth-covered tables, and those who were not official guests ate their meat with their fingers as they wandered about or stood in little groups and the juices ran down their chins and along their arms and onto the ground where the dogs lapped it up and whined for more. Eleanor ate very little. The sight of so many slabs of meat, so much juice running down the chins of so many people, shrunk her throat. The meat turned sour on her tongue. Her stomach shrivelled.

'We make our own relish, Mrs Dunlevy,' announced the lady mayoress. 'It has junipers in it, of all things!'

'How charming,' said Eleanor, not taking any. On her left the mayor was explaining to her husband some new method of irrigation and she watched Alasdair give the man his full attention, offer up some appropriate comment, give the scheme his full consideration, when she could see he was no more present than she herself was, could see some metronome beating time behind his eyes. He exchanged glances, often, with Greensmith, who looked more wretched by the hour.

'But why, Mr Dunlevy, should the capital of our nation not be right here, in Penrith?' demanded an alderman seated on Eleanor's right and leaning over her so that he almost dislodged her hat in his eagerness to gain an audience with her husband, the minister.

'Here?' said Alasdair. He smiled. 'Why, sir, because it is not the required hundred miles from Sydney, that is why. The bill is quite clear on that point, and Penrith cannot be more than thirty miles at most.'

But the man would not be put off.

'I have heard the people of Goulburn were not the required distance either, that they were only some ninety-six miles from Sydney, but they got the under-secretary to resurvey the map and found that their city was a hundred miles distance after all, that it was in fact a hundred and four miles!'

'Yes, I had heard that,' Alasdair admitted. 'And in the process they found that Bathurst, their most bitter rival, was suddenly a mere ninety-eight miles distant and so no more in the running.' He allowed himself a smile at the petty jealousies of the regions. 'But I doubt the most obliging surveyor in the colony could find you another seventy miles, sir.'

The alderman sat back, deflated and defeated by geography.

'That is my youngest,' said the lady mayoress, indicating a bare-foot child of indeterminate sex some little distance away. Eleanor looked and saw the child in grubby whites, licking its fingers, and she did not know if she was meant to congratulate or commiserate or merely to observe. She smiled and said nothing.

The mayor stood up, and those who had voted for him in the recent mayoral election clapped and cheered, and those who had not jeered and turned their backs, and those from outlying stations or who had travelled down from the mountains that morning to attend the event looked on indifferently or helped themselves to more meat, for there was plenty left over.

'Friends,' said the mayor, holding up his hands for silence. 'We are fortunate to be joined today by the Honourable Mr Alasdair Dunlevy, member of the Legislative Assembly, minister and promi-nent supporter of the Federation—'

At which a great shout went up.

'—and should the men of this great colony of New South Wales decide to vote in favour of the Federation, which I am certain we shall—'

Another shout, louder this time.

'—then he is sure to take up a seat at the new federal parlia-ment—wherever that may be!'

There was laughter now, but also a rumbling of discontent.

Alasdair stood up and the mayor sat down.

'My fellow New South Welshmen,' he began. 'My fellow Australians!'

And as the men surged closer and the cheers followed, the minister settled into his speech and Eleanor watched her husband's shoulders go back and his chin come up and his chest puff out and she remembered the early days. She remembered campaigning for his first seat in places just like this, or worse, where the men came just so they could have an excuse to stand around and drink a bottle of beer, and if a fight did not break out it was only because not enough men had come. Town after town, speech after speech, and she had stood at his side and afterwards cleaned the blood and the spittle from his clothes and from his face. There had been an untamed, frontier feel to the colony in those days. On election days they had witnessed voters being beaten, they had seen drays filled with people paid to go from one polling station to another to vote, changing their clothes and voting sometimes more than once in the same place. There was nothing to stop them. Alasdair had lost. Time after time Alasdair had lost.

And she had stood at his side.

'This is our time!' said Alasdair. 'History is ours for the taking!'

'*It is a sellout!*' came a loud voice from the front of the crowd and a man lunged forward, a settler, a huge man but hollowed out and weather-worn and crushed by years of drought and taxes and hard work. The crowd surged and swelled around him. 'You think you can come here from the city and tell us what is good for us? What is good for our families? *You know nothing of us!*'

The man swayed drunkenly and the fury swelled in his veins so that the beer bottle he grasped shattered in his hands. The crowd opened up around him.

'I know enough to know when a fellow is drunk and needs his wife to take him home,' retorted Alasdair and the crowd laughed, though some did not. Some muttered angrily and went to the assistance of the man who may not be their friend but who was their neighbour, nonetheless, and whose drought they had shared and whose funerals they had attended.

'And why was the Premiers' Conference held in Melbourne?' called out another man. 'Why behind closed doors in secret? *What were they hiding?*'

'The bill is the same as it was last year *and we rejected it last year!*'

'What about *our rivers*? There is no protection for us New South Welshmen to control *our own rivers!*'

But these were lone voices and the crowd moved around them, jostling and enjoying the fun. An ibis that had wandered into the crowd in search of food got itself trodden on and flapped noisily into the air, squawking indignantly, and the people around it laughed.

It was an afternoon's entertainment. History was in their hands, these people who laughed at a silly bird and who wandered about foolishly like children at a party.

But Alasdair smiled at them good-naturedly. Until one man called out, 'Your fancy wife looks like she ain't never done a hard day's work in her life but because she shares her bed with a politician that gives her the right to sit up there all high and mighty, does it? Let her spend the night with a real man and I will teach her a thing or two about wifely duties!'

For a moment no one spoke. The crowd seemed frozen as in a montage, the cockatoos fell silent and the kangaroos in the next paddock lifted their heads, their noses twitching.

Eleanor, too, lifted her head though it felt strangely heavy and the air around her had a viscous, glue-like quality, and she looked to her husband. But he, like herself, was frozen. No words came from his lips. No anger sprung to his eyes. No muscle moved on his face. He remained silent.

Beside her the mayor scrambled to his feet.

'You are a *disgrace*, sir. Leave at once or you will find yourself in a cell overnight. This lady is our most honoured guest and our treatment of her will be no less than it would be were the wife of the Governor himself here, or Her Majesty the Queen,' and he bowed low before the minister's wife as if she were indeed the Queen, sweeping off his hat and resuming his seat. The crowd, released from its horror by the mayor's gallant rebuttal, cheered and went about its business and forgot what had been said a moment earlier by someone in their midst.

But Eleanor sat quite still.

And when it was time to go it was James Greensmith, her husband's secretary, who held her arm and escorted her to the carriage, and with such a look on his face one might believe he would gladly have hunted down and killed with his bare hands the man who had insulted her.

# CHAPTER EIGHTEEN

# DO NOT TAKE
# OUR WORD FOR IT

*I shall be glad to take the infant,* Mrs Flowers had replied in a hand that was cramped and consequently a little difficult to read, for she had, it seemed, much to convey and the square of the notepaper she used was small and rather cheap. A sum was mentioned and a meeting place proposed two days hence at Sydney Terminal Station at a very late hour appropriate to a transaction such as this. Alice must come alone with the child and bring any clothing the child might have. And the money, of course. The foster parents, she was assured, were a good Christian couple who lived on a parcel of land outside of the city. The child would thrive, the child would be happy and healthy, and Alice would be provided with regular accounts of how it fared. She need have no concerns.

Alice sat at the rear of a tram, the letter in her pocket. She had brought it with her as proof that the woman, Mrs Flowers, existed. She was going to show it to Milli, though how good Milli's letter reading was or if she would be allowed to read a letter at all Alice did not know, but she had brought it anyway, for luck. As proof.

For Milli did not even know her baby was rescued! She did not know her baby lived. She would be frantic, and Alice imagined herself saying those words, *I have saved the baby, Milli!*, and she imagined Milli's face, her tears. Alice's heart swelled with the joy she was bringing.

She gazed out of the window at the squat workers' cottages of Darlinghurst. She clutched her ticket and leaned her head against the glass. The day shone brightly but the inside of the tram was musty and dirt-encrusted, and tobacco and spittle had turned the floor to a sticky brown glue. The tram had trundled its way around Potts Point and into Woolloomooloo and was now rattling down Riley Street as though it had all the time in the world and Alice regretted already her decision not to go on foot. The tram was an extravagance but the letter in her pocket, the news she brought, had made her reckless, had made her extravagant. She had never been a bringer of joy before; it was not a role she had ever imagined for herself.

The tram rattled on its way, stopping every hundred yards or so as the people shuffled off and other people shuffled on. The gaol was just a mile or so from the streets she and Milli had grown up in, but everything about this journey was strange and unfamiliar. She may as well have been visiting Milli on the moon, or in Melbourne.

It would become familiar though. *Three years' hard labour.* She had said the words over and over in her head until they became an invocation, until they had ceased to have any meaning at all. She made herself think about it now, about the three years' hard labour.

But she could not do so! She saw the people seated all about her. She saw the mean little dwellings of Riley Street. It would become real only once she had visited Milli there, seen that dreadful place with her own eyes, was witness to Milli's ruin. Afterwards, she would always picture Milli there, no matter where she was or what she was doing. It would be her punishment. For escaping that life.

The tram lurched forward and the people stood in the aisles as there were no more seats. It stopped outside a Jewish candle maker with a tailor's premises upstairs. Alice knew this shop, this corner. They had walked these streets as children, hurrying home in the dark from somewhere, carrying something, a loaf of bread, perhaps, still warm from the baker's oven, on one occasion squabbling about a coin found on the ground or left over from the purchase. And Milli, who was taller and stronger, had easily held the coin out of her reach and Alice had jumped up and down and cried with frustration. When they had got home Mr Purley had taken the penny and struck Milli so that blood poured from her mouth and Alice had run and hidden under the stairs. It was the first time she had hidden there, but Milli had found her. It was the first time Milli had said, *I will not let him hurt you, Alice, I will not!*

The tram rattled on its way. 'He is not our real dad,' Milli had said, often, as though she worried Alice might think Mr Purley was their father, though Alice never had, not for a moment. Milli remembered their real dad, or said she did. Was he a good man? Alice had wondered, but she had never asked, afraid of the answer. No man, in her experience, was good. Father McCreadie, perhaps, but that was different—and she had heard things about him, though he had always been kind to her. And Mr Dunlevy, she supposed, was good, though the rules of good and bad seemed to apply differently to he and Mrs Dunlevy, and she only dimly perceived them. But their real dad, had he been a good man? It had troubled her as a child.

The tram shuddered to a halt. She had taken the tram because it would take her far out of her way and delay the moment of arriving, she saw that now, but the moment was upon her. Here she was already walking up Forbes Street and there was nothing could stop her. Except perhaps herself.

The gaol filled the sky. A place so large in her mind and now in reality that Alice could not fix her gaze upon it. Instead she turned her gaze downwards to the pavement, to the swishing skirts and lace-up boots of two young women walking ahead of her who had got off at the same stop. They came to the entrance of the gaol and the two women walked past and onwards and Alice followed, walked all the way to the corner of Burton Street. Here the two women turned and were soon gone, their lives going in a different direction. Alice kept on walking. She walked the circumference of the prison and found herself lost because it had not four sides but five. A pentagon, of sorts. As though the normal rules of construction had been abandoned here. Or perhaps it was merely an awkwardly shaped piece of land and an unskilled workforce. A watchtower nestled in the curiously angled corner where two sides of the five-sided building merged. Alice felt the gaze of the prison guard perched high up on the platform of the watchtower.

She found her way back to the entrance. Here two vast turrets the height of six men or more abutted the doorway. They had slits cut into them at intervals, behind which, in another century and in another hemisphere, a medieval archer might have crouched. Ornamental, Alice presumed, or perhaps a warning. The walls of the prison were carved from great slabs of sandstone that shone like blocks of gold in the afternoon sunlight. The marks of the convicts' tools could be seen in many of them, scratches and sometimes

initials. *I was here*, the convicts' marks said, *and do not forget it.*
The doors, black and solid, were firmly closed. And it was here, not
so very long ago, that the people of Darlinghurst and beyond—for
it was a great spectacle—had stood to watch murderers hanged.
There had been a platform for the hangings over the doorway so
the people below could watch. Her mother had come here as a girl
to view a famous bushranger hanged. ('We was not so civilised in
them days,' though she had spoken with wonder of the bushranger's
legs kicking in the air.) The platform was gone now and in its place
these turrets built, and above the door a magnificent prancing lion
and a unicorn, carved out of the stone right where the platform
had once stood, as though such beasts, such craftsmanship, were
proof of the civilisation of the people, of the city.

Alice held her tram ticket tightly as one might a rosary or a
good luck charm. While she still held it in her hand her journey
had not ended. But she was ashamed of her dread; it seemed a
poor thing indeed for a visitor who was here for an hour and then
gone to be afraid when Milli was inside, a prisoner.

She gazed up at the door. And her heart broke. The women
prisoners had their hair shaved off, she had heard. But she thought,
too, of the joy she was bringing.

She knocked loudly on the door.

Some small portion of the door—for she was not significant
enough to warrant opening the whole thing—was slowly eased
open and a sharp face observed her. What type of a man it was
who worked in such a place seemed clear at once from his crudely
carved features and the grim, grey uniform that clothed him, from
the great slab of a paw that pulled open the little door and the
small, black eyes that crawled over her person, at once suspicious
and speculative. He stood barring her way, but as Alice could see

other people like herself gathered in a little huddle beyond she
saw that the man only stood in her way because it pleased him
to do so.

The door closed behind her and she stood in a tiled hallway,
black-and-white squares beneath her feet, steps leading upwards
to her left, a guards' room to her right and another set of doors,
closed, before her. Notices and signs every way she turned warned
what she might do and what she might not do. Dire penalties
were invoked. Were the men still flogged? Alice wondered. Or
the women?

It was not so long ago they had been a penal colony.

The hall was uncomfortably crowded. A silent, shuffling,
fidgeting crowd who stood about loosely or leaned against the
wall scratching and picking at themselves. Their boots had holes in
them and their heads were covered with shawls; they clutched sad
little baskets of food close to their chests; they were reeling drunk.
One—a young man in a torn shirt—held a Bible and murmured
to himself; another—a youth with a lame leg—concealed a razor
blade in his shoe and when the guards found it the boy was beaten
and thrown onto the street. No one seemed surprised. No one
watched. Alice was searched too, a giant of a man in a straining
grey tunic with tiny staring black eyes and large callused hands
who patted her roughly and thrust a hand inside her clothing
and another up her skirt, turning her about this way and that as
he pleased, laughing when she tried to stop him. No one seemed
surprised. No one watched. The man smelled of damp earth and
rotting food and stale sweat. When he had finished with Alice
he thrust her away.

A window was cut into the wall of the guards' room and here
a third guard was stationed. Behind him a small wood-burning

stove smoked quietly, the remains of a meal could be seen. Hanging from the walls were truncheons and various other implements that might be pressed into service to supress a man or many men. And a telephone, incongruous amid the paraphernalia of an earlier and more brutal century.

'What prisoner?' the man demanded of her. He clasped a pen in his fist.

'Milli Nimrod,' Alice said. She spoke in a low voice, wanting no one else to hear her sister's name spoken in such a place, though what difference it made she did not know. 'Millicent.'

The clerk wrote this down with a laborious hand, his pen scratching audibly on the thick parchment of his ledger.

Another man appeared, more senior perhaps, for he looked over the man's shoulder at what he had written and swore at him and pulled at the man's arm to drag him away. Alice was left to wait, but it was not long before a door was unlocked and the sorry little crowd shuffled through to another place. Alice attempted to follow but the guard barred her way. He locked the door and leaned against it and looked at her. Now the hall was empty, just herself and him.

And suddenly Alice was frightened.

The guard pushed himself up off the door and his eyes did not leave her face. He took a step towards her and his gaze slid slowly over her. The smell in the small room had changed subtly. There was an acrid smell. The smell of fear. Her own fear. Alice kept her eyes on the man's face, not for a moment leaving it, but another part of her, the part that had grown up on these streets, that had lived all those years in a room with Mr Purley, darted left and right about the small room, assessing it, taking in the two locked doors, the pen that the clerk had used and had left on the desk—was it within her reach?—and the walls themselves, thick and solid enough that a head bashed against it would render a man insensible for a time. She had nothing on her person save for the letter from the woman, Mrs Flowers, and her tram ticket. The ticket fluttered now to the floor.

The guard had come no closer; he appeared to be waiting. There would be others then, not just one. Alice felt the panic rising in her. When the two guards who had left reappeared she braced herself, heard her own breathing, quick, jagged. Her fingers closed into fists.

One of the guards put his head through the hole in the wall and indicated to her. 'You! Come here.'

She did not move.

He shrugged. 'Suit yourself.' He consulted the ledger. Looked up. The other guard stood at his shoulder, ignoring his colleague and watching her, studying her it seemed. The first one spoke again. 'Millicent Nimrod, was it?'

Alice waited, then nodded.

'Deceased,' he said, closing the ledger with a snap.

For a time no one spoke. None of the guards moved. They just watched her, in a detached way; curious, it seemed. And slightly amused.

'No,' said Alice, shaking her head. 'She is here, my sister. Milli.'

'No, she ain't. I just told you. She is deceased. Dead. Hung herself. This morning. Found in her cell.'

'Do not take our word for it. You shall read of it in tomorrow's paper,' said the guard who stood behind him and who seemed fascinated by the young woman's reaction to the news.

'Here is her things,' said the first man, pushing a meagre parcel tied with string through the opening. 'Take it.'

But Alice could not take it. Alice could not move.

'Give her some brandy,' said one of them. 'Oh, but I clean forgot—we are all out of brandy!'

And they laughed.

Alice took the parcel. She left the prison and walked down Forbes Street and this time she did not take the tram. This time she walked.

CHAPTER NINETEEN

# OFFENCES AGAINST THE PERSON

'Will you go to the police, sir, with the letter that warned of the accident on the line?' said James Greensmith as they sat in the compartment of the afternoon express train on its return journey to the city.

And thus was the existence of the letter, delivered that morning by the secretary's own hand and up to this point kept from her by her husband, made known to Eleanor Dunlevy. Not the details of its contents, perhaps, but enough for her to understand it predicted dire calamity should the minister and his entourage venture to the west that day. The unfortunate Greensmith, whose indiscretion this was (earning him a look of furious disbelief from his employer), fell silent. He had stopped short of producing the letter—an illiterate missive penned in a childish hand that one no more heeded than a child's toy hurled in a tantrum—but there was little point now in denying that the letter existed, that its warning had almost come true.

No one spoke.

Eleanor said nothing. She sat staring out of the train window and Alasdair was witness to every sort of emotion that now flitted across his wife's face; indeed he could feel each one, her fury, her disbelief, her fear, perhaps (though of this he was less certain), and the compartment fairly crackled with it all the way home.

As the front door closed behind them she turned to him, her anger white hot. 'You *knew*? You had received a warning but *you did nothing?*'

And it was as well that the maid, who ought to have opened the door to them but had not, was nowhere to be seen.

'Of course I did not know!' Alasdair replied, his justifications already prepared, for it had been a long train ride home. 'Certainly I received a vague threat in an anonymous note, which is nothing unusual in my position, though I do not always choose to share it with you. If I acted on every crazed threat that I received I should never go anywhere and these malefactors would have their victory.'

She seemed hardly to hear him, was half turned away, her jaw set tightly, but now she spun back to him, her eyes flashing furiously. 'I understood it was not a vague threat at all but a most precise threat concerning our train journey today.'

And Alasdair damned his imbecilic and imprudent secretary.

'I would not say so—'

'Show it to me! The note: show me!'

It crossed his mind to refuse—it was his right to do so—but the absurdity of this was too great and so he retrieved it from his pocket and handed it to her.

She took the letter and opened it and her hand, he saw, shook a little. She read it quickly, for there was not much there other than the threat to their lives. And it proved her point, of course, that the threat was specific. She crushed the note in her hand and again turned away from him.

'You would put all our lives in danger,' she said quietly, but the fury had not gone; if anything, it was deeper now. 'Not just yours and mine and James's—'

James, was it!

'—but everyone on that train, every man, woman and child.'

She did not look at him as she said this, but her fury was gone and he realised, finally, that his wife had been frightened.

Alasdair located spills and a box of matches and after a few false starts lit the fire in his study, watching as the coals finally caught and began to glow. The night was noticeably milder here on the coast than it had been at Penrith earlier in the day, but he needed this fire. Yet the coals seemed to emit no heat, he felt nothing, neither heat not cold, not the carpet beneath his feet nor the spent match in his hand. He crouched before the fire, a little mesmerised by it, and the maid's absence, an annoyance at first, no longer seemed so. He wished this fire to be his alone and no one else's.

After some little time, during which no thoughts disturbed him and his mind was still, he stood up. He rubbed his eyes.

Someone had laid a pylon on the railway line with the sole intention of wrecking a train, or at least derailing it. And not just any train either: *his* train. They had not succeeded, but for those few precious seconds when the driver had spotted the obstruction and had slammed on his brakes, as the train had screamed to a stop and life—*his* life—had been held in the balance, he had experienced a feeling almost of euphoria. He had thought, *What if it is to end now, what of it?*

But it had not. Life continued. His, Eleanor's.

He went to his desk. He retrieved a small key and opened each drawer in turn and went through its contents, pulling items out and, with a rapid appraisal, studying each and every one: parliamentary papers, old speeches, drafts and notes for speeches never given, correspondence with constituents, with secretaries, with other parliamentarians, with family members now long dead. There were scrawled notes, envelopes, bills, dockets, tickets, invitations, personal and ministerial diaries going back a decade and more, the original documents and plans for the house, his marriage certificate, a studio portrait of his mother and father—yellowed and mottled with age. And when he had gone through each drawer he started on the polished walnut bookshelves that lined two walls, floor to ceiling, and that contained volumes of parliamentary records and constitutional law and political biographies, and in among them old maps of the colony, school-era Latin and Ancient Greek texts, even some old sea charts and his worn and much-annotated copy of Watkin Tench's explorations. He pulled out each book, searching inside their covers and behind them.

Nothing. There was nothing.

He stood in the centre of the room. The sweat glistened on his forehead and pooled on his upper lip and at the back of his neck, his shirt was damp and clung to his skin but his body felt cold. Clammy.

He would not panic. Alasdair Dunlevy, Secretary for Public Monies, was not that sort of man, yet it was hard to ignore the myriad hectic thoughts darting about like tiny fish in a pond inside his head, and he could not catch a single one nor make sense of them singly or collectively.

He went to his dressing room and rummaged through each trouser pocket, each coat pocket—but it was absurd! Anything left in his clothing would have long ago been found by the maid and, if not her, then by the laundry.

If he *had* left something in a pocket . . .

No, there was nothing, he was certain of it. And last night he had gone through this same exercise at his office in Richmond Terrace, just as thoroughly, just as frenziedly, and finding only what he had known was there—the original letter from the Woolloomooloo letting agent agreeing to Alasdair's terms and delivered to a box at the post office and addressed to a name that was not his own, receipts for each month's rent of the Woolloomooloo apartment (paid in cash, in advance), and one or two, perhaps five or six, notes from Verity herself, receipts and bills for items he had purchased for her and that was all—and all now destroyed. He had gathered it all up and gone into the park under cover of the early winter darkness and found an incinerator and had tossed the few items into it and watched them ignite. The embers had glowed then floated up into the night air and vanished. He had thought he would feel relief but instead, somewhere inside him, a voice had cried out in anguish.

There was nothing of Verity Trent here at his home, he was sure of it, yet the fear that he had missed something had gnawed away at him all day.

Alasdair pulled up a chair and sat down. He thought about lighting a cigar but something about the act smacked too much of self-satisfaction and he did not feel self-satisfied. A drink then. He dug out an unopened bottle of malt whisky from the bottom of a cupboard and a tumbler and poured himself a quantity.

There were no documents left that might incriminate him, but what of those who had witnessed him, the people who had seen him and could connect him with Verity? The man, Orange, the letting agent, who knew him by sight, certainly, but not by name. The same could be said for the two neighbours, the elderly woman— who in any case was blind or close to it—and the rather helpful, rather too curious Miss Tiptree. He worried about Miss Tiptree. Had anyone seen him at the house during the months he had visited Verity there? He thought not, but how could one be sure? His visits had mostly been at night but not always, not that last time. That had been morning, broad daylight.

And the folly of this struck him. Well, there was no helping it now.

Then there was the elderly hospital clerk. Alasdair had sat across a desk from the man and conversed with him, told the man he was a minister of state (though not given his name, lied about his constituency) and provided a plausible reason, a justifiable reason even, for his interest in the girl. Surely he could only be implicated if all these various persons were brought together and connected to him, and why should they be?

He wondered if there might be anything at Verity's apartment.

He knocked back the whisky and walked to the window. The curtains were drawn. It was the first thing he had done on entering the room but now he tweaked the curtain aside and peered out into the darkness. He saw only his own reflection. The windowpane was cold beneath his fingers and his breath created a smear of mist on the glass.

There were notes he had written to her, a dozen at least he estimated, mostly arranging appointments, some accompanying flowers and other gifts, but never signed, never with an address. In his handwriting, of course, but who could prove it? One of those notes to Verity, the last one, had gone missing. He wondered about that. She had claimed not to have received it. A ruse, presumably, so that she could miss the appointment with him. So that she might, instead, attend her own appointment with this . . . doctor.

There was nothing else.

He turned back to the room, surveyed it.

He thought: Verity has done this, not me. The crime—an appalling crime!—had been committed by her, along with whatever unscrupulous doctor she had unearthed and colluded with. He, Alasdair, had not been a party to it.

But had he, unwittingly?

He returned to the bookshelf and pulled out a volume of criminal law. The Offences against the Person Act, 1861, Section 58. He could not recall ever reading it before. *Any woman being convicted of offence of using drugs or instruments to procure abortion shall be liable to be kept in penal servitude for life.*

*Life!* And this was an amendment to the 1837 Act, which had previously specified the death penalty.

He stood up and took a turn about the room. But there was more. Section 59 stated that anyone found to be supplying or procuring poison or instruments for the purpose of criminal abortion should be liable to be kept in penal servitude.

He thought hard. He had not supplied her with anything— except money, on a number of occasions. Money which she, presumably, had spent on this appalling act. Did that make him liable or not? He thought not, but he wasn't sure. He pulled the book towards him and read and reread the passage but the words did not change; they said each time penal servitude for life.

He was unable to take it in. Ought he to consult his solicitor? Good God no, that would set him on a path he did not need, nor wish, to go down. He had already done all he could to mitigate his risk.

He closed the volume and carefully replaced it, replaced it all so that anyone coming in here—and who aside from the maid would come in here?—would see nothing out of place. He ran a hand along the spines of the beautiful leather-bound volumes of constitutional law. The law had been his friend, in an abstract way, but now it had turned on him.

At a sound outside he lowered the light down to almost nothing and tweaked aside the curtain. Someone was down there on the path. It was Alice, returned late. As he watched she stopped, seemed to stumble and crouched down, her hands on the ground, her head lowered. What was she doing? Was the girl ill? He stepped back from the window and replaced the curtain before she saw him.

He crouched again before the fire. He had wished this fire to be his alone and no one else's so that he could feed it with his memories, dead memories, memories that might cost him dearly, cost his reputation, his career, his marriage, his freedom even, but he had found nothing to burn. All the memories were here in his head and in his heart and he could not burn them. He had no wish to burn them. He did not want to abandon her.

Even though she had taken their child.

CHAPTER TWENTY

# THE LETHARGY OF INDIFFERENCE

Two mornings later the first post brought a note from Marian Dempsey proposing Eleanor accompany her to the anti-bill demonstration arranged by the Women's Suffrage League at Darlington town hall that evening and at which Miss Dempsey's brother was to speak.

'How extraordinary!' said Eleanor, frowning over the note. 'Surely Marian Dempsey understands you are an ardent supporter of the Federation, Alasdair? And yet she would invite me to an anti-bill demonstration.'

And she passed the note to him, offered with it her brightest smile, yet her words sounded brittle even to her own ears, and the smile froze a little on her face. They had spoken on a handful of occasions since Wednesday evening and on each occasion her words had been thus, brittle, unnatural, and her husband's replies terse, his fury suppressed. Though it was herself, surely, who ought to be furious?

Why was it always herself brokering the truce, placating?

Alasdair did not take the note. He did not look up from the morning newspaper.

'Perhaps she believes you do not share my views,' he said.

'I have never said as much.'

'And do you?' He lowered his newspaper paper and regarded her. 'Share my views?' There was something rather cold in his question, and in his eyes.

'Naturally. I am your wife.'

After a moment's silence he went back to his newspaper.

Alice came in then, going to the fire and stoking it with a poker. It was the first morning they had had the fire lit over breakfast and Alice seemed unable to judge its efficacy as she returned continually to refuel it and nurse it. The girl gave a violent shiver that was excessive, or seemed so to her mistress, for really the morning was quite mild. The flames leaped up now and Alice moved a firescreen before it.

And Alasdair did not stir, studying the newspaper as though it were a sacred text.

'Is your speech at Penrith reported?' Eleanor enquired.

'Naturally,' he replied, echoing her own response of a moment earlier. Usually it pleased him to have his movements, his speeches, reported in the newspaper.

'Will you not read it to me? You used to.'

She wished at once she had not said that, *you used to*. It sounded plaintive, reproachful. She warmed her words with a smile that she did not feel and that he did not see.

'If you wish so much to read it then do so.' He sat back and tossed the paper across the table at her.

Eleanor took the paper, holding it tightly in her hands for she did not have her spectacles and could hardly make out the words.

But here it was, a brief paragraph headed DUNLEVY ARRIVES LATE AT PENRITH DUE TO DELAYED TRAIN, and it went on to describe the very tardy arrival of the ministerial party due to a mishap on the railway line that had severely delayed the train. There was no mention of train-wreckers. The speech itself was not reported, though the outburst of the vulgar man was, described as a single dissenter subsequently removed from the proceedings.

'How unfortunate,' Eleanor observed, and the events of two days ago, which up to that point had seemed a trial and a challenge but ultimately a duty performed (if not an absolute success), now seemed farcical, a failure. She was uncertain if she shared in that failure or if she mocked it. She said nothing further on the subject.

And on the same page she read: *Early in the week a Women's Federal League was formed at the Sydney Town Hall with Lady Harris (the Mayoress) president and the following vice-presidents: Mrs E. Barton, Mrs G.H. Reid, the Premier's wife—*

And on it went, listing in exquisite detail the names of the wives of most of the prominent ministers of the Legislative Assembly and the Council, all of whom, it appeared, had also been in attendance. The object of the newly formed league was to assist in the securing of a large majority for the bill. It was to meet the next afternoon at the town hall.

'But how extraordinary!' Eleanor exclaimed. 'I knew nothing of this. How was it I was not invited?' She read again the list of names. 'Mrs Price is to be honorary secretary, Mrs Forrester honorary treasurer! It is preposterous! What can Mrs Forrester know of accounting and finance? Can they have forgotten to invite me? Alasdair, do you not think it extraordinary?'

What if she had not been forgotten? What if she had been deliberately excluded? The spectre of Miss Trent, always present though occasionally silenced, materialised once more, immense and menacing. For if Eleanor had found out about Miss Trent, why should others not have done so, too?

It gripped her throat. An invisible hand clutching at her windpipe. Panic, and out of proportion to the situation, she saw that, but here it was. To be never free of this woman. To exist in the shadow of her own fear.

She reached for the bellpull.

'Alice, has any letter arrived for me in the last week that you have failed to deliver to me?'

'No, madam.'

'You are certain? Nothing has come that may have dropped and become hidden? Nothing still on the letter tray? Nothing you have given to Mr Dunlevy in error? Think carefully, girl.'

Alice shook her head. 'No, madam. I am certain of it.'

'But how can you be certain unless you have looked? Go now, and search in the hallway and see if there is anything. And search thoroughly, mind.'

'Yes, madam.'

'There was an invitation, I believe,' remarked Alasdair, when Alice had gone. He paused to pour milk into his coffee. 'It came to my office some days ago.'

For a time neither of them spoke. The sound of furniture being moved about could be heard from the hallway. Something clattered to the ground.

'Then, as they are to meet again tomorrow,' Eleanor announced, 'I believe I shall go.'

'As you wish,' Alasdair replied, and still he did not look at her. 'Though it is of no account. What can they achieve, I wonder, these women?' He reached over and reclaimed his newspaper. 'A wife's proper place remains at her husband's side. That is where she can achieve the most.'

'Really? You are to attend a meeting at Marrickville this evening, are you not? And yet you have not asked me to accompany you.'

And the truce she had attempted to broker crumbled to dust in the face of her fury.

Alice returned a little time later to announce that she was very sorry but no letter could be found. Should she continue searching elsewhere?

∞

'I am delighted you accepted my invitation, Mrs Dunlevy,' said Marian Dempsey that evening as they arrived at the town hall in Darlington. 'I had thought you were entirely caught up with the pro-bill set.'

'Really? Then why invite me?' said Eleanor, who was a little uncertain herself why she had accepted the invitation. She feared it was perverse. Alasdair had gone to his meeting at Marrickville and she had stood, once again, at the upstairs window and watched his departure, and the only person who had observed her was James Greensmith as he had stood holding the door of the cab.

'Because everyone else was otherwise engaged,' replied Miss Dempsey, with a candidness and simplicity that might have been utterly guileless. 'Thank you, my dear,' she said to the ardent young women who stood at the doorway to the hall and handed her a pamphlet.

Marian Dempsey was dressed in a neatly tailored slate-grey suit and a discreet little hat that was conservative and formal and entirely appropriate to a Women's Suffrage League meeting—which, perhaps, suggested she dressed otherwise at other times, which she did not. Miss Dempsey rarely looked her best in formal evening dress, or at her ease. The triviality and frivolousness of dinner conversations strained her innate earnestness and the extent of this only became evident when one witnessed her in the daytime at a meeting or a rally or organising and cajoling her brother, a task of which she never tired and at which she excelled. That she would have made the better parliamentarian than he had been observed many times and was perfectly true. It did, however, on occasion, make her a little dull. Eleanor had dressed in a suit too, but hers was lavender and her hat had a fascinating little gauze veil that she wore pulled down over her face.

Together they moved into a large room and looked about for a seat and Eleanor felt a sudden heaviness descend on her. Fury had carried her this far, but faced with yet another cheerless municipal hall, another platform of speakers, another hard-backed uncomfortable chair, her spirits waned. Must democracy be always so dreary?

And must it, always, be held in such wretched places? Darlington was a place of poorly built workers' dwellings, factories and workshops piled one on top of another with little thought for fresh air or sunlight. As their cab had swung into Darlington Road it had hit something which the driver said was a woman lying in the road, though he thought her already deceased on account of her not objecting when he ran over her. A crowd had quickly gathered and Eleanor and Miss Dempsey had abandoned the cab and gone the rest of the way on foot.

'I am attending the Women's Federal League tomorrow afternoon,' said Eleanor, arranging herself in a chair and looking around to see who else was here. There was no one—or no one whom she recognised. This was a relief. 'They have only recently formed and it is to be their first official meeting,' she went on, though at this moment the thought of it—of further democracy—appalled her. That meeting, at least, was to be held in the more salubrious surroundings of the Sydney Town Hall, and this appeased her. 'Lady Harris, the mayoress, is president and Mrs Reid and Mrs Barton shall be there.'

'Hedging your bets, are you?' said Miss Dempsey, nodding wisely. 'Or is this evening a chance to spy on the opposition?' And there was a gleam in her eye just as though it were all some childish game and Eleanor heard again Alasdair's words at breakfast: *It is of no account. What can they achieve, I wonder, these women?* And perhaps he was right: what could they achieve? Though his words had stung, as they were intended to.

'Should you find you require anonymity I am quite prepared to shield you with my parasol,' Miss Dempsey offered.

'I am intrigued to learn why Ned consented to speak here, Miss Dempsey,' said Eleanor, choosing to ignore what she took to be a facetious remark. 'Can it be he is secretly a champion of women's suffrage?'

'My brother is no champion of women's suffrage, you may be assured of that, though on this one issue his views and theirs do happen to coincide. There he is.' And Miss Dempsey nodded.

Eleanor looked though she could not, for the moment, make out Ned Dempsey. There were a great many women in the hall and all the seats were taken and many late arrivals stood at the rear and still others were trying to come in.

How extraordinary it was! These women stood about in excitable huddles, greeting one another, and proudly sporting their Women's Suffrage League sashes. They gathered close to the large platform and at the entranceway, accosting new arrivals and urging pamphlets on them or deflecting the crude jibes and catcalls of the young men who passed by outside or who ventured into the hall to ridicule them. One or two gentlemen, come legitimately to the meeting, shook the women's hands as though the ladies were gentlemen like themselves and they uttered gruff words of support or spoke loudly and pompously as though it were their meeting and they were the main event. And now Eleanor picked out Ned Dempsey, sometime member of the Legislative Assembly—though currently between constituencies—attired in his most formal suit and an old-fashioned silk cravat and spats, a top hat on his head, a cane in his hand, standing in the centre of the room talking in a loud voice and congratulating everyone, though nothing had been achieved yet and the meeting not yet begun.

Beside her Marian Dempsey sat proudly in her seat waiting for her brother to acknowledge her. She was always touchingly proud of him when he did little, other than his own unerring loyalty to her, to warrant it.

'Who is that fellow?' said Miss Dempsey.

Eleanor had just observed George Drummond-Smith in the entranceway to the hall, puffing a cigar and looking about him with slightly narrowed eyes as though he was taking the measure of the place. He swung about and looked directly at her but Eleanor ducked her head. Her flesh prickled and she had an uneasy sense of the room shrinking around her. Short of running into Alasdair himself, Drummond-Smith was the last man she wished to encounter here.

When she ventured to look again he had gone.

But evidently it was not George Drummond-Smith Marian Dempsey had meant, for a young man in the ill-fitting suit and bowler hat of the clerical classes was hailing them from across the room and now began to make his way over. He was upon them before Eleanor could reply, a slight figure with a thin, hungry face and bright, rapidly blinking eyes, clasping a notepad and a small stub of pencil which he licked as though he was about to take their order in a rather cheap hotel.

'Mrs Dunlevy,' he called as he approached, waving a hand to get their attention. 'Peters of the *Mail*. I did not expect to see the minister's wife here at an anti-bill demonstration.' And having located her, the blinking eyes latched onto her face and scrutinised every part of it as though he might find that which he most desired there.

Eleanor turned her head away, feeling a little sliver of ice prick her heart. 'We do not subscribe to your newspaper, Mr Peters, and consequently have nothing to say to you,' she declared, and proceeded to ignore him.

'Really!' said Miss Dempsey, when the young man had given up with a shrug and darted off. 'One does not expect to be hailed in a crowd as though one were a hansom cab.'

But the meeting was beginning and a small group had disengaged itself and was mounting the platform at the front of the hall. A number of chairs and a lectern had been positioned there and below them the rows of chairs were clustered very close to the front of the platform as though the person who had arranged the room did not expect any of the women to speak loudly enough. The speakers were introduced: the chair, the secretary, the honoured guests, a Miss Hickman and a Miss Scott and a Miss Jessup and Miss Taylor and a Miss—

But Eleanor found it was too many names all at once and, now that she studied them more closely, they all looked astonishingly similar. All spinsters, every one of them, past their prime and into their middle years or beyond, plainly dressed in brown and grey as though suffrage could come in no other colours but these. As though suffrage must be dull and dreary. And self-important and quite, quite irrelevant, and Eleanor sighed a little to herself for it was a little absurd and a little pathetic. And beside her Miss Dempsey, though she was no suffragist, leaned forward expectantly, breathlessly, but then Miss Dempsey was a spinster too. She too wore grey.

The chairman, a Miss Hickman, stood up and Ned Dempsey stood up too, and called loudly for quiet though the hall had largely fallen silent. Miss Hickman ignored the nod he gave her to proceed and began her address. It was a short address of welcome and high hopes and ended with an entreaty: 'Electors of this colony, in your own interests and in the interest of those to come after you, vote *No* on June twenty!'

*This was met by applause, both sustained and enthusiastic, and one or two of the younger and more ardent women in the hall rose to their feet and then sat down again, a little self-consciously.*

And Eleanor thought it was all very well her urging them all to vote *No*, but had it escaped everyone's notice that not a woman among them *could* vote? One might as well sit and lecture a roomful of blacks on the finer points of the constitution. It was absurd and, yes, a little pathetic. She smiled to herself because it was always pleasing to feel a little superior.

Miss Hickman resumed her seat and Ned Dempsey leaned over and patted her arm and uttered something encouraging.

A second speaker was introduced, a Miss Scott, who took a moment to compose herself; who looked about her, awed, perhaps, by the enormity of the hall, of the audience, of the task before her.

'Ladies,' she began in a clear, calm voice, 'unlike the women of South Australia *we have no vote!*'

'*Shame! Shame!*'

'Yet we are taxpayers. And we are law-abiding citizens—more law-abiding than most men are!'

There was laughter here, and applause. Ned Dempsey frowned, but in the saddened way of a disappointed parent.

'Let these men divest themselves of the ridiculous old-fashioned idea that a great nation is made out of huge national debts, standing armies, expensive buildings, much territory, artificial sentiment, fat billets for some people, while others starve.'

'*Hear, hear!*'

'A nation can only be great inasmuch as the whole of its people enjoy that greatness, feel that greatness, and can leave it as an inheritance to their children.'

Miss Scott paused and looked at her audience. She leaned forward. She abandoned the lectern entirely and walked to the edge of the platform.

'Ladies, is there anything in the bill that will make the people—the many, not the few—happy and prosperous? Certainly a few people will walk the floor of the proposed new two-house parliament, a few people will draw handsome salaries, a few people will rejoice in a great increase of power. We, the people, will be taxed to pay for all these things and as compensation we will have the pleasure of trying to make ends meet, a thing politicians never do. Ladies, I urge all of you to have *nothing to do with this unjust bill!*'

The room erupted and all but a handful were soon on their feet, hats in the air, feet stamping the ground so that the very foundations of the hall shook.

'Really!' said Miss Dempsey loudly in Eleanor's ear. 'Have you ever heard such wantonly militant, such deplorably misguided nonsense?'

As the roar went on and on, and it seemed for a time that order would not be restored, Ned Dempsey heaved himself to his feet and acknowledged the applause, and when the hall had fallen silent he placed his thumbs in his waistband and threw back his shoulders and cast a shrewd eye at the expectant onlookers.

'Ladies of Sydney,' he began, and there was more applause. 'The ordinary healthy, happy woman is generally an uninterested conservative. Home and friends, perhaps husband and children, fill up the measure of her desire, and she sees no reason for wishing to alter the old ways, which have brought her satisfaction. But when a great subject is under discussion, when a great movement is afoot, she must wake from her lethargy of indifference!'

A silence followed this, then a smattering of applause, not least from Miss Dempsey who was fervent in her enthusiasm, but it was a brave gambit, indeed, accusing one's audience of lethargic indifference and Eleanor, peering at the speaker in some astonishment, was surely not the only person in the hall to recognise that his entire opening speech had been lifted word for word from Tuesday's *Herald*.

The remainder of Mr Dempsey's address fell rather flat, urging as he was the ladies of the colony to encourage their menfolk to vote against the bill while at the same time declaring that their place was in the home supporting their husbands and their husbands' views. It was a contrary position to take and the applause he received was, accordingly, somewhat muted and Miss Dempsey, who expressed herself quite offended, proposed they depart at once.

The road outside the town hall had cleared and the woman who was run over, if it had been a woman, was gone to the morgue or to the hospital or back to whichever gin house she had stumbled out of. A young Aboriginal boy took the penny that Eleanor offered and went off to secure a cab for her, returning triumphantly a few minutes later. There was little point in taking Miss Dempsey with her, for the Dempseys lived in another part of town entirely, Ned Dempsey's loss of his cabinet post and any attendant income necessitating a sudden and dramatic change of residence. But twenty years a politician's wife had taught Eleanor that these things

279

were not irreversible—a year from now Ned Dempsey might be Attorney-General or Premier (though one hoped not), and it was as well to maintain some connection with his sister in the meantime. So Eleanor kissed Marian Dempsey warmly on both cheeks and left her on Darlington Road to fend for herself as best she could.

The ride home through the darkened streets was exhilarating. Rain had been forecast, though there was no sign of it yet; it was a cloudless night, cold and still, and the moon hung in the eastern sky, casting a glow over the rooftops.

And Eleanor was elated. The reason for her elation remained elusive, yet she felt it was tied up somehow with these women at the meeting who wished to vote at the referendum and, if they could not do so, then they wished to have nothing to do with it. It seemed to Eleanor churlish and not a little ridiculous, for the referendum would go ahead regardless, yet they spoke as though this state of affairs—paid employment, voting, the payment of taxes—was something to aspire to.

And she could not agree, she could not understand it. Her own mother had worked in paid employment—cleaning and gutting fish down at the quay when little more than a child before the schoolmaster, John Bass, newly arrived in the colony, had offered her a life of modest respectability in Balmain: a respectability her mother had grasped at with both hands and clung tenaciously to, and when she had found herself widowed and her children dead and that respectability threatened, she had married the retired Captain Tremaine and moved into his cottage and raised a child she could enrol in piano lessons and take to edifying lectures at the local town hall. No, there had been nothing in her mother's grim childhood to which one might aspire.

And there was even less in that of her grandmother, Molly Dowd, a domestic servant in a merchant's house in Liverpool,

England, and transported at the age of eighteen for some undefined misdemeanour in the first decade of the century, arriving in the penal colony already six months pregnant with Eleanor's mother. She was an elusive and shadowy figure this Molly Dowd, the year of her birth and the date or place of her death being unknown and unsubstantiated. She had disappeared very early from Eleanor's mother's life, the misdemeanour that got her transported being sometimes euphemistically referred to by her mother as theft and other times as lewd and licentious behaviour though it seemed clear to Eleanor, now, that her enterprising grandmother had been caught selling the one thing she had—herself—right under the roof of the merchant's house. Again, hardly something to aspire to.

Next month her mother would be twenty years dead and there was no one now who remembered that Eliza Tremaine had ever been Eliza Bass, and one would have to go far back into the annals of the colony to connect Eliza Bass, schoolmaster's widow, with Eliza Dowd, daughter of a felon. No one ever *had* made this connection, so far as Eleanor knew, and for this she was thankful, for while it was fine to live in a colony that had sprung triumphantly from the quagmire of a penal settlement, it was quite another to have a grandmother who was a convict and, in all likelihood, a prostitute.

But yet Eleanor was elated. To attend a political meeting on one's own was, it turned out, invigorating. She had sat through hundreds of dull political meetings in her time, always as Alasdair's wife, always with the single thought on her mind: was it enough to get him elected, was it enough for him to retain his seat? She had rarely, if ever, considered what Alasdair said at such meetings, what the other speakers said, what might be at stake. For if one had no power in a society, why should one concern oneself with its politics? She did not know the answer to this but it troubled her. Her elation waned a little.

The cab plunged downwards towards Elizabeth Bay and she called out instructions to the driver. He pulled up at the house and leaped down to open the door and pull down the step. At the same time the front door opened and Alice burst out, hastening to her with an unfurled umbrella though the sky was still clear, perhaps a cloud or two rolling in now from the west, but there was certainly no need for the umbrella. And Eleanor said, rather curtly for her elation had faded now, 'No, Alice, it is not raining. Please take it away. Though it is rather cold. I shall go up to my room directly. Is there a fire lit? Then do so, and I should like a warm drink, perhaps a coffee.'

She went into the house and disgorged hat, gloves and coat and Alice dropped first one glove and then the other, then, realising she had left the front door wide open and the cold air coming in, attempted to close it and only succeeded in dropping all the items she held. She seemed close to tears. This was irritating, for one does not want a maid who cries.

'Your clumsiness does not improve, Alice, though I had fervently hoped it would,' sighed her mistress, who at that moment loathed the enforced dullness of forever maintaining a house, of forever maintaining a front before the servants. 'Help me off with these boots. We encountered the worst kind of streets this evening and were obliged to walk some distance and I fear it has spoiled the leather.'

'Yes, madam. And, madam, Mr Dunlevy is in the drawing room,' said Alice.

'Eleanor.'

Alasdair called to her from the drawing room and she stood up, the boots now removed, a soft pair of house shoes in their place.

Eleanor smoothed down her lavender skirt and studied herself in the mirror that filled one wall of the hallway. She remembered she had felt elated in the cab.

'Thank you, Alice, you may go,' she said, and she waited for the girl to curtsy and depart before entering the room. 'Alasdair.'

He stood with his back to her at the fireplace, though no fire was lit, and perhaps he had not long returned for the room was cold, his gloves laid carelessly on an occasional table as though he had come home in a great hurry and there had been no time for Alice to put away his things. He turned and studied her silently, as she had just studied herself in the mirror, and under his gaze she swept into the room and sank down on a chair.

He said nothing, though he had called for her, and she could not quite read him; there was a tension that she recognised, for it had been present a great deal recently, something held tightly in check.

'You attended the anti-bill meeting this evening,' he said at last.
'I did.'

He turned back to the fireplace, looked down at his feet, one resting on the brass fender, then he turned back.

'And do you not think—' he paused, appeared to be searching for the right words, and went on '—that for the wife of a pro-Federation minister to attend a vehemently and very public anti-Federation demonstration might be highly compromising and extremely embarrassing? That it might, in fact, be considered an act of disloyalty, of betrayal? That it might harm, irreparably, your husband's career?'

'No, I had not considered that. I do not consider it now.'

'Indeed!' He threw back his head, disbelieving, it seemed, her calm denial.

How had he found out, and so quickly, before she was even returned? Someone had seen her at the meeting (the reporter perhaps—Peters of the *Mail*, or some other). She realised she had not intended to tell him, or perhaps that she might wait until the referendum was over and done with and then she might reveal it, amusingly, triumphantly, over breakfast. But Alasdair had found out and it was somehow not amusing, it was not triumphant.

'Alasdair, you did not wish me to accompany you to your meeting tonight so I went, instead, to my own. Is that so very wrong?'

His head swung around and he stood over her. 'You did this to *spite* me? Do you think this is a *game*, then? All that I have strived for, that this colony has strived for, democracy, the Federation—is it merely a child's game to you?'

'Until I am allowed to have my say in the new nation, yes, I rather think it is.'

'Your *say*?' And he laughed. 'So now you are a suffragist? Good God, this is not about votes for women, it is about building a nation! It is bad enough that these foolish women choose to appropriate the Federation for their own ends, but to have my own *wife* fall under their spell, to publicly throw in her support for them—it is *intolerable*!'

'I did no such thing! I merely sat in a chair—'

'Do not pretend to such naivety, Eleanor. You are a minister's wife and when you attend a meeting like that it will be assumed you support it. And you *were* seen, make no mistake about that.'

'And tomorrow I intend to attend the pro-Federation league at the town hall. Surely that—'

'*No!* You will *not* attend any meeting, for or against. You will remain in this house and receive no callers. You will speak to no one until the referendum is over.'

She gasped, half laughing. 'You are not serious, Alasdair? I am to remain here, a prisoner in my own home, for—for ten days? Do not be absurd. It is monstrous! Preposterous!'

'It is my will. If you have engagements, you may send word that you are indisposed. I will not be challenged on this.'

Eleanor stood up. She walked a little away and then she returned. She stood before him. '*You* would censure *me*?' And when he made no reply, 'You have made a grave error of judgement, Alasdair, if you insist on this.'

'I am your husband and I *do* insist on it.'

They faced each other in the very centre of the room, in a yard or two of empty space in a room that positively overflowed with chairs and many little tables and a glut of paintings on the walls and vast lustrous ferns in great pots that they had selected together, she and he, and arranged for their comfort and pleasure and so that others might see and appreciate their good taste, and it was all rendered redundant. Their very furniture mocked them at this moment, or so it seemed to Eleanor. She had no use for it, for this room.

'You leave me no choice,' she said, and she spoke only in part to her husband, and in part to the furniture and the room that contained it. 'I know about Miss Trent.'

# CHAPTER TWENTY-ONE

# DECEIT

And yet Alasdair's evening had begun well enough. The Federation meeting in Marrickville. The town hall crowded, lively even. The rain, threatening all day, had held off. And he had no sooner arrived than a note from the Premier was thrust into his hand by a parliamentary messenger requesting his presence on the three-day tour of the southern districts. They were to depart on the morrow and if this short notice implied someone else had fallen ill or was otherwise indisposed and himself a last minute replacement, what of it? It was an opportunity and he would grasp at it.

After such news it had proved no easy task to turn one's thoughts to the meeting. One of the speakers had failed to turn up but this was not necessarily a bad thing, for the minister who did put in an appearance, the Secretary for Public Monies, now assumed centre stage; gave the final speech of the evening and accepted the applause, the accolades. The event ended with welcome promptness, even a little early. Then, right at the very close of the meeting, some grog-soaked wretch in rags who had haunted the rear of the hall throughout the meeting and been noisily ejected at one point had reappeared, this time clutching a screaming brat in her arms, had come up to the stage and thrown herself at Alasdair, hurling some incomprehensible invective and, when this failed to have the desired effect, spitting on his face and lapel and having to be forcibly manhandled away by three attendant constables.

Alasdair had no sooner extricated himself from his outrage, pushing the flustered Greensmith aside and tearing off his soiled coat, than his eyes had fallen in astonishment on the grizzled face of Gregson, the hospital administrator.

For a moment he had stared at the man—those bushy white whiskers, the stiff high collar, that old-fashioned frockcoat, those absurd pince-nez—appalled, as though he had been caught out in a lie. Which, he supposed, he had. Certainly Gregson had every right to be here; it was a public meeting and this was, presumably, the man's domain. But Alasdair was appalled. His anonymity, or the illusion of it, was shattered.

'Come away from this circus of madness, Dunlevy, my carriage is outside.'

This, perhaps, was the most unlikely turn the evening had taken: George Drummond-Smith appearing at his elbow and offering an unlikely escape. And himself accepting, though in his disorientated state Alasdair had not so much accepted the offer of escape as found himself bundled into a waiting hansom cab, the door slamming shut on him, and himself and Drummond-Smith fleeing the scene.

'Your meetings are, by some measure, the most entertaining, Dunlevy,' Drummond-Smith declared as the cab set off northwards along Illawarra Road at a brisk clip, and he had settled himself into his seat, the better to observe his fellow passenger. 'Didn't the last one descend into pitched battle?'

'Hardly that!'

Now he had caught his breath a little, Alasdair sat up, rearranged one or two items of apparel that had become disarranged, and began to consider how he might, with dignity, extricate himself from the cab. Even five minutes in the confined space of a hansom cab with this man, Drummond-Smith, was not to be borne.

'I have amused myself greatly this evening observing, first, Henderson's meeting at Erskineville then Arnold's meeting at St Peters,' Drummond-Smith continued. 'I have heard Arnold spoken of as a future premier but after this evening's performance I am afraid I simply cannot see it. *Dull.* Utterly turgid, staid and dull. Your meeting, however—' at which point he actually leaned over and tapped Alasdair on the knee with his cane '—a positive riot of exuberant spirit! Speaking of which, my evening began with the delightful ladies of the Women's Suffrage League who met at Darlington to speak against Federation—but of course, you already knew this, Mrs Dunlevy being counted among their number.'

Alasdair had extricated himself from the cab at that point, his dignity no longer a priority. He had come home on his own. He had awaited his wife's return.

It was a lengthy wait. For much of it, Alasdair sat perfectly still on the armchair that his wife usually favoured. He did know why he had chosen this armchair.

They were all his armchairs, of course. Paid for with his money.

It was the ride home with Drummond-Smith. It drove the breath from his body. Made him feel as though he might break every stick of furniture in the room. Forced him to recall, in every tormenting detail, the incident last year, the accusations that had followed it.

He stood up, unable to remain stationary any longer. He walked about the room.

But was it not almost exactly a year since Eleanor had lost the child?

This pulled him up short. He thought back. Realised the anniversary had come and gone nine days ago, unnoticed. By himself, at least. And three days later the vote had been lost.

He took up his pacing again, but slower now. It was not a time he wished to recall. Eleanor had been bedridden for some weeks afterwards and he had been a little afraid of her, he realised, during that time. His wife facing an enemy he could not defeat—her own body, God's will, call it what you may.

After a time she had rallied and one evening—weeks later, for it had been late October by then—they had attended a reception at Parliament House. Eleanor's first engagement since the loss of the child, though neither of them had spoken of it in those terms. And he had understood—of course he had!—that it would be arduous for her. Women felt these things more keenly than men. He would be at her side to guide her through it. But in the end he was delayed, a meeting had gone on longer than anticipated, and he arrived at the Assembly lobby some minutes after the hour they had arranged to meet.

After some little time, when he felt at first concerned by his wife's non-appearance and then foolish, thinking she had changed her mind and fled home, he saw her emerge from the ladies' lounge. He started forward. But then he checked himself. For Eleanor had a curious flush on her face and her eyes were quite strange to him. A moment later George Drummond-Smith emerged from the same room, pulling on his gloves and walking with a kind of swagger, as was his wont, but that evening the swagger was accentuated. And any number of others witnessed it, the lobby filling up with parliamentarians and their wives. The looks they exchanged . . .

Alasdair felt himself shrink and become quite still. That curious, almost feverish look in his wife's eyes as she came to him and placed her hand on his arm, turned him utterly cold.

'What were you doing, alone, in a room with that man?' he asked her, and she stared past him as though she had not heard. Her first engagement since the loss of the child. He had thought to make himself particularly solicitous of her needs, to guide her through it. Now, he wondered. Now, he felt himself a fool.

How much of a fool? Had his wife merely been careless? Indiscreet? It was contemptible of him to imagine anything more— she had just lost the child, had been bedridden!—but yet he *had* thought. He *had* wondered. Had felt an ice-cold seed of doubt take root deep within him.

The following morning, though surely he had not sought him out, he saw Drummond-Smith in the chamber. Alone. He hesitated on the threshold and in that moment Drummond-Smith saw him and the mocking smile on the man's face sealed his fate. Perhaps all their fates. A confrontation could not be avoided. Alasdair marched boldly in.

'What do you mean, man, following my wife about like that last night? It is unseemly at best—'

Drummond-Smith sat back in his seat, shuffled together a pile of papers, settled his gaze on the man before him. '*If* your wife has shown a preference for me over her own husband, I cannot be held responsible—'

'How *dare* you—'

'—and I would advise you, Dunlevy, not to make a fuss. I hold in my possession certain letters from your wife to me that are, shall we say, less than discreet.'

'I do not believe you!'

At this Drummond-Smith shrugged, delighted it seemed. He crossed one leg over the other as though he were watching the final overs of a particularly intriguing test match.

'Then by all means go to her,' he said. 'Go to your dutiful wife and demand the truth.'

Alasdair tossed off a laugh at this. At the absurdity of it, the arrogance of the man. But the laugh died, almost at once, on his lips. The enormity of Drummond-Smith's words—

That thing that he most feared—

Even the suggestion that it might be so—

An indiscretion. A liaison.

He could not speak. He could not think.

A liaison between his wife and this—this man!

There were no letters, of course. Eleanor was not so stupid. But to think that was to admit her capacity for subterfuge, for deceit.

He could not catch his breath.

He turned around. He walked away, a pace, perhaps two. He turned back.

Drummond-Smith just sitting there, observing him.

*By all means go to her!*

The words taunted him, as they were intended to do. He would not go to his wife with such an accusation. He knew it, instantly and as surely as Drummond-Smith knew it. No marriage could survive such an accusation. He could not countenance her denial, would know at once that she lied. And if she did *not* deny it . . .

No, this thought was the most terrible to him.

That she might be innocent of the charge had become, already, an impossibility and he wondered at how far he had travelled so quickly without even knowing he had departed.

He turned on his heels and left.

But something had changed. Some small but vital part of him that had survived the death of the child, the loss of the vote, had succumbed. He had thought about his wife with George Drummond-Smith, whose walrus moustache rivalled that of the Premier himself.

What he had laughed off as absurd had become tangible. Become the Truth.

'I know about Miss Trent.'

These words, flung at him by his wife, echoed about the drawing room; they ricocheted from one wall to the other. They silenced the great clock in the hallway and the one on the mantel. They expelled all other thoughts from Alasdair's head and for a time he was insensible.

He had misheard, surely? Had inserted these words into the space between them because they were so much on his mind. He had invoked them. Invoked Verity.

*I know about Miss Trent.*

Thoughts crowded and jostled, spilling one over another until he was bewildered. Until his only recourse was attack: 'How *dare* you! You would accuse me—my wife!—in my own house?'

She did not flinch but faced him with a fury that, for a moment, took him aback.

'I have seen you with her! I know where she resides! Here, I have the letter you wrote to her, arranging your tawdry little liaison!' And with a trembling hand she pulled from her reticule a crumpled envelope and shook it in his face: 'Do you deny—'

'Hypocrite!'

The word fell, crashing to the floor, and the cockatoos in the ancient fig outside erupted into screaming flight.

He repeated it—

'*Hypocrite!*'

—and at least had the satisfaction of seeing her step back, the fury turn to—what? He could not guess. But before she could think to summon a reply he caught her by the arm, just above the elbow, holding her fast and speaking in a low voice: 'I am well aware what you did last year—and as we still grieved for our lost child!'

The charge was made and in her face he saw—

But he could no longer read her face, the mask she wore. The strangeness of her, it felled him. And when she began to reply—

'*No!* Do not speak another word. I will not hear it. Your behaviour is utterly, utterly beyond the pale. I forbid you to speak of this. I forbid you to leave this house or to speak of this to anyone!'

CHAPTER TWENTY-TWO

# ANY TRAIN TO EMU PLAINS

The rain began as soon as Alice had closed the front door following Mrs Dunlevy's return. Great fat drops, slowly at first, but with a quality to them that, you knew, meant a downpour, steady and drenching and prolonged. Already Alice could hear it rattling on the roof tiles, dripping into the gutters, pattering onto the leaves of the great fig tree outside.

She gazed at the discarded items—hat, gloves, coat, the soiled boots—but she did not tidy them. She went to the kitchen. There was a back door here, accessed from the outside via a passage down the side of the house. The grocer's boy used it, and the coalman and the butcher's boy and everyone, really, who came to the house who was not Mr or Mrs Dunlevy or one of their guests. Mrs Flynn had used it an hour or so ago, wrapping a shawl over her head and clutching some of the leftover loaf and some of the side of beef and wishing Alice a good night and hurrying out into the darkness.

Alice shivered, for the nights had grown darker. She no longer saw the twinkling of lights on the harbour from her attic window, she no longer saw the stars on a cloudless night. Or perhaps they were still there—the lights on the harbour, the stars in the night sky—and it was simply that Alice no longer looked for them.

She went to the back door and she paused, drew breath and opened it cautiously, just a crack, and peered through into the night and only then standing aside and letting the damp figure who was outside come in.

'Why'd you leave me out in the rain?' said Mrs Renfrew indignantly, and she handed her bundle to Alice and shook the raindrops from her shawl.

Alice took the bundle and cradled it in her arms. Then she began to cry, silently and piteously, turning away so that she might not be observed. After a moment she stopped. She lifted the blanket from the baby's face and stared at it. Its face was a mottled yellowish-pink hue, the dark fuzz of hair on its head a little thinner than it had been. The baby stirred and snuffled, balling up a fist and screwing up its face, but otherwise made no sound.

'Is he alright?' she asked dubiously.

'Blessed if I know,' said Mrs Renfrew. 'He's alive, ain't he?' She stood, looking about her. 'Coo,' she said.

She may or may not have noticed Alice crying silently a moment or two earlier.

Alice looked around her. 'This is the kitchen,' she said, feeling some explanation was required.

Mrs Renfrew had brought with her an odour, something earthy, pungent, like the thunderboxes of the many houses Alice had lived in as a child. It was a smell the Dunlevys would notice at once, if they had a mind to come this way. She must hurry Mrs Renfrew out again, though she hesitated to do so because it was something,

wasn't it, having someone here to visit her? Not someone delivering the groceries or the meat or the coal but here to see her, Alice
Nimrod.

'You been to see her, then—your sister?' said Mrs Renfrew.

Alice buried her face in the baby's blanket, feeling the tiny thing
squirm and wrestle for a moment with the bindings that held it.

*No, Milli is dead and gone, killed herself.*

But the words did not form in her mouth and could not be
uttered, not now, perhaps not ever.

So Alice said nothing and after a time she patted the baby
gently on its back and took a turn about the kitchen.

'I have found the baby a home,' she said, but Mrs Renfrew
stopped her with a gesture.

'Do not tell me. I do not wish to know. Whatever is the poor
wee thing's fate, it is no concern of mine.'

And so instead Alice said, 'You have been a true and good friend
to me and my sister, Mrs Renfrew, and I am grateful.'

These words felt awkward and oddly shaped in her mouth for
Alice had few occasions to thank others.

But Mrs Renfrew dismissed this too.

'I do not want your thanks. I want my money and whatever
food these folk can spare.' She ran a starved, almost manic eye
over the cupboards and the door to the scullery. Her arms were
so thin the bones themselves seemed to have shrunk, as though
she had the skeleton of a bird, and how much nourishment she
can have provided to the baby, who knew? The baby was alive and
that was all that had been asked of her.

Alice put the baby against her shoulder and reached into the
pocket of her dress and offered up a small pile of coins over which
Mrs Renfrew cast a practised eye, then she went out to the coal
scuttle and brought in the basket she had filled with all the leftovers

she had been able to get her hands on that she thought no one would notice, though she was pretty certain Mrs Flynn had got wind of what was going on for she had turned the place upside down this evening looking for the remains of the roast duck from the day before, and when Alice had suggested a possum had got it or a fox, perhaps, she had raised a sceptical eyebrow.

Mrs Renfrew surveyed the goods critically but, perhaps realising there was no more to come, neither food nor money, she accepted it without complaint, pulled on her shawl and made for the door.

'Listen, girl, you better warn that sister of yours to be careful,' she said after a moment's hesitation. 'Them people she borrowed from is still looking to make good on their loan and her being in Darlinghurst Gaol ain't gonna keep her safe. If they catch up to her in there, they shall slit her throat, sure as sure, and if they cannot find her, they will slit yours instead.'

But Alice walked up and down the kitchen with the baby and the words *My sister is dead*, which might have changed something or might have changed nothing at all, remained unsaid.

'Suit yourself,' said Mrs Renfrew, and she was gone. But the odour she had brought with her remained for a long time.

For a moment Alice did not move. Her sister's baby was a weight in her arms so heavy she could hardly bear it and at the same time was so light, so tentative, a thing of gossamer and air, that it seemed it might slip away and be gone, and how these two things could both be so she did not know.

A noise from the main part of the house stirred her and a fear that lately was always present, if occasionally dulled and vague, flared. If Mrs Dunlevy came into the kitchen now—

But Mrs Dunlevy never came into the kitchen. Why should she come now, today?

Alice crept into the hallway, kissing the crown of the baby's head though hardly aware that she did so. She heard voices from the drawing room, Mr and Mrs Dunlevy, and she darted past the door and up the stairs and no one came out, no one called her name. When she reached her own room at the top of the house she paused, calming herself, waiting for the baby to wake, but it did not.

She lay the baby in a drawer, lining it first with newspaper. She left it sleeping and went downstairs and she wondered why it was that God had chosen her, why Father McCreadie had come for her and not for Milli, why it was she who was saved. And the baby too; perhaps the baby was saved. It was strange to her.

In the hallway Alice took up the boots Mrs Dunlevy had discarded and studied them. They were covered in mud. It was a shame, for they were lovely things. If she could she would make them nice again. If she made the boots as good as new, and if she thought very hard about how God had saved her, how God had saved Milli's baby, then it was alright that later tonight she was going to hand the baby over and not see it again for years, perhaps. She wondered if this was why God had saved her: so that she might save Milli's baby. If Father McCreadie was here she would ask him, though she had not set eyes on him in five years and had never wanted to ask him a question about God before. She imagined herself asking her question now and she tried to think what answer Father McCreadie might give.

He would not know the answer. He would make up some lie.

She knew this with a certainty that stilled the heart and made her wonder why she had not known it before and how she knew it now. But she *did* know it and she could not, now, unknow it.

She picked up the boots and stood up to return to the kitchen.

'*I know about Miss Trent.*'

Alice froze midstride, and her heart, which had lurched and shook and caused her all manner of trouble all day, quivered at these words. It was no name she knew, but the voice—it was Mrs Dunlevy's—cried it the way Milli had cried out the Lord's name in the courthouse as the baby had ripped her open in its hurry to reach the world.

'*Hypocrite!*'

This was him, Mr Dunlevy.

And then:

'No! *Do not speak another word. I will not hear it. Your behaviour is utterly, utterly beyond the pale. I forbid you to speak of this. I forbid you to leave this house or to speak of this to anyone!*'

The door flew open and Alice flattened herself against the wall as Mr Dunlevy burst from the room. If he had paused to look around he must surely have seen her there, the muddied boots clutched to her breast, but he did not stop, he did not look around. He went straight up the stairs, his footsteps thudding with each step, and a door slammed. Its echoes filled the hallway, filled the house, long after he was gone.

The house now screamed out its silence, it reverberated off the walls, it shook the very foundations, it pinned Alice to the floor and for a time she forgot to breathe.

But was that the baby crying, two floors up, distantly? Oh, it could not be!

Alice cried out, a sob of dismay, and her hand flew to her mouth to stifle it. She dropped the boots and sprung from her hiding place at the exact moment Mrs Dunlevy came out of the drawing room and they all but collided. They came face to face, the mistress and the servant, and whose face it was that was the most ashen, whose eyes it was that showed the most dismay, was impossible to say. Alice saw Mrs Dunlevy's face and she heard again the words her husband had spoken for she could not unhear those words and she could not pretend she had not heard them, and she saw that Mrs Dunlevy knew this too.

There was no place to hide. All was laid bare.

And what now? For no servant should see her mistress's shame, should witness her mistress's disgrace. No household can endure it.

Alice did not wait to find out. She fled up the stairs, past Mr Dunlevy's closed door and up to her own room at the top of house where the baby had awakened. She pounced on it, scooping it up and clasping it to her chest to quieten it, to quieten her own beating heart.

The baby wailed and she pressed its face to her breast and felt its tiny fists push against her flesh. The amount of time she had left with it could be countered now in hours, in minutes.

At midnight the house was heavy—not with sleep, for no one slept, but with silence, with misgivings, with passion spent and with passion unspent, with so much emotion, indeed, that the air was dense with it and Alice found it difficult to catch her breath.

She sat on the bed, cradling the baby but not looking at it. She had put on all the warm clothes she possessed and now her heart pounded the blood about her body as though she had fled in fear of her life though she sat perfectly still. She must go, must leave this minute or the moment would be lost. She must leave!

Alice raised her face to the slanted square of ceiling. The rafters were low enough to touch.

*What should I do, Milli?*

But Milli did not speak to her. No one spoke to her. Of course they did not. Alice was quite alone. Except for the baby, whose fate—

But the baby's fate was God's decision, not Alice Nimrod's. God had let Milli die. God had put Mrs Flowers in her path. Alice thought of Moses in the basket. The slave girl. The child floating down the river to its destiny . . .

The baby wriggled. It tossed its head, becoming restless. In a moment it would awake and cry. It would wake the whole household. It was this and not God, not Moses in the basket, that decided her.

She leaped up. She wrapped a scarf about her head and one about the baby and slipped down the first flights of stairs. On the landing, she paused. The floorboards in Mr Dunlevy's room creaked as he paced but his door did not open. No sound came from Mrs Dunlevy's room. Alice slipped down the second flight and let herself out of the side door.

The rain did not let up. Alice hurried with her head down and her scarf over her head but the scarf was soon soaked through and the rain drove directly into her face and into her eyes. She could not shield herself as her arms were full and the package she carried was more important than the rain lashing her face.

The streets were empty save for the occasional cab setting up a terrific spray as it passed. Alice slowed her headlong dash lest she slip in the mud and in the fast-running gutters. She lost her bearings at one point; she knew the area as well as anyone, but in the darkness of a moonless night and in the driving rain familiar streets became unknown and strange. She thought she must be on Devonshire Street and, yes, here were the railings now on her right and on the other side of the railings the old cemetery. She followed the line of the railings and she prayed she did not mistake her way and was someplace else entirely. The graves in the old cemetery emerged intermittently out of a low-hanging mist, only the tops showing, made grotesque by the darkness and by her fear, for it was known that on the wettest nights slimy and putrid matter seeped out of the ground and onto the neighbouring pavements. But now she saw on her left the lights of the great railway station and she let out a little gasp of relief. It was tempting to pause for a moment to catch her breath but she was late, or she had a sense she must be late, for the journey had taken longer than it ought due to the blackness of the night and the encumbrance of the rain. Half past midnight was the time of the appointment and somewhere far off a church clock chimed, hollowly, forlornly, spurring her onwards.

The baby was an awkward size and had grown heavier at every step so that her arms had begun to ache almost at once and now they burned with pain, and as she held him to her breast she could not feel his heartbeat so that the thought that she might be carrying a dead thing struck her with horror. But there! He had moved. That was all she needed. She covered him again with the old blanket and set off once more.

She was close enough now to make out the stone-and-brick building of Sydney Terminal Station and its brightly lit entrance hall, and she hurried towards it. The sweep of roadway leading to the station was deserted, no horse or carriage stood waiting and none arrived to drop anyone off or pick anyone up, and she wondered just how late it was. In her urgency she almost slipped, throwing out a hand to the wet ground to save herself. Even here, where the road was properly paved, the rain had turned the ground to mud. She steadied herself and made one last final dash, landing up in the entranceway where she came to a halt.

Even at this late hour and on such a dreadful night people gathered, made sluggish by the rain, lugging great boxes and trunks, dragging crying children, pausing in the entranceway to open and close umbrellas and shake sodden hats or just taking shelter, putting off the moment when they must leave the station and go outside. The rain had created great puddles that splashed mud up over the women's skirts and over the men's boots as they ran through them. A porter hurried past with head bent and hat pulled low. He glanced at Alice with her bundle as he passed but did not stop her; no one's gaze lasted more than a second. It was not the night to be asking questions. And perhaps many young women came alone to this station late at night clutching babies to their breasts.

I am late, thought Alice, but she did not move. She stood in the ticket hall, patting the baby's back and gazing about her, struck dumb for a moment, for this was the station of their dreams, where she and Milli had come often as children. The station was new then, the fearful old shed that had stood for twenty years replaced with this stone-and-brick creation, all archways and beautiful brickwork and big solid walls. Like a church, Milli had said, except that here no one told you what to do or think. Here was a place that made no demands on you and instead offered you the chance of escape, or at least the chance to dream of escape. They had never once taken a train, but they had watched the people who had journeyed here from Penrith and Bowenfels and Mount Victoria, the trains that had come over the mountains. They had stood at the departure board and Milli had said, 'I shall catch any train, Alice. Any train to Emu Plains,' for that was where the trains went, and together they had imagined a place called Emu Plains. Milli had caught a train, years later and all the way to Melbourne, and whether she had ever gone to Emu Plains Alice did not know.

She did know that this station would be gone soon too, the whole thing pulled down, all these archways and this beautiful brickwork, though it had stood barely twenty years, and a new station, much grander, would be erected right where the old cemetery stood. Mr Dunlevy had talked of it over breakfast. A grand new station built on a cemetery.

A clock chimed the quarter hour and Alice picked up her skirts and ran towards the platforms, passing each one until she reached platform 14. It was the last one, squeezed in as an afterthought, the furthest away, the hardest to reach, the least used.

Not a soul about. No train waited at the platform, no passenger came or went. On the neighbouring platform a solitary station official carrying a hurricane lamp, checking and locking up, glanced at her across the deserted railway tracks but did not stop, and he was too far distant for her to see his face nor him to see hers.

The baby began to cry. If it was hungry it was no wonder. She had tried to give it bread soaked in water to suck on, and who knew if that was enough to keep the poor little thing from perishing? The baby did not thrive but it was not dead. She held the little bundle close to her own shivering body but, as she was soon to hand him over, she held him a little less tightly. She turned her face away from him. She placed herself far away, on that train to Emu Plains.

'Miss Hills?'

It was strange to be addressed by a name that was not your own and Alice started and for a moment could not speak.

'Mrs Flowers?'

For here finally was the name in the newspaper, the illegible signature on the bottom of a scrawled note, the person who, until this moment, existed only in the imagination, as a saviour, perhaps.

Salvation, yes, but did the person who offered salvation also offer damnation? It seemed so to Alice.

The reality of this Mrs Flowers was a stout, black-clad figure, short and squat, in a large shapeless bonnet of no obvious colour and tied beneath her chin by a tattered ribbon, with a heavy black coat that reached almost to the ground and beneath which the toes of mud-plastered boots were visible. Her face was at first in shadow and seemed at home there but she lifted her head and the light caught her then let her go, for there was something a little curious about her eyes, blankly hidden behind little round spectacles that yet summed up in one swift glance all that there was to know about Miss Hills (not her real name) who had got herself into trouble and was desperate enough to arrange this meeting. Having appraised Miss Hills, she pulled back her lips in a smile that showed one or two teeth, no more, and she nodded as though she had seen all she needed to see.

'How old is the baby?'

'Five days.'

'Boy or girl?'

'It is a boy.'

Mrs Flowers nodded. 'Good. It's easier to place a little boy.'

'You said there is family all ready for him?'

'So there is. A good Christian couple out in the country. On a farm. Childless. They are awaiting him this very moment.'

It was exactly what the advertisement in the newspaper had said: a good Christian family of moderate but honest means. It was exactly what Alice wanted to hear.

But she hesitated.

'There has been a change. The mother, she—the mother is no longer living and will not want the baby back at the end of three years. It will need to be fostered for longer, till it is six or seven, maybe. If I could have it myself I would but I cannot. I have a position . . .'

'The cost will be more,' said Mrs Flowers, and this, probably, was her reply to any change in circumstances.

Alice stared at her helplessly. 'I do not have it.'

But this was no barrier, it seemed. 'When will you have more?'

'I do not know. In a few weeks, months . . . I do not know.'

Mrs Flowers nodded. 'It will have to do.'

'It is my sister's child,' Alice said, though she had hoped not to say this. 'Shall I be able to go out there to visit, if I wish to?'

'Not at first. The baby must be allowed to settle in for a time. They will write to me, for they are educated people, and I will forward the letter to you if you have a mind to read it.'

This was as sentimental as she got, Mrs Flowers; this was the limit of her compassion. Now she was brisk, businesslike: 'Give me the money. Quickly now. Three pounds. And it is ten shillings every month after that. You must pay it to the post office at Pitt Street. Do not miss a month and do not be late; I cannot answer for the baby's welfare if the money stops.'

The flare of the gaslight struck the blank discs of her spectacles and bounced right off, unable or unwilling to penetrate further.

It did not quite make sense to Alice that the baby's welfare would be in jeopardy if she was late with the money—had Mrs Flowers not said the people were a good Christian family?—but everything came down to money, in the end, didn't it?

Alice pushed her fears aside. She would not let them in. There could be no suggestion of danger, despite Mrs Flynn's warnings, despite what she herself knew of the world. If she let in even the possibility of danger it would all collapse in a heap and that could not be allowed to happen. It could not.

She reached into her pocket and pulled out the money. It was a significant sum—but it was a significant transaction.

She pushed her fears down.

Mrs Flowers took the money and counted it quickly, peered at the notes, holding them up close to her short-sighted eyes, biting each coin with her few remaining teeth. And then the money was gone, inside the capacious black coat. 'Hand it over then.'

She meant the baby. Held out both hands to take it.

A train pulled into the platform opposite with a screech of brakes and couplings and wheels. Great clouds of smoke and smut and steam filled the air. Doors opened and a handful of tired passengers emerged, a porter came running. Alice handed over the baby and by the time the doors of the carriages closed again and the train had gone to the sidings for the night Alice was already hurrying back to Elizabeth Bay before she was missed. And the baby was—

Well, who knew where the baby was?

CHAPTER TWENTY-THREE

# DECEIT II

Eleanor did not sleep. She sat at her desk, protected by the darkness. She listened to the rain on the windows and on the roof, so insistent and unceasing that the days of blue-skied sunlight seemed like they belonged to another city in another climate. She pressed her fingers into the flesh of her upper arm and felt the tenderness there in the shape of a man's grip.

She heard the sounds of the house, at one point imagining footsteps on the stairs, the sound of a door far off at the rear of the house closing, and had leaped up, confused, the blood roaring in her ears, but not going to the door, not going to the window. Simply standing in the darkened room, waiting, every nerve raw. After a time, and when it became clear she had imagined it, she sank down once more to the chair.

The clock in the hallway struck and chimed its way around the hour and on to the next hour, charting a passage through the night.

What had she done?

A year ago, when they were still grieving the loss of their child. She had no idea at all. She had remained in bed for a time. A long time. The vote had been held and lost and Alasdair had moved into the second bedroom. After a time she had got better, or that was how the doctor had described it: Mrs Dunlevy getting up from her bed, getting dressed, venturing outside, accepting one or two visitors. Getting better.

After a little more time she had attended a reception at Parliament House, her first engagement since the loss of the child, arriving by cab to meet Alasdair there but arriving too soon and finding, quite suddenly, that it was more than she felt able to do, entering the reception on her own. It was too soon—though the doctor had assured her she was better. She must enter the room on her husband's arm and that way, if there was sympathy, if there were silent looks, she could endure it, she felt.

But she had arrived too soon.

There was no sign of Alasdair and all about her people were massing, cabs were pulling up outside, more and more of them. In a moment someone would see her.

There was a lounge where she might sit and wait for him. She crossed the lobby and entered the room and stood, a little breathless, a little dismayed. It would pass, of course, this terror. But until it did she found herself dismayed.

The oppressive little room of gilt cornices and thick carpet and massive leather sofas added to her dismay. There were few spaces in this building where a lady might go, this stuffy little lounge being one of them. The host of dead parliamentarians whose portraits crowded the four walls made it clear that even this small square of government was but grudgingly granted.

When the door behind her opened and closed, she turned to Alasdair with a smile because this fracture in their marriage had not yet appeared, though they had lost the child, though he had moved, by then, into the second bedroom.

But it was not Alasdair. It was George Drummond-Smith.

'I—Oh!' she said, confused.

Drummond-Smith, whom she had known, a little, over many years, who had dined on occasion in their home, whose wife one had met perhaps twice in ten years. A man who spoke of trivialities to her and of world events to her husband, which did not mark him out from any other gentleman of her acquaintance, but whose fixed, unwavering gaze when one was speaking or from across a room was unsettling. He was wearing evening dress that night, all the gentlemen were, and gloves, which he now pulled off. A cane, his top hat. He removed that too. He did not seemed surprised to see her, just as though they were meeting by arrangement. He smiled, gave her that fixed look, advanced towards her. He pulled his gloves off—she particularly remembered that—just as though he had some important business to attend to.

'Eleanor,' he said, though he had never used her name before nor been asked to. She did not like that, nor the way he said it.

'Mr Drummond-Smith,' she replied, meeting his gaze, making a point. 'I am awaiting my husband.'

'Indeed? But he is not here, I think.'

It was, she thought, a curious thing to say.

He stood before her very close, too close, and the light was reflected brightly in his eyes, it bounced off his forehead so that his flesh appeared not quite human. His great walrus moustache; he took such pride in it. She imagined him combing it, grooming it. He reached out and took her gloved hand, not taking his eyes from hers. He raised her hand to his lips, at the last moment undoing the little button at her wrist and sliding the glove from her hand, kissing her fingers. She had a sense of something supressed in him, an energy barely contained by his clothes. It radiated out of him. He did not take his eyes from hers.

And, stupidly, dimly, up to this point she had not understood his intent. He had followed her into the room, she realised.

She pulled her hand sharply away. Or tried to. He clasped it more tightly. He slid his arm about her waist, pressing it against the small of her back to pull her towards him.

'Come, Eleanor, do not be coy. You are hardly a blushing virgin.'

'How *dare* you!'

She snatched back her hand and made for the door and there was a moment when she thought he would spring after her, that he would prevent her from leaving.

Instead he let out a hard little laugh: 'Leave, if you must, my dear!'

And then, as she reached the door: 'I do not take kindly to being made a fool of!'

Outside Alasdair was standing at the reception desk. He gave her the queerest look as she burst from the lounge, furious and flustered.

A moment later Drummond-Smith emerged, pulling on his gloves.

'That man is odious!' she declared, shaken, and she took her husband's arm.

Alasdair stared at her as though he had not heard. 'What were you doing, alone, in a room with that man?'

What had she done? Eleanor did not know. But why, then, did she remember that one evening? She wondered if perhaps she did know and her unease grew.

As the dawn crept in she arose from her desk and went out of the room and to her husband's door. It was half open. There was movement within and she stood, uncertain, then pushed open the door. Inside Alasdair was dressed, or completing his dress: knotting a tie, buttoning a waistcoat, smoothing down his hair. A trunk stood open upon the table with items already inside and Alice, the maid, stood midway between wardrobe and trunk, a pile of shirts in her arms. The girl stopped dead and stared, her eyes quite wild and terrible, as though she knew all that went on in the house. Alasdair stopped and stared too; his eyes were fearful and furious and then nothing at all as he turned from her.

Eleanor wondered how, after twenty years, she could know someone so little.

'Leave us, Alice,' she commanded, and the girl all but dropped the pile of clothes in her haste to get out. Eleanor closed the door behind her. The trunk on the bed. Alasdair's clothes in the trunk. And a portmanteau, fastened and bulging, by the door.

'You are going somewhere?'

She felt something rise within her. Her words so calm, so quiet, so reasonable, but something was rising. It frightened her a little.

'The Tour of the South with the Premier.'

'I did not realise you were to accompany him—'

'I received word yesterday. What is it you want, Eleanor?'

Already he had turned back to the mirror, his fingers fumbled with the myriad tiny buttons on the waistcoat.

He had told her nothing of his intention to accompany the Premier on this tour. And she was to believe he had only learned of it yesterday? Was everything he now said to her a lie?

For a moment Eleanor could not speak. The words rose in her throat, but they were all in a jumble, choking her one moment and then tumbling out any which way: 'You accused me, Alasdair, of being a hypocrite for something I had done last year. You said—'

He rounded on her, the fury returned. His eyes seemed black to her, when no one's eyes were ever really black, were they? And yet they looked so, at this moment.

'I *said* I would *not* discuss it!'

He threw down his tie. He leaped forward and in that instant she was fearful, but he brushed past her and stood on the landing and called out for the maid. '*Alice!*'

'Surely I have a right to know of what I am accused!'

'Take the trunk downstairs and get a cab. I leave at once.'

'Alasdair! I have a right—'

He spun around to face her and there was fury still but also, she saw, dismay, disbelief, hurt. He looked as a man might whose wife has let him down in the most profound way, and now she wanted to shake him, to strike him, for it was *she—she* who had been wronged!

'*I saw you!*' he cried out, taking her by the shoulders then at once letting her go. 'With that man. With Drummond-Smith—'

She gasped, let out a laugh.

'—with my own eyes. Your . . . liaison! My *God*, at Parliament House!' He turned away but at once turned back again, clenched both fists tightly of front of his face. 'Did you really believe I would not realise it? How could you be so *stupid*, Eleanor, so *indiscreet*? How many people, do you think, saw you come out of that room with him that night?'

Eleanor stared at him. She shook her head. 'You are mad! There was no liaison! How could you think such a thing?'

'The man has letters that *you* have written to him!'

'But he cannot, for I have never written a letter to that man. Ever. He is lying, Alasdair. He has deceived you—'

'Ha!'

'—because I rebuffed him, and in no uncertain terms. He threatened—oh, I did not take the threat seriously at the time, but here is what he has done: poisoned you against me with these lies!' It was as simple as that and she laughed, though it was a bitter laugh.

'He has letters!'

As though she had not spoken. As though Alasdair had not heard a single word. It struck her, then: 'But this was your excuse, wasn't it? All the excuse you needed to be with this woman! Your justification for an affair.'

'No!' He walked away from her, shaking his head. 'No. You cannot deceive me anymore, Eleanor.'

'It is not *I* who has deceived you! Only one of us has been unfaithful in this marriage, Alasdair, only one of has broken their vows, has lied to other, and as God is my witness, it is not I!'

'*No!* Leave! Leave this room *now*!'

He looked stricken. She must look much the same, she presumed. As though they had plumbed some depth. Could not sink any further. It seemed they must, at last, understand each other.

Eleanor spoke now in quite a different voice: 'Do you care, then, so much for this woman, Alasdair—'

But he cried out in exasperation and pushed past her and plunged down the stairs. She followed a step behind, but only as far as the top of the stairs. Heard the front door open below.

'—that you would sacrifice *everything*?'

But the door had closed.

CHAPTER TWENTY-FOUR

# FLASH FLOOD

The rain did not let up the following day or for the two after that. Within hours of the cloudburst the gutters in the streets of the city overflowed. By the end of the day they had turned to rivers. Great torrents of water cascaded down Macquarie Street, bringing with it tree branches, mud, sodden newspapers, broken umbrellas and the overturned refuse of every domestic and mercantile premises on the way, even one or two bloated animal carcasses, to be spat out into the quay and swept into the harbour and beyond. Rain lashed the windows of Parliament House, the Treasury, Customs House and Government House; it buffeted the bows of the steamships and the colliers as they attempted to dock at Woolloomooloo and it drenched the men on the dockside. Earthworks loosened and trees were unrooted. Roofs leaked and some collapsed. In the poorer districts, whole buildings were swept away and some of the residents along with them. Beyond the city the rivers swelled and burst their banks, the roads became impassable, the settlements and outlying stations became inundated. The sheep and cattle that had withstood the drought were lost.

Alasdair's newspaper declared it a disaster. Not the loss of life or livestock or property, but the referendum which was now just a week away. How would the men get to the polling stations, it asked, when the rivers had burst their banks and the roads had become impassable? Their drays could not ford the raging waters and their horses had perished. What were they to do?

Alasdair read of the disaster in the dining room of a hotel, on a train, in the dining room of another hotel. The city was being washed away but the referendum would still go ahead. Polling arrangements were advertised. Whole pages were given over to the debate, the speeches, the nightly meetings held in hotels and town halls and council chambers across the city and in country towns the length of the colony. The Premier was here and he was there—six thousand heard him speak at Newcastle, a smaller number at Darlington, his speeches were reprinted in full, with almost as much space given to Mr Barton. A tally was kept of how many attended this meeting and how many attended that. Was the spirit in the colony for Federation or was it against? The anti-billites could be dismissed, said the newspaper, the motion was sure to carry. The anti-billites were a growing force, said the same paper, and nothing was certain, they could yet spoil the day. The editorials were daily more imploring, the letters to the editor ever more impassioned. An effigy of the Premier was set alight outside the meeting at Darlington and the local constables had to act promptly to put it out.

Mr Dunlevy, the Secretary for Public Monies, reported the *Herald*, had attended a meeting at Marrickville and at Drummoyne, he had been at Waverley and Ashfield, he had been at Parramatta and Camperdown and Waterloo, and now he had left the city to accompany the Premier on his tour of the southern townships. It was a wonder, the paper said, that the people still came out, night after night, in all this rain.

Alasdair stood beside the Premier on a stage at Albury that was built for three, four at a push, but the Premier was so generous of girth there was barely room for the two of them and when the Premier took a step forward or used his arms to make a point, which he did repeatedly and expansively, Alasdair was obliged to duck and step back and the stage shuddered and threatened to collapse altogether.

'I have this day received word that our colleagues in Queensland have carried the Federation Enabling Bill!' the Premier declared, holding in his fist this very telegram and the people cheered. 'It is a Major Step Forward!' he added, thus securing a further cheer.

The Premier had been handed this same telegram three days earlier and he had given this exact same speech at Newcastle that evening, but the people of Albury were not to know this. He knew how to play a crowd, did Reid; he knew how to use a prop.

They were at the Mechanics Institute and a thousand or more men had filled the hall to hear the Premier speak and a few hundred ladies filled the gallery above, and this despite the weather so dramatically and unceasingly inclement. The hall in which they stood was a vast, cavernous and high-ceilinged place, no doubt cool on a summer evening but on this wet wintery day it was bitter—though the perspiration glistened on the bald head of the Premier and gathered in little droplets on his magnificent walrus moustache.

'Those who sneered at the smallness of some of the colonies are guilty of snobbishness,' said the Premier, 'and those who fear their honesty are unjust.'

And the people applauded. It was sometimes a little difficult to follow his exact meaning, but the gist, surely, was clear enough.

'It is no argument against the honesty of the other colonies that they have not got as big a land revenue as we have. Once it is admitted that the people of Australia are honest all round, half the objections to the bill disappear.'

Again the people cheered their approval. Alasdair cheered too, though he had heard the speech already on the train down. They had arrived at Albury by the mail train at noon and the mayor and most of the town had been at the station to welcome them. They had travelled by carriage to their hotel and the main street had been festooned with bunting and flags and a great banner had stretched across the street proclaiming, with unrestrained optimism, ALBURY: THE NATION'S CAPITAL. At a reception speeches had been made and the Premier's health drunk, and in the afternoon they had been driven about the town in a carriage venturing as far as the border, where the good folk of Victoria had been almost as vociferous in their welcome and good wishes for the Premier as had the people of New South Wales.

'Now I come to the question of the federal capital,' said Mr Reid, 'about which Albury has never shown any warmth of feeling,' (great laughter). 'It was a bitter pill for Victoria that Mr Turner, their premier, gave the capital to New South Wales,' (cheers) 'but having barred all Victoria he determined that Sydney should not have it and he is quite justified in doing so,' (hear, hear).

'Albury for the capital!' cried the crowd, boisterous in its enthusiasm.

And *would* Albury be the capital? Alasdair wondered. It had made a good case, as good as any other place. He thought of the long and uncomfortable train journey they had endured to get here, of the cattle wandering unheeded down the main street, of the farmers and landowners riding into town on horseback and his heart sank. It was a loathsome place! They were all loathsome places. When he envisaged the nation's capital he imagined himself in an elegant house on Flinders Street overlooking the Yarra. He imagined himself in Melbourne. Was he the only one who dreaded the idea of a capital out here in the middle of a barren nothing, built on dirt and fit only for squatters? Why, look at the mess the Canadians had made of it! Mr Dibbs, the anti-federalist, had visited that country the year before and had found Ottawa, their newly built federal capital, to be a small place with no decent hotel and a railway station smaller than many of Sydney's suburban stations. When he had enquired where the people of the capital were to be found, he was told they were out of town as parliament was not sitting.

Was this their future then? Had the people of New South Wales learned nothing from the blunder of their sister colony across the sea?

The elegant house overlooking the Yarra. It had grown and grown in his imaginings over the months until he could picture the wallpaper in the breakfast room, the carpet on the staircase, the light fixtures, the entrance hall. Even down to the ivory-topped cane in the hallway that the servant would hand to him and the walk he would make along the river towards the new parliament— all of it, every unspoiled, incredible detail. And the woman who sat opposite him at that breakfast table, he had pictured her too. Of course he had! She had been the crowning glory, the queen at the heart of the palace he had built!

Now, when he attempted to look into the eyes of his queen, his eyes slide from her face. Try as hard as he might, he could not see her. She no longer had a face. She no longer had a name.

And somehow a whole week had passed since he had gone to the hospital and he had made no enquiries since. If Verity lived or not, he did not know.

There was no way back, he saw, aghast. No way at all.

'Gentlemen,' said the Premier, and the buttons of his waistcoat strained, 'the struggle which is to culminate on June twenty is going to be victory for Federation!'

The floor erupted into wild applause and the Premier beamed and allowed himself to be slapped on the back and heartily congratulated.

And this was the man who, a year ago, had been so unable to commit himself to Federation he could speak for two hours on the subject and at the end of that time one still did not know if was in favour or against. The papers had dubbed him 'Yes-No Reid'. Could this man one day be Australia's prime minister? wondered Alasdair. The fellow was a great orator—the finest in the empire if you believed what some said, but his enormous girth (which one was hard put to ignore), that absurd moustache, the monocle he affected to wear, all of it made him less the eminent statesman and more the comic figure of vaudeville. Yet look at the people—for they were now taking a vote: for or against? And here was the response: all of them to a man in favour of Federation. But, no, one fellow here at the back voting in the negative. Still, all but one in favour. Resounding cheers all around the hall and a vote of thanks from the mayor. Alasdair slapped the Premier on the back, he offered his heartiest congratulations.

How did Reid do it? The man was in his mid-fifties if he was a day, he had just returned from a gruelling tour of the Northern Rivers, an engagement at Sydney, then he had shot back up to Newcastle and now here he was at the start of a Tour of the South yet he looked as fresh as a batsman at the start of an innings. Alasdair had barely attended a meeting outside the city before today yet he felt close to collapse. Was superhuman endurance the mark of a premier, he wondered, of a potential prime minister?

He did not know. Whenever he imagined that man, Australia's first prime minister, it was not Mr Reid, his own leader, whom he pictured in the role, it was Mr Barton, and that was awkward. He did not voice these thoughts, naturally, but there was no denying that the leader of the Opposition—who had chosen to remain in the city and was speaking at Waverley this very evening and who was drawing crowds every bit as large as the Premier's and delivering speeches reported every bit as enthusiastically in the *Herald*—looked the part, he spoke the part, he *was* the part. And perhaps Alasdair was not the only man who thought so. Even so, it was awkward.

'Congratulations, sir,' said Alasdair again, in case his first congratulations had not been quite hearty enough.

They were travelling to Junee that night then on to Cootamundra and Goulburn. Alasdair had found it necessary to get Greensmith to consult a map of the colony to locate Junee, and even after studying the map they had been none the wiser.

It was a long time to spend on a train with any man, not least the Premier.

A crowd had gathered now about the Premier: local business-men, landowners, half-a-dozen pressmen, the entire town council, and a not insignificant number of ladies, who had come down from the gallery and were fluttering their fans in his direction as though it were a summer's evening and Mr Reid a dashing young nobleman at an assembly ball and, frankly, there was something undignified about the whole thing.

Alasdair turned to the mayor and he shook the man's hand and said something appropriate; he stood at the Premier's side as the explosion of a photographer's flash-lamp momentarily blinded them; he dashed through the rain to the waiting carriage; he sat opposite the Premier and talked of great and important things as they made their way back to the hotel. The main street was turned to mud in all the rain and quite deserted, the bunting and the flags sodden now in the deluge.

'This town will not be our nation's capital,' said Reid, speaking in a low, measured voice quite different to that of the great orator of an hour ago. He leaned back in the carriage and peered out of the window at the darkened, deserted streets.

'You think not, sir?'

'Not one of these places will be our capital, Dunlevy. A new place will be chosen, virgin soil. A new town for a new nation.'

It sounded good, statesmanlike even, and Alasdair nodded, but he was thinking of Ottawa.

'A British journal has proposed our new capital be named Britannia,' he said.

'That will happen over the dead body of myself and every other true and right-thinking Australian man,' Reid replied, not turning his gaze from the window.

And on that they could agree.


They would not be staying overnight at the hotel. It was merely a place for refreshment, to wash and change their clothes. They were to travel on to Junee that night.

It was a small party that made its way to the station an hour later, the mayor and the lady mayoress riding in the carriage to officially see the party off, a small crowd of well-wishers gathered on the platform and those of the press who were covering the tour and would be boarding the train with them. Reid was in high spirits, offering farewells and accepting thanks with all the bonhomie and triumph of a man who has already won an election. But once on board he disappeared into his sleeping compartment and was seen no more. Alasdair had a compartment next door and before the train had long left the lights of Albury behind he heard the Premier's roaring snores through the wall.

Was that the secret then, an ability to shut off and sleep at a moment's notice? An ability to clear one's mind of all troubling thoughts?

Alasdair pulled down the sash window in his own compartment and stuck his head outside. A rush of cold, smutty air hit him and he closed his eyes and let the rain fall on his face.

A week had passed since he had gone to the hospital and if Verity still lived, he did not know. This not knowing, it was an iron hand at his throat, its fingers slowly squeezing.

And three days had passed, too, since Eleanor had flung her accusation at him and he had countered her with his own accusations. There was no part of that encounter he wished to relive. That his wife knew of his most private dealings with Verity—his love-making! It was horrifying to him.

As horrifying as knowing of her liaison with another man.

And this astonished him! That he had, at last, found the courage to charge her with it and her deceit, a thing he had nursed and carried in his heart for eight months, was finally made real. It seemed incredible to him that he no longer bore it alone. That she now must assume the burden.

But she had not assumed it. Eleanor had denied it with a vehemence and a simplicity that had shaken him. He had long ago abandoned the possibility of her guiltlessness. Now—

He pressed his hands into his eyes to scour out the image. This new burden. A groan escaped his lips, to be whipped away by the wind.

It could not end well and this extended train jaunt into the interior was merely putting off what seemed inevitable: there could be no happiness for any of them.

He was stunned for a time at this revelation: that what he sought was happiness, a thing so intangible, so elusive, he had hardly believed in its existence before. Now he sought it with all his being but in the bitter knowledge it was denied him.

He opened his eyes to utter darkness, no light showed. If there were settlements out there no lights burned, and the cloud cover meant no moon and no stars. A perfect void. The rattle and hiss of the steam engine and the straining of the wheels and the couplings as the train negotiated an incline filled his head, the smoke filled his nose and his eyes. He slammed the window shut and sat on his bed.

He knew he would not sleep.

Their train was due in to Junee at two in the morning. They would be met at the station, have an early breakfast and go directly to their first engagement. It seemed monstrous, this two am arrival. If one was arriving somewhere at two in the morning one at least wished it to be Berlin or Vienna or Geneva, not this unknown place, this Junee.

He lay down on the bed and turned down the lamp. It was not possible to clear one's mind of all troubling thoughts. No matter how many miles a man travelled he brought such thoughts with him.

There was smoke in his eyes and though the lamp emitted a faint glow he could not see.

He was awoken by a jolt that almost threw him from his bunk and onto the floor. It was only by flinging out an arm to the wall that he saved himself from this indignity.

The carriage juddered and shook, a second jolt followed the first, and his trunk slid from the luggage rack and crashed to the floor. The train had come to a dead halt and Alasdair heard a rush of steam and the screech and grind of metal on metal, then silence.

He lay quite still in the bunk and his heart thudded so loudly it filled his head and his chest ached and strained.

'*It is a great log laid across the tracks,*' cried Greensmith, bursting into the compartment—

But Greensmith did not burst into the compartment. No one did. There was no sound, no voices, no panicked shouting up or down the train. And a moment later the couplings strained and went taut, the wheels engaged and the train moved off once more.

Alasdair found himself standing up, though he had no memory of leaving his bunk. He stood for a moment before dropping back down onto the bed. The train had braked suddenly and that was all, a kangaroo or a steer on the line. There was no log on the line, the train was not wrecked. But his body was damp with perspiration.

The compartment had a small sink in one corner and beside it a little cupboard containing a jug of water. He got up and lurched across the small space and got the jug and drank down a quantity of the water and splashed the remainder on his face. He stood for a time breathing slowly. The Premier's snores continued from the neighbouring compartment. It was doubtful the man had even woken. Alasdair opened the window again and stood letting the cold air calm him. He dimly made out a flurry of movement in the darkness. A mob of kangaroos startled by the train. In a second they were gone.

But his hands shook.

# CHAPTER TWENTY-FIVE

# INDISPOSED

'We heard you were indisposed, Eleanor. Are you unwell?'

Cecily Pyke had called and she had brought her eldest daughter, a tall girl called Marguerite who was of the age where girls wished to emulate their mothers and also despised them. They had arranged themselves, mother and daughter, on the settee and Alice had been dispatched to the kitchen.

*Was* Eleanor indisposed?

For four days she had made no calls and she had received no calls, and not because Alasdair had forbidden it, or not directly. It was simply this: the words they had spoken to each other, she and Alasdair, on Friday night and again early on Saturday morning would not let her alone. They could not be unsaid; they could not be bidden away. They had lodged somewhere very deep. They prevented Eleanor from leaving the house, sometimes even from venturing out of her room. They had made her turn callers away. It was an agony to be alone with those words echoing unceasingly inside her head but the agony of being in society seemed infinitely worse. So she drank tea alone, she read the newspaper, she organised the household accounts, she scrutinised the tradesmen's bills. She wore her spectacles almost all the time. She undertook all manner of everyday chores but the words remained. They would not be dislodged.

This morning, a Wednesday, Cecily Pyke had come to the door, an emissary from the outside world, and Eleanor had let her—and her daughter—in. She could not say why today particularly when every other day she had refused callers. She felt as though she had been away a long time though it had only been four days.

She had greeted her visitors cordially, she had seated them and herself, and now she poured tea with a steady hand.

'I am quite well, thank you, Mrs Pyke,' she said.

She had worn ivory and grey and oyster for four days, but this morning she wore a gown of the richest ultramarine Indian silk and she sat in her drawing room among the giant ferns. 'Like an exotic bird!' the daughter, Marguerite, had exclaimed, as though she had previously considered all her mother's cronies rather dull. And then she had coloured.

Eleanor smiled at the daughter from her place among the ferns. The ultramarine gown rustled faintly as Eleanor poured the tea, drawing attention to itself as a well-made garment should, with delicacy and subtlety. It was certainly not a gown of someone indisposed.

'Well. This is good news indeed,' said Mrs Pyke after a moment or two, when it became clear her host did not intend to expand upon her answer and the mystery of her alleged indisposition must remain just that: a mystery.

*But can you not see it?* cried Eleanor across the void that separated her chair from theirs. *Can you not feel it?* And all that she held tightly within herself was so great at that moment it threatened to spill out unchecked.

But, no, they could not see it.

'We have been reading of Mr Dunlevy's endeavours,' said Mrs Pyke. 'He is with the Premier, is he not, on the south coast?'

'So I am led to believe.'

'You do not accompany him?'

'No.'

'Fraser is at Waterloo this evening,' Mrs Pyke said, leaning forward a little as if this were classified information, though it had been reported in the newspaper that morning. 'He was with the Premier at Newcastle on Saturday night, of course, where they had upwards of six thousand, I understand.'

'He is not concerned?' Eleanor enquired. 'Waterloo is very near to Darlington, where they set fire to an effigy of the Premier and the police were obliged to put it out.'

'Was the Premier burned?' asked Marguerite, glancing up fascinated.

'No, dear,' said her mother. 'The Premier was not burned, thank the Good Lord, an *effigy* of the Premier was burned. It is quite a separate thing.'

Marguerite looked disappointed. 'Then what is it for?'

'To frighten people,' said Eleanor. 'Though I am sure no one was frightened. It was a very stupid thing to do. We had our own fright on our journey to Penrith. A log was thrown across the tracks and but for the quick thinking of the train driver we should have been quite derailed or worse.'

'Goodness!' said Mrs Pyke.

Marguerite adopted a considered expression, as though she were weighing up the probability of such an incident genuinely resulting in major calamity. 'Goodness,' she murmured at last, echoing her mother. She took up her mother's hand and began absent-mindedly to twist the rings on her mother's fingers.

'Were you frightened?' asked Mrs Pyke.

'I was a little. Not at first, but afterwards.'

Mrs Pyke nodded. 'That is how it is sometimes,' she said, as though she had experienced many such incidents in her time.

Alice came in. She deposited tea and a plate of Mrs Flynn's scones, and Marguerite observed her for she was of that age where all things were curious to her and none more so than herself so, when she observed the Dunlevy's servant, it was to see how the maid might view herself. But Alice left and so her impressions of Marguerite, if indeed she had any, remained undetermined.

'Oh! Mrs Flynn's scones! There is nothing like them,' declared Mrs Pyke. 'But, Marguerite, you must watch your figure—you are quite tall enough.'

'I like being tall,' said Marguerite, selecting the largest and most perfectly buttery and floury scone on the plate.

'Yes, dear, but your husband might not,' said her mother, patting her knee.

'Then I shall marry a tall husband. Or I shall find a short husband who does not mind his wife being taller than he.'

'I doubt there is such a husband,' said Eleanor, observing curiously, as she always did, the communication between mother and daughter. It was more curious to her now that her friends' daughters had reached this age where they accompanied their mothers on calls and where they came to picnics in pretty white dresses and sat under trees and no longer ran about underfoot as they had only a year or so earlier.

Eleanor smiled at the child and offered her another scone. Marguerite was only a few years Miss Trent's junior. In a year or two her husband, any of their husbands, would look at the girl quite differently. The girl's obliviousness as she sat playing with her mother's rings, her utter guilelessness, now appeared disingenuous and so Eleanor smiled at the child. She offered another scone.

'Marguerite, why not go and thank Mrs Flynn for the most excellent scones she has baked for us?' said Cecily to her daughter, which was a curious thing for her to suggest—certainly her daughter appeared to think so, for she looked blankly at her mother but was persuaded, finally, on this mission and departed.

No sooner had she quit the room than Cecily shot forward and asked breathlessly, 'You have seen the newspaper?'

She fired off her question so suddenly Eleanor was taken aback, and the look that accompanied it was pregnant with meaning, though what that meaning was Eleanor could not begin to guess. Unless . . .

Miss Trent. The arrest, the abortion, the police constables, the hospital, the doctor, her own husband—all of it swam before her eyes in large black bold letters on page five or perhaps page six of the *Sydney Morning Herald*.

'Poor Adaline!' said Cecily. 'There were all manner of lurid and sensational details about the divorce in this morning's paper—you must have seen it?'

Eleanor had seen it but could not, for the moment, speak.

And so Cecily went on, 'The housekeeper was revealed to have had a child! Can you imagine? Its paternity is not definitively stated—for lawsuits are pending—but the inference was clear. Adaline's children, or at least the two little girls, have been shipped already to grandparents in England and further lawsuits are anticipated . . . though one wonders who there is left to sue.'

She paused, and seemed at once to regret her gushy relaying of the events. Colouring a little, she sat back and arranged her hands on her lap, the pastoralist's wife once more.

'It is . . . dreadful,' said Eleanor, and she could think of nothing further to add. Their friend's downfall, terrible and spectacular and seemingly unstoppable, hung in the room between them.

'I called on Adaline,' said Cecily, after a little pause. 'It seemed the charitable thing. And she was so kind and gracious and made no reference at all to any of it. It was really rather sad.'

Eleanor moved her arm and heard her blue gown rustle noisily. She lowered her arm and sat perfectly still.

To be pitied. The horror of it took her breath away.

Marguerite returned from the kitchen, sullen and complaining from her encounter with Mrs Flynn, and her mother, skipping briskly from the Jellicoe divorce said, 'We read of you, too, in the newspaper, Eleanor, attending the Women's Suffrage League meeting against the bill. I rather expected to see you at the town hall with the Federal League, and instead there you were throwing in your lot with the opposition! I confess I was quite thrilled that you had done such a thing, and that Mr Dunlevy had allowed it.'

And so this was the purpose of the visit. But Cecily Pyke was not an unkind person; she suffered occasionally for the poor and the less fortunate. If she had called on her friend it was as much to see that all was well as it was to uncover secrets. But of all the preoccupations that smouldered within the heart of her silent and silk-clad host at this moment and that might, at some distant time, be revealed, it was humiliation and shame that burned the most fiercely and that would never, could never, be brought out into the daylight. And so Eleanor said, 'My attendance was at the behest of Miss Dempsey to support her as she supported her brother, and so Alasdair had no cause to say anything about it.'

Mrs Pyke was silent for a moment, and if she did not believe this or was disappointed by it, or if she was merely considering a third scone, was not clear.

'Well,' she said finally, 'I do think it very high-minded of Mr Dunlevy to agree to it. I am not certain Fraser would have, and he is a very high-minded man.'

And beside her Marguerite sighed and looked bored by the idea of her father being very high-minded.

∞

People were gathered outside Parliament House—for no very good reason that Eleanor could see, though it was certain to be connected in some way to the Federation. The crowd was small and, despite the rain, appeared to be settled in for the day.

But what can be achieved? thought Eleanor, whose patience with it all had run its course.

She had defied her husband, and she had defied herself. She had refused to remain at home another day and had come out. The visit from Cecily Pyke had shattered but also to some degree mended her. There was unfinished business and so she had come to Macquarie Street.

And almost immediately she saw her husband's secretary, James Greensmith. He emerged from the crowd, buttoning up a coat, papers under his arm and with a sense of purpose in his stride, but when he saw her—which he did, though she had done nothing to attract his attention—he stopped dead so that a man walked into him.

The crowd surged and swelled, and in another moment Mr Greensmith was gone from sight and Eleanor, who was not going that way at all, but who was instead going into the hospital next door, and who had come out in defiance of her husband, was uneasy.

For did Mr Greensmith, too, believe her to be indisposed? The thought unsettled her and she hurried a little with her head down. She did not know how much her husband's secretary might know of his employer's personal affairs, how much the young man might report back to him. She did not know very much at all about Mr Greensmith, she supposed. He played things very close to his chest, though he was always extremely well turned out and she suspected him of harbouring some very great ambitions, politically.

And then she dismissed Mr Greensmith from her thoughts, though the nagging doubt remained that he had seen her.

'My dear Mrs Dunlevy, this is a delightful surprise. Please do sit. Allow me to offer you some tea.'

'Ambrose. You are too kind.'

Eleanor allowed herself to be ushered to a seat and for tea with lemon to be administered to her and almost at once she began to feel better, for there is nothing like being administered to, especially by a wealthy, much older gentleman, and Ambrose Winks was undoubtedly both of these.

Winks had been, in some distant past, deputy superintendent of the hospital, though now he filled his time as chairman of its Benevolence Committee, a committee on which Eleanor had, for many years and with varying degrees of enthusiasm, served. He was an octogenarian, almost as old as the original hospital, and a man who dressed as though frockcoats, stovetop hats and untamed white beards had never gone out of fashion. His manners, too, had something of the arcane about them: when he spoke of Her Majesty, which he did often, it was as if she were eternally the girl of seventeen just ascended to the throne and he seemed frozen at that point, somewhere mid-century. But he was a dear man, and he always had time for Eleanor. For any lady, really.

'You are looking radiant,' he declared, which was perhaps something one said to a younger lady, not one just past her fortieth year, but from Winks's great age the difference between twenty and forty must seem very slight. 'I have been reading of your husband's endeavours,' he went on. 'He is with our dear Premier on this Tour of the South?'

And when she nodded,

'You do not accompany him?'

One never knew with Ambrose if a simple enquiry was just that, or if there was something more to it.

'He will have his hands full managing the Premier,' said Eleanor, keeping her eyes level with his. 'He does not need the added burden of a wife in tow.'

'I am sure you could never be a burden, Mrs Dunlevy.'

She smiled. 'You take gallantry to a higher elevation, Ambrose.' But she basked in it, a little.

'I try to, dear lady, I try to. Now, what may I do for you?'

'Intelligence. No, do not pretend you are not the repository of all that is, was and ever will be in this hospital, for I will not believe it.'

'Now *you* flatter *me*.' But his eyes sparkled.

'I speak no more than the truth.'

And now came the moment when pleasantries ended and the purpose of her visit must be revealed. And how extraordinarily hard it was to bridge that moment—for to reveal the purpose of her visit risked revealing herself. Her mouth had gone dry but she did not take up her teacup again, fearing her hand would shake.

But on she plunged for she was set on a certain course and would not waver from it.

'I am curious about an unfortunate young woman who was brought into the hospital in the custody of the police a week or so ago and whose future, we are led to believe, is in a precarious state, not least because she is gravely ill and does not wake.'

Winks nodded slowly as she spoke, and he now sat back in his chair and placed his hands together over his stomach. The lines on his face were deep and numerous like the rings of an ancient oak.

'I know the particular case of which you speak. It is, as you say, a most unfortunate case. What is it you wish to know?'

'Does the woman live?'

And thus was the most momentous question asked in so simple a way, as though it meant little, as though nothing at all hung on the reply.

'Yes. She lives.'

The reply came and nothing changed in the world and nothing changed in Eleanor's expression, although both had altered in a subtle and infinite way.

'A recovery appears more likely than not,' said Winks. 'She was insensible for some days but now has regained a little of her wits. Though her condition is still grave and may yet prove fatal.'

Eleanor was silent for a time. She did not know if she had desired Miss Trent to die or to live. Now that she had her answer she realised that what she desired meant nothing, that it would not alter the course of any lives, except perhaps her own.

'Is she aware of her surroundings, of her . . . predicament?'

'That I cannot say.'

'And what of that? The police charge? It is an extremely serious one?'

'Indeed. As I understand it, the charge—' And here the old gentleman hesitated delicately and gave her a look he might have reserved for the seventeen-year-old monarch were she here in his rooms. 'Eleanor, I do not mean to be coy, but you do understand the nature of the charge?'

'I do.'

He nodded. 'That is as well—I do not like to use euphemism when plain speaking will suffice. I understand the charge against the young woman will likely be dropped.'

Eleanor was not sure she had heard him correctly. 'But—that cannot be so!'

She felt herself disorientated and the great injustice that had been done to her seemed, by his words, to be condoned.

'The unfortunate young woman was arrested at her home and not—' he coughed delicately '—whilst the act itself was being performed. And the doctor—whoever this devil is—cannot be located. Absconded.'

'And so she gets away with this . . . this *abhorrent* act?'

Winks took a conciliatory approach: 'It is for God and not us mortals to sit in judgement.'

But Eleanor wondered if God did indeed sit in judgement of Miss Trent. It seemed to her he favoured her; that his justice, if one could call it such, was partisan and arbitrary.

'And for all we know,' said Winks, oblivious, 'it may have been a simple miscarriage.'

'You cannot seriously believe that?'

For a moment Eleanor was too stunned to think. And Winks offered no reply to her question.

'And what of the other party—the man?' she persisted, when she had calmed herself a little. 'We know she is not married. What do we know of him?'

'I do not believe we know anything of this man.'

'And so he gets away with it too. Scot-free.'

'Again, we may only speculate. Perhaps he colluded with Miss Trent in this terrible act and perhaps he is utterly ignorant of it.'

'If a man is utterly ignorant in a matter such as this it is because he chooses to be.'

Eleanor stood up. She went to the window. It afforded a view of rooftops, chimneys, the wall of another part of the hospital—the boiler room, perhaps, as great bellows of steam erupted periodically from a series of vents. When he had been deputy superintendent, Ambrose had had rooms overlooking Macquarie Street. He had had two secretaries. Today she had walked straight in to see him. She did not know why she thought of this, the thought crowded into a head already crammed to bursting.

'Ambrose—' she turned back to face the ageing administrator '—would you know if any man had visited her during her time here?'

'I would not. But I do not believe she would have been allowed any visitor during this time that she has been on a police charge.'

'Is she permitted visitors now?'

He regarded her with eyes almost as old as the century. 'You wish to visit her, Eleanor?'

'I feel it my duty, Ambrose. She is clearly a lost soul.'

Miss Trent, who had been abandoned by God or favoured by him, depending on how the thing was viewed, lay in a bed at the far end of a long and overcrowded women's ward on the second floor of the hospital. She lay unmoving and with her eyes closed. She did not look like the same woman whom Eleanor had helped up the stairs to her apartment and left seated on the settee as she was beginning to haemorrhage. This woman looked smaller, slighter, more fragile. It was still a rather plain face: too pale, too narrow, too sharp where it might have been better softer. Her eyelids were a shade of mauve and they flickered as though the eyes beneath the lids moved constantly in some hectic dream. Otherwise she did not stir.

There was nothing very appealing about her—there had been nothing then, there was nothing now. If Miss Trent held some secret allure, then she held it very close.

But Eleanor could not draw away.

There was unfinished business. Not the unfinished business she had anticipated, which was to hear of the girl lying in the morgue, halfway dispatched to some meagre and anonymous plot of land in a nearby churchyard; nor the alternative—shackled in a cell at the mercy of constable, prison warden and judiciary. But neither outcome, apparently, was Miss Trent's fate.

The door which Eleanor had expected to close remained firmly open.

She could not, for the moment, muster her thoughts. She studied Miss Trent's hands. They lay, or had been placed, on her chest as though she were dead. One finger twitched. These were not aristocratic hands but neither were they servant's hands. Something between. A governess, a shop girl. If these hands had scrubbed wooden tables and emptied slops or gutted fish it had been a long time ago. But who knew the truth of Miss Trent's former life? Miss Trent was recently arrived in the colony, which meant she was free from the curse that dogged every Sydney-born man and woman. No one would ever wonder if Miss Trent's people had arrived here in chains on transport ships, their backs seared and split open by the lash; no one would wonder if her grandmother had been a convict and a prostitute. Fortunate Miss Trent.

'You may sit,' said one of the nurses, indicating a chair, her eyes sweeping over Eleanor's face, but Eleanor did not sit. She was, after all, not a visitor and she hardly cared if the patient lived or died. Instead she studied Miss Trent, whose life she had, inadvertently, saved. She could go no nearer and she could not draw away, for it is a terrible thing to save the life of one who is despised. It is a burden.

The mistress lived.

Even if her child did not. Had Alasdair known about the existence of the baby or about the abortion? Had he arranged the abortion—paid for it, even? For he had gone to her at her home in the hours before she had had the abortion. A bastard child, unwanted. Perhaps he had demanded she rid herself of it. Perhaps the child had not been unwanted.

These were questions no wife should ever be called upon to consider.

This feeling that welled up inside her now, it was nothing so simple as hatred, and she stood, dumb. She would not allow it to overflow or consume her.

Miss Trent had not told Alasdair about the baby, about the abortion. Eleanor felt certain of this as she stood looking down at the girl. Or perhaps she merely wished it to be so. And Alasdair did not visit her in the hospital. Surely that meant—

She could not say what it meant. That he did not know she was here? That he was afraid to come lest he be seen? He was with the Premier in the south while his mistress lay prostrate and helpless. Perhaps it simply meant that the Federation meant more to him than Miss Trent did.

This made her suddenly a little giddy, made her wish to laugh out loud. Made her wish to reach out and strike the face that lay so still on the bed. But the nurse had returned and made a second sweep of Eleanor's face and so Eleanor turned and left the ward.

In the corridor outside the ward she found James Greensmith clutching a portfolio of papers and a telegram, now opened, and the expression on his face was no longer that of a secretary.

CHAPTER TWENTY-SIX

# NO BABIES HERE

Clouds blew in over The Gap and rolled over Watsons Bay and Bondi, for occasionally, and confusingly, the weather came in from the ocean and not from the west at all. Rain splashed onto the doorstep of the minister's house at Elizabeth Bay and the cook, Mrs Flynn, stood at the back door watching it. She was an uncomplicated soul who wasted no energy contemplating the differences between herself and her employer or, by inference, the differences between any two groups of persons in her city, wretched or wealthy or anything in between. If a person made a wrong step in their brief time on earth that was their lookout. She felt no compulsion to point out their error or to offer what little assistance it might be in her power to give. But this morning, these last few days, she found herself unaccountably uneasy.

She spat a stream of tobacco into the camellia bush outside, closed the back door and returned to her kitchen and the pastry she was rolling out.

Alice Nimrod, kneeling before the stove scraping and cleaning furiously, sat back on her haunches. She waited. But Mrs Flynn said nothing. She had said nothing for five days, and after a moment Alice went back to her work.

It was only once the pastry had been completed to Mrs Flynn's satisfaction and laid inside a pie dish with stewed apples, when two cloves had been placed just so and a dusting of cinnamon sprinkled on top and the pie deposited into the oven, that Mrs Flynn spoke. 'I hope you do not live to regret it, Alice, and that's all I have to say on the matter.'

'And why should I regret giving the baby a chance of a better life?' cried Alice all in a rush and jumping to her feet, for these words had been ready and straining to be released these five days and more.

'Because that baby is no more on a farm in the country with cows and sheep and what have you than it is with Her Majesty at Windsor Castle.'

'You do not know that!'

'Don't I?'

For a time neither spoke. Mrs Flynn pulled out a chair and sat down on it. She sighed—and she was not, as a rule, a woman who sighed; she was a woman who got on and did what needed to be done. But today she sighed. 'You have lived on those streets, Alice Nimrod. You know what kind of place this is, same as ever I do.'

And Alice did know. But sometimes to know a thing did not help. Sometimes it made things worse.

Alice went upstairs and she beat the curtains in Mr Dunlevy's room and she dragged the carpet sweeper over the rugs and flung open the windows to air the place, and the rain thundered onto the roof and the guttering and onto the sill so that she had to close the windows again almost at once.

Mrs Flynn thought the baby was dead.

Alice pulled the layers of bedding from Mr Dunlevy's bed and bundled them up and placed new ones on. She put away the gloves and collars and shirts that had returned from the laundry and noted which had a mark on them the laundry had missed and which were not starched just right. She polished the bedheads and she dusted the desk and the shelves and the drawers and the pictures on the walls and the photographs in their frames.

And she saw that everything had been moved about in Mr Dunlevy's room. The dust was disturbed, things had been taken up and replaced in a slightly different way: drawers, books, everything. She wondered if Mrs Dunlevy had done it, though why Mrs Dunlevy might do such a thing Alice did not know.

They had avoided each other since Friday evening, and five days was a long time for a servant to avoid her mistress and an even longer time for a mistress to avoid her servant, but they had managed it. This was, in large part, down to Alice, who spent a great deal of her time scurrying back up the stairs and darting into rooms and turning about and walking back the way she had just come, and she did this because she had no wish to witness her mistress's shame for she had found that, inexplicably, she shared in it.

This was confusing to her and she wished Mr Dunlevy would return from his trip, though she could not see how this might improve things. But she felt the awkwardness of her situation.

The one o'clock gun sounded at Fort Denison and the second post came and then the third, and in the scullery Mrs Flynn's apple pie cooled on a tray. The clocks in each room chimed and chimed again, marking another hour, marking the end of another day. Five days had already passed since Alice had handed over the baby. The moon came up before the afternoon was even half done, for the June days were almost at their shortest, and soon it would be six days. When she saw the moon, when she counted the days that had passed, Alice was filled with such a great terror she forgot to breathe.

Mrs Dunlevy dined alone and did not eat even a single slice of the apple pie so that Alice took it back to the kitchen.

'What can be done?' she said to Mrs Flynn, and she was not referring to the uneaten pie. She rarely asked anyone for anything, for you almost never got what you wanted or, if you did, then the cost was likely to be more than you could afford. But tonight she asked Mrs Flynn.

Mrs Flynn, who thought the baby was already dead, said, 'Go and get it back, Alice Nimrod, if you are able.'

'And then what?'

'Leave it outside the orphanage where it should have been all along.'

'And never see it again?'

'And know it lives.'

At half past midnight on platform 14 of Sydney Terminal Station everything was as it had been five nights before—the rain came down in sheets, a porter stalked the empty platforms with a lamp held high, the last trains arrived and the passengers moved silently about in the great billows of steam and smoke like exhausted, ancient ghosts. And a girl with a baby waited in the shadows, shivering with cold and fear as though she did not know if she feared salvation more than she feared death.

Though neither came.

Alice watched her. The girl wore a rain-soaked sagging straw hat and she turned this way and that, starting at every sound and occasionally wiping a sleeve over her nose. She waited, but how long she would wait depended on many things and some of them Alice could guess, others she could not. A train whistled distantly and approached the station and the girl cocked her head, and in another moment she and her bundle would be on the tracks beneath the oncoming train and both their miseries would be over.

But here, now, was Mrs Flowers emerging from the steam and the smoke and the shadows and offering her own particular brand of salvation. She called out to the girl, approached her and spoke again, sharply. Alice pressed herself into the shadows and heard nothing of the transaction. In a moment it was done, money and baby exchanged, the bundle wrapped tightly inside the older woman's coat, and all of their destinies forever altered—the child's, the girl's, possibly Mrs Flower's too, though this seemed less certain.

Mrs Flowers walked away at a rapid pace and did not look back and was at once swallowed up in the darkness and the smoke so that her brief presence had an unnatural and unreal quality to it, like a spectral visitation.

The girl, having handed her child over to a stranger, stood quite still with a hand pressed against her mouth. She walked blindly away and there seemed every likelihood her night would end beneath the wheels of a train; or, if not this night, then another.

But Alice Nimrod did not stay to observe it. She set off after the hurrying black figure of Mrs Flowers, skirting the puddles and leaping the overflowing gutters, startled by the speed at which the woman moved, and with a baby in her arms.

They left the station, heading eastwards along Devonshire Street and making a series of turns down ever narrower and darker laneways so that Alice, who had grown up in these streets, hardly knew where they were. When they had reached the darkest, the narrowest laneway at the heart of a maze of such places—a laneway so narrow you could touch both sides at once without even stretching, a place so foul that the pigs which roamed other Surry Hills laneways, rooting out and consuming its refuge and detritus, were here quite absent—Mrs Flowers reached her destination. She pushed at an unseen gate and was gone and she did not pause, not even for a moment, to look behind her, for Mrs Flowers did the work of the devil and so she had little to fear from mortal souls.

She had little to fear from Alice Nimrod, whose soul was of the most mortal kind and who was but a few yards behind and so reached the place a moment later.

Alice found the gate with her hands for the darkness was all-consuming and unforgiving. The gate was not latched; indeed, it was barely attached to its hinges at all so that, when she pushed it and slipped inside, it almost clattered to the ground.

Beyond was a space filled with dark shadows and unpleasant odours, a tiny yard, overgrown and piled high with whatever such places were piled high with. It backed onto the rear of a dwelling, which in this neighbourhood was a crumbling and single-storey worker's cottage.

No light showed. Someone in one of the neighbouring cottages sang loudly and drunkenly and further away men's voices were raised in dispute and something smashed, a bottle or a window. A bat flew overhead with a great flap of black leathery wings and Alice stifled a cry. Something scurried over her foot.

From the cottage there was no sound at all, no baby crying, nothing.

Alice waited, straining to hear, gathering her courage about her. There was a cesspit here; she felt the muck oozing beneath her feet and she wondered what else it was in this yard that emitted such unpleasant odours. A dead dog? Animal bones and butcher's offal and other rubbish from the house, human and animal, which, if you lived among it long enough, you no longer noticed? But what if it was not the corpse of a dead dog?

She hammered on the door and prayed she would not die this night.

After a long moment the door opened a crack.

'Who's zere?'

It was a man's voice. She had not anticipated this. Hoarse and rasping, and with it came a gust of stale tobacco, unwashed bodies, smoke and something that had been fried a long while ago and still lingered.

'I want my baby back,' said Alice.

She could see almost nothing of the man, for the interior of the cottage seemed darker even than the night, but at her words she sensed a quick movement of his head, a sucking of his teeth, the rustle of layers of coarse clothing. She sensed his astonishment.

'Git outta here!'

'I want my baby back,' said Alice a second time.

'No babies here. Gorn, scram!'

'Yes, there is,' Alice persisted, though she felt that something must give—her courage or her bladder. Her legs perhaps and her heart too. All seemed on the verge of collapse. 'I gave it to Mrs Flowers Friday night and now I have followed her here with some other woman's baby and I want mine back.'

At this the door opened abruptly and the man stumbled out, so that Alice stepped back with a gasp and threw out a hand to steady herself. She felt his breath on her face

'Ain't no Mrs Flowers here. Ain't no babies here.'

A baby cried then from somewhere behind him inside the cottage, a wail that split the night in two, and for the length of the cry they both stood in frozen muteness.

And then the wail stopped and the man's arm shot out and grabbed the back of Alice's neck and a blade flashed in the moonlight and Alice felt its edge at her throat.

'I said *no babies here*. You show your face here again I will slice it right off.'

He let go of her and Alice fell backwards into the muck and the rubbish. She scrambled to her feet and fled.

CHAPTER TWENTY-SEVEN

# LARGE EVENTS AND SMALL DETAILS

The Premier's party took the midnight train from Cootamundra, arriving at Goulburn in the early hours. The mayor and various aldermen held a reception for them upon their arrival and members of the local Federal League gave a welcome address. The party lunched at the council chambers, attended by a hundred local gentleman and waited on by the ladies of the district. Toasts were drunk and the Premier made a speech. In the evening the Premier spoke at length at the Oddfellows' Hall, which had been extravagantly hung with bunting and ribbons and flags, and the large crowd applauded him, and themselves, enthusiastically.

And afterwards what Alasdair remembered was the way an alderman's wife had stifled a yawn at their pre-dawn arrival at the station and how a cockerel had crowed as they had sat in the carriage and travelled through the deserted streets. He remembered the line of native paperbarks behind the single row of buildings in the main street and the Premier stumbling as he entered the hotel and two porters exchanging looks of mutual disappointment that the Premier was, after all, just a man. He remembered the plate of mutton a woman had placed before him at the luncheon and the slight crack in the plate's rim. He thought of the button that had come loose on his topcoat as he dressed and of the green baize that covered the speakers' tables at the Oddfellows' Hall and that hung in great folds and rubbed against his knees. He remembered that, as the Premier explained to the people why it was he had rejected the Federation bill a year ago and why he supported it now, a small piece of bunting above his head came unstuck and drifted to the floor.

For life was made up not of large events but of small details, and today's receptions, the many speeches, though they may appear of vital importance at the time (otherwise why the rush to catch the midnight express last night, why all those aldermen up before dawn dressed in their finery, their wives yawning?), would not be remembered in a hundred years. There had been a referendum last year and when it had failed it had seemed nothing short of a catastrophe. But in the end it had not mattered, for here they all were, a year later, holding another one.

As he had boarded the express at Cootamundra an official had handed Alasdair a telegram. He had stuffed it in a pocket of his coat and boarded the train and overseen the stowing of his bags and gone to the Premier's compartment to discuss some point of issue for the following day. He had bade the others of their party goodnight and retired to his compartment with the telegram still in his pocket just as though such telegrams came every day and did not mean very much.

He had sat on his bed and adjusted the light and pulled out the telegram—sent from Sydney a few hours ago in reply to the one he himself had dispatched earlier, and reaching him only due to the greatest good fortune, for he had been at Cootamundra no more than a few hours—and his hand shook.

It was from Greensmith. It said simply: PATIENT TRENT CONSCIOUS THOUGH STILL ILL STOP DOCTORS HOPEFUL OF RECOVERY STOP AWAIT FURTHER INSTRUCTIONS STOP GREENSMITH.

The minister had folded the telegram in two and then closed his fists around it. He had slid off the bed and dropped to his knees and crouched with his forehead touching the floor. And when, a few hours later, the train had rattled into Goulburn, he had stood at the window and the dawn had glowed orange and a vast flock of white cockatoos had risen to the air and filled the sky.

The Tour of the South was completed. The party left Goulburn by the last train and would arrive in Sydney at midnight. They would sleep in their own beds that night.

As the train plunged northwards through the dark, the gentlemen sat facing one another, the mood at first loud and boisterous—for the tour had been a success—and later contemplative and silent as they were rocked by the motion of the carriage. They thought about the wives awaiting their return, the urgent papers requiring their attention, their beds and a pipe or a good cigar by the fire.

The Premier leaned across the small space and patted Alasdair's knee and said, 'Come on with us tomorrow to Bathurst, Dunlevy—there is space enough and it will be a big event. You shall be my opening speaker.'

And this was a triumph for Alasdair, hard-earned and a long time coming. He swelled, a little, with pride.

The Premier added, 'Though do not bring that wife of yours—we do not wish an anti-billite in our midst!'

It seemed that the Premier might laugh now to indicate that this was a little joke, but the Premier did not laugh. It was not a little joke, and Alasdair's triumph, hard-earned and a long time coming, turned to cold dismay.

But the telegram smouldered in his pocket and Miss Trent lived. He touched the telegram and his fingers glowed warm. The train to Bathurst would depart mid-morning the next day so he would have only a few hours in Sydney, but that was all he needed.

They arrived at Sydney Terminal at midnight, and though the hour was late and the train had been delayed, men were there from the press, and a number of other gentlemen and even one or two wives, though Eleanor was not among them. The Premier gave an impromptu speech on the platform, which a number of the gentlemen of the press copied down and others did not, for nothing was said that had not been said on other platforms and at other stations. And Alasdair wondered what it would be like for the Premier, sometime hence, to exit a train and not be greeted by the members of the press and not be called upon to make an impromptu speech—for such a time would surely come.

He left in a cab at the first opportunity, observing those members of his party whose wives had ventured out in the dark and the cold and the incessant rain—it still rained here in Sydney!—to meet them. It was very strange to know that his wife was not among them and perhaps (for all kinds of vague but extraordinary ideas now eddied about his head) never would be again. He stared out of the window of the cab and thought how strange it all was.

The house in Elizabeth Bay was in darkness and no one waited up for him. He hammered loudly on the door and a light came on upstairs. In a moment the door opened and Alice stood there in a nightgown and a shawl, holding a candle. She threw up a hand to cover her throat as a lady would who had mislaid her pearls and her face was frightened.

He got her to fill him a bath and find him some refreshment for he was hungry, he realised, though he did not know what he wanted. In the end he accepted a piece of cold apple pie and a glass of port in his study, where he sat, warm from the bath and exhausted, but fearing he would not sleep.

He did sleep, awaking at dawn to a clear sky and a shaft of early daylight that struck his pillow an inch from his head. He lay for a moment, as one did as a small boy on birthdays and other import-ant days, not wanting the day to start and fearing it never would. He must tell Alice he would need a new set of clothes for the trip to Bathurst, and whether the Premier intended that Alasdair continue on with him to Wellington and Orange he did not know but it was well to assume he would.

The importance of it, this building of a nation and his part in it, struck him afresh and he basked, for a moment. The Premier's comment about his wife could be ignored, could be discounted for the joke it undoubtedly was. It would not spoil this moment.

And Alasdair lay, stunned by the sunlight, by the clearness of the sky, by the chorus of jubilant currawongs outside his window. When at last he sat up it seemed to him that the room must have changed in some subtle way as he had changed, but there was nothing different. He dressed and roused Alice for his coffee and his breakfast and gave her instructions for his departure. She got in a muddle with it all as though she did not have the space in her head for more than three things at once. She had a small cut, he saw, on her throat, and the imperfection of her, of Alice the maid, was for a moment dispiriting. When he had sent her away he got up and went to stand at the window so that he might view the bay through the bare branches of the winter frangipani, something he had never before done.

It occurred to him he must be gone before Eleanor came downstairs, and now that he had had this thought it became, suddenly, imperative. He chased and cajoled the unfortunate Alice until all was done to his satisfaction then sent her out to find a cab. He stood at the front door surrounded by his bags. He listened for Eleanor's door to open upstairs but no sound came. Was she awaiting his departure, he wondered, before venturing downstairs? And, perversely, he had a mind to hold off his departure.

But the cab was here and his bags stowed. He climbed in and told the driver to take him to the Sydney Hospital.

'Driver, wait! Alasdair! Where are you going?'

His mind was far away and Alasdair could not, at first, make sense of these words, he could not identify the voice that spoke them. When he had swum across the ocean that separated his thoughts from the place where his physical body was, he saw it was his wife who addressed the cab driver, who stood at the door of his cab without hat or gloves or even a coat. She shivered, her arms hugging herself as though it were a winter morning in some cold place and not a Sydney morning with the sun already high in the southern sky warming the earth.

Her eyes searched his face. They peeled back layers of skin revealing the soft tissue beneath. His flesh burned.

'I am going to the station,' he replied, indignant, as might any man be at such a question. He was on official business. He was to join the Premier.

But they had passed this point. They were already halfway down a path that was uncharted and brutal and had no place for denials. And so he added, in a quite different tone, 'And to the hospital.'

These words, freeing him.

A vaguely quizzical look came into Eleanor's eyes and he thought for a brief, bright, extraordinary moment that she had accepted what he said, but the look was gone almost at once, leaving no look at all, a blankness. Calm acceptance, he took it for. But he was wrong.

She grabbed the handle of the cab door and jerked it open and began to get in.

Dismayed, he held her off.

'What are you doing, Eleanor? For God's sake!'

He wrestled the door from her and she fell back, stumbling a little. Behind her he saw the cab driver, who had jumped down from his perch and had his mouth open and the whip in his hand, and Alasdair stared at the man's stupid face rather than at his wife's. He resumed his seat. He pulled the door shut and shouted at the man, 'What do you wait for?'

The man sprang back up to his seat and cracked his whip and the horse started awake and the cab jerked forward. Alasdair stared straight ahead.

At Macquarie Street the clerks and lawyers and government officials strolled towards their places of business, the usual morning industry made languid by the suddenness of sunlight after so much rain. The people shone and the streets, submerged by the deluge only hours before, were bone-dry.

Alasdair viewed them across a great distance. The horror of it wrapped him in a mantle that pinned his arms to his sides and dulled the thoughts in his head.

It had come too soon, the confrontation with Eleanor. He was not prepared. He had meant to do it on his terms not hers. He wished very much to be angry at her for that appalling scene, but for the moment the horror of it precluded his fury.

The cab pulled up outside the hospital and Alasdair gave the driver a large sum without once looking at him. The man's gaze was a torment to him. He instructed the man to wait here, with his bags, until his return. It would be a short visit, but the moments on which a man's life turned *were* short—for how long did it take to fall in love, to propose marriage, to receive a firstborn in one's arms, to fall out of love?

Miss Trent was in a women's ward on the second floor and he wondered if he might be prevented from seeing her but no one questioned him. A nurse bid him a good morning and another offered a smile and pointed out to him a bed at the far end. 'There is a chair,' the nurse said. 'You may sit if you wish.'

Alasdair walked towards her. On each side tall windows looked out on colonnades that ran the length of the ward, dappled in the sunlight, like a viceroy's residence. The ceiling, distantly high to catch the breeze in summer, made him reel. And here, finally, was Verity. She made a still, slight figure barely distinguishable from the large hospital bed and the coarse hospital sheets that trapped her. Her face on the pillow was white and as contemplatively still as an angel on a tomb.

He thought, She has died, and no one even noticed!

But her face slowly turned towards him.

He stumbled. Those final few yards that separated him from her were infinite and terrible, her eyes on him as he crossed that unimaginably vast space made him feel his nakedness, and he crossed the remaining few yards quickly, coming to her side, pulling up the chair and taking her hand.

'Verity,' he said. His voice came from some deep place.

Now all the hours and the days that he had not sat with her at her bedside, that he had spent in other places and in other towns, in hotels and trains and town halls, all the mementos of her that he had scoured his drawers for and burned, all of this was manifest in his face for her to see. His shame laid bare.

'Will you forgive me?' he whispered.

She frowned at this, her brow creasing, the eyebrows arching, as though she did not understand what it was she must forgive, as if she had thought it was she, not he, who must ask for forgiveness—for their baby that she had destroyed.

Or this is what he thought, for she said absolutely nothing. He squeezed her hand.

At last she spoke. 'You know, of course, why it is that I am here?'

He did. He could not unknow it.

'I told them it was a miscarriage,' she said, her voice very low and quite without emotion. 'Though it was not.' And she turned her face away and towards the window.

'Yes,' said Alasdair. He would have liked to say, *I understand*, but he could not say it for he did not understand. Their child, destroyed.

'The police have left me alone. I am not worth their while,' she said.

At this, Alasdair sat dumbfounded.

'You did not know?' she asked, turning to him and scrutinising his face. 'I thought that was why you were here.'

'No, I did not know.' He took a long breath. 'I came here to say I will do whatever can be done. I will engage the best lawyer in the colony to defend you.'

For a time neither spoke.

'Well, now you shall not need to,' she said. 'But it was a kind thought.'

'A kind thought?'

He stood and turned about. A nurse further down the ward, tending another woman, looked up and stared at him. He sat down again.

'It was not a kind thought, Verity. It was necessary. To save you.'

He flinched at the melodrama of his own words, at the assumption that he could save her. But he had not said yet what he most needed to say.

'Verity, it is no longer possible for me to continue in this manner. Indeed, I do not wish to. We cannot marry but we may be together—if not here, then in another city. Melbourne. London. Wherever you wish it to be.'

His words burst from him, the more so for being so long contained, and once they were free, he was free, and a world of possibility opened before him. Before them both.

'If I must retire from public life I will do so, gladly.' He gave a little laugh, afraid that he might not be able to express what was in his heart. 'All those things that mattered to me I no longer care for. They are like . . . dust. I will find something else to do. With you at my side.' He touched her face. 'Verity, there will be other children.'

∞

The hansom cab into which the minister had climbed had gone some little time ago, in a flurry of whips and shouting and the clatter of hooves, and a quiet calm had then descended on the peaceful little bay so that it was once more like any other morning.

But it was not like any other morning, for the minister's wife stood in the road, her arms by her side with no hat and no gloves. With nothing.

A face had appeared briefly at an upstairs window of a neighbouring villa, a servant stood at an opened back door and paused in wonder, but now both were gone. Elsewhere blinds were closed, curtains drawn, doors were closed. After a time Eleanor turned and went back inside.

A short time later Alice emerged and went off up the street, returning with a second cab. Eleanor came out of the house and this time she wore hat and gloves and coat and got into the cab.

'The Sydney Hospital,' she said to the driver, and the driver, who had just finished a morning cup of tea and had enjoyed a bit of a break, shook the reins of his horses and said, 'Giddup,' and thought nothing of it.

They arrived at the hospital and Eleanor went to the ward she had gone to two days earlier. The same nurse or another one smiled at her as she passed. They smiled a great deal, these nurses, though all one could see of them, due to the nun-like wimples that covered their heads, was the smooth white oval of their faces. Eleanor felt she did not quite trust their smiles, that they hid something deep within themselves. She passed the nurse coldly and did not meet her eye.

She walked a little way down the ward but she went no further than, perhaps, halfway. She could see her husband beside the bed at the far end, seated on the chair the nurse had bade she herself sit on, and she could see the figure prone on the bed, awake, now, and listening. Or not listening, she could not tell.

She could not see her husband's face, only his back, his shoulders, his hands, his head. Every part of him was turned towards the woman on the bed, every muscle and fibre of his body was taut as he cleaved to her.

'All those things that mattered to me I no longer care for. They are like . . . dust,' he said to her, as a man does who tears open his soul and offers it to another.

A nurse spoke to Eleanor, came and stood beside her, calm and white and complacent, opening and closing her mouth. 'Who is it you wish to visit?' the nurse repeated.

'I will find something else to do. With you at my side.'

Said her husband. Eleanor watched him reach out and touch the face of the figure on the bed.

And at the touch of his fingers on this woman's face he rendered all the things that had mattered to him to dust. His wife, watching, was rendered to dust.

Eleanor swung her gaze away from the scene at the bed and into the watching face of the nurse, who remained doggedly at her side. Whose hand gripped her arm at the elbow, whose hold prevented her, it seemed, from falling. Guided her towards a chair, her expression curious, kind, concerned, wishing nothing more than to assist.

But it was not in her power to give the assistance Eleanor required. Eleanor shook the woman off. She walked towards the door.

From the far end of the ward her husband's words followed her: 'Verity, there will be other children.'

∽

The ward had an easterly aspect and through the tall windows slivers of brilliant white light struck the ceiling far above. Cathedral-like, thought Alasdair, though he was not a religious man. If he had been he would not have compared a hospital ward to a cathedral, but he was in that place where men looked for, and saw, what they needed.

'I do not want other children,' said Verity.

Alasdair lowered his gaze from the heavens to her face.

'Perhaps not at first,' he said.

Alasdair stroked the back of her hand with his forefinger, noticing the delicate blue veins just below the skin, the way her fingers lay spread out on the sheet as though she pressed down on something but how one finger—the little finger—lifted off the bed involuntarily. His heart danced inside him and his ears rang.

She pulled her hand away. 'I do not wish to have a child. Why do you not take my meaning?'

'Because I hope that you will come to change your mind.' And it hurt him, unaccountably, that she had withdrawn her hand, though it was a small thing in itself.

'You think you know my mind better than I do?' And she turned to look at him, her eyes curious, intent.

He smiled. 'I think many young ladies do not know their own minds.'

She turned away again. 'That is what John used to say.'

He did not anticipate that. 'You mean this clerk fellow, John Brewster, your fiancé?'

'John said, *It will be better for you, Verity, if you stay in England whilst I go and make my fortune in the colonies. It will be better for you if you do not follow me. It will be better for you*—and, of course, what he meant was, it would be better for *him*—if I gave up any idea of marriage altogether.'

And again Alasdair was at a loss. What did it mean that she talked to him of this man, the dead clerk?

'And, of course, I did know my own mind and John did not,' she said, as though she had scored a victory, somehow, over her dead fiancé.

Though this man had not, it now seemed, been her fiancé. The man, Brewster, had thrown her over. But she had come out after him. Pursued him. And again Alasdair did not know what it meant.

'John was the reason I came to this place,' she went on, 'and now I wish to return home. If you believe that I am indebted to you, then you may cast an eye over my present circumstance and reconsider.'

'Verity, if you wish to return to England, then I shall accompany you. I have already said so.' And Alasdair was glad to be able to offer his sacrifice to her a second time.

'I wish you to arrange my passage but I do not wish you to accompany me.'

Some dim sense of her meaning now reached him and a fissure began to appear in the new world he had created for them both. Perhaps she sensed it, for she went on without awaiting his reply. 'I do not wish to be your mistress. I do not wish to be any man's mistress. It suited me, I believe, for a time, and perhaps I allowed you to convince me that it was in my best interests, or that it was, in fact, my only option. It is not. I can return home a free woman, unencumbered, and that is what I wish to do.'

The fissure widened and a tiny trickle of his life blood spilled into it.

'I love you, Verity,' he said simply. 'It is a love that consumes me. It has changed my life. Changed me. Do you not see it?'

He had imagined, many times, saying these words to her, and in his imagination they came, always, as a triumphant culmination. They were not like this: an entreaty, a beseeching.

Verity struggled to sit up, her face level with his, and her face was like that of another woman entirely.

'I believe I have grown to despise you,' she said. 'I do not know how much more plain I can be. If I have deceived you in this, then

I say you have deceived yourself. I despise the role you have created for me, second to your wife, whom you would desert in a moment but to whom you would remain married. And I despise this place.'

She looked about her at the ward and the prostrate people in it, but her look stretched far beyond the hospital.

'It is a savage and uncivilised place and its people strut about as though they have the most magnificent city in the world when most have never set foot in London or in any great capital. They think their city is paved with gold when it is thick with sheep and flies and the children of convicts. It is as wretched a place as ever I saw.'

Each word struck its blow and Alasdair did not move. The words nailed him, without mercy, to the chair.

They rained down on him and he was powerless to deflect them.

She despised him, and this was as wretched a place as she ever saw. He did not know which revelation shook him the most. If she had told him night was day and the sun was the moon he might have been less astonished. Less destroyed.

He rose from the chair. He nodded stiffly at her and turned away, and as he left the ward a nurse looked up and smiled at him hopefully but he did not see her.

CHAPTER TWENTY-EIGHT

# THE BABY FARM

'I warned you!' Mrs Flynn had said unhelpfully, when Alice had come to her the morning after, still shaken and with a scratch on her throat where the man's knife had nicked her. But she had sat the girl down and administered a nip of gin, watching silently as Alice swallowed it and choked a little.

'You must go to the police,' Mrs Flynn declared with a conviction admirable in someone who, not ten days earlier, had stood in this same kitchen and laughed at the notion the law might protect them.

'No!' Alice cried, jumping up so that the chair crashed to the floor. 'It is 'cause of the police that things have got to where they have.'

Mrs Flynn gave her a look that suggested this was an interpretation of events to which she did not subscribe, but Mrs Flynn did not know all the facts. And Mrs Flynn had not known Milli. There would be no police.

'Then what is to be done, Alice? What is to be done?' And Mrs Flynn went off shaking her head.

What *was* to be done? Alice did not know and she went through her day and into the next day believing the baby already dead, steeling herself to believe that this was the best thing—for the baby, for everyone. But it is a terrible thing to deaden your own heart and sometimes the heart will not be deadened.

'I shall go back to the house. Perhaps it is not too late,' she announced finally, on the Friday morning, and she stood in the middle of the kitchen in defiance of Mrs Flynn as though the older woman might try to prevent her, when in fact there was no one who cared enough about Alice Nimrod to prevent her walking into danger or to offer comfort when she did.

But Mrs Flynn was concerned, for the household routine was threatened.

'*Now?*' she said, astonished. It was the middle of the day. She had never heard of such a thing. But Mrs Flynn, perhaps remembering the revolutionary corsets and seeing that the world was no longer a place she knew, sighed. 'Go then. If the mistress asks where you are I shall think of something to tell her.'

And so Alice had gone.

And in the daylight she hardly recognised the place. She picked her way along the narrow and cluttered lane through the refuse of a dozen households and the rats did not scurry away at her approach and a dog, rabid and diseased, worried at her heels.

But selecting one dilapidated gate from the many such gates hanging limply from their broken hinges in a wall of crumbling brickwork was no simple matter.

She decided at last on one and eased the gate open. Yes, here was the yard, seen now in daylight, squalid and strewn with rubbish. From a fence post a brace of dead rabbits hung by their feet swinging gently in the breeze and festering with maggots.

The yard backed onto a squat and crumbling single-storey cottage built of disintegrating sandstone and dating from the earliest decades of the settlement and unlikely to make it into the new century. It was a building as unlovely and unloved as any in the colony. The sort of place folk gratefully left behind in their overcrowded and wretched cities in the old country and then, inexplicably, set about re-creating in this new land. It had a solitary window which was boarded up. The back door, its timbers rotting, was approached by a step that was all but crumbled away. Above, a precariously leaning chimney, from which no smoke came, poked uneasily from its roof.

This was surely the place, though the cottage next door or the one beyond that could just as easily be it too, for the uneven rows of houses went on and on, and the people who lived in them went on and on, and the horror Alice Nimrod felt was the horror of someone who had escaped.

But the cottage was strangely silent.

And that was odd, for all about the laneways teemed. Not with life, exactly, but with the half-living that passed for life here—the drunk and the insensible and the destitute and the dead all piled one on top of another, some in silence and others in an ecstasy of commotion, enough to pierce the ears and bring the crumbling buildings crashing about their inadequate foundations.

But this cottage was silent.

Alice went up to the door and listened. She pulled the door and it creaked, opening perhaps halfway before becoming stuck in its ill-fitting frame. The smell, too, was different this time. No smoke or cooking or the stale odour of unwashed bodies, just a foetid, rotting stench of decay and human waste and the mustiness of rodents. Alice waited. She listened for the slightest sound that might indicate someone lurked within. But nothing stirred.

Except for a scratching and a rustling. And so Alice forced her body through the gap and half-a-dozen rats scurried into the shadows.

Light spilled in behind her and she saw that she stood in a mean little kitchen or scullery, now abandoned. Some previous occupant had installed shelves, a lop-sided cupboard and a three-legged table. Piles of rubbish—food scrapings, old newspapers, spilled wax, straw—covered the floor and the one or two surfaces, but nothing of value had been left behind. She stepped cautiously in the half-light, going through to a second room at the front of the cottage. This was a larger space, she sensed, and similarly abandoned, but it was in darkness, the window boarded up, the door onto the street shut.

She heard again a scurrying of rats startled by her presence.

She plunged into this second, larger room and thrust out both hands into the blackness making for the door, feeling for a handle or a knob or a latch, finally just grabbing the wood and pulling and pushing, and eventually it dislodged enough to swing open and a shaft of daylight pierced the room behind her. She turned about, fearful of what she might see, but this room was empty, a floor covered with loose boards, some scraps of matting strewn with rat droppings, a crudely constructed and empty fireplace and bare, stone walls.

But Alice had seen something in the corner of the room that stilled her heart.

It must be a piece of rubbish. Yes, surely that was it. But she knew it was not. She walked over, not quite touching the floor, not touching anything, separate from the world around her. She stopped two feet away.

It was an arm. A tiny newborn's limb, bloodied and dead and showing the gnaw marks of the rats that had taken it.

She spun away, stumbling and blinded, and when she had reached a wall against which she might throw out a shaking hand, she vomited. When she had retched herself hoarse and the rats had begun to circle, she stood up, shouting at them and kicking until they scurried away once more.

She went back to the dead thing, her hand clamped firmly to her mouth. But this was just a single arm when there were two babies here, at least. Milli's and the other girl's. Where was the rest of this poor infant, and where was the other baby?

In the far corner of the room a floorboard had been dislodged. She went over and crouched down, pulling at the boards and finding beneath them a hollowed-out place and two bundles, one bloodied and butchered, and she cried as with a shaking finger she pulled the torn rags away and saw the remains of the thing that a day or so earlier the terrified girl had handed over, in her innocence, to a murderer. She flung the rags back over the horrid thing to cover it. She turned to the second bundle, but now her fingers shook so much she could not grip the cloth that covered it. Steeling herself, she poked it and it did not stir.

It did not stir.

She took hold of the cloth and pulled it, finding inside the bundle a baby, a tiny, unspoiled baby boy, quite still.

She let out a sob and scooped up the dead thing.

And when she felt the tiniest beat of a tiny heart, still fighting despite all that the world had done to stop it, she gasped and could not see for the tears that ran down her face and fell onto the baby's forehead.

A baptism, almost.

When she was able, she got to her feet and fled.

367

CHAPTER TWENTY-NINE

# STAGE FRIGHT

The Premier's train left mid-morning heading westwards. The mood in the carriage was jocular—the job was almost done, the prize was almost theirs. But as the train crossed the Nepean River at Emu Plains, leaving the scattered outposts of the city behind and beginning its ascent, the mood changed. From the window they saw blue gum-covered crests and gullies that rose and plummeted in a breathless infinity. Those who had never before made the journey over the mountains fell silent; those who travelled this way regularly felt a pride in their country that they would have blushed to express in words. The most hardened parliamentary soul was stirred by the sight.

At Katoomba the train stopped briefly so that the people could cheer and the officials from the local Federal Executive could greet the Premier, and so that the members of the party could exit the train briefly to stamp their feet on the frozen ground, slap their hands briskly together and watch their breath turn to vapour before their eyes.

And now the train began its slow and winding descent to the plains below, arriving into Bathurst in the late afternoon. Here more crowds awaited them, another mayor, yet more aldermen, and both the district and the city bands played a triumphal welcome. The procession to the town hall was led by the fine strong men of the Bathurst Fire Brigade and behind the official party the people followed on foot, counting in their hundreds. At the town hall there was champagne enough for a great many worthy persons' health to be toasted, after which the party dined at a local hotel. The culmination of the day was the address that evening to be held at the School of Arts, where upwards of twelve hundred persons awaited and where every prominent citizen and his wife was soon gathered on a platform that creaked beneath their combined weight.

The hall was festooned: ribbons and bunting and flags hung from every place that it was possible to hang something, and pretty young ladies wore Federation ribbons pinned to their breasts and the mayor and his many aldermen fairly swelled with civic pride.

The Premier was in fine spirits, shaking every hand and slapping every back and kissing every lady's hand. He exchanged hearty words with the massed gentlemen of the press and he posed for a photograph.

'Gentlemen, please take your seats,' cried an official who wore a large watch on a chain and being the only gentleman in the room who did not smile and make jocular declarations for his job it was—and a thankless job too—to keep the address to time. There was another train to catch, if not tonight then early on the morrow. 'Gentlemen, *please!*' he urged.

And the platform creaked as the Premier took his chair.

The mayor spoke first—it was his town, after all—to give the official welcome and thanks. This was a Federation town, he declared, and if it should, one day, become the nation's capital then it would be as well for the nation! The people cheered (perhaps unaware their town was now officially only ninety-eight miles from Sydney and therefore no longer eligible). They were honoured this evening, the mayor said, not only with the Premier's presence but with that of a number of his ministers too, the first of whom, the Secretary for Public Monies, the Honourable Mr Alasdair Dunlevy MLA, he was pleased to invite to the podium now to address them.

Much applause greeted this announcement, not because Mr Dunlevy was to speak (as most did not know who he was) but because the mood was jubilant and the people of Bathurst had waited a long time to take centre stage.

Mr Dunlevy, who was seated close to the Premier, now rose and approached the podium. He carried his speech notes and he placed these notes on the podium. He adjusted them. He lifted his head. The hall, and the twelve hundred people inside it, fell, for the most part, to a hushed quiet—though when the mood is jubilant hushed quiet is no easy thing and one or two cheers persisted and some irreverent comments shot back and forth from the galleries to the floor and back again and a ripple of laughter followed them. But eventually they fell away and the hall was silent.

And the people waited.

But the minister did not speak.

The people shuffled, they became a little restless, one or two called out. A nervous laugh came, an insult from far to the back of the hall.

But still the minister did not speak.

Those on the platform exchanged looks, shifted in their seats. And down below the platform the people seated in the front rows could see the gleam of perspiration on the minister's forehead and the grey pallor of his face. And they saw how his hand shook at his side.

Stage fright, they said later.

CHAPTER THIRTY

# UNTETHERED

Eleanor sat at her writing desk. Her journal lay unopened before her and she ran her fingers over the soft calfskin cover to anchor herself to this place, to this world, but she did not open the journal and as the room had settled into evening and was already in semi-darkness she could not have read the words she had once written even had she wished to.

The fire was not lit, the curtains were not drawn and the light from the street outside bathed the room in a not-unpleasant glow, enough to make out shapes and shadows well enough though not to read or write by.

Outside there seemed to be no stars in the sky and she could not recall the last time she had searched for them. One night, she could not have been more than seven or eight, her father had come to the room in which she slept and had woken her in the darkness and taken her up to the roof where they had lain for an hour or more with blankets covering them, for it had been a cold, clear night, and watched a meteor shower overhead. Tiny points of light bursting into life and shooting across the sky then blinking out of existence, one after another in every part of the sky, so fleeting you caught them in the corner of your eye and they were gone. She remembered how it felt to share this secret with him, for it had seemed, at the time, like a secret.

And then he had gone, and so long ago that his voice, his smile, his smell, was as fleeting as those shooting stars had once been. Her mother had gone three years later of a silly nagging cough that had seemed little enough at first but which worsened and in a fortnight had carried her off.

They had been a safety net, her mother and father, she saw. A fixed point upon which to anchor oneself, and when they were gone that anchor point was gone too, and one drifted, untethered, with nothing beneath. And sometimes that was liberating and other times it was terrifying.

Your husband becomes your safety net, that was what her mother had said. It was the sort of thing she might have said, at any rate. Though in her case both her husbands had, one after another and some years apart, and through no fault of their own one presumed, deserted her.

But they had died. A different form of desertion. After which one might don widow's weeds, accept condolences and, after an appropriate period, move on.

Eleanor pondered the time, estimated it to be seven or perhaps eight o'clock. Certainly long after dusk and yet her fire was not lit and her curtains not drawn.

Afterwards the two things seemed connected in her mind: her realisation about the fire and curtains, and a moment later, almost simultaneously it seemed, the sound of a baby crying upstairs. But it might not have happened like that; it may have been some little

373

time between the first thing and the second. Afterwards, it was difficult to recall with any certainty.

A baby was crying upstairs. It was such an unlikely sound that it took an absurdly long time for Eleanor's brain to register and make sense of it. She got up. She left her room and stood on the landing, looking upwards.

*Could* it be a baby? It must, surely, be a bat or a possum outside.

She put a hand on the bannister and a step on the first stair, listening. For a moment there was silence, but then she heard it again and she went up the stairs, though it had been five years, perhaps, since she had last gone up to the maid's room and then only briefly to ensure the maid who had departed had taken only what was hers. She reached the top of the winding wooden staircase and stood on the little landing just long enough to understand something was very wrong. She threw open the door.

Inside the room the maid, Alice, stood wide-eyed and holding in her arms a baby. It was wrapped in a shawl of some description and its face—a tiny red, wrinkled face—was screwed up mid-scream. Its fists were clenched in fury, its limbs so diminutive they seemed little more than a doll's. A newborn or, at most, a few days old.

And Alice gaped at her in mute horror.

Indeed, the horror seemed to rise up from the floor, it seeped out of the walls, it poured down on them from the ceiling. It drenched them and Eleanor reeled. The baby's cries came to her from far away and the words that Alice spoke did not come to her at all. She had entered a quite different world, where the things that she had known—about herself, about the people around her—were quite false and other things were now shown to be true. She said to the maid: 'This is my husband's child.'

Her words cut through the fog that surrounded them both and hung there, momentous and terrible. 'This is Mr Dunlevy's child, is it not? Tell me.'

Alice took a step away from her, her mouth agape. And now something got through, the sound of Alice's words, if not their actual meaning.

'*No*, madam, indeed it is *not!*' she cried. 'It is my sister's child. She has died suddenly and I have saved her child. I am sorry, madam, for I know I should not—'

'It is my husband's child. And you have hidden this from me, the two of you.'

'No, madam, I swear on the child's life—'

Eleanor put her hands over her ears and turned away from the girl's denials. She was going to fall, or to faint, she did not know which. She put her hand on the doorknob and held very tightly onto it and the girl's denials went on and on.

'She went into labour because of the sentence, madam. Three years' hard labour, it was, and I could not save her, and before I could visit her in the prison she had done away with herself, though it is a wicked mortal sin and the baby would surely perish—'

'*Be quiet!*'

Alice was quiet. The words froze in the space between them.

'You will leave this house. *Now.* This minute. Before my husband returns. *I will not have you in this house one more minute.*'

'Madam!'

The clock on the landing below struck the quarter hour and Eleanor flung the door open wide and stood with her back to the room and to the horror of that scene.

'You shall leave this house before the clock strikes the hour or I shall telephone the police.'

Eleanor went back downstairs and her hands shook on the bannister and she stumbled once but righted herself. She went all the way down to the drawing room.

It was later than she had thought; the clock had chimed a quarter before nine o'clock. So be it. The girl and the child would be gone by nine. She sat and waited.

And it is a long time to wait, a quarter of an hour, when broken down into each component minute and second and beat of the heart. Eleanor sat and she waited. She thought of very little and she thought of everything. She understood, at last, what sort of a man was her husband, that he would kneel at the bed of one woman to profess his love and at the same time impregnate a servant girl—as Leon Jellicoe had done, or worse! Were all men such, then? Their baseness and treachery indistinguishable from one another? That he would accuse her of an affair so that he might hide his own transgressions. And she understood, too, the deceit of the servant who colluded with the master of the house to hide her sinful state. She saw that it was in the nature of such people to beget a child through deception and duplicity, to hide a pregnancy, to bear a bastard child in shameful secrecy in an attic room.

It was astonishing how clearly she now saw the world.

So Eleanor sat and she waited.

She heard every sound. A carriage rattled up to the house and she feared it was her husband returned. But it could not be, as he was with the Premier at Bathurst. And sure enough the carriage soon passed and was gone. A wind rustled the leaves of the giant fig and caused the branches of the frangipani to tap against a windowpane. The house creaked and groaned and resettled on its foundations like a very old man in a chair who has seen all that life has and wishes to see no more.

But even the slowest quarter hour must submit eventually, and she heard footsteps on the stairs. Her hands closed slowly around the arm of her chair. She stared straight ahead.

She heard a sob outside the door.

'*Please*, Madam, I beg you not to do this. I have no place to go, and there is the baby, it is so small and I have nothing to give it.'

Eleanor sat and waited.

'Madam.'

After a time she heard the front door open and then close. A moment or two after that the clock on the landing above chimed the hour, followed a few seconds later by the other clocks in the house.

Then there was silence.

CHAPTER THIRTY-ONE

# WATERLOO

Alasdair returned early from the Tour of the West at the Premier's suggestion. Was it a suggestion or more a request, an order? The words 'complete rest' and 'exhaustion' hung over him as he stood at the window of his room at the hotel and watched the porter pack his clothes, as the man stepped into the street and hailed a carriage to take him to the station, as he boarded the train, alone, and the rest of the party continued on to Wellington.

'No Wellington for you, Dunlevy; more a Waterloo, I would think,' the Premier had said, and he had laughed at this most excellent joke.

And his minister suffered the ignominy of the train journey with every station he passed through. At Katoomba only market-goers and early sightseers waited on the platform. The excited crowds of the day before were just a paragraph in the newspaper today. The descent of the train through the winding ridges and gullies was made at a great speed when the day before the train had strained at every incline. Every now and then he glimpsed the smoke haze of the city floating distantly on the horizon. He did not wish to reach his destination.

How would he explain himself? And to whom?

The clouds, rolling in from the west, overtook him at Penrith and the distant city vanished in a hail of new rain. It was a Saturday morning. At each station the people jostled on the platforms with crates and livestock, which they loaded into the third-class carriages, dashing from place to place beneath rapidly retrieved umbrellas. A crate overturned and a host of small yellow chicks ran in all directions. After a delay the train set off once more.

The referendum was in three days but the people loaded live-stock onto trains and ran in all directions after escaping yellow chicks. He wondered what was the truth: the vote or the people going to market?

He arrived at Sydney Terminal Station at the same time as the Premier's party was due to arrive in Wellington. He got a cab and rode through the streets feeling he had been absent a great many days and not just overnight.

He went straight home. He did not linger very long on the thought that a little to the north, at the hospital, Verity lay. He did not think about that at all.

The cook, Mrs Flynn, opened the door to him. She had a pinched look about her, as though she had leaned too close to the stove and her face had become flushed from the flames. But as she habitually spent her time in the kitchen and he was very rarely in her presence, he presumed this to be her natural state.

'Oh, sir!' she said, and again he assumed this to be a natural thing she might utter. At any rate her hand went to her mouth and she stood back to let him enter, offering no further utterance. She seemed dismayed by his umbrella, by his dripping coat.

'Mrs Dunlevy is here?' he asked her.

'Yes, sir. Upstairs, sir. In her room.'

Mrs Flynn had a way of opening her mouth as though intending to say one thing and then saying quite another thing altogether.

He left her contemplating his bags in the hallway and wondered where the maid was and what the implications were for lunch if the cook was playing at housemaid today.

Or had he missed lunch?

He went to the drawing room and sat down heavily on the first chair he reached and put his head in his hands. He had thought he was done with maids and lunches and cooks, with everything connected to this life. He had given it up; though his sacrifice, in the end, had come to nothing. Had been thrown back in his face. But to have come to that decision, to have reached that place, and now to find oneself exactly back in the spot one thought one had left forever was—

Beyond anything.

To lose her was—

But there was nothing, he realised, to compare it to.

After a time he lowered his hands from his face and sat calmly. And he did feel calm. For there was the present to deal with. There was Eleanor upstairs in her room and he would explain things to her. Explain some things, at least. Not all.

But he sat calmly and did not move.

The door opened and Eleanor came in.

Alasdair turned and looked up at her with his new calmness. He did not smile or offer a greeting but he did look up, he was calm. And now, at any rate, he could explain things to her.

But it was she who spoke first, and he remembered thinking afterwards that Eleanor did not once ask the reason for his early arrival home. But it was possible he had never shared his schedule with her or given her a date for his expected return. Yes, very likely that was it. Possibly it was no concern to her when her husband returned or even if he did. That was likely too.

But Eleanor spoke: 'You are leaving then?' she said.

And he saw that his explanation to her was going to be no easy thing.

'No,' he said.

And, in that one word, all that had happened was explained. He would not be leaving. He look a long breath. He wished she would sit down. Or go, now that things were clear again between them. Instead she stood before him, she loomed over him.

She was speaking again and it seemed at first inconsequential, talk of the servants, but after a long moment her words penetrated.

'I have sent Alice away. Her and the child.'

He looked up at her. 'Child? What child?'

She did not answer at once, then, 'Do you deny all knowledge of it?'

'My dear, I have not the slightest idea as to what you are referring.'

At his words, she turned away. Whatever passed over her face in that moment she did not wish him to see. And when she turned back there was a coldness to her, a bitterness.

'First this woman, this Miss Trent,' she said, 'who must break the law in the most appalling way to rid herself of your bastard child, and now the maid—*the maid, Alasdair!*—who presumably had no option but to expel the wretched thing, and right here under our very roof for all I know, though the idea of it is quite repellent. Well, now she is gone and the child too.'

He could not speak. And this was as well for she had not finished.

'The *hypocrisy* of it! That you should accuse *me* of infidelity—' She stopped herself. Took a deep breath. 'I believe you should go, Alasdair. I do not wish us to continue as we are.'

He struggled to his feet. How could she know all this about Verity? As for the rest of it!

'But you are *deluded*, Eleanor. I do not deny this . . .' He paused. He could not find the word. When he did find a word, he closed that part of himself that shrank in shame. '. . . this *incident* with Miss Trent. Indeed, I am come here today to discuss it frankly with you and to beg your forgiveness. But this other accusation about myself and the maid—the *maid*, Eleanor, good *God!*—and a child, it is preposterous. *Deranged.*'

But she stood before him, resolute. And he saw that it was not her strength or her resolution that kept her standing there, it was her dismay, and the slightest movement of the breeze would see her crumble into powder before him. But still she stood before him, resolute, despite him. Despite herself.

'Eleanor, what child, for God's sake? Look about you. There is no child. There never has been a child.'

CHAPTER THIRTY-TWO

# THE TRANSIENCE
# OF ALL THINGS

A short time later a carriage drew up outside the house, a dark green brougham pulled by two perfectly matched bay cobs and carrying Mrs Henry Rothe.

Mrs Rothe, whose husband kept his own carriage and stabled his own horses, sat and waited, staring straight ahead and pulling at the fingers of her new gloves, for they had been made a little tight. After a time, and as no one came out to her, she sent her groom to the house. The groom, too, was in dark green. Mrs Rothe, who laughed a great deal at the world but who suffered the same insecurities all people did, pulled at the fingers of her new gloves and so did not observe the confused exchange between her groom and the Dunlevys' cook. For Mrs Flynn, after a lengthy delay, had heard the man at the front door and had come to see who it was and what it was they wanted.

The groom returned and, after a not-inconsiderable time, Mrs Dunlevy herself emerged from her house and the groom jumped down and went to open the door and lower the step so that she might enter the carriage. The two ladies greeted one another and no mention was made of Mrs Dunlevy's tardiness or her high colour or her distraction as the carriage made its way the short distance to the town hall at Paddington and Mrs Rothe understood that some crisis had occurred.

So she talked of inconsequential things in order that Eleanor might sit in silence and stare out of the window, and she saw in her friend's eyes the brittle light of glass about to shatter. And Mrs Rothe talked, and wondered.

They arrived at the town hall and it was festooned—everywhere now, it seemed, was festooned—though the rain guaranteed the flags and bunting that hung outside were bedraggled and sodden before the event was even begun. A great many people, most of them women—for this was a meeting of the Women's Federal League—were similarly bedraggled and sodden as they had arrived on foot and Mrs Rothe's carriage, pulling up right outside the door, splashed those young women unlucky enough to be standing near to the kerb. The two ladies, sheltered by the umbrella of the Rothes' coachman, swept up the steps and into the hall and exclaimed loudly about the weather, though they were the only two people in the place who were dry.

That is, Mrs Rothe exclaimed loudly about the weather.

Eleanor Dunlevy stood quite still in the foyer as a great many people swirled about her.

There *was* a child. To deny its existence, to deny one's part in its existence, was perfidious.

But someone was talking. Eleanor looked about. She felt very small, very transparent. She wondered if she had, in fact, come to the town hall with Blanche Rothe or if she imagined the whole thing.

'I am quite surprised you dare show your face at a Women's Federal League address, Eleanor, after your dalliance with the anti-billites,' said Mrs Rothe, as though she had rehearsed this line on the carriage ride over and was not about to forgo the pleasure of repeating it now, and in the presence of a number of other ladies of no small import who happened to be within earshot, simply because her friend was, apparently, in the midst of a crisis.

But her remark fell a little flat when none of the ladies present commented on it and Eleanor made no reply.

'Mrs Dunlevy? I thought it was you! Is it true your husband froze and could not speak a single word at the Premier's meeting at Bathurst last evening? It is reported in this morning's *Herald*.'

And thus was Mrs Rothe trumped, and by Mrs Parkes, who, while she was not strictly speaking related to the great man, did at least share his name.

Eleanor thought, That is why Alasdair returned so suddenly from the west this morning. She had thought it was because of Miss Trent. And perhaps it was still because of her. Perhaps everything her husband did now was because of Miss Trent.

It was news, too, to Blanche Rothe, she saw, as that lady's gaze fixed on her own face, hoping to see a husband's public disgrace there, perhaps even a little glad, for Blanche herself had felt the sharp pinpricks of public humiliation in the past. How easy it was to read all this, in an instant, in the other woman's face, thought Eleanor.

As for Mrs Parkes, who came at her through a large crowd, pushing her way through and swollen, it seemed, with her eagerness to make her cruel remark, the lady had nothing but a name shared with a great man three years dead and to whom she was not actually related. Her husband, a superintendent of works, resided apart from her in some other part of the city.

'My husband is not with the Premier, Mrs Parkes; he is here in Sydney,' Eleanor said, which was sufficient to cast doubt on the story. But she was dismayed at how her voice shook—though it was possible no one but herself noticed.

The crowd that gathered in the foyer had now reached such proportions that conversing with one's neighbour had become impractical and it was acceptable to simply stand and say nothing, to look at no one. The ladies of the Women's Federal League bustled hither and thither greeting and organising, and presently they urged those gathered to move into the hall. They were to be addressed by Mr Barton himself, which was a coup and a feather in a number of people's caps, though Mrs Rothe, perhaps perceiving she had an audience, declared she did not particularly care for the gentleman.

Mr Barton arrived rather late due to another engagement elsewhere in the city and due to the rain, but he did, at last, arrive and several of the ladies present, many of whom had grown-up children, felt their pulses flutter and their faces flush as Mr Barton took to the platform. His magnificent stature and his smooth, clean-shaven cheeks, his boyish fair hair and his clear and ardent voice was enough to stir the most unromantic heart, young and not so young. And when he exhorted them, 'Ladies, you cannot vote in Tuesday's referendum, but it would be a great thing if you could influence your husbands, brothers and friends,' they applauded and it did not, in that moment, appear an injustice to call on their help while denying them the vote.

But later, when Mr Barton has gone, when they have made their way home, dashing over puddles, to make their husband's tea, will they pause to consider what has been asked of them? Eleanor wondered, will they feel just a little cheated?

Otherwise she thought very little. The applause swelled and rippled about her but did not touch her. She observed the hat worn by the young lady in front of her, a very wide-brimmed hat adorned by an ostrich feather that hung limply and was ruined by the rain. She noticed Mrs Rothe, seated beside her, pulling at the fingers of her gloves. She thought: If we lived separately, Alasdair and I, I shall be no better than Mrs Parkes—pitied, talked about, cruel. She thought: Shall I be forced, then, to go and live quietly in some other place? She thought of Balmain, where her father's stone cottage had once stood. But she had left all of that. She had climbed her way out of it and she would not go back.

People would find out. One person already knew, for they had sent her the note. And the cook, Mrs Flynn, she must know.

Then Mrs Flynn, too, must go.

Eleanor understood that this was just the start.

The ladies around her jumped to their feet and clapped enthusiastically, and Eleanor also rose to her feet, or her shadow did, an echo of Eleanor Dunlevy, whose face was turned towards the gentleman on the platform but whose eyes stared down a very long and very dark tunnel.

She left then, pushing past the ladies beside her and walking out of the hall, and Mrs Rothe, who was rather taken with Mr Barton though she had dismissed his charms not half an hour earlier, did not notice until after the meeting that Mrs Dunlevy had gone.

In the foyer of the town hall Eleanor saw Cecily Pyke and one of her daughters, not Marguerite, shaking umbrellas and hats and full of the excitement of a journey made in the rain.

'Heavens, the rain!' exclaimed Mrs Pyke. 'We are dreadfully late. Have we missed Mr Barton? Helena is most anxious to see him.' And Eleanor remembered that this daughter, the second-eldest, was called Helena. This Helena was perhaps a year or two the younger and her cheeks more flushed and her excitement less contained than that of her elder sister.

'It was because of the baby,' Mrs Pyke went on. 'He upset something or other and Nurse got quite cross with him and it was quite a to-do and hence we are late.'

For Mrs Pyke had given her husband a brood of offspring covering a whole range of ages, the youngest of which was but a year old and still in the nursery.

And Alasdair had impregnated two females, thought Eleanor. Two that she knew of.

Eleanor left Mrs Pyke and her daughter to face the almost certain disappointment of having missed Mr Barton's address and went out into the evening rain.

∞

*Eleanor, what child, for God's sake? Look about you. There is no child. There never has been a child.*

Alasdair stood at the window, dazed, and watched as the green-liveried carriage that carried Mrs Rothe and his wife to their engagement turned around and shot back up the hill. It occurred to him that he had forbidden Eleanor to leave the house or to attend any engagement until after the referendum, and yet here she was defying his instructions.

How powerless he was in the face of her opposition. In the face of any woman, if she truly set out to destroy him.

And this raving about a child—his child!—and the maid! It was madness.

But where *was* Alice? he wondered. He had not seen her all evening and he realised now he had no wish to come face to face with the girl, not after his wife had made such an appalling

allegation. The shame of it must, surely, stain any future inter-
action he had with her.

Dear God.

He was glad, now, that he had permitted Eleanor to attend
her meeting. He could show reason in the face of this mania; he
could retain the ability for rational thought, even if she—if any
female—could not.

Eleanor had left her reticule behind. She had fled the house
so abruptly, in such a state of nerves, she had left it on the table.
He snatched it up and undid the fastening and turned it upside
down. It was empty. Not believing this he thrust his hand inside
and felt around. Nothing.

It was perfidious. Chicanery. What did a female carry in such
things? He did not know. Had bought one once, an expensive one,
for Verity without the faintest notion as to what she might keep
in there. A handkerchief, he had assumed. And his wife—twenty
years his wife!—had never once offered to show him the contents
of her reticule until that evening eight days ago when she had
pulled out a crumpled envelope and waved it in his face, crying
triumphantly, *I have the letter you wrote to her, arranging your
tawdry little liaison.* Where was that letter now? Was its existence
a figment of her imagination, as the crazed story of the baby was,
or had someone really sent it to her?

Who?

He flung himself out of the room and up the staircase and into
his wife's room. He went directly to the writing desk and pulled
at the drawer, exclaiming aloud when he found it locked. It
seemed further evidence of her perfidiousness. Her chicanery. He
scrabbled about among her things for the key but did not find it.
He exclaimed again, stood in the centre of the room, curious bolts
of energy shooting the length of his arms and back up again so that

he could not stand motionless a moment longer. He grabbed the handle of the drawer, took up the paperknife that lay, as though awaiting him, on the desk, and attacked the lock, pulling and twisting until finally it gave with a dull snap. The drawer shot out of its slot with such force he almost fell backwards.

Inside was a journal.

Did Eleanor keep a journal? He'd had no idea. Well, he was certainly not going to waste his time browsing her various thoughts and observations on himself. He thrust it aside and here, nestling underneath, was a letter. Just the one. It occurred to him, only at that moment, that he would find letters from Drummond-Smith.

He pulled back his hand as though he had found a funnel web lurking there, overcome by an aversion to finding any such letters.

Extraordinary, how this felled him—utterly—for a time.

He shook off the feeling and took up the letter. There were no others, just this one in a plain envelope, cream in colour and of good quality and addressed in blue ink in a workmanlike hand to his wife here at their home.

Whose hand? He did not know. A man's or a woman's? He could not even guess. The single sheet of notepaper contained within was the missing note he had scrawled to Verity three weeks ago arranging his visit.

He let out a shout of laughter. He shook his head, held the note at arm's length, turned it over as though it might divulge its secrets, provide some clue.

There was nothing. Just the note. Written by himself at his office, addressed by himself on some other envelope entirely and sent to Verity. And now it was here, in his wife's drawer.

Verity herself must have sent it.

Another laugh. He could not find it in himself to be dismayed. He was beyond such things. He sat down on the bed.

After a time he got up and searched through the remainder of the drawer. There was nothing at all from Drummond-Smith but this reprieve brought no release. It brought nothing.

Finally he pulled out his wife's journal and began to read.

∽

Sunday morning dawned grey and overcast, and the crowds, upwards of twenty thousand, began to gather in the Domain, it being the last Sunday before the referendum and there being little else to do on a wet Sunday morning unless you counted church, which most did not. For it was a much greater sport to splash through the puddles and slip in the mud on the water-logged grass, to dash from one platform to another and hear the words of one speaker after another, cheering and laughing and haranguing and slinging great clods of mud as the mood took them. If this was what was meant by Federation, they liked it. They embraced it!

In Elizabeth Bay Alasdair was standing before the mirror contemplating the futility of his Ascot tie when his wife walked into the room.

He spun about, unprepared. It was a violation, a transgression. But it was only the latest in many such violations and transgressions.

'Tell me how many there have been,' she demanded, pausing a yard or two short of him. 'I no longer wish to live in ignorance.'

She was splendid in her fury, though there was a fragility and a desperation at the edges of the splendour that sent a chill of fear through him.

Was it hysteria? he wondered. Had she lost her reason? One heard of such things, a sudden derangement of the mind caused by some great distress, such as the loss of the child a year ago—had it affected her more than he had realised? The female mind was weaker than the male. He thought of asylums. Doctors.

'For God's sake, Eleanor!' he replied and he turned back to the mirror. His fingers shook a little.

Could a man be a minister of the Crown, could he hope to hold any sort of parliamentary office, if he had a wife housed in an asylum?

'No! I will *not* be put off!' she said, advancing on him. 'You will tell me.'

Alasdair put down the tie that refused to be tied and whose very purpose no longer seemed clear to him and turned again to face her. It seemed important to speak very calmly, very firmly to her, though he felt the house loosen on its foundations and quake around him. He felt the insubstantiality and transience of all things.

She wished to have him abase himself before her. Very well, he would.

'I have admitted my transgression with Miss Trent, towards whom I did, I admit, experience some feelings for a time. Though that is now passed.'

What it cost him to say these words. It seemed to him his broken heart must show as vividly as a scar upon his face. He looked directly at his wife, begging her to see it, his broken heart, terrified lest she did.

'There has been no other,' he said.

But he was a little frightened of her. She seemed to be someone he did not know. He saw again, around the edges of her, some strange madness.

'I do not believe you. The child—'

'The *child*,' he interrupted, reaching for the newspaper, last Wednesday's newspaper, and thrusting it into her hands, 'is not mine.'

She continued to stare at him. Finally she looked down at the newspaper in her hand, at the page it was folded to. On a little chain about her neck hung a pair of wire-rimmed spectacles that he had never seen before and that she placed now on her nose. She made no comment as she read, but he saw from a faint rippling of the muscles around her throat, from a stiffness that came into her spine, that she understood.

Her face had gone quite white, even her lips.

When she had read it she turned about and left his room. Alasdair reached behind him for his chair and sat down and did not stir for a time. He ought to be angry with her, furious. But instead he reached for the newspaper. The story was an insignificant piece; variations of it—a different name, minor details altered—appeared in the newspaper every day. But this one had made him stop and read:

## SUICIDE OF A PRISONER

Yesterday an inquest was held at Darlinghurst Gaol on the body of Millicent Nimrod, whose death took place at that institution on Wednesday last. Evidence showed the prisoner had committed suicide by hanging herself in her cell using lengths of sheet tied together to make a rope. Deceased was sentenced to three years' penal servitude for malicious damage to property, her third such offence, and had recently given birth to a child, the fate of the child being unknown. A verdict of suicide while insane was returned.

He folded the newspaper and put it away. The story saddened him. He had not known the woman but her sister had, presumably, been their maid, Alice Nimrod, and now Alice was gone and he had an idea his wife had been responsible for the girl's sudden departure.

∞

Much later, when the crowds at the Domain had begun to disperse and the platforms on which the speakers stood had sunk into the mud and were beginning to be dismantled, Mrs Dunlevy came into the kitchen. This, like her husband's bedroom and the maid's attic room, was a space into which she rarely ventured, but it seemed that all such demarcations within the house had broken down.

She stood for a time in the doorway and when Mrs Flynn, who was engaged in a tricky manoeuvre with a leg of lamb and the stove door, realised she was there she almost dropped the lamb and the tray and burned herself.

'Lord, missus, you gave me a start!' she exclaimed with a jollity she did not feel, for Alice was gone and the poor wee baby too, and here was Mrs Dunlevy in the kitchen doorway and it was all very unsettling. And then she said, 'Oh, Mrs Dunlevy, are you sick? You do not look at all well,' though it was not something she ought to have said to the mistress of the house. But the mistress *did* look unwell, all grey and fainting, as she described it later to Mr Flynn. 'Though I oughtened to have said so,' she had added.

And what Mrs Dunlevy had asked her was, did she know where Alice might have gone to?

Just as though Alice had upped and left of her own volition— and perhaps she had, for now Mrs Flynn was no longer sure of anything.

'And so I told her, *Surry Hills, Mrs Dunlevy.* That is what I said,' she reported to Mr Flynn later that evening, 'and then she was gone. What do you make of that?'

But Mr Flynn, who worked on the wharves and was enjoying the last few hours of his Sunday off, did not make anything of it.

∞

Eleanor left the kitchen and went up the stairs to her room and softly closed the door. The room was quiet, dark. She made no attempt to turn on a light or to light a candle.

Alice was gone and she was responsible for the girl's sudden departure. This was not in dispute. Her accusation of the child's paternity, her utter belief that the girl had colluded in a sordid affair with her husband, these now appeared . . . less certain. It was possible—likely, even—that the child belonged to the girl's sister. And that this wretched female was indeed now deceased.

But still, it made no sense to Eleanor how the child had ended up here, in the upstairs attic room.

The moon was newly risen and still low in the sky and a strip of moonlight struck the floor and a corner of the bed, reaching as far as the writing desk. She saw that the drawer to her desk was slightly open when she had certainly locked it the day before. She touched the drawer and found that the lock was broken. She ran her fingers along the bevelled wooden edge of the desk, along the jagged metal of the broken lock.

Alasdair had done this. She could not tell when. Last night, perhaps, while she had been out. And she had not noticed it when she had come home. She sat on the bed. She could not imagine what it was he looked for.

She felt that she was not sure what either of them looked for.

And all this time there had been a child, secreted upstairs. The wonder of it struck her.

But how had the child come to be here? She saw, in her imagination, Alice, dashing through darkened streets in the rain, wrapped in a sodden shawl, holding the newborn to her breast. Bringing it, for safety, to this house. (For where else could she take it?) This vision, of the young girl and the infant at her breast, so vivid, so compelling. It seemed to Eleanor almost biblical in its time-lessness. Its sadness. She could not rid herself of it.

The thought that she had made a dreadful, dreadful mistake crept in around the very edges of her consciousness. That she had treated the girl shamefully, or worse, circled around and around her head.

Mrs Flynn knew it. Had been flustered and embarrassed in her attempts to hide her knowledge from her employer. It had been a mistake to ask Mrs Flynn for Alice's whereabouts.

The household was destroyed, Eleanor saw. She did not see how it could ever be salvaged. If she located the girl, if she rescued Alice and the child from whatever miserable place it was they sheltered in, well, there could be no question of offering the girl her position again. That was quite impossible, and Alice would not expect it. But she might offer help. She might offer money, a testimonial. She saw that this was the very least a Christian woman could do.

Eleanor stood up.

She realised she was crying, had been crying for some little time, the tears running silent and unbidden down her face. She did not want to care what happened to a wretched maid, but she saw that, if she saved this girl, she might also save herself.

∞

Night came upon the city, bringing with it the army of rats that in the daylight went unseen but as the darkness spread swarmed along every inch of the waterfront from Watsons Bay to Drummoyne. In a small number of suburbs the night brought on a fairy tale of electric-lit drawing rooms and dazzlingly brilliant dining rooms, but in the majority of places the darkness sucked the life out of the streets and the people retreated from it.

In one of these streets a hansom cab crawled. It had come from Devonshire Street, turned into Crown Street and back into Fitzroy. The cab had crossed many of these same streets already, crossing and recrossing Surry Hills from Elizabeth Street to Bourke, from Cleveland Street to Foveaux. Every so often the veiled lady within the cab called out an instruction—slow down, not here, go this way, stop here, go on—and the cab stopped and started and turned back on itself and slowed down and sped up so that the cab driver shook his head and muttered to himself, though it would be a good fare. But have a heart, lady, he thought to himself as they turned once more into Riley Street.

They were seeking someone, he understood that, for the lady sat forward and leaned out of the window when they passed some destitute young girl, or some drunken mother or some down-on-her-luck gin house whore, so that he wondered what exactly she might want with such a person—not that it was any concern of his.

'Stop! Driver, stop!' she cried and he called out, 'Woah!' to his poor worn-out horse and stopped the cab on the corner where some poor unfortunate soul lay on the ground. But the sky had long since turned grey and then black and you could no more see who it was than you could see the face of the lady beneath her veil.

'No, go on,' she said, very quiet, and he sighed and urged his horse on again.

When they approached the corner of Riley and Albion and he saw the great dark mass that was Frog Hollow ahead of them he flicked his whip at the lumbering animal, urging it to hurry past, but the lady called out, 'Stop! Stop here!'

'Not here, lady. Ain't safe.' And he urged the horse on.

'I command you to stop!'

And so he did stop.

'What is this place?'

'No place for you, lady. You get out here I cannot answer for what might happen and I will not be here waiting when it does.'

Though he would be sorry if it did, for they had spent a time together, he and she, and he had listened to the gathering anguish in her voice and he had an idea that beneath that veil was something so out of his reach it might just break his heart.

And here they were, just as he had foreseen: unearthly figures emerging from the depths of the great pit like ghouls in a cemetery. Or like rats, circling and sniffing the air, and he took a tight grip of his whip and with his free hand he reached behind him for the cosh he carried for emergencies. This felt like it was about to become an emergency. He could see their pale faces, the light glinting in their ghoul eyes.

Perhaps the lady made some movement, for they switched their attention away from him and the horse and towards her. One made a lunge at the door and almost got it open. He heard her cry out and he struck the horse and shouted, '*Giddup! Giddup now!*' and the horse started up, terrified, and they were gone at a trot. The driver did not slow until they had reached the lights of Crown Street.

He thought this would have frightened the lady but all she said was, 'Take me to the asylum.'

She meant the Benevolent Asylum at the junction of Pitt and George and Devonshire streets, where the old tollgate had once stood and where the women—since as far back as he could remember and far beyond that, for the building was convict-built, he was sure—went for their lying-in, those that had no bed of their own and often no husband either. He knew the place, all the cabbies did, though most of the women who went there went on foot.

He reached the place and waited in the rain as she went inside. He crouched over his reins, pulling the collar of his coat up higher, but his coat was soaked right through and the rain ran down his neck and into his ears and filled his boots, and he thought with a kind of despair that he would die right here on this cab this very evening and that in Heaven, if there was a Heaven, it would be raining there too.

Presently the lady came out and he saw from the way she held her head she had not found what she sought.

'Home, lady?' he called out, because all that mattered now was getting to his own home, unharnessing the horse and getting himself into bed as quickly as possible, with a warm mug of milk and a nip of rum to help him on his way.

'Yes, alright,' she said in a voice quite different now, a voice that was very low and tired and beaten. She still wore that veil, though he wondered why she bothered when the night was as black as a priest's hat and a man could no more see the lady's face than he could see into her heart. Though it was black, he decided, her heart. But the way she had said, *Yes, alright,* that made him wonder what she did look like beneath that veil, and the part of him that was still wistful and that remembered how it felt to fall in love thought of all the beautiful things in the world that he could not have, and his bed, which a moment before he had wished for, now seemed a cold and lonely place.

# CHAPTER THIRTY-THREE

# ASYLUM

The deputy superintendent at the Benevolent Asylum, an ardent young man named Quinn whose soft edges were steadily being hardened by the work he had chosen, knew Mrs Dunlevy. Or, rather, he knew of her. The wife of the minister was a long-serving member of the asylum's Ladies' Committee and so he did not hesitate to show her, at her request, the records of recent admissions. And if he privately considered it odd she make such a request late on a Sunday evening and clearly in a state of some agitation, he kept such thoughts to himself.

He watched her, though discreetly, and the soft glow of the desk lamp cast a shadow over one side of her face and illuminated the other so that he thought of Renaissance paintings and the sufferings of saints and a great many other things about which he knew almost nothing but which seemed to him at that moment fateful and immense. If the minister's wife searched the records for a particular name, she did not deign to share it with him, and when she closed the book and looked for a moment, searchingly it seemed, into his face, he said nothing and showed no surprise. It was evident she had not found that for which she searched. He watched her depart into the rainy night and a waiting cab.

He wished very much he had been able to assist her.

It occurred to him that many of the women—the unmarried ones, that is—provided a false name when they were admitted and he wondered, on reflection, if he might have mentioned this to her. Indeed, the thought now took such a hold of him that he started towards the door to follow her but could see, already, Mrs Dunlevy's hansom moving off and the moment was past. So he gave it up and instead returned to his little room upstairs and the warmth of a wood stove and a nip of rum.

And this was a pity, for a cursory study of the admission records would have shown him that a Catherine Foley, a young woman nineteen years of age and with an infant a week or two old, had arrived at the asylum's doors very late on Friday evening.

Catherine Foley was still here, her name invented—borrowed, perhaps, was a fairer description—but her predicament real enough. Common enough. For the asylum was full this night and every night. Catherine was the name of Alice's mother, Foley her maiden name, a girl from the west of Ireland and, though she had been dead these five years, Catherine Nimrod could, in this way, help her daughter.

And Alice Nimrod needed help. She lay with her dead sister's baby on a tiny cot in a long and echoing ward crammed with such cots rammed up against each other, leaving not an inch of space between, and the hundred and more women who filled this place tossed and turned, cursed and wept. Some of the women had their babies with them and some did not. Some of the women had lost their babies, and in another ward not too far away were the babies who had lost their mothers. There was little talking among the inmates; each was wrapped tightly within her own separate world. This was not to say the place was quiet and calm, for misery is rarely quiet and here, where so many souls, their spirits and their bodies broken, gathered in a single space, the misery leached out of the walls and echoed in the very rafters, it rose up out of the floor. It was made manifest in the legion of vermin that crawled and burrowed through the soiled bedding and over the scabbed bodies of the women.

But there was order, of a kind, among the misery. The women— those who could stand, who could walk a few yards unaided—had attended the service at the chapel that morning. A Proddy service, it had turned out, and Alice Nimrod, who had never been to such a thing before, had sat and wondered at it, at the emptiness of it, as if they were addressing a different God entirely and not the God she was used to; one who was very far away and who seemed untroubled by earthly failings. And in her mind this distant Proddy God became confused with the Dunlevys, who were equally grand and distant and untroubled by things that tore other people's lives apart.

She did not feel the injustice of her situation, for it seemed to her that if you stood too close to these distant gods, the Dunlevys, you might get burned and she had got burned. It was the way of things.

But she was frightened. She had come to the asylum late at night and been provided emergency refuge. Tomorrow the admissions committee would consider her case. She could not sleep for worrying about it. If the horror of leaving was any worse than the horror of staying, she did not know.

In the morning the Protestant chaplain came to her and said some words of comfort and blessed her, though Alice was uncertain what his blessing meant for he was not a priest, he had no rosary, no Hail Marys, nothing. He was unarmed.

She waited all day. She had prepared a story of a husband who had deserted her, the circumstances of the baby's birth. She had no papers to prove her story, but did any of these women? They would discover she was not the child's mother, this was her great fear—was it possible a doctor would examine her? She thought of strange hands touching her. She did not know if a crime had been committed. She had taken her sister's baby.

Late in the afternoon two police constables came into the asylum. A man had come into the place and broken the jaw of one of the women, his wife, and in another ward a woman had smothered her newborn and been dragged out screaming and cursing, but these two constables just arrived looked straight at Alice. She had not been summoned yet to address the committee and when, now, a young man called out her name, instead of answering his summons she took up the baby and fled out of the door and no one came after her.

Outside the city was heading into evening, the streets surrounding the asylum already dark with occasional pools of light. But gas lighting frightened Alice now and she avoided it. She went from place to place, drifting as one did drift when one's destination was unknown, and the faces she sometimes saw were not friendly. She thought after a time that she must come up with some plan. She thought she could perhaps go to Mrs Flynn, who had helped her and had been her friend, after a fashion; who at least believed in a sort of justice. But she did not know Mrs Flynn's house and she wondered if she would go there even if she did know it. She thought about returning to the Dunlevys and prostrating herself at their door. But she did not turn in a northerly direction. Her body took her away from such places as the Dunlevys inhabited. She thought of how Milli had hidden her face in the shadows, ashamed of her downfall. Alice had not done the wicked thing Mrs Dunlevy had accused her of and she did not know why she might be accused of such a thing, but she had done other things. She had stolen the baby.

The night lengthened. It was as unending as such nights must be. Alice walked and hour followed hour, unmarked and forgotten as soon as it was past, for each was the same as the last. She walked and she clutched the baby. They seemed to have become one, she and the baby, and she would not abandon it now even if it meant they both must perish. But she had thought this vaguely, in an abstract way, while she was lying on the cot in the asylum. The reality of walking the dark streets in the rain with a baby was quite different. She feared for her resolve.

'Zat Miss Nimrod? Thought it was.'

A face emerged out of the night so suddenly and at such close quarters Alice started backwards. The cold and the wet and the distress of her situation had dulled her thoughts, and for a time she could not place the face or the words it spoke. And when her numbed thoughts assembled themselves and she saw that it was Mr Renfrew, clothed in the remnants of a suit that had once belonged to someone else and with the water cascading from his hat, she was confused. The only other time they had met he had struck his wife and demanded money from her.

She stared at him, dumbly, helplessly.

'Look like you could use some help,' he said, as though a young woman clutching a baby in obvious distress on a dark night was the natural state of things, and in the world the Renfrew's inhabited no doubt it was. But kindness came in all packages, the Bible taught you that—though if you read a few pages further on the

Bible told you something else again, or that was Alice's recollection of it.

Mr Renfrew had frightened her a little the only other time they had met, but Alice had lost too much to remember her fear. He was a man with a wife and a clutch of children whom he had not entirely abandoned, which put him above most men. He was a little drunk, she saw. A glistening in his eyes, a slight unsteadiness to his step, suggested this was so. And the fumes of some sly grog consumed illicitly, yes, she could smell this now. Some men were better after a drink or two, it softened their raw edges, and Mr Renfrew was, perhaps, one of these. It hardly mattered, she realised.

It took all her strength not to fall at his feet.

'Come on home with me, lass,' said Mr Renfrew, patting her arm. 'My missus will take care of you. You are among friends now.'

And he gathered her up and led her to salvation, of a kind.

CHAPTER THIRTY-FOUR

# BITTER

On Tuesday morning the greatest fears of the federalists seemed
realised. The day dawned grey and overcast and the city was
lost in a fog from Bondi to the lower mountains. But before the
anti-federalists could thrust aside their curtains and leave their
houses to herald this late and much-needed intervention the sun
rose above the horizon and the early fog melted away. By the
time the clock at the GPO struck eight and the polling booths
opened the sky was a clear blue as far as the horizon extended.

Voting began sluggishly in the city, though in the suburban
polling stations queues formed even before polling opened and the
early risers—the men who worked in the factories and warehouses
or with deliveries to make, the tradesmen, some on foot, some in
their drays—waited for the doors to open so that they might get
on with their days. The pro-federalists were up early handing out
cards and leaflets at the tram stops and the railway stations, urging
the reticent to do their civic duty. For nothing was certain—a year
ago less than half the electorate had voted, a year ago the promised

majority had not materialised and the day had been lost. If it failed again today, there would be no third attempt. There would be no Federation.

The anti-federalists were out too, and if they could not win by rational persuasion they would resort to scaremongering, and a cart was seen circling the busier city streets sporting a huge banner that showed a menacing swarm of Chinamen in northern Queensland surging, via a newly built federal railway, towards the white dominions of New South Wales and Victoria—for this would, surely, be the colony's fate if it chose Federation. At some point during the afternoon the banner was set alight and onlookers cheered as they watched it burn.

The biggest crowds gathered at Castlereagh Street and Hunter Street, where platforms had been erected and the two leaders of the parties and those members of the Legislative Assembly and the Council not at their own constituencies congregated, some to urge the people to vote and others, like Charles Booker-Reid, who had not the least wish to visit his distant constituency, to enjoy the spectacle and, he trusted, the triumph. George Drummond-Smith, whose constituency was similarly remote, had also chosen to remain in the city during the whole of the campaign and was not about to leave now that victory was in sight. Henry Rothe, whose constituency was conveniently placed at Potts Point, welcomed his constituents personally with his wife at his side and enjoyed the harbour views with a glass of breakfast champagne and a jaunty wave to the occupants of the fleet of small craft that had taken to the water for the occasion. The Fraser Pykes were at Parramatta, having packed into two carriages before dawn and travelled to the west so that Fraser could urge on his own electors with the aid of his entire family, nurse and baby included. Ned Dempsey, being temporarily without an electorate, stood firmly with the anti-federalists at the busier city polling booths, offering warnings that were dire and, as the day wore on, increasingly fatalistic. His sister, who had decided she quite approved of the idea of Federation, stood beside her brother encouragingly while not actually agreeing with a single word he said. In an electorate even further west than Fraser Pyke's the widower Everett Judd clasped the hand of each man who had come to vote, regardless of how he had voted, and thanked him and did not dwell on the fact that at every previous election his wife had stood by his side.

Alasdair Dunlevy was also at his constituency in the south-west, though his wife did not accompany him. Instead it was his secretary, Mr Greensmith, very neat today in a pinstriped suit and pale grey silk Ascot tie, who stood at his side. Volunteers from the local branch of the party had set up stages outside the largest polling stations and Mr Dunlevy was shuttled from one to the other throughout the day on a dray festooned with bunting and pulled by two horses donated by a local brewery. Spirits were high in the south-west, the public holiday and the cessation of the rain almost certainly being the cause of it, the prospect of a newly federated nation coming a distant third, and as Mr Dunlevy took to the stage some wag called out, '*Will he speak or will he just stand there?*', for word had got around—thanks to the *Herald* report—that Mr Dunlevy had frozen at the Premier's event at Bathurst. It was repeated throughout the day at each polling station he arrived at, and Mr Dunlevy suffered it with good grace, for what else could he do?

'*Don't forget to say something! Only politician I ever heard of who could not speak!*'

Mr Dunlevy ignored this fresh intervention, ignored the heckler, ignored them all. He turned instead to his secretary, Greensmith, who was witness to his humiliation but who stood, reassuringly, at the edge of the platform. A young man of ambition, and exceptionally well turned out, who had reworked the minister's speech even as they had sat in the train together that morning and whose notes, written in blue ink in a workmanlike hand, filled the pages he now held before him.

And here Alasdair understood that the only person who could have intercepted a note he had written to his mistress, who could have opened the note, understood its contents and redirected the note to the one person to whom it could do the most damage, was his secretary. Was Greensmith.

He remembered the young man's gallant taking of his wife's arm at the Premier's reception and again at Penrith, his dismay that morning on arriving at the house to learn Mrs Dunlevy would not be accompanying them. He saw that ambition formed only one small part in the man's motivation. That the main reason was desire.

Alasdair delivered his speech. He did not need to refer to the notes. He was a parliamentarian of twenty years standing, he could exhort these men to their civic duty simply by opening his heart and his soul to them! For he had realised it could not touch him, this final betrayal, coming as it did so soon after other betrayals that had cut so much deeper and that would require so much more time to heal.

Afterwards men cheered, though he did not wait to hear their cheers. He left the stage, left the handwritten pages of his speech where they had dropped, abandoned, to the floor, and when his secretary stepped forward to shake his hand, the minister swept past him and went, alone, to his next engagement.

∞

At the house in Elizabeth Bay Eleanor Dunlevy stood at her window. In the street below people came and went, some in carriages, some on foot, going to the polling booths and returning.

Eleanor did not accompany her husband, though it was a day they had both worked towards for a year. More than a year—for much of the last decade. This was the culmination of that endeavour, the long-awaited triumph after so many hours of toil, and she would not be there to see it nor to share in it. Indeed, she was no longer certain what it meant to share in her husband's triumph, or in his failure. Both seemed remote to her.

She had gone to his room late the previous night, when they had managed to avoid one another for most of the day, and said, 'I shall not accompany you tomorrow, Alasdair.'

And he had said, 'As you wish,' and that had been an end to it.

They had not spoken again of the maid or the baby. Eleanor had not said, *I accept now that the child was not yours, I was wrong to accuse you,* for the baby's paternity no longer seemed important. And he had not asked her, *Where is she now, the maid, Alice?* If he had, she would have said, *There is nothing we can do for her, we cannot possibly have a maid with a baby.* But Alasdair had not asked. And Alice had not been found.

Eleanor no longer knew why she had gone out and searched for the girl—if her purpose had been to give her money, or to provide the address of the asylum, she had failed to do either. But girls like that knew where the asylum was. And there was no question of taking Alice back, with or without the baby, not after what had been said.

Eleanor would go into the agency tomorrow. She would find a new maid. Still, she had a sense she had not done all that she might. Though what else she could have done she did not know.

She saw that the hoped-for salvation—of the girl, the baby, of herself—had not occurred.

She thought, Alice should have come to me for help. And this put the blame squarely on the girl's shoulders. All that had followed lay at her door.

But *would* I have helped? Eleanor wondered.

The government had decreed the day a holiday but not everyone was enjoying the holiday and not every place was closed. The telephone rang in the hallway of the Dunlevys' house in the middle of the afternoon, which it did rarely enough even on a normal day, for the number of subscribers was small still and so there were very few whom one might telephone and very few who might telephone one. But today the telephone rang.

Eleanor waited for a time to see if the telephone would cease to ring of its own accord, and when it did not she went downstairs and picked up the telephone receiver. She held the instrument close her ear and said, clearly and distinctly, 'This is the Dunlevy residency. Who is calling, please?' because there was no maid to answer the call and Mrs Flynn had not come in today so that they were, effectively, on their own.

'I am afraid I do not understand you. Who is calling, please?'

She did not recognise the voice, a man's, and rather muffled and faint, as if he called from a great distance, though in fact the man who telephoned was less than a mile away.

∞

At Sydney Hospital, which was less than a mile from Elizabeth Bay as the southerly blows, though rather more than that if one is required to follow the circuitous route taken by the meandering

411

roads, Miss Verity Trent dressed herself, a little painfully, stopping once or twice to catch her breath.

Her time at the hospital was at an end, her place soon to be taken by another. Someone more deserving, certain of the nursing staff thought privately and some not so privately; the reason for Miss Trent's illness was generally known and those among them who believed in Sin and Wickedness did not bother to hide their judgement as they tended to her, and those who believed in Charity and Forgiveness did not judge at all and offered kindness with their ministrations and, oddly, both factions read the same Book and considered themselves of the same faith. Fortunately, their faith was broad enough to encompass both schools of thought.

Miss Trent's time on the ward, her time in the colony, had not been a pleasant one. She was relieved to be going. She dressed herself painfully but she did not ask for help and none was offered.

∞

The government had decreed the day a holiday and the city's cab drivers had included themselves within the spirit of this decree so that Eleanor had a great deal of trouble finding a hansom to take her to Macquarie Street. When she did locate one the driver was garrulous and full of opinions that he was inclined to share with her, though mercifully a stiff breeze off the water whipped his words away as soon as he uttered them and Eleanor was spared.

*Was* she spared?

The cab drew up now before the front steps of the hospital and Eleanor climbed down, needing the man's hand as she descended but dismissing him at once when she no longer had need of him.

She did not go up the steps. Instead, she made her way around to the rear where the hospital buildings merged with the great and sweeping expanse of the Domain. Here the romantic whimsy of the place, which elsewhere was held in check, erupted with unrestrained abandon in the form of a delightful if incongruous three-storey turret better suited to a medieval castle than a colonial hospital. This piece of architectural caprice housed the hospital's modern and new operating theatre on its uppermost floor, the elegantly proportioned Chapel of St Luke in its middle floor, and at ground level, accessed by a small and insignificant green door, the morgue.

'Please mind your head!' cried a young clerk starting up in alarm as Eleanor appeared in the doorway.

It was a cramped and low-ceilinged place, squeezed awkwardly into a circular interior that defied rooms and corridors or anything really that demanded corners and right angles as their foundation. Some attempt had been made to compartmentalise the place, and Eleanor was led along a short and dimly lit passage by the young orderly, who walked on tiptoe and who ducked his head and twitched his hands, and whether the man's chronic and unceasing nervousness was due to an unease of the dead or of the living, or by the cramped conditions in which he worked, could only be guessed.

'This is Mr Erasmus,' said the orderly, handing her over and darting gratefully away.

Mr Erasmus, who appeared to have been awaiting her arrival, stood by a closed door, his hand on the doorhandle. All that Eleanor understood of this man was the old-fashioned mutton-chop whiskers he sported and the waistcoat he wore. It had mother-of-pearl buttons on it. He did not speak and so she was forced to look into his face. It was the face of a man much younger than his whiskers suggested. His face showed no expression and she could not guess at his intent, though his silence, the lack of an expression in his eyes, somehow implied a great deal if one could but grasp it.

Mr Erasmus indicated then with a movement of his hand that she should follow. It was a gesture both perfunctory and kindly: a man who dealt daily with tragedy. Or that was how Eleanor interpreted it. Perhaps it was just a gesture.

He opened the door and a smell seeped out. It had been there in a more subtle form from the instant she had crossed the threshold, though she had barely acknowledged it. Now it shouted its presence. A sweet, cloying odour not at all what one thought death must smell like, not decaying or foetid or rank at all. And unforgettable, though she did not understand this until later.

The room was tiled on floor and walls like a bathroom in a good hotel and yet it was nothing at all like a good hotel. The air was markedly cooler than the outside temperature. In the centre of the room was a table upon which a body was laid, covered by a sheet.

The man, Mr Erasmus, stood unmoving beside Eleanor. He waited for a moment then pulled the sheet aside with a tight little flourish as might a sombre magician who has tired a little of his profession but has no other means by which to make a living.

'This is her?' he said after a time, and when he had waited long enough for Eleanor to speak.

'Yes. Alice Nimrod. Our maid.'

But how different she looked. And perhaps that was death. It wiped away all disappointments and triumphs. The girl's face was a blank, it said nothing about how she had got here, it offered no excuses and no recriminations. It was strange to gaze so long upon the face of a maid; it was not the correct way of things. What colour eyes had the girl had? Eleanor wondered. But she did not know. And now the girl's eyes were closed.

A mother should be standing here, thought Eleanor; instead it is an employer. A former employer, though she did not say this to the man, Mr Erasmus. She had claimed Alice as her maid and denied the dismissal as though she could deny her own part in this death.

*I believe I may be in some way responsible for this girl's death.*

But she could no more say these words than Alice could sit up now and accuse her. Alice did not need to accuse her. Eleanor pitched forward and put out her hands to the table edge to steady herself and Mr Erasmus leaped forward to take her arm, alarmed, she sensed, surprised—it was a maid, after all. But she wanted his pity, Eleanor realised, she yearned for his solace, his sympathy. The man must have it in him.

But it was only a maid.

She turned away and the man replaced the sheet over Alice's face. And something about the way he had shown her only the girl's face, not an inch more, troubled her.

'I wish to know—can you tell me what happened to her?'

'Her throat was cut.'

The period of time—a handful of seconds, no more—after which he said this did not exist. Eleanor found herself outside in the corridor.

He had come outside with her, this Mr Erasmus, he had closed the door behind him. He regarded her and his face, too, showed no excuses, no recriminations.

'She was your maid,' he said.

'Yes.'

But it had not been a question. He had in his hand—crumpled, five years old now but still with its original envelope—the letter from the agency with the Dunlevys' address on. Why keep such a thing? Had Alice had it with her when she died? Had she had all that she owned with her when she was killed?

They stood in silence.

415

'When was she brought in?' said Eleanor.

'First thing this morning. Probably it happened last night.'

'But—' and Eleanor turned and looked directly at him '—there was a baby.'

∞

At six o'clock the polling stations across the colony closed to loud cheers, and in the city the people began to gather in great numbers outside the offices of the *Herald*. The first results came in at six thirty, and as each new telegram arrived an employee of the newspaper hurried out and posted *Yes* or *No* on a board outside and a cheer went up, no matter the outcome; the people just wished to cheer, they did not discriminate. And it was no certain thing as, for a time, the *No*'s came in thick and fast only a little behind the *Yes*'s. But by eight o'clock it began to appear that a win in favour of the Federation was likely. At ten o'clock the result was all but confirmed and a win declared, and the cheering in the streets was long and hearty, after which the crowd dispersed, for tomorrow was another day.

∞

Eleanor got home long before her husband for her journey was shorter than his. But it was dark as her cab drew up outside the house and it took her a moment or two to disengage herself from its interior and negotiate the door and the step. And then she must find some coins for the fare and all the while balance this bundle that she held.

The cab dispatched with, she walked up to the front door and the baby in her arms made no sound and it was Eleanor herself who cried a little as she went into the house.

# CHAPTER THIRTY-FIVE

# FEDERATION

It had been a mild winter after all, though it had not seemed so at the time—and, really, how cold could it get, in Sydney?—and then a whole month early, in the second week of October, the jacarandas exploded into bloom across the city, and if one was fortunate enough to be alive on such a day it was impossible not to feel the joy of it. When a southerly struck, late one afternoon towards the end of the month, the whole lot was gone in a moment, blown off the trees for another year and, for a few glorious days, the streets of the city were paved in mauve blossom in the same way that, as children, we had believed the streets of London to be paved with gold, though we had learned as we had got older, that this was not true.

The Federation vote had been a success, though many towns and suburbs had voted against it. But the majority had been secured and the first federal election was to be held in two years' time. And somewhere along the line, in the few short weeks since the referendum, the Premier's government had been swept aside and Mr Lyne—about whom no one had heard very much at all during the referendum—was the new Premier, though how this had occurred, or why, most people in the colony could not say. For there had been no election, yet a number of important men in parliament now sat in different seats to those they had occupied in June, and a number held quite different offices and some held no office at all. Such was the life of the politician.

In one of his first acts as Premier, Mr Lyne had discontinued the Office of Public Monies. It duplicated much of the work of the Colonial Treasurer and the Secretary for Public Works, after all. The Secretary for Public Monies now found himself without office, position or staff, but as he had expectations of being appointed Minister for Federation the loss was, it was hoped, only short term. Mr George Drummond-Smith had also lost his position with the formation of the new government, but as he now, unaccountably, sported a black eye and a dislocated jaw—the origins of which were the source of much speculation but little in the way of hard fact—his temporary withdrawal from public life was prudent. One of Mr Lyne's former ministers sported a badly bruised hand but as no one, not even this gentleman's wife, put these two incidents together, it was not remarked upon.

At the house in Elizabeth Bay the frangipani had burst into life, sprouting a host of new buds, and the view down to the bay was gone now until April.

Eleanor Dunlevy stood at the window with the baby in her arms. He was awake, his eyes focusing on her face, or appearing to. Really, it was hard to know but she fancied he knew her face, now. And she pointed out to him the things she saw from the window—the new buds on the branches of the frangipani, the carriage that came down the hill and went on to the water's edge, the currawongs in the branches of the old fig tree and the cock-atoos circling overhead. All of it was new for spring, all of it was new for the baby.

Alasdair came in dressed in his best suit and smartest tie and a new pair of gloves, for there was to be a reception that afternoon at the governor's house.

'Are you ready? Come, let me take him,' and he took the infant from his wife so that she could prepare herself. He took the baby upstairs and returned it to its nursery, laying it down in its cradle and tucking the blanket around it, and as the nurse was out of the room for the moment, it did not matter that there was a tear in his eye as he did so.

# AUTHOR'S NOTE

Whilst the pivotal characters in this novel are entirely fictional, a number of the lesser characters are real, as any student of Australian history will know. The Premier of New South Wales, the colourful and larger-than-life George Reid, and his opposite number, Edmund Barton—who did indeed go on to be Australia's first prime minister—are two obvious examples. Others are: Mrs Reid and Mrs Barton (their wives); Miss Hickman and Miss Scott of the Women's Suffrage League; William Lyne, the premier who succeeded George Reid; William Wentworth, the explorer and statesman; and John Blaxland, the landowner and merchant. Most—though not all—of what these people say in the novel is taken from speeches and addresses they gave at the time and were reported in the press of the day. Many—though again not all—of the Federation meetings and events and speeches in the novel are taken from real events of the day and were reported in the newspapers though, for plot purposes, I have taken occasional liberties with the dates and ordering of some events. There was no Secretary of Public Monies with offices in Richmond Terrace in Reid's administration; it is an entirely fictitious ministry.

Frog Hollow, as many Sydneysiders know, is a real place and has featured in several histories of the area, though nowadays the Hollow is a pleasant little park more likely to be frequented by office workers (myself included) eating their lunch than it is by razor gangs and grog-soaked prostitutes, though a small sign at the top of the escarpment discreetly reminds visitors of the park's colourful and not-so-distant past. The Benevolent Asylum at the corner of Pitt and Devonshire streets provided essential indoor and outdoor relief for Sydney's poor for almost a century until it was demolished in 1901 to make way for Central Railway Station, but extensive records still exist both of the asylum's day-to-day workings and of the many thousands of unfortunates who used its services over the years. No anarchists were operating in Sydney at the time that this novel is set (though the burning of the effigy of the Premier at Darlington was an actual event), however a (somewhat amateurish) gang of anarchists called the Broad Arrow Gang were active in Melbourne during this period and have, in part, inspired incidents in this novel. Baby farming was, sadly, common enough in both Sydney and Melbourne in the early part of the 1890s, less so in the later years of that decade when new protective laws came in, and was well documented in the accounts of the day and in a number of books written since that time. And, finally, the 'great man' alluded to in chapter 32 was, of course, Sir Henry Parkes, Premier of New South Wales for much of the 1870s and 1880s, and often referred to as the Father of Federation for his early championing of that cause.

*Maggie Joel*
*Sydney, 2019*

# ACKNOWLEDGEMENTS

I have been blessed in the writing of this book by the help of Wendy Holz, a dear friend of many years' standing and also—by happy coincidence—a librarian at the State Library of New South Wales who assisted me in negotiating that library's archives and online systems and left no stone unturned in her pursuit of sources, suggestions and references. Also, my grateful thanks to Caroline Wilkson, historian at the Sydney Hospital, and Rosemary Sempell, parliamentary archivist at New South Wales Parliament House, both of whom so generously shared with me their time, knowledge, resources and enthusiasm. Thanks are due also to the staff of the Mitchell Library and at the Benevolent Society, Sydney; to my publisher, Annette Barlow, and my agent, Clare Forster, for their continuing support, guidance and belief in me; to my editor extraordinaire, Ali Lavau, who always cuts so incisively right to the heart of the matter in ways that challenge me to be a better writer; to my dearest friend and supporter, Tricia Dearborn; and to all the wonderful people at Allen & Unwin and Curtis Brown for their assistance, support, expertise and encouragement during the editing and publication of this book. And, lastly, to that fine institution, the Australia Council for the Arts and its people who continue to provide me with encouragement and inspiration and who—when we are not too busy—allow me the space to write, in particular Carolyn Watts and Michelle Brown.

The following publications, histories, memoirs and online resources proved invaluable in the writing of this book:

*Australia's First Hospital: The First 100 Years* by Caroline Wilkinson (Friends of Sydney Hospital, 2005).
*Australia in the Victorian Age: Life in the Cities* by Michael Cannon (Thomas Nelson, 1975).
Darlinghurst Courthouse and Residence, NSW Government, Office of Environment and Heritage website: http://www.environment.nsw.gov.au
*Fractured Families: Life on the Margins in Colonial New South Wales* by Tanya Evans (UNSW Press, 2015).
*Guide to the Records of the Benevolent Society of New South Wales, 1813–1995* by Paul Scifleet (Benevolent Society of New South Wales, 1996).
Hansard: Eighteenth Parliament, Second Session, 21 February to 30 March 1899.
Hansard: Eighteenth Parliament, Third Session, 11 to 21 April 1899.
Map of Sydney and Suburbs Showing Tramway Lines and Stopping Places 1894, National Library of Australia website: http://nla.gov.au/
*The History of Parliament House, Sydney* by J.R. Stevenson (*Royal Australian Historical Society Journal*, volume 42, 1957).